THE INTERPRETER FROM JAVA

In which the recollections of a heffalump
and the memoirs of a wartime interpreter,
hammered out on a typewriter,
are interrupted by the stories,
letters and mutterings of their eldest son,
with commentary from his brother.

ALFRED BIRNEY

THE INTERPRETER FROM JAVA

Translated from the original Dutch
by David Doherty

HEAD of ZEUS

An Apollo Book

First published in Dutch as *De tolk van Java* in 2016 by Uitgeverij De Geus

This is an Apollo book. First published in the UK in 2020 by Head of Zeus Ltd

9 7 5 3 1 2 4 6 8

A catalogue record for this book is available from the British Library.

Typeset by Divaddict Publishing Solutions Ltd

ISBN (HB): 9781788544320
ISBN (XTPB): 9781788544337
ISBN (E): 9781788544313

Printed and bound by CPI Group (UK) Ltd, Croydon, CR0 4YY

MIX
Paper from responsible sources
FSC® C020471

Head of Zeus Ltd
5–8 Hardwick Street
London EC1R 4RG

WWW.HEADOFZEUS.COM

This publication has been made possible with financial support from the Dutch Foundation for Literature.

Nederlands letterenfonds
dutch foundation for literature

In memory of my parents,
who were once Baldy and the Heffalump.

There are no mistakes in life
Some people say
It is true sometimes
You can see it that way

Bob Dylan
('Man in the Long Black Coat', 1989)

CONTENTS

I

DISSONANTS

Guitar and typewriter

As a young man in Surabaya, my father saw the flying cigars of the Japanese Air Force bomb his home to rubble, he saw Japanese soldiers behead civilians, he committed acts of sabotage for the Destruction Corps, was tortured and laid in an iron box to broil beneath the burning sun, he saw Japanese soldiers feed truckloads of caged Australian prisoners to the sharks, he saw Punjabi soldiers under British command sneak up on the Japanese and slit their throats, he learned of the death of his cousin on the Burma Railway, heard how his favourite uncle was tortured to death by Japanese soldiers on his father's family estate, he betrayed his 'hostess' sister's Japanese lover, he guided Allied troops through the heat of East Java, where Indonesian rebels were hung by the ankles and interrogated while he – an interpreter – hammered away at a typewriter, he helped the Allies burn villages to the ground, heard the screams of young rebels consumed by flames as they ran from their simple homes into a hail of gunfire, he learned to handle a gun and, at a railway station, riddled a woman and her child with bullets when a Javanese freedom fighter took cover behind them, he led an interrogation unit in Jember, broke the silence of the most tight-lipped prisoners, he was thrown 250 feet into a ravine when his armoured vehicle hit a landmine, he was ordered by a Dutch officer to supervise the transport of inmates from the municipal jail in Jember and, arriving at Wonokromo station in Surabaya after a nine-hour journey, he dragged the corpses of suffocated prisoners from the goods train, he found the body of an Indo friend who had blown his brains out because his girl had slept with a Dutch soldier, and, amid the chaos of Bersiap, he killed young men with whom he had a score to settle. But for him the worst thing was when the neck of his guitar broke.

Or did that last detail slip your mind, Pa? Perhaps because you made it up?

It happened during the First Police Action. Two convoys travelling in opposite directions passed at close quarters. Some squaddie left the barrel of his machine gun in harm's way and you the neck of your guitar. The make of the machine gun is unknown, but your guitar was an original US Gibson: every Indo's dream, played by all the greats. A prize you'd have given anything to own, even the sweetest girl in all Croc City.

You were a big man in my eyes, a fearsome figure, and you smiled as you told me this tale in a chilly Dutch living room. The guitar had been a faithful companion to you and your soldier buddies, though you never mention it in your writings. And, as long as that instrument survived, the war still resembled a *Boy's Own* caper: tearing around, feeding your face, serenading the village girls, spying on women as they bathed in the river. Night after night as a kid, I had to listen to those ripping yarns of yours. While your Dutch mates in their green berets plastered their tanks with pin-ups, you hung a portrait of their queen at the foot of your bed in Surabaya. Your lofty dream of Holland was just a decent pay packet to most of those guys or, to the psychos among them, an adventure. That first batch of Dutch Marines had been trained in America – to you they were heroes. And, pig-headed as you are, you continued to watch those mindless American movies all your life, films in which war is for heroes and peace is for cowards. Refused to grow up, didn't you, Pa? You always remained that boy of twenty.

At the pictures

Out of the blue – I must've been about eighteen – you decided to take me out one night. A rare occurrence. Granted, it had been five years since we'd lived in the same house, since Child Services had taken me from you at the age of thirteen and – in your words – 'deported' me to the children's home. Dutch grub was all they fed us there, but when it came time to leave, the authorities saw fit to lodge me and my brother Phil with a family steeped in the ways of the Indies. Our landlady swanned around as if the sun had never set on the empire. What the hell were Child Services playing at? Five years of knuckling under to a Dutch regime only to be handed over to a family stuck in the colonial past.

It was the same old battle cry every time you visited us at the children's home. You insisted you wanted your kids back, that you were fighting one court case after another, that we were 'your blood', that we belonged with you… there was no end to it. Phil tried to warn me, but I ignored his brotherly advice. I fled our stifling Indo lodgings and headed straight for the place you told me I belonged. A tram to The Hague, a bus from Staatsspoor station via Voorburg and Leidschendam to a brand-new housing scheme in Voorschoten, where I stood and rang your bell in a bleak and spotless doorway less than a mile from my old children's home. You opened the door with an unforgettable welcome:

'*Why did you forsake me?*'

Jesus calling out to God the Father. Back then you were sleeping with the Bible under your pillow, you crazy bastard. The worst of it was, I honestly believed I *had* forsaken you. My photo pressed between the pages of your Bible – what was that about? Was I a bookmark in place of your dagger? You didn't think I'd believe you were praying for me, did you? Later I became convinced you stuck pins in that photo. I told that to two girlfriends of mine after I fled your home once and for all, and it made them cry. They thought I had lost my mind, though by that time they knew you weren't exactly sane yourself: I brought those sweet American hippies back to your place one day and you took them for a couple of floozies, sent them packing without a second glance. You turfed out an American-Dutch friend of mine too. And all because he was black, racist loon that you are. That same friend later told me you were a madman, just like Ma had always said. I didn't want to believe it then. I'm afraid I still don't.

And so you took me out that Tuesday night. Who goes to the pictures on a Tuesday? We caught a bus in Voorschoten, got off at Staatsspoor station and walked to the Odeon on Herengracht. They were showing an American action flick: five death-row inmates offered one last chance at freedom if they rescued some military boffin from the clutches of the Vietnamese. Raising hell as they roared through the jungles of Vietnam on their motorbikes, the convicts were picked off one by one but against all odds the scientist was saved. You stared spellbound at the screen; you and a handful of other simple souls dotted about the cinema. You were forty-five, give or take – an age for contemplation, for self-reflection – yet you sat there like a little kid next to a son who loathed motorbikes, who squeezed his eyes shut when one of the heroes was shot to pieces, snared by a vine, strung upside down, impaled on a bed of bamboo spears. Those Viet Cong and their booby traps! Grisly tactics aside, I secretly cheered them on. To me they were the underdogs, my blood brothers on the silver screen. You rooted for the gung-ho Yanks. Unease was all I felt sitting there next to you; perhaps you felt uneasy next to me. On the bus back to Voorschoten not a word passed between us. I suppose you were trying to coax me out of my shell, stuck on my own in that suicide flat of yours listening to the radio all day while you were out at work, no clue what to do with my life. Puccini Crescent: what a grim corner of the commuter belt that was, a horseshoe of four-storey flats in a satellite town wedged between Leiden and The Hague, home to lonely men and women too timid to say hello when they passed on the street, office drones who spent their evenings watching TV alone.

Guess what, Pa, life in Holland hasn't changed. Thanks for settling in this cold country where life is good as long as you have no need of warmth. Wise of you to live out your days in Spain. Or is it just cowardice? Fear we might come over and do you in? It's still three against one, pal. Only we're bigger now, stronger, a far cry from the little lads we once were. I'm a halfway decent jujitsuka. Phil is a killing machine with a handful of black belts. Arti is a streetfighter. Give it your best shot, old man. During your last year in Holland – South Haarlem, another desperate hole – I heard you slept with an axe under your bed, scared Arti would turn up one night and punch your lights out. I heard that from Ma and she heard it from one of your daughters, Mil most likely, your favourite, named after some old flame, an Aussie girl you picked up in your Java days. You can thank your lucky stars I only took up martial arts late in life. I'm not the killing kind, Pa, but even now you deserve a one-way trip to Intensive Care courtesy of my own bare hands. Twenty-five years of groaning under your iron fist, your paranoia, followed by twenty-five years writing it all down in an unfinished book might seem like a balance of sorts, but I'd rather have spent forty-nine years living life to the full and one year behind bars for inflicting grievous bodily harm on a former marine. No such luck: I am a noble being, a pen-wielding samurai who walks a gentler path, who strums his guitar and makes people smile. I have been cursed with an inquiring nature, naive enough to think I can fathom the inner workings of an unhinged fascist. Perhaps you deserve that too, if only because the pages that comprise your monument may yet expose Dutch history for the lie that it is.

The movie is over. The director chisels his heroes' faces in the clouds.

THE END
(complete with bombastic crescendo)

In your boyhood dreams, you must have pictured your own face up there. Forget it, Pa. The war-movie heaven those heroes fly off to only ever existed in Hollywood.

*

When I was twelve, you gave me a pen. An old-school fountain pen, complete with ink pot and pen wiper. A gift to assuage your guilt after you kicked me down the stairs and back up again in that sad little two-up two-down of ours in The Hague Southwest. One of those jerry-built neighbourhoods that would end up housing society's outcasts fifty years on. Even so, you knew what you were doing when you gave me that pen. You saw more in me than you ever let on, with those oblique Asian ways of yours.

You didn't stop there. When I turned twelve you began to inundate me with books about the war. A slew of aircraft carriers, jet fighters and bombers in black and white. Honestly, Pa, I could see no beauty in those photos. Later, much later, I found out that not one of those history books could be trusted. Lousy propaganda, in praise of the technological advances in killing machines. They spoke of Police Actions: a veiled term for colonial war that no researcher, journalist or writer has succeeded in scrapping from those worthless schoolbooks. Dutch colonial history is filed away in a separate set of bookcases. And then there are the hordes of Dutchmen who think history begins with World War Two and are happy to consign the rest to antiquity. These are the people I live among. How's that for a life sentence? They think World War Two ground to a halt on 5 May 1945. Sure it did, for the Dutch behind their dunes.

Say, Pa, your mother was Chinese, wasn't she? That makes you half Chinese and me a quarter, following a path in my own DNA by nosing around in the *I Ching*, that mysterious *Book of Changes*. Hexagram 29 has this to say: 'It is only through repetition that the pupil makes the material his own.'

Critical self-reflection is hard to come by here in Holland. The Dutch bang on about slaves, coolies, migrant workers and the children of colonial love. Your lot arrived here as first-generation migrants from the Indies and the Dutch scattered you throughout the land: back in the fifties one Indo family to every street was pretty much the quota. If only they had stuck you all in a ghetto. The Hague Southwest would have become the place to be. We, the generations that followed, would be leaning out of windows and lounging on balconies, the mixed-blood remnants of the Dutch tropics, alive and still kicking. Saturday night would be one big jamboree, complete with Hawaiian music, Indo rock, kite flying and a tombola. Now the place is home to every ethnic minority under the sun and police patrol cars blight the streets.

Cesspit

Even before the Allies had liberated the southern provinces towards the end of World War Two, the old slogan 'If the Indies fall, disaster calls' echoed like a mantra through the Netherlands. The first shiploads of volunteer soldiers, recruited in Brabant and Limburg, were nowhere near enough to save a colony and a swift amendment to the constitution was needed to put conscripts in the firing line. Among them was my mother's brother, Uncle Jan. Very much against his will, 'Our Jan', as they called him back home in Helmond, found himself in the self-proclaimed Republic of Indonesia, feigning stomach cramps, nausea, headaches and a complete aversion to the tropical heat from the second he arrived.

My father was around twenty when he saw the Allies' armoured cars roll into Surabaya, the city of his birth, and offered his services as an interpreter. Once the Japanese had capitulated and the Dutch arrived to take over the reins from the Allies, he took up with the Marines. Regular Dutch soldiers played bumbling bit parts in his tales of heroism, unlike the Brits, Australians and above all the Gurkhas he encountered. Those Dutch dopes – Belandas in the local lingo – thought nothing of lighting a cigarette in the pitch dark with the Indonesian enemy just a stone's throw away. Razing villages to the ground didn't count as heroism. That was just part of a marine's job, nothing romantic about it. Romance only reared its head when a village *wasn't* torched.

'No, don't. I've got a sweetheart in that *kampong*!'

'Hey, a girl there swears she's had a baby by a cousin of mine, ha ha! Those Belandas fuck themselves silly over here. Will us Indos get the same privileges in Holland? Weird, isn't it: the Belandas don't hit their women. Hear that? In Holland the women hit the men! The girls over there are tough as nails, *aduh*!'

East Java. Bodies never floated in the *kali* for long. Crocodiles still swam there. By the time Police Action No. 1 was under way, Our Jan had found himself a berth on a ship bound for home, the sly dog. He wiped the crocodile tears from his kisser and whistled tunes of mock nostalgia through his porthole. From the truck that drove him down to the docks, he had chucked his correspondence book at a bunch of local interpreters for a laugh. It eventually fell into my father's hands and became his most treasured possession. The lads from Limburg and Brabant loved to wave those books around, brimming with photos and addresses of beguiling Dutch girls eager to write to brave young men out in the tropics: goddesses in the eyes of every Indo.

My father's Chinese mother had given him a Germanic name: Arend, which means eagle. But Java being a place where names are readily corrupted, most people just called him Arto. It was only in Holland that his birthname was restored to him, by us, his children. We added the definite article for good measure: the Eagle. Calling your father by his given name was unheard of. Back then, we didn't even call him Pa. He was something else entirely.

Before we arrived on the scene, dashing Arto had managed to charm no less than three Dutch women with the photos and letters he sent from East Java: a cultured lady from Amsterdam who had her picture taken on a soaring staircase in a high-class photo studio; a middle-class woman from The Hague who posed with a parasol in front of the splendid Kurhaus Hotel; and a heffalump with a cheery smile from the southern town of Helmond, the Kediri of the Netherlands if you will. Kediri being the town in East Java where Arto's mother was born.

The lady from Amsterdam sent impeccably calligraphed letters in green ink, tied with lilac bows. The woman from The Hague used a typewriter on which the *e* and the *o* had worn away, a shortcoming made good by the fact that she could reach speeds of up to two hundred strokes a minute, or so she said. This was a skill Arto envied, since the interrogation reports he had to bang out on rolls of paper were often the length of his arm, verbatim accounts of the agonized cries of Indonesian resistance fighters as they were tortured by the Dutch marines and their interpreters.

Arto belonged to a group of 'native' interpreters. He could speak and write Dutch, English, French, German, High Javanese, Middle Javanese, Low Javanese, Madurese, Sundanese, Chinese Pidgin, Cantonese, Japanese, Arabic and, of course, Malay, the *lingua franca* of the Archipelago's coastal regions. The heffalump from Helmond was wowed by Arto's linguistic prowess. He in turn was taken aback by her childish handwriting, idiotic punctuation and inane comments. He let a marine chum from Brabant read her letters and he said she must be left-handed, explaining that in Holland everyone who wrote with their left hand was made to switch to their right. It was the Brabant boy's considered opinion that left-handed women made the best lovers. He based this assertion on his own experience and even went so far as to spurn the advances of right-handed women.

The Helmond heffalump had a couple of sisters, the prettiest of whom was determined to find herself a dashing young man from the tropics. Her name was Riek and she dictated choice phrases to her elder sister, the heffalump, such as 'them eyes o' yours don't half make me melt like butter'.

'That's barely even Dutch,' grinned the marine from Brabant, sitting beside Arto as they barrelled along in an armoured vehicle during Police Action No. 1. Seconds later, dashing Arto hit a landmine and was thrown 250 feet into a ravine. To his dismay, the spinal injuries he sustained prevented him from taking part in Police Action No. 2. For a time he lay low at Willemsoord Barracks in Surabaya, going out on the town once in a while, until he began to hear his name carried with increasing frequency on the wind that was stirring in Sukarno's back yard. He was on a blacklist. The war had been decided, Arto had lost, decolonization could begin. Ship after ship packed with servicemen and civilians left for Dutch shores. Dashing Arto was ordered to remain within the confines of the barracks. Help came in the shape of a Dutch captain, a shadowy figure without whose network he would never have been able to escape his homeland, where the only future that awaited him was in the belly of a crocodile.

Days before his departure, during the quiet, less dangerous hours of the afternoon, Arto said farewell to his mother, the cook and the housemaid. The rest of his family were absent. That evening he sneaked out of the barracks with Ben de Lima, an Ambonese pal, who knew a good Chinese place on Embong Malang. Ben swore they served the best pork in town, perhaps in East Java, if not the whole island. He also claimed to know the Chinese chef's secret, but he chuckled and kept it to himself.

'I'll find out,' said Arto. 'Just you wait. There's no keeping a secret from me, you know that. Whenever you couldn't get those bastards to talk you came to me, remember?'

Arto was referring to the interrogation techniques he employed to loosen the tongues of Indonesian prisoners. In that respect, he had always been superior to good-hearted Ben de Lima. The two men had a long voyage ahead of them. There was more than enough time to make Ben spill the beans.

Ben nodded indifferently; all he wanted to do was to eat and forget. Before long, Arto was forced to admit his friend was right: he had never eaten more succulent pork in his life. It was a small, nondescript restaurant, a little off the beaten track, with a side entrance you would walk right past if you didn't know it was there. Beyond the dining room was a courtyard teeming with cockroaches. Night shadows crowded around the dim light of bare bulbs orbited by buzzing insects. Nothing unusual about that, but Arto had been rattled by the news that people were out to get him and had to suppress the urge to ask Ben to escort him to the *kamar kecil*.

The toilet had a wooden door with a heart-shaped hole at eye level. Ben had told him the Dutch marines called it a cesspit and that the restaurant's Chinese owner had done his best to imitate the Dutch experience. It was lit by the feeble glow of an oil lamp and contained a raised pot with a lid on it, something Arto had never encountered before. He removed the lid, sat down and set about his business.

He counted three before he heard the turd land far below him. As he scooped water from the pail beside the pot to rinse his backside, a noise beneath him made him jump. Hurriedly, he pulled up his trousers. As he wiped the sweat from his brow, the noise came again: the contented grunting of pigs down in the depths. He felt a stab of anger at Ben for making a fool of him, but putting the lid back on the pot, he decided there were worse things in life. An arse riddled with bullets, to name but one.

Arriving in Holland after his long voyage, Arto's first impulse was to leap into the water. His second was to turn and run back up the gangway and into the belly of the Great Bear, the troop ship that had carried him to the Dutch coast in six weeks. As the ship's librarian, he'd had a decent enough time. The lads from Brabant and Limburg he met on Java had told him a thousand times that the sun did not always shine in Holland, but he had never wanted to believe it. Now, looking down at the quayside shrouded in mist and the sombre figures in thick woollen overcoats – men in hats, women in headscarves – a joyless, irrevocable future flashed before his eyes. His mother had given him a set of six ivory table knives to take with him, knives that severed the physical ties between Arto and Java forever.

As Arto was setting foot on the IJ docks in Amsterdam, five *pemudas* armed to the teeth were paying his mother a visit. These young Indonesian freedom fighters had tied red bandannas around their fevered brows, Japanese warrior style. They did not take the trouble to enter by the gate but leapt – no, flew – over the razor-sharp teeth along the top of the fence, spikes Arto and his brothers had once filed down with the patience of angels to make sure that any would-be intruder would end his life as satay. The five *pemudas* laughed at this notion but were denied the chance to blast open the lock on the front door with the guns they had stolen from the Japanese capitulators.

Arto's mother had appeared in the doorway, with a searching look that somehow made her small frame tower high above them. Her *sarong* was the earth, her *kebaya* the sky, her brow the heavens.

The five *pemudas* greeted the Chinese woman with the traditional Indonesian *sembah*, and, apologizing profusely, explained why they had come.

'Go on then, shoot me,' she said.

'Mrs Sie, we are very sorry. We have come for your son, your last-born. It's Arto we want.'

'Arto is in Holland.'

'What? Has Arto fled to Holland?'

'Listen, you bunch of jessies, your friends have come knocking on my door before now. What was Arto supposed to do, sit here and wait for your bullets?'

One of them lit up a *kretek* cigarette. Pensively, he blew the clove-scented tobacco smoke into the air and said in melodious Dutch, 'Mrs Sie, it would have been better if you had handed over your son to be tried by us. Then our dead could have slept in peace.'

'In that case, take my life instead of my son's.'

'Thank you, Mrs Sie. You are a good person. We will pray for you.'

They quietly opened the gate and backed away over the porch in single file, clasping their hands as they took their leave of the Chinese woman. Once they were out on the street, they turned their backs on the house at number 5, thrust their weapons in the air and yelled 'Long live the Republic of Indonesia!'

Some 18,000 nautical miles away, dashing Arto had been housed in the Alexander Barracks behind the dunes that shield The Hague from the North Sea. In the city centre, he met up with people he knew from the Indies. No one ever called it the Dutch East Indies and it was never, ever referred to as Indonesia. Years later I see a young man, barely twenty-five years old, posing in full dress uniform with a former comfort girl beside the kiosk designed by Berlage. A postcard-sized black-and-white photograph, never sent. The young man believes the citizens of The Hague will hold him in high esteem for his wartime deeds of heroism, while the young woman hopes to erase her shameful past as a plaything for Japanese officers in a new city where no one knows her name. But both are looked on with suspicion. Holland has barely recovered from German occupation and whatever happened over there in the Indies is of concern to no one but 'the colonials'. Those foreigners have bags of money, after all. They can bugger off back to whatever island they came from. There's a bloody housing shortage as it is, and those darkies stink as bad as that muck they eat, reeking of garlic and that shit they call *trassi*.

The misguided notion that 'the colonials' were loaded with money had also occurred to the lady friend Arto went to meet in Amsterdam. He felt distinctly out of place in the starched-linen restaurant she had chosen, understood very little of the menu and soon began to wonder whether the woman had rehearsed her lines in advance. Her words seemed to have been dictated to her and reminded him of the green ink and lilac bows of her letters. Lilac was also the colour of the bow that adorned her hat. He had to make a conscious effort to follow her as she spoke of all kinds of writers who didn't interest him in the least. At school he had got no further than *Don Quixote*, *Moby-Dick*, *Robinson Crusoe* and a handful of other Western classics. Fortunately, he was able to tell her a thing or two about his father's family, a subject about which she was more than curious. They were well-to-do, unlike him, the bastard son, who had to live on bread and water for a week after the starched-linen restaurant handed him the bill.

The second candidate from his list of female penfriends was a good deal cheaper. They arranged to meet at an establishment in Scheveningen, where they drank tea together. A solitary biscuit was served with the tea, a cultural difference that received ample coverage in one of the many letters he sent to his family in Surabaya, half of which never arrived. The lady from The Hague spoke in a different accent to her rival from Amsterdam, more regal. In other ways too, her bearing was a touch more formal, but thankfully she spoke of things he knew: typewriters, mostly. She worked at a notary's office and he asked her whether that was more prestigious here in Holland than working for the government. When he signalled to the waiter to bring extra sachets of sugar for his tea, the lady from The Hague's neutral expression soured somewhat. He explained his request. 'Us chaps from the Indies like our tea sweet.'

'Oh yes, I understand. So you drink tea there too?'

'Tea grows on Java. As does sugar. And coffee.'

'Oh. Yes. And what about typewriters?'

'Typewriters do not grow on Java.'

Unable to gauge his intonation, she did not know whether to treat this as an attempt at humour. The best course of action, it seemed to her, was to glance at her wristwatch and postpone the stroll they had agreed to take until another day.

Relieved, Arto was now free to wander the length of the busy promenade unaccompanied. He looked around constantly, keeping an eye out not only for Indos, but also for Indonesians. He had heard about traitors coming to Holland as stowaways, men who, as far as he was concerned, should be throttled without a second thought. He wondered whether buying a hat might help him escape the notice of all these people who were staring at him so strangely. Even the sea seemed to greet him with a filthy grin.

His final trump card lay in Helmond, and a slow train took him to this provincial southern town on a summer's day in 1950. He relished the punctuality with which the train pulled into the station, not one minute sooner or later than the arrival time announced at Hollands Spoor station in The Hague. Try telling that to those Indonesian layabouts on Java.

Helmond was small. Even quieter than The Hague, which itself was a mortuary compared to the bustle of Surabaya. There was no one at the station to meet him, he had told no one about his trip. All he knew was the heffalump's address: Beelsstraat 1, where her father had a cobbler's shop. Arto approached several people to ask for directions. Friendly though they were, they proved even more difficult to understand than the marines from Brabant he had hung around with in East Java.

Beelsstraat was a thoroughfare by Helmond standards but, in his eyes, it was a poor excuse for a street. Even the corner property at number 1 looked like a doll's house. A matron with a greasy, checked tea towel knotted to her apron opened the door to him, uttered a cry of alarm and bolted back inside. Then the sharp, birdlike face of a wiry man popped out of the adjacent cobbler's workshop and shouted indoors in a calm voice. Three girls, the man's daughters he surmised, appeared in the doorway and giggled as they examined the East Indian – which was what people called his type at the time – from head to toe.

He looked down at the tips of his shoes, gleaming in the afternoon sun of Helmond. The crease in his trousers was as sharp as when he had left, despite the train journey. Only a sliver of cufflink glinted below the sleeves of his jacket. What was there to giggle about?

Was his hair out of place? Had he overdone the brilliantine?

People from the Indies were apt to bemoan the penny-pinching ways of the Dutch, but in Brabant this was less of an issue and Arto sat down to a generous lunch. The heffalump said very little; in fact, she said nothing at all. Every now and then her sister Mies would give him a fish-eyed stare from behind her thick glasses and ask him a question about the tropics, but most of the talking was done by Riek, the tallest sister and, with her bouncy hair, the prettiest of the three. Her thick Helmond accent meant he understood very little of what she said, but she sounded amusing. Our Jan was not around, a matter of some regret to the cobbler, because Our Jan had such great stories about the Indies. 'Or is it called Indonesia now?' he said, mainly to himself and oblivious to the sensitive chord he had struck in the young man from the tropics sitting opposite him.

Following an odd meal consisting of soup, bread, cold meats

thinly sliced, a boiled egg that had to be eaten with a spoon, tea and an orange, it was time for the three sisters to leave the room. This they did in the wake of the speechless matron, still in shock at the presence of a young man from the tropics in her own home.

But before dashing Arto came to sit face to face with the man of the house, he asked in flawless Dutch if he might avail himself of the toilet.

As it turned out, the cobbler's family did not have the kind of modern toilet he had become accustomed to in The Hague. They still had what might be referred to as a cesspit, in an outbuilding accessed through the garden. As he approached it, Arto was reminded of his farewell meal at the Chinese restaurant in Surabaya: the incredibly succulent slices of roast pork, coated in seasoned flour and accompanied by a red sauce made from tropical fruits.

It was the height of the afternoon, time in fact for a siesta in the tropics. But by now he had learned that, even here in the provinces, people did not have outhouses where guests could lie down and rest for a few hours. He felt his muscles tense. The painted door to the cesspit looked exactly like the one at the Chinese restaurant on the eve of his departure for this peculiar country. An open heart in the dark-green wood beckoned.

Inside, he lifted the lid and stared into a dark hole. He listened closely but could hear nothing, only the buzzing of a fly or two. There was no pail of water for rinsing his behind. No matter: he had learned to cope with the strange Dutch phenomenon of toilet paper.

And on that summer's day in 1950 in Helmond, buttocks spread on the wooden seat in an outhouse that was spick and span, he relieved himself and counted the seconds as the turd left his body and fell earthwards. But he heard nothing, not even after he had counted to ten! Even more alarmed than he had been at the Chinese restaurant in Surabaya, he leapt off the toilet. Keeping one eye on the mysterious dark pit, he fumbled nervously with the toilet paper.

Back in the living room, with its ill-fitting cloths on polished tables, pots of geraniums on the windowsill and cuckoo clock nailed to the wall, he took a seat opposite his future father-in-law.

The man offered him a cigar.

After taking one from the blank wooden cigar box held out to him and lighting it, Arto glanced over his shoulder towards the garden. What strange, silent breed of creature did they keep in the depths of their cesspits here in Helmond?

The cobbler, in his civvies, blew a smoke ring at the ceiling and quietly observed the young man from the tropics, who stole another look over his shoulder. Then he asked dashing Arto the one, prescient question that his bride-to-be, listening furtively at the door, would never forget.

'Listen fella, are they out to get you or something?'

Recollections of a heffalump (1)

'No-oo, that's not how it went the day he came to Helmond... Annie van Asseldonck comes to see me and says do you want to write to a lad over in the Indies, so I go over to hers and she's got a stack of photos of exotic young blokes and I says, crikey, he's a looker, he'll do for me, I'll write to him all right. Oh yes, your Pa was a fine-looking man in his day! Anyway, she gives me his address and passes my address on to somebody or other and sure enough I get a letter from Pa and we start writing to each other. That went on for a year or two and then he came to Holland. He was stationed with the Marines on Van Alkemadelaan in The Hague even though he came here as a civilian. He didn't have time to visit me straight off – it must have been a month or two later. Because... well, he had to acclimatize and that, and he'd gone to Amsterdam to see that other girl who wrote to him and to Limburg or somewhere, I don't know, and he went to Lunteren to see that other marine, the lad from Gelderland who kept chickens. Then one fine day someone turns up at the shop. I was upstairs or outside at the time, so my father comes and says Annie there's a visitor for you, that chap of yours has turned up, that East Indian fella! "What?" I said, and Riek was there too and she's up at the mirror in a flash doing her hair. Anyway, I went down to the shop and there was your Pa with that bloke from Lunteren. No, he didn't come alone, I don't care what you say, you or that father of yours. He came with that poultry farmer, I know for a fact.'

'Had a chicken under his arm, did he?'

'Don't be daft! What kind of man brings a chicken along on a Sunday when his pal's out to marry some girl… Joop! That was his name! Or Jan. Joop van den Burg. Or Jan van der Burgt, something like that. My mother wasn't home and my father said go and sit in back with him, I've got customers.'

'On a Sunday?'

'Well, then it must have been Saturday, I can't remember exactly. Anyway, I know he didn't want the customers to see we had a darkie in the house.'

'Was Pa a *darkie*?'

'Anyone that wasn't white was a darkie, that's how backward we were in those days. By this time my mother's turned up and she doesn't know what to do with herself either. And Riek keeps on exclaiming "Oh what a handsome lad! Oh what a handsome lad!" I was fat back then and Pa called me a heffalump right off the bat. He kept flirting with Riek, but she was only sixteen and that was still too young. Anyway, we had sandwiches and coffee and then my father tells him he should call again. And to make an appointment next time, if he didn't mind. A few Sundays later he's back, with another ex-marine this time, a lad from Tilburg, I don't recall exactly. A Dutch lad, a Brabant lad I should say. And at the end of August 1950 – five months he'd been in Holland by then – he turns up on his own one day. He'd moved out of the barracks to a place on Trooststraat in The Hague. Can't say I was in love with him. Riek was head over heels, not me. We went for a walk down to the Vrand, a big park, over the bridge and along the paths by the Tea House. "That sister of yours is a fine-looking girl!" he says. And I say, "Well, don't go trying anything on with her, she's only sixteen." I didn't feel anything much for him, but he asked me over to The Hague one time. My Aunt Annie was living on Troelstrakade at the time so I stayed with her and it was like I was drawn to him, like a force was tugging at me, all mysterious, like in those books by whatsisname, that writer, Couperus is it? Like a force it was, even though I had a will of my own, you know, had my head screwed on, I did. My parents were dead against me going to The Hague, but the more they protested the more I was drawn to him. I was working in the cardboard factory at the time, packing boxes, checking things off, getting deliveries ready, that sort of thing. One Thursday they hand me my pay packet and the next day, instead of turning up for work, I get on the train. I go to Aunt Annie in The Hague and tell her I've run away from home 'cause they're all against me and I'm always getting told off. Annie says don't go and see him whatever you do, stay here with us for a bit. But her son sneaks me over to Trooststraat one day. Yes, I asked him to. And that's when it all began. Your father wasn't working; he was still living off handouts from the Marine barracks. We went cycling together and visited folk he knew from the Indies, Aunty Lieke and Aunty Thea and the rest. On my side we went to see Aunty Fien. Fien lived on Van Alkemadelaan back then, not far from the barracks. She warned me about your father, said he was wrong for me and things would never work out between us. She thought there was something strange about him. He was always looking over his shoulder and my father would say, "Hey, no one here is out to get you…"'

'"I know," your father would reply, "but I've been through so much." He was always afraid of being attacked but I didn't see the paranoia in him. It was a thrill, going into town with such a handsome, dark-skinned lad, that was something out of the ordinary, something no one else had! Even so, there was something a bit off-putting about it, a bit peculiar. I was nineteen and I'd never been to bed with a boy and I wanted to be a virgin bride, pure as the driven snow. But one day I'm back at his place on Trooststraat. Pa had an upstairs room to himself. Quite a few lads from the Indies would hang out there and they used to have a good laugh 'cause I couldn't understand a word they said. They drank fruit squash or coffee, never alcohol. Once they gave me a glass of that cordial to drink – *susa, soso* – something like that. Pa's friends left and, what came over me I'll never know, but suddenly there I was stripping off! I forced myself on your father. I was all hot and bothered and having a fine old time to myself and it was only later I found out they always had a little bottle of Spanish Fly with them and they had slipped some into that... that...'

'... *susu*, Ma... rose syrup... cordial...'

'... they slipped it into my drink! I never touched the stuff again. Cordial or not, to me that rose syrup is nothing but a tropical love potion. Kees Stokkermans, or Joop Stokkermans, whatever his name is, that marine from 's-Gravenzande, he told me those lads used that stuff to drive me crazy and he should know 'cause he was stationed in the Indies and he said that's what they do, drive each other mad with herbs and potions and *guna-guna*, even kill one another with that hocus pocus. It's a different world, you know. Here they just blow one another's brains out. I hadn't a clue, I mean I was still a virgin but one slug of that muck and you're shagging yourself silly! So that was my first time but there was no blood and your father didn't believe me and called me a liar and refused to accept I'd had an examination down there and that they'd pierced the hymen. When his Indo pals came back, I heard them say half in Malay, half in Dutch that he'd have to marry me. If you ask me that's what he was after, 'cause he didn't have an official passport then, just some kind of green card from the Marines. And, my God, wouldn't you know it, one time and that was me pregnant! And your father and those boys just sat there laughing and Stokkermans said not one of them Indos is any good. The pregnancy made me sick and I didn't dare tell Aunt Annie. I found myself a bedsit on Van Zeggelenlaan. I told your father about my condition and he didn't bat an eyelid, the creep. It was all part of his little scheme, if you ask me. He wanted us to live together – 'shacking up' we called it then – 'cause marriage wasn't an option, he was in a jam, didn't even know whether he'd be allowed to stay in the country. December 1950, January 1951 this was, and I was queasy and achy the whole time. We moved into a ground floor flat on Gouverneurlaan, fifty guilders a week, half board with a landlady. I was working at a printer's shop, Rijmenam on Hofwijckstraat, and your father volunteered half-days on Van de Kunststraat as a lathe operator and a draughtsman. When the sickness got so bad I couldn't work any more, your father began to hit me. The landlady heard me crying often enough and one evening she even sent for the doctor. He didn't see that I was expecting twins and left me none the wiser as to why I was so sick. Yes, the pair of you made me sick. Sick as a dog!'

'Even back then?'

'Yes, even back then, you little prick! I went on the sick and when your father was at work the landlady used to knock at the door and check on me. She saw from my face that he hit me and told me he should keep his hands to himself, that she wouldn't stand for it in her house. I can see you're from a decent family, she said, so pack your things love, and to hell with him.

'"But I'm expecting!" I said.

'"Oh God, that too! How far along are you?" she asked.

'"Three months. I have to get married or I'll bring shame on the family," I said.

'And then one day my mother came to The Hague to visit Aunt Annie on Troelstrakade. That was all Annie's doing, 'cause she thought I should make a clean breast of it. She wasn't going to tell tales, I had to speak up for myself. I kept my mouth shut the whole afternoon. It was only when I took my mother back to Hollands Spoor station that it came out, in a fit of tears. She wasn't the least surprised. A week later, Aunt Annie put your father and me in touch with Reverend Lelie. He was from Helmond, too. Pa asked the vicar if he would wed us, but he refused unless I went to Sunday school first. There was no way Pa would marry a

Catholic girl, 'cause his mother'd had him christened a Protestant during the war and herself along with him. Something to do with the Chinese being in danger if they believed in Confucius or Buddha, I don't know the ins and outs. So, Sunday school it was, at a community centre type place. At first, your father came along to make sure he approved and after a while I went by myself. Aunt Annie put Reverend Lelie in touch with my parents in Helmond. They talked and talked and when he came back, Reverend Lelie told me my parents were still dead against us getting wed. Not only that, but he had made inquiries in Indonesia and it turned out your father had got up to all sorts over there and so he thought my parents had every reason to oppose the marriage, that it would be a one-way ticket to misery. But I was blind with love and pregnant into the bargain. Reverend Lelie suggested I go into a home for unwed mothers. You two would've been taken away from me as soon as you were born, and I'd never have seen my children again, never even know their names or where they were. You'd have gone straight to a Catholic orphanage, been put up for adoption. Two weeks they gave me to think it over, then I had to go to Helmond and tell them my decision. Your Pa knew nothing about it. The day dawned and off I went to see my parents and I was supposed to call on Reverend Lelie that same evening. Of course, I told them I couldn't bear to have my child taken away from me and to pretend I'd never even had a baby. I still didn't know I was expecting twins. Life might be difficult, I said, but I want my child to have a father. I was nearly five months gone by this time and Pa and me still couldn't get married, 'cause we'd found out he wasn't a proper Dutchman. He had been in Indonesia but here in Holland it was different and they needed proof from Surabaya. And he still bore his mother's name – Sie – 'cause his father hadn't recognized him as his own. Pa told me to persuade my parents to give their permission for us to wed. When I came back and finally told him about Reverend Lelie's plan, he threatened to kill him with his Marine dagger. I swear, he was all set to slit Reverend Lelie's throat with that dagger of his, you know the one, in that leather sheath, the one he always kept within reach, crazy bastard that he was, and he smiled and told me there was still blood on it, and then you know the score 'cause horrible things happened over there in the tropics, worse than over here, way worse than here. Not like with the Jews, mind, that was different altogether. But at last the papers arrived from Indonesia and they were enough so we could be married by the magistrate.'

'Oh, so Indonesia saved the day?'

'No, I'll get to that in a bit.'

'That can't be right. In Holland they tell him his papers are no good, so they leave it up to the Indonesians and they decide it's all fine? Since when did a Dutchman ever take an Indonesian's word for anything? What kind of bullshit is that?'

'Pipe down, will you? Let me finish! What do you know about it? It must have had something to do with him being a political refugee, with him having to flee the country all of a sudden. Anyway, the papers meant we didn't need my parents' permission to marry. We were wed on 28 March 1951. Two witnesses: that marine from Tilburg and your father's bosom buddy, Sundahl, the one who ended up emigrating to America. But here's the best bit, it turned out your father still wasn't a Dutch national. In Indonesia he was registered as Chinese, so while we were waiting for him to be nationalized or naturalized or whatever, I became a Chinese by marriage. The one and only Brabant-born heffalump registered in The Hague as a Chinky!'

'That's not what Pa says. At the end of his memoirs he writes… Here, read for yourself…'

'Memoirs? You have his memoirs? How did you get your hands on them?'

'I'll tell you later.'

'But no one's supposed to read them!'

'Why ever not?'

'They're secret!'

'Not secret from you, surely?'

From Baldy's memoirs (1)

Soil of the Fatherland

On 14 April 1950, I first set foot on the soil of the Fatherland. A military band was lined up on the IJ docks, playing popular tunes of the day to welcome the homecoming soldiers. For me, it was one surprise after another. Everything was new and strange. Once our transport ship, the *Great Bear*, had docked, I disembarked with my fellow marines. We walked down the long gangway to a large warehouse on the quay. Barriers held back the cheering crowd. Among the throng, a mob of young Communists began shouting abuse at us, calling us mass murderers, rapists and hurling other choice epithets. The marines up ahead were so angry they dropped their duffel bags and dived into a fistfight with those scum. I was ordered to join in, whether I wanted to or not. I did not hesitate and began to lash out. The Military Police soon arrived in a bid to calm things down but they were not much help. By that time, the regular soldiers had disembarked and they waded into the fray. The arrival hall was one big battlefield. Eventually, the troublemakers took to their heels and order was restored.

I recovered my suitcase and joined the marines queuing at the tables of refreshments, where helpful ladies stood waiting with apples and packets of sandwiches. A charming little Red Cross nurse handed me a packed lunch with the words, 'Welcome to your Fatherland, East Indian marine.'

I was so nervous and surprised, all I could say was, 'I thank you.' Never in my life had a white Dutchwoman greeted me with such friendliness, such warmth. In the Indies such humanity would have been unthinkable, since we, the product of the Indies, were third-class citizens, the dusky dregs of society. We were on the same level as the natives, the people they used to call *inlanders* and now refer to as Indonesians. And if they found out you had been born out of wedlock, you were treated as a pariah.

Waiting for the rest of my baggage in the arrival hall, I joined my mates Ben de Lima, Harry Rijckaerdt and Jonker Laperia, and we found a quiet corner where we could enjoy our packed lunches. A little while later, a couple of Dutch pals came over and treated us to bottles of beer. I decided to go for a wander and bumped into a number of porters. Among them were a few old friends who had made the voyage before I did. When I asked if there were no better jobs for them, they told me work was thin on the ground and began banging on about the good old days.

It was late afternoon by the time our baggage was loaded onto the waiting buses bound for various destinations. I said farewell to my friends and boarded the bus to The Hague. There I was housed temporarily in the home of Thea Kötner on Parallelweg. Thea was a divorcée whose ex-husband had been given custody of her three children. The very next day I had to move to a boarding house on Oostduinlaan, run by Mrs Essenberg. She came from the Indies, but sympathy and solidarity were not in her nature. Money was her sole motivation for taking me in. Another day passed and I reported to the municipal offices on Goudenregenplein. There I handed in my green passport. The desk clerk, a demobbed soldier who had served in the Indies, took the document and bitterly cursed the old colonial system that had fobbed me off with a green passport and the status of 'Dutch subject'.

'I'll get you a full Dutch passport within a week,' the clerk said. 'A blue one. It's a bloody disgrace, if you ask me. The emigration office in the Indies should have given you Dutch nationality on the spot.'

Before my first week in the boarding house was over, I received a phone call summoning me to see the paymaster at the headquarters of the Marine Corps in Rotterdam. I took the next train and after a long search finally found the place. There I met Piet Dikotta, my former commanding officer at the Marine Brigade Security Service in Surabaya, who had landed a cushy job at HQ. He escorted me to the paymaster's office.

The paymaster was a lieutenant commander who had seen active service in the tropics. He invited me to sit down and asked me where I was staying and how I was doing. I told him I had to pay Mrs Essenberg 150 guilders a week for board and a humble breakfast. A bath cost fifty cents extra. On hearing this, he all but exploded. He grabbed the telephone directory, found her number and unleashed a barrage of maritime expletives down the phone at her. Fuming and red in the face, he slammed down the receiver. This did me the power of good. He ordered me to leave the boarding house immediately and to report to the naval barracks on Van Alkemadelaan in The Hague. There I could stay free of charge until I was able to pay my own way. And so I stumbled from one dubious adventure to the next, until I married one of the many girls who had written to me.

Recollections of a heffalump (2)

'Ha! "One of the many girls!" He should have been so lucky!'

'Ma, it's his nationality I'm trying to get at. I always thought he had dual nationality: Chinese and Dutch.'

'Yes, come to think of it, you're right. There was that time – this was years later – when I got a visit from the immigration office. Knocked on the door of my little flat in Zoetermeer they did, suspected me of being in the country illegally. Showed me a paper that said I was Chinese. Me… a Chinky! So I pull my eyes back, all slanty like, and we have a good laugh about it, me and the two blokes from immigration. Never heard another word about it.'

'That makes sense. When Nana went to the post office to apply for her ID card, the girl behind the counter asked her which nationality she wanted on the card: Chinese or Dutch… "What?" Nana says. "Am I Chinese?" "Yes," the girl says. "Can I have both?" Nana asks. Yes, no problem. I always envied my little sister because I wanted dual nationality myself so I could travel to China without any hassle. Life's all about the paperwork, eh Ma?'

'Huh? If only! There you go, talking bollocks again! So you think you lot are Chinese, too? Wouldn't that be something! Well, you'd pass for Chinese sooner than I would, that's for sure. But to get back to my story: we got out of that filthy, whore-ridden neighbourhood near the station, thank God, and found ourselves a place on Bilderdijkstraat. That's where the real trouble began.'

Matagora

The photo from Bilderdijkstraat was taken not long before my birth. It's the only photo I have from that time. My mother is heavily pregnant with us, the twins. Near her stands a friend of the family. He and my mother are smiling broadly. Their smiles are real, not pretend; the mood one of mutual sympathy my parents could never attain. A length of striped cloth hangs from a rod at the window, an improvised curtain. The stripes are horizontal and make the place look shabby.

Before I was born, my parents were living in an obscure little hotel opposite the public library on Bilderdijkstraat in The Hague. The place was always full of actors, some of them famous at the time.

Years later, the hotel became the kind of seedy establishment where lovers meet during office hours. An attractive Indo woman with a paranoid streak and a deep-seated fear of parting with her address once proposed we go there together. The rooms were rented by the hour. But I was daunted by the idea of making love in the place where my mother's waters had broken one sultry afternoon, to say nothing of doing the deed within sixty minutes at a given time of day.

As my mother tells it, she and my father only stayed there a month or two. The room in the photo bears all the hallmarks of my father: a bookcase cobbled together from old crates and stacked with ring binders; the bound, embossed volumes of an encyclopaedia; a stack of textbooks topped by a ticking alarm clock. A medicine cabinet on the wall. A *batik* cloth struggling to liven up the wallpaper, a light switch made of Bakelite. The smile the man and woman share is baffling.

'Who's that guy again?' I ask.

'That's Matagora. He was in love with me.'

'Matagora... Christ, I'd forgotten that name. What do you mean he was in love with you?'

'Just what I said! You've heard of people falling in love, haven't you?'

'Why would Matagora be in love with you? Who falls in love with his best friend's pregnant wife?'

'Oh, I wouldn't say Matagora was his best friend. Sundahl was your father's best friend.'

'Was Matagora a marine, too?'

'No, Matagora was with the East Indies Army.'

'Did he kill Indonesians? I heard all those KNIL blokes did was shoot in the air.'

'How should I know? God, you ask the daftest questions sometimes. Your mother was nowhere near that stinking war, remember? I was back here in Brabant. Besides, Matagora never wanted to talk about the bloody war, not like your bloody father with those non-stop bloody stories of his. He was a very nice man. Handsome too.'

Matagora is wearing a trench coat and woollen gloves, about to leave by the look of things. For this farewell snapshot, his elbow is resting on a stack of books and he is looking straight into the lens and smiling. Friendly are his dark, sculpted features, typically Ambonese traits. Bright are his teeth. Ma-ta-go-ra. His name has the ring of a magic spell. He was alone, no wife, no children. Thirteen years on, that hadn't changed.

My mother is closer to the camera, her swollen belly rounding out a drab maternity dress. It's around this time that my father begins to hit her. He kicks that belly of hers. I must have felt it; we can't have had a peaceful time in there, my twin and I. We grow impatient, start hammering on the wall of her womb. My mother goes through hell and we are born early. Four weeks early according to my father, five according to my mother. Or one says six and the other eight, whichever number suits them best.

A black paraffin heater stands between Matagora and my mother. If the heater was burning, it must have been a cold spring; we were born in the summer. The corner of a bed edges into the frame. It must have been one of those bedsits where you do everything in one room, including washing yourself at a cold-water tap.

The photographer can only be my father. He loved taking photos, sent entire series to his family in Indonesia – independent of the Netherlands by then – in the hope they would arrive. My mother is looking to the side and smiling at Matagora, who in turn smiles at the camera.

'He warned me about your father,' she said.

'What do you mean "warned you"?'

'What do you think I mean? Lost your memory all of a sudden?'

'What did he say to you?'

'What do you think he said? That I should leave him, even before you two were born. He was willing to take me with him, to rescue me and the two of you from your father's clutches. He knew your father was off his chump. Knew ever since they met in that stinking East Indies of theirs.'

'And the war didn't send Matagora over the edge?'

'It's nothing to do with the bloody war! That father of yours was crazy long before the war broke out. And he knew that, Matagora knew.'

'So that's why he hung around with Pa? Fancied being best mates with a guy who was off his chump?'

'You can be friends with someone who's not right in the head, can't you? What about that shower you hang around with? Are they all normal? What if one of them commits a murder, what then? Would you just drop them?'

'I wouldn't run off with his wife and kids, that's for sure.'

'If only I'd done it! Think of the misery I'd have been spared with that father of yours.'

'Maybe Matagora would have hit you too.'

'Matagora?'

'Isn't that what they say? That Ambonese men knock their wives about?'

'Not Matagora! He was gentle as can be!'

It's true, he was a gentle man. I never saw much of Matagora. But I often heard his name, back when my father used to visit him. I never went along; my father never took any of his children to see Matagora. Perhaps Matagora lived in some ten-by-ten backstreet dive and was ashamed of his situation.

The last time I saw him was the summer I turned thirteen. My father had laid into me and I had run into the bathroom. Hunched over the basin, I watched the tap water carry off the blood that dripped from my face. Strange, but I saw beauty in my blood mixing with the water, the evidence diluted and draining away. Someone came into the room. I did not have to look up to know it was my father. Matagora appeared too. His voice was soft and calm, an incantation almost. My father left and I looked into Matagora's troubled eyes. It felt safe with him standing there, as if to protect me from another of my father's outbursts.

Matagora at the bathroom door. About to leave, like the photo of him and my mother, taken thirteen years earlier. My mother shooting him a loving look. That's what it was. She was smitten. With Matagora, who became a buffer between me and my father, until it was no longer needed or it no longer mattered. I never saw him again.

But wait, was there one last time? One Sunday a few years later, during visiting hours at the children's home in Voorschoten. As we said goodbye, that father of mine suddenly started blubbering. An embarrassing spectacle, watching that brute bawl his eyes out. My friends obligingly turned their heads away. Matagora put his arm around my weeping father's shoulder and together they walked away, out through the gates of a home where no war was raging. Was it Matagora who was with him that day? Whatever happened to that gentle man?

Recollections of a heffalump (3)

'Pa was working full time by then. And in the hotel you had Jan Retèl and Sigrid Koetse – she was still under age, so there was some funny business going on there – and a whole bunch of other actors who hung around with them, you know what it's like with those celebrities. Jan Retèl was a big name in those days, believe you me. They'd help me down the stairs, 'cause I could barely manage with that big belly of mine and Jan Retèl said to me, "Oh, what a waste – you should've been on the stage." And he meant it, you know. I'd always wanted to be a comedy actress.'

'Was your young man from the tropics still knocking you about in that hotel on Bilderdijkstraat?'

'No, your father and me were getting on fine then.'

'Are you sure? You told me once he kicked you in the belly not long before we were born.'

'No, that was earlier.'

'With you it's a different story every time.'

'By then your father was paying me no heed at all! Always out gallivanting. Had his papers by that time. He was safe here in Holland but in Indonesia they'd have chopped him up and had him for breakfast, he knew that for sure. But instead of leaving the war behind him, he was wedded to it. One morning at the crack of dawn he left for an air show in Ypenburg. You remember how ridiculously early he used to get up – never shook those idiotic tropical ways of his. He collected books about planes; obsessed with them he was. War planes of course, not passenger planes but jet fighters and bombers and helicopters and God knows what else. When he left I told him I wasn't feeling well in that stuffy little attic room but he couldn't have cared less. A little cot was all set up for you two and your little clothes were ready because by then we knew you were twins – your father had twins in the family, Ella and Ina, his sisters – and all of a sudden the blood started pouring out of me. I panicked, staggered out onto the landing and screamed, but there was no one around, no Alice, no Sigrid, no Jan Retèl. An old couple lived next door but even they weren't home. And the hotel was closed on Sundays, so the owner wasn't there either. I had to get down those steep stairs with that big belly of mine, one foot at a time, to get to the telephone in the hall. I slid ten cents in the slot and called Aunt Annie, 'cause she liked to move with the times and already had her own phone. It was seven in the evening by the time Annie came thumping up the stairs with a taxi driver in tow. We packed a few things and the cab took us to the maternity clinic on Prins Mauritslaan.'

'Ha! Not far from the house where Tjalie Robinson would end up living, writing and working on his hopeless dream of turning a bunch of Indos into something that resembled a people.'

'As if I'd know anything about that. There you go again, with your books and your writers. I never knew musicians read so many books. My father never so much as opened a book. He played his music and kept his mouth shut the rest of the time. Anyway, somehow the police managed to track your father down and give him the news and he arrived at the clinic just as you were being born.'

'So he didn't arrive till half past two in the morning? That must have been one hell of an air show!'

'No, he turned up at one. God only knows where he'd been. Might have been half-twelve even. You were a breech birth, so I was already half-dead. You came out feet first so they shoved you back in and then you came out back first. Phil was lying crossways and you were already half an hour old when they decided to get him out by Caesarean. "You or the baby?" they asked. I can't remember what I said. Later they told me the doctor thought I was a goner – it happened a lot in those days. At death's door, I was. Phil too. It really was him or me. You came *this* close to having no mother and no twin brother. Your father all to yourself – how would you have liked that? Well, the clinic had just been reopened and you were the first twins and the whole ward was waiting for you. The pair of you were laid on a little bed with hot water bottles and a glass top. An incubator, yes, very high tech in those days and it had wheels so you could sleep next to my bed.'

'An aquarium.'

'Aquarium? What are you on about?'

'I suddenly thought of Pa's obsession with that aquarium, a mania he passed on to me.'

'I can barely follow you at times, do you know that? You and that brother of yours. Sometimes I think they beamed you down from another planet, I really do! I spent a couple of days in the delivery room 'cause I wasn't breathing right. You were wheeled from one end of the ward to the other. Everyone wanted to see you, 'cause you were the only brown babies in the place, a sight to behold. Three weeks passed and then you came home with me, back to Bilderdijkstraat and that attic room at the hotel.'

'Hey, Ma, did you know that hotel became a knocking shop? Number 12 Bilderdijkstraat. According to house numerology, one plus two equals three, and any house with the number three is a proper fuck palace.'

'Less of the language!'

'Come on, it's only a bit of fun.'

'But now you mention it… a knocking shop… I can't say I'm surprised. There was nowhere to put your things and the beds took up half the room. That didn't matter to the actors of course – they were on stage every night. During the day I had artistes rinsing out your nappies and waiting on me hand and foot. If you cried in the middle of the night, the old folk next door would come and complain. But what was the owner going to do, throw us out on the street? Pa wrote to the Queen, the Mayor and God knows who else. Never stopped banging away at his typewriter, telling them all how he had fought for the Dutch red-white-and-blue as a marine. Don't you remember him typing away all the time? Sometimes I thought he'd type himself silly, and the pair of you into the bargain.'

'There was a Dutch writer whose cat always lay next to his typewriter. That moggy got addicted to the tap-tap-tap. In the end it went doolally. I swear… doolally tap.'

'I'll take your word for it. Anyway the typing paid off, 'cause they offered us a house on Schermerstraat, not far from Zuider Park. But it was still being built and one night I came down with a high fever. The artistes called a doctor and he said get her over here quick and two of the actors put me in a cab to the hospital on Zuidwal and went back inside to take care of you two. At the hospital they told me I had mastitis and they had to keep me in. They brought you over the next day and the whole ward went daft when they wheeled in two brown kiddies. They gave you a pink wristband and Phil a blue one, or the other way around, I can't remember exactly.'

'That's important to Phil. He wound up believing they swapped us around at that place: that he became me and I became him, astrologically speaking.'

'Him and his star signs. Does he ever see people as people? I knew damn well who was who – I didn't need a wristband to tell me that. And what does it matter anyway? You get one life and that's your lot. Those nurses fell in love with you two, by the way. Spoiled you rotten, they did. You slept in the same cot. And that father of yours didn't know what was going on, came marching in bold as you please and demanded to take you home with him. As if he had the faintest idea how to take care of you. It took a whole army of nurses to calm him down and tell him that wasn't the way it worked in Holland. Well, he swore he would come back every day, but of course he didn't, the lying sod. Had to work overtime, or so he said. God only knows where he was hanging out. He was busy trying to sort out that house on Schermerstraat and when he did visit he always brought someone with him. Once he turned up with an Indo woman who said you'd have a sharp tongue when you were older because it had a deep groove in it. And another Indo woman said you had the second sight 'cause you were born with a caul and your fontanelle took ages to close. You were sickly and spent half the time sleeping, while Phil was a fierce one and could bite really hard. You had to take turns at the breast and there was a woman who'd had a stillbirth and she was allowed to give you the bottle, first one then the other. Cheered her up no end. Then they'd take you back to the baby ward and that's how it went for three months there on Zuidwal. By the time they discharged me our house was ready, but I went back specially to the hotel on Bilderdijkstraat to say goodbye to those lovely actors. Kind folk they were, so kind.'

Incubator

In the beginning my parents created the heavens and the earth. The earth was savage and then tranquil and the spirit of my parents hovered over the waters. 'Let there be light!' my father said and flicked the switch on his desk lamp. And he saw that the light was good, and he saw that his typewriter was good and he separated light from darkness. Light he called the tedium of day, darkness the playground of love. And there was evening and there was morning, the first day. 'I feel a vault within my body,' said my mother. And so the heavens and the earth were separated. Neither she nor he had power over the vault within her belly and they both named it hell, for soon they would no longer be alone in that shabby, cosy little bedsit in the gloom of Bilderdijkstraat, where rain poured and snow turned the pavement slippery and passers-by saw this couple as strange, for they looked nothing like the couples with hats, headscarves and umbrellas who peopled the streets. They were the whore and the stranger from the East. They were slaves to their desires, worse than the Jews who had been driven in their thousands from the city's streets to its cold, damp stations, where long trains stood waiting to take them to places far worse than hell, where they were gassed and incinerated and where years later swollen cabbages sprouted from soil made fertile by those who had choked to death in gas chambers.

My father had another war in his head, a war no one in this city seemed to know. In Holland, the war had been reduced to the bitter winter of 1944–45 and the hunger and desperation that came with it. Not a word about the Jews. And the colonies were just far-off places where greedy Dutchmen gave Indonesians a taste of the lash, rode the native girls and fathered half-breeds who have been called many a name through the centuries. Coloured they were, blue even.

They were creole, half-bloods and half-castes, injuns, East Indians, Indos and Eurasians. The words came thick and fast, in Dutch that bastardized Malay and Portuguese: *klipsteen*, *liplap*, *sinjo*, *nonnie*, *petjoek*, *serani*. *Mesties* they were, and *poesties* and *kasties* and *toepas* and *cristietsen*... until finally, in post-war Holland, they settled on 'Indo-Dutch'. A label my father clung to for dear life. A label that sticks in my throat.

He wanted to be like his wife, except for her complete lack of intellect, and he called this land of hers heaven, though it was cold as hell and he had to pile on thick clothes to shield himself from wind and weather. For his wife, Indonesia must have seemed like paradise, with its palm trees, blue skies and sunshine, but her husband no longer knew of such things. He spoke constantly of the war and when she asked him to stop he flew into a rage and hit her in the face. And when her belly grew so big that the heffalump began to resemble a beached whale, he kicked it. At times she denies this, at times she does not, depending on her mood.

At these blows, the vault turned strange with fluid and noise, and we grew restless and wanted to escape the stifling belly. We fought for our place at the aperture and in the final struggle I ended up below and my brother above. I pressed my feet against the opening and pinned my brother above me, sideways so he had no escape. Someone yanked me out with a pair of forceps, then wrestled with the problem of how to shift that other unwanted knot of gristle from one hell to another. My mother was given a choice: his life or hers. She raved that they had to get him out – what would the neighbours say if she chose to save herself – and they sliced her belly open and freed him from that bomb shelter where it had never been safe. My brother lived. My mother too.

My brother and I were unusual twins due to the enormous time difference of thirty-five minutes. Our astrological ascendants are not the same: mine is Cancer, his is Leo.

In the beginning, it was formless, dark and full of shadows. Sometimes there was strange music, all echoes and humming dissonants. My mother later claimed that these sounds made me cry as I lay in my cradle. And my father kicked the cradle until I was quiet again. And so there was no difference between belly and cradle. The incubator, an aquarium without water, surrounded by the kindness of nurses… that I cannot remember. It is a fantasy at best.

Once I was a fish.

The fish is.

Now that I am human, I shun daylight and would rather sleep on a couch by the radio than in a bed in a darkened room. I am a musician. I come to life in the evening, live by night. For years I could not bring myself to play jazzy dissonants on my guitar. They unsettled me, stirred up memories I could not pin down.

Recollections of a heffalump (4)

'Remember Ollie Plomp? She was from Suriname – not many of them in Holland back then – and married to a Dutchman from Gelderland. She lived next door on Schermerstraat by Zuider Park. One evening she came to the door with one of those wide prams. Over the moon, I was. It meant I could go for walks with the two of you. You turned brown as a berry in the sun; Phil was always paler. We knew a lot of nice people: the De Niet family, Aunty Fien, Aunty Lieke, Thea Buren or Bürer – never could remember her name – all from the Indies, except Aunty Fien of course. Everyone loved to see you and by that time we had more or less patched things up with my parents. But people on the street would stop and stare or they'd stop me and ask: are you married to one of them blokes from the Indies? I felt so ashamed pushing that big pram of yours. They looked at me like I was a whore. Not Ollie Plomp, of course, 'cause she was black and married to a white chap so that was different. And it was better to be a black woman married to a white man. She knew what she was doing, Ollie Plomp. That father of yours couldn't stand your wailing at night but he wouldn't let me pick you up. Sometimes he got so angry he'd shout, "For God's sake! I've got to be up early!"

And he'd go over and kick your cot. That soon shut you up. A man from Gelderland would never have done that. But when your father finally nodded off, I'd sneak out of bed every now and then and take a look at you. One day, I was feeding the two of you in the playpen when he came home from work. He had forgotten his keys, so he rang the doorbell. I didn't know it was him, so I didn't answer because he had told me never to open the door to anyone. But the bell kept ringing, so eventually I went to take a look. I opened the door and without saying a word he hit me right in the face. With his fist, mind! My cheek swelled up so bad I couldn't go out for a week. Ollie Plomp did my shopping for me and took you out in the pram. That's when he really began to scare me. He used to go to bed early, always complaining about his back, about falling into that ravine in his armoured car. Luckily, we knew the Van Mouriks, a big Indo family on Erasmusweg. We would go over there on a Sunday and there was always food on the go and lots of people chatting away in Malay, playing cards, singing, strumming guitars, not just Malay songs but Jim Reeves too – the Indos loved that soppy stuff, lapped it up they did. One of Van Mourik's cousins married a Dutch girl, so I finally had someone to talk to. Marietje van Mourik had the gift of the gab and she'd picked up that mix of Dutch and Malay they all spoke. She nattered on at a rate of knots and one time out of nowhere she said: "Annie, you know why you had such a terrible time giving birth? Because the two of you aren't suited." She just came right out with it! Meanwhile, I was expecting again.'

'Burst condom, right?'

'How do you know that?'

'Pa told me.'

'Oh, that father of yours is off his chump! But, fair do's, it might have been. You had to rinse them out and re-use them. Useless bloody things.'

'I remember them lying on the washbasin…'

'What? At that age?'

'Phil saw them too. I think we even played with them. But that was after the others were born.'

'Bloody cheek! Anyway, that house on Schermerstraat was much too small, what with Arti on the way, so we moved to Melis Stokelaan on the other side of the park. Another tenement flat but with an extra room. The day before Arti was born I had eaten a whole bunch of grapes. And the next day it was thunder and lightning. Arti arrived during the storm. The heat was killing and I had the runs. Arti came into this world covered in shite, I swear, absolutely covered in shite.'

'We say "shit" in these parts.'

'Oh, do you now? Well, at home we always said "shite".'

'Not exactly an auspicious omen.'

'Omen? What are you on about?'

'A sign of things to come. That boy has spent most of his life in the shit, Ma. Figuratively speaking. Why did you call him Arti, anyway? One letter removed from Arto.'

'I think he thought Arti would be our last. Something like that. I don't really know, I didn't have a say. He wanted to give you all American names. You know how he always wanted to emigrate to America. Come to think of it, he was the youngest, too.'

'A family of five, like us. He was the fifth.'

'We'd have been better stopping at two, 'cause your father had more and more trouble coping with family life. He started evening classes to become an engineer and got a job as a draughtsman at the Public Works department. But he had a hard time working his way up the ranks. He thought Holland was like the Indies and it was all about who you knew, but of course that's not how it went. There were bust-ups with his colleagues and he took all that out on us. When Mil was born, the house got too small for him, so he moved his desk into the bedroom and holed himself up in there. If you lot made a racket, he'd come storming out and bang your heads together or bang them against the wall – he couldn't stand your noise. And then you'd be whining in bed and I'd have to tend to you with cold flannels. I don't think I got to watch a single thing on TV without being interrupted. Remember how he knocked your mother out with a dumbbell? I landed on the girls' bed – yes, it was after Nana was born – and Pa filled a bucket with cold water and threw it in my face, the filthy sadist. Another time he whacked me on the arm with the lid of the wash-boiler.'

'I remember, all right. Phil and I tried to stop him and he belted us from one end of the flat to the other. And the next day it was, "Get the washing done, you two. Your mother's got thrombosis."'

'Yes. The insurance man who came to collect the monthly payments said once, "Goodness missus, where did you get those bruises?" I said nothing, of course, or your father would've killed me. Things went from bad to worse at the Public Works department and he was on the sick for a while. By then we were living on Hoogveen, in that nice little terraced house where you had your own room. But he got more aggressive, even the extra space didn't help. Always moaning about his back, not that it stopped him training with dumbbells and lifting those weights on a pulley. And tinkering non-stop with that filthy moped of his in the living room. The blue one. A Zone-dup.'

'Zündapp, Mam. It was German.'

'German? That greasy blue thing that stank of petrol? The whole room reeked of it. I could've sworn that man thought he was still living in the Indies. Garden doors wide open in all weathers.'

'Nice house. It was quiet up in my room. Though I remember putting my foot through one of those glass doors, in a rage because my brothers locked me out. Spent all summer with my leg in plaster.'

'Yes, I remember that all right.'

'Pa knocked a gap in the hedge so he could drive his moped through. I remember him driving it right into the house and sitting there just gazing at it once he'd finished polishing. The local kids didn't like us – we only had proper playmates after we moved to that evil little flat by the park. That's where it ended. Where it all fell apart, I mean. We were never together again after that, not all of us. No matter what the occasion, someone was always conspicuous by their absence. The family curse, we call it.'

'Who's *we*?'

'We, the children.'

'Oh, and what does that make us?'

'Who do you mean *us*?'

'Your father and your mother!'

'You're you.'

Heads

One day my mother came out with a mantra she would inflict on us for the rest of our lives. 'The two of you are from another planet.'

From an early age, my twin brother was fascinated by the laws of gravity, by rockets and UFOs, while I turned to the Bakelite radio to help me forget the harrowing war stories my father told. As long as my brother and I played side by side, all was well. The moment we played *with* each other, a fight would break out and my father would bang our heads together.

When I was around twenty-five years old, a woman told me she had seen stars once after her husband hit her. She told everyone. Till then she'd thought seeing stars was something that only happened in cartoons. This surprised me. Stars can take on many forms, depending how hard you are hit. Seeing stars isn't so bad. When you see meteors coming at you and feel sick to your stomach, that's when it gets hard to stay on your feet.

The worst thing was the moment before our heads collided. In a split second you look deep into the eyes of your terrified brother. And he looks into yours. I can't remember the last time we looked into each other's eyes. I'm afraid we never really have, afraid we've avoided each other's gaze our whole lives long.

Seeing stars is nothing. Never daring to look your brother in the eye again is something else. It's better when your head hits the wall. It feels different, harder, but you don't see your brother's terrified eyes coming towards you, becoming and then being your own. A wall is dead. A wall is not a mirror.

My room has one window and four bare walls. The room where

I am writing these words, I mean. I don't know why I never hang anything on the walls. I don't want to think about it. That's just the way it is.

Guitar Indo (1)

Hey Pa, in that one photo you took of your pregnant heffalump on Bilderdijkstraat I see all kinds of stuff on the floor and on the walls, but no guitar. In those early years in Holland, did owning a camera and a typewriter mean more to you than owning a guitar?

An Indo without a guitar is a weeping willow, Pa.

From the house on Schermerstraat – our first official residence – only a few photos remain. Snapshots of the street, a picnic with Granny Helmond in Zuider Park, us twins in the playpen. But from the flat on Melis Stokelaan, our family hell at number 1394, I have a shoebox full of photos: black-and-white, many in the standard format of the day – 3.5 x 3.5 inches – the odd one enlarged, some with wavy edges. Almost every photo you took in that place features a guitar, a cheap thing that hung on the wall, opposite the portrait of your mother. The guitar on the wall and your mother on the mantlepiece, directly above the coal fire so she wouldn't feel the Dutch cold. No laughing matter, eh Pa?

You seldom strummed that guitar. I only remember one evening, sitting around your bed with the others, singing from the stencils you kept in that no-nonsense, grey folder with the black linen spine. One of the rare evenings when you were a father, not a camp commandant. Yet you didn't play a single folk song from your motherland. There was no 'Terang Bulan'. No 'Nina Bobo'. No 'Bengawan Solo'. None of that stuff. Your favourites came from Jim Reeves, the syrupy nostalgia so popular among Indos of your generation. Followed by a parade of corny American songs you must have picked up from your Allied buddies back on Java. 'South of the Border' serenades a lover in Mexico. Mexico of all places! You cherished The American Dream, but your heart was drawn to Mexico, perhaps because you thought an Indo might blend in better there. You had a point: today the world's largest Indo community can be found in Los Angeles. The Indos there are mistaken for Mexicans all the time, so they grow a moustache, speak Spanish and borrow an identity more easily than they ever could in Holland.

What a visionary you were, to want to emigrate to California. As a child, I shuddered at the thought. Ma and I were the stick-in-the-muds who wanted to stay in Holland rather than make the leap to the land of fairy tales where a bartender can end up president. If I'm honest, it's something I regret when I look back. Sorry I was such a scared little boy, Pa, though I can't say whether it was America that scared me or the ocean I would have had to swim to escape you. Escaping, getting away from you, *that* was something I longed to do before I could crawl, you worthless fuck.

There I go again, hurling abuse. Sorry, Pa. But I swear with considerable restraint, don't you think? Why did I hear the slug of your typewriter more often than music from your guitar? Perhaps you played quietly, something many Indos do, so as not to wake the kids or the neighbours. Sometimes your guitar was missing from the wall and I knew it must be somewhere in your bedroom. To touch it was forbidden. Even as a small boy, I wanted to learn to play but to you it was more important to keep it free of scuffs and scratches. Your guitar was barely an instrument at all, more of a showpiece, and that's how it was treated. You rubbed it with teak oil on a regular basis, the worst thing you could have done. The moisture bent the neck out of shape. Well done you. You might as well have oiled your typewriter with Castrol GTX... Not that your failings ever stopped you making fun of me in front of the others. 'Cackie' you called me on a daily basis. Short for cack-handed. As if your fingers were so nimble. Were you really so afraid I'd end up dropping your guitar if I got my paws on it, or did you suspect I might outshine you as a musician?

Your bedroom, the place where you raped and abused your wife, was strictly off limits. If I ever ventured in there, I would drop to my knees in front of the guitar, take it gingerly by the neck to make sure it didn't fall over and run my thumb gently across the strings. That strange modern tuning was enchanting and frightening at the same time. E A D G B E… a world away from the harmonious *kroncong* or Hawaiian tuning. Even now, the sound of those open strings stirs memories in me of the war books stacked around that wide bed of yours and of the cold Marine dagger under your pillow, there in case some Indonesian freedom fighter appeared one night out of nowhere to slit your throat in revenge for everything you did back there, once upon a time on Java.

The guitar was mandatory, part of the furniture, a bare necessity for every Indo. I longed to hear music sounding in its belly, balm for the bloody tales of war you sent echoing around the living room night after night. There wasn't much music in your head, to say nothing of your hands. Why did you never stop counting your victims? Why could you never be quiet and simply play your guitar like your friends did? Why couldn't you live up to the cliché of the Indo? Oh, pardon me, you are not an Indo. Then what *are* you? An Indo-Dutchman? Congratulations on your title. Shame you had to fight so hard for it. But amid all the blood and guts, a decent yarn would cross your lips once in a while, thank Christ. Kids want to hear fairy tales, Pa, not war stories.

Pah Tjillih

Pah Tjillih was an old man. Lame, half-blind and always armed with a staff. He was known to possess special powers and in his younger days, it was said, he had learned the secrets of the martial arts from a venerable Chinese master. In line with the punishment he wished to dispense, one judicious blow from his staff was enough to paralyse the recipient's arm or leg for a week, a month or three months. A slow death lasting anything from three to six months was also part of his repertoire. This was done with a blow to the chest. But the worst thing Pah Tjillih could do was dispatch someone to the great hereafter with a curse uttered in Javanese.

Like all masters of the martial arts, Pah Tjillih also understood the extraordinary art of healing. With a laying on of hands he could work miracles. The potions and ointments he concocted were eagerly sought after throughout the region. And like all great minds, Pah Tjillih understood the art of being alone. He lived in a small house on the edge of Surabaya, where he tended his plants each day until the clock on the mantle struck six. Then night fell, and the jungle began to sing to him.

Long after the war and his flight from Indonesia, the news of Pah Tjillih's passing reached my father by letter. According to the old man's neighbours, the clock on the mantle stood still at the hour of his death and the plants in and around the house died with him.

Hello, Papa!

We could have done with more stories like that one, Pa. The letter must have been addressed to our family hell, that cramped four-room flat of ours. Did it feel lonely not to be able to share the memory of Pah Tjillih with your heffalump, a woman interested in little more than canned-laughter comedies on a black-and-white TV? Where did you open that letter? At your desk in the forbidden zone? Was it really a bedroom you shared with your heffalump? Or was it more an office-cum-torture chamber that just happened to contain a bed?

That room at the back of the flat, with its view of the perpetually deserted communal garden behind our block, was your domain. Ma's was the Formica chair in the kitchen, where she smoked the cigarettes she lit on the pilot light of the boiler. We sat down to eat in the living room at six on the dot, not a minute later. If you were late we waited, even if the food went cold, and when you came through the door, we greeted you in unison. 'Hello, Papa!'

The greeting was compulsory. Just as you once had to bow to

the Japs. We greeted you out of fear, as if you didn't know. And, to be honest, we sat there waiting for the day when you would not come home at all. Never again. When you would drive your moped into a canal and be dredged up days later by the fire brigade, your coffin dispatched on a special Royal Air Force plane back to Java, where it would be lowered into the water from the Red Bridge in Surabaya. Crocodiles would swim towards your coffin, almost as if they knew who you were, what you had done and how much pleasure they were about to give your Javanese enemies, who would watch the wood splinter and your corpse being torn to pieces. A wonderful island indeed where such things were possible. Man in harmony with nature. All very different to The Hague, where us Indo kids had to find a way to survive, living cheek by jowl with those oversized Dutch lads. Ma was always kicking us out onto the street to play. She didn't like children, doesn't like children, will never like children, that child-woman who rattles on but never quite says anything. Did her father like children, I wonder? Strange how that man down in Brabant could feel so much more distant than our dead grandfather on your side, lying in his grave on Java.

Weighing out nails

My maternal grandfather grew up in a Brabant orphanage and became something of a celebrity in Helmond when he won the state lottery twice in a row. He used the capital that landed in his lap to set himself up as a cobbler. I remember the dimly lit workshop, the smell of leather and out in the street the glint of cobblestones baking in the summer sun. I was only ever there in the summer holidays and the sun always shone. I don't remember it ever raining, nor do I remember Grandad Helmond ever coming to visit us in The Hague. He drove a black Citroën Traction Avant. Oh, the smell of that car! Leather upholstery, wooden dashboard, cigar smoke. The windscreen wipers were upside-down. Grandad

Helmond always struck me as good-humoured and even-tempered, and yes, come to think of it, I do remember rain: a huge cloudburst above De Peel, where we had been swimming in the crystal-clear peat lake. The whole car shook as it battled through a thick curtain of rain. One of the wipers snapped and I stared at the sole survivor as it sent water arcing across the windscreen, on tenterhooks wondering whether it would give out before we made it back to the cobbler's home.

As well as outings to De Peel, Grandad Helmond kept us amused by tapping his boiled egg against his forehead at breakfast, before spooning out the contents seasoned with pinches of salt. He said nothing at the breakfast table, barely spoke a word at all. Instead, he played the conjurer.

The eldest of the three boys, I was sometimes allowed to help out in the cobbler's workshop, where the smell of shoes and polish and animal fat created an air of devotion in the diffuse light that filtered in through the small windows. I had the honour of weighing out nails, sold to customers in a paper poke for fifteen cents so they could hammer the soles of their own shoes back into place.

The weights were ranked in order of size on a wooden block next to an intriguing set of scales. What a pleasure it was to be allowed to place one, two or three weights on the left scale, to scoop up the cobbler's nails with a handsome metal implement and let them slide onto the right scale. I would spend minutes on end fiddling till the two sides were perfectly balanced.

To begin with, Grandad Helmond would put up with my painstaking attempts to level the scales by adding or subtracting a single nail. But there always came a moment when he could stand it no longer. 'It don't have to be down to the last nail,' he'd say, 'long as it's right more or less.' And he would fill ten pokes in a minute where it would have taken me an hour. Gone was the enchantment of the gently rocking scales and the pleasure of calligraphing the price on the brown paper pokes with a soft pencil. I was crushed, my summer holiday knocked out of whack. What is a shoemaker without a heart for beauty and precision?

Recollections of a heffalump (5)

'The stifling heat had been building all day and that night a ferocious thunderstorm let rip. I was born amid thunder and lightning on 30 August 1928 and they named me Johanna Henrica van Kerkoerle. My mother was twenty-four and my father was twenty-eight. I came after my brother Jan, their first daughter. My father was overjoyed and tied one on, 'cause every bar in town had to hear the good news. My parents had a little shop and cobbler's workshop on Heistraat. Helmond was a factory town and everyone worked hard for a living. My mother used to go round all the customers to ask if their shoes needed mending and my father was known as the best shoemaker in town and he worked day and night. It was his dream to own a big business one day. I was still a babe in arms when he won the jackpot in the state lottery: 100,000 Dutch guilders. He moved to bigger premises, bought a car, got his driving licence from the mayor in exchange for a box of cigars and the customers started coming to us instead of my mother having to chase them down. At the weekend, my father played in a band that performed in the surrounding villages. Accordion and fiddle he played, and he would give his bandmates a lift. He drove them home too, much the worse for drink, and one night he ran his black Citroën Traction Avant straight into a canal, with four of his bandmates inside, that's how drunk they all were. They crawled out and when my father came home he said his car had drowned. He bought a new one a week later, another black Citroën Traction Avant. Raised an orphan, he had been booted from one foster home to the next and he was determined never to scrimp and save again, especially when he won the lottery a second time and banked another 100,000 guilders. His band played polkas, mazurkas and waltzes, and of course they belted out a tear jerker or two. We had one of those old gramophone players at home with records by Mario Lanza and Caruso. You had to crank it up and the needle always needed replacing. Mies wasn't long born when the Depression hit: the poor workers queued up at the soup kitchens pan in hand, and when Jan and me were driven to school, the poor buggers used to pelt the car with whatever they could lay their hands on. Money got tighter for us too, and we moved to a rented place with a shop on Mierloseweg. I was six and I had a swing up in the attic. We didn't have it so tough. When Riek, our crazy Riek, was born, we moved to Beelsstraat. A busy street it was, with a butcher's and a greengrocer's opposite, and just down from us was Van Asseldonck's bakery and the chemist's, and right next door was a builder's yard. There were some lovely lads working there and sometimes I'd climb onto the roof and call to them and when they looked up I'd duck out of sight. The contractor complained to my father and after that I wasn't allowed on the roof any more and I had to help in the workshop.'

'Grandad used to let me weigh out nails in the workshop.'

'Did he now? The folk across the street were mad about you lot, you know. They thought you were so cute, a bunch of little brown kids, and they stuffed you full of sweets.'

'Yeah. They didn't hit us or yell at us or lock us in the cupboard.'

'Oh, come off it! Who in Helmond ever locked you in a cupboard?'

'Your mother.'

'Well, you must have been asking for it.'

'Was she in the habit of doing that? Locking kids in cupboards? Did your mother ever lock you in a cupboard?'

'Not that I can remember, but then I did as I was told. I did well at school. No great shakes at Dutch and arithmetic, but I was good at geography and history. And yes, times were bad, there was still a lot of poverty, but as a little girl all that went over my head. When I was around ten, I heard talk of Hitler. As a child you were never allowed to hear anything about politics, it was nothing but say your prayers, go to school, say your prayers, go out to play and that was that. You had no idea what went on in the big bad world. It was a sheltered life we led at home, at school too. Till I came home one day and my parents were huddled by the radio, I'd never seen them so worried. I asked what was wrong but my mother put her finger to her lips, as if the Germans could hear us. "War's broken out," she said. I was twelve and before we went to bed that night someone on the radio said just go to sleep as usual, no cause for alarm. In the middle of the night we woke to the drone of hundreds of German planes and in the morning we heard shots fired in the street by a handful Dutch soldiers. What a useless shower they were! The Queen gave a speech on the radio and told us the invasion had begun. It was a week before we could go outside again. There were tanks and German soldiers everywhere. But they tried to build a bit of a rapport with us and in the first few months it didn't seem so bad. Things got worse when they brought in a seven o'clock curfew: anyone who couldn't identify themselves was shot dead on the spot. We were ordered to black out the windows and in the daytime Germans soldiers came to confiscate all our copper and brass: jugs, pots, vases, egg cups, tobacco jars… anything made of copper had to be handed over. If you hid it and they found it later, they stood you against a wall and shot you. I was in an awful state about our copper cigar box, 'cause Father always let me open it and fetch a cigar for him or if a gentleman came to call, and I was always so careful when I lifted up that lovely lid and then I'd lay eyes on those beautiful cigar bands and the smell was wonderful! So I hid that beautiful copper cigar box under the divan to keep it from the Germans and oh did I get what for – the only time in my life that my mother gave me what for. But I knew why, 'cause if the Germans had found it they'd have lined us all up and shot us full of bullets and you'd never have seen the light of day!'

'God, if only the Germans had done that.'

'Oh, for crying out loud! How can you say such a thing?'

'It's a joke, Ma.'

'Call that a joke? You're a weird one, you are! From another planet… do you hear me? Another planet! Off your head, just like that crazy brother of yours, always peering through that telescope of his in Geneva or God knows where he's hanging out these days. At least he was always civil to me, not like you. Always treat me like a stupid cow, you do. Like I'm a child, you little prick! Anyway, the occupation wasn't so bad to start with. But then the rationing got worse and you needed coupons for everything. You had coupons for bread, cloth, shoes – though when that came in people went back to wearing clogs. I used to have to queue for hours with those coupons when I came home from school. Veg and potatoes weren't rationed in the first year and a lot of black-market dealings went on and people hoarded like mad but the Huns put an end to that and then we were back to queueing up for a bunch of leeks and a kilo of spuds for ten cents a go. Meanwhile, my father would call on the farmers and exchange shoes for flour, milk and grain. The baker's van was a moving target. They'd block the road, steal his bread and knock the living daylights out of him. After a while you had to queue from six in the morning to have any chance of a bite to eat. The Huns were hungry too, of course, and if they saw you walking along with bread and cheese they'd nick the lot and leave you empty-handed. They left the kids alone, which is why I was always sent out to run the errands. But then the British started bombing German targets at night and we had to take cover in the air raid shelters. They often warned us when the British were coming – I can't remember how exactly – and the Germans began to fire off them V1s of theirs. When it was all over, you'd come out and find bits of rocket in the garden but a cousin of mine in Eindhoven was in a shelter – a trench in the sand covered with boards down at the bottom of the garden – and she got hit by a stray V1 and died on the spot. So your father can bang on about his family and his eight cousins beheaded by the Japs, but we lost a cousin too. And all the able-bodied lads were sent off to Germany to work in the munitions factory or on the roads. They made my father repair a lot of the soldiers' boots. Oh, they paid him all right – they were good like that, the Huns. The winter of 1943 was bitter cold, twenty below freezing, and the moon and the stars twinkled in the sky. From the shelter, I would look up at the stars and keep very still and pray to God that no bombs would fall on our house. The schools were closed to save on fuel. One day a young German soldier – couldn't have been a day over eighteen – came to pick up his boots and stood there crying in the shop. He showed us photos of his parents and his brother and his little sisters. "I never wanted this war," he kept saying. "I love my family and I want to go back home." Broke my heart it did, and after that I stopped hating the Germans. A lot of fancy houses had been commandeered and later it turned out they were houses that had belonged to Jews who'd been taken away and put on one of those trains. Never saw them again. And ordinary German families came and lived in those houses because things were bad in Germany too. British bombers were blowing everything to bits, so what else were they supposed to do? And you'd hear the planes coming over at night, heading for Germany again, so it was no picnic for them either. One day the Germans came and confiscated all our radios. No one, not a single one of us, was allowed to hear another word about the war, but lots of people had a receiver tucked away somewhere and at night messages were broadcast by some kind of secret service about how things were in Holland and that was when we heard how Rotterdam had refused to surrender and how bad they had it there. We didn't know till later that they'd borne the brunt of it – all those bombs, all those people killed – and that's why some folk took to calling Rotterdammers "cockroaches". Sick, isn't it? Calling your own countrymen cockroaches because they were bombed to a pulp? And after the radios we had to hand over our bikes. Some of those Germans had never ridden one before and had to learn, but what did I care about my bike? I wanted to be an actress! At school we had a little theatre group but I fell off the high bar during gym class and sprained my ankle and my best friend got the lead part and I was miserable 'cause I was a damn sight better than she was – Jan Retèl saw that straight away all those years later in that hotel on Bilderdijkstraat. Oh, if only I'd wound up there without your father, I could have been a TV actress. What about that? Your mother on the telly? Of course, you wouldn't have been around to see me, but still. Anyway, where was I? Oh yes, 1944. Well, there were all kinds of rumours that the Tommies were coming. That's what we called the British.'

'After Thomas Atkins, a soldier who died fighting the French. Thomas perished in the arms of the Duke of Wellington and they say it was his doing that Atkins came to represent the British soldier. In both World Wars, friend and foe referred to the Brits as Tommies.'

'How do you know all that?'

'Listen, Ma, I've immersed myself in that bloody war of yours more than you ever did. The fate of a post-war kid who thinks his future is determined by the past of his forefathers.'

'Ah, what are you on about? You didn't have to live through the war! And if I were you, I'd be glad of it.'

'That war of yours filled our house for thirteen years! Till Child Services came and got us out of there.'

'Oh, and I suppose the war never got a mention at that children's home in Voorschoten?'

'Of course it did. The head there gave us that "you lot never lived through the war" schtick often enough. We weren't allowed to *have* problems, never mind cause any. We were supposed to be happy, because we hadn't lived through the war. We were raised by war children, so what right did we have to complain? Phil and I never complained, by the way, at least not when we were younger. Remember how you used to lay our duffel coats on top of the blankets because the winters were so cold? We were eight and you had us dragging those bloody great sacks of coal through the snow and I had to get up at the crack of dawn to stoke the fire while you and Pa were still in bed. And if I turned up my nose at a meal it was all because I hadn't lived through that war of yours.'

'That was your father! He was the one always on about the war! Like the only war was in Indonesia and nothing happened here. But those Huns got more vicious as the war went on, more likely to put you up against a wall and gun you down for no reason. And Jews were still being carted off, though we had no idea where to, of course – we had other things to worry about.'

'An entire section of the population is dragged off just like that and no one has an inkling?'

'We thought they were being put to work in Germany!'

'Men, women and *children*? A kid at a lathe, making warheads?'

'How were we supposed to know about the death camps? Why would we even *think* something like that? Gas chambers! That's not something that enters your head, is it? Well then! And in the summer, and the summer was scorching one year, we had to gather wood in the forest to stock up for winter. Try that instead of lugging a few sacks of coal.'

'I never complained. I only wanted to remind you. You never seem to remember a thing when it comes to us.'

'Would you rather have sat there in the cold, you daft lump? So what if it snowed? A little snow never hurt anyone... Those filthy Huns laid landmines in the woods, so you had to watch your step when you gathered firewood. That's a damn sight worse than slipping in the snow with a coal sack on your shoulders. And sometimes we'd queue for hours for a bit of bread and the Germans would come along and take it all for the top brass and put a sign in the window: *SOLD OUT!*

'That said, we never went hungry at home, 'cause my father kept on trading shoes with the local farmers, so we always had beans, peas and barley, though the pickings got very slim that last year. But by then there were the rumours that liberation was on the way. There was fighting over by the canal and a few bombs were dropped. One morning, we heard an awful racket and peeked out to see the Huns goose-stepping past like prisoners of war with their hands clasped behind their heads...'

'Was that soldier among them? The German boy who cried about his family in the shop when he came to pick up his boots?'

'... and there were Allied tanks, and people put flags out and there was cheering and singing 'cause Limburg and Brabant had been liberated. Up north, they had to wait. The likes of The Hague and Amsterdam still had the Hunger Winter to get through. The Tommies took it in turns to lodge with us. If the soldiers needed a rest, they got a week off. They brought their own sleeping bags and food, cigarettes and, best of all, chocolate. We couldn't speak any English so it was all nodding and pointing and waving your arms about, but they were nice, the Tommies. They'd fix a lamp for you, stuff like that, and they were always listening to the radio, but after a week they were on the march again and sometimes we'd get one back and he'd be sobbing his heart out 'cause he'd lost a pal of his.'

'And his other pal was busy shagging the woman next door, I bet.'

'Oh, give over! And what of it? Some of those lads were proper handsome.'

'And *did* you ever see that soldier, the German boy who was crying in your workshop?'

'Who? Oh, *that* boy… They shot him most likely, I don't know. How would I know that? The Brits and the Americans were much nicer, and yes they got off with the prettiest girls, and I was pretty all right, so my father made me stay indoors. When they'd all gone, you saw girls in the family way here and there, and I thanked my lucky stars I wasn't one of them. I was seventeen when the liberators left and at last I was allowed out with Our Jan to the Sunday night dances. The Brits had brought all kinds of new dances over with them, so us Dutch yokels finally learned a decent move or two. That's how I met Peter van der Hurk, at Drouwen's dance hall, up by the bridge, knocked down years ago. There was live music, dance bands that played foxtrots and waltzes and tangoes and rumbas and God knows what else, and Peter came up and asked me to dance and we agreed to meet the week after and before we knew it we were going out together. After the dance, we'd take a walk in the park. He always wore plus-fours and with his hair cut short he wasn't much of a looker but I was soft on him anyway. Then one night he told me he wanted to be a priest. He was going away to a seminary and we sat and cried on a bench in the park and then he left and I never saw him again. But by the end of the week I'd forgotten all about him and I fell for a musician, an accordion player, but he had wandering hands so I dumped him. That's the way it was back then. You could be sitting on a park bench kissing in the dark and a priest would jump out from nowhere and shine a torch in your face and start bellowing at you: "How old are you?" and "What are you doing out at this time of night?" and "Get yourself home this minute!" I was still only seventeen and my mother sent me down to the dairy every week to fetch ice cream. There was a sawmill next to the dairy and the lads used to shout, "Hey, milkmaid!" 'cause I had a nice pair of tits on me, or they'd say I had false teeth because they were so white, and when I got mad and bared my teeth at them they'd shout, "Blow me, them fangs of hers are real after all!" And then a nice lad came up to me and said, "Don't let it bother you, they're only having a bit of fun." And I was soft on him from then on. One day he asked me out to the pictures, there was a love story on, and after we went dancing. His name was Tom so I called him Tommy, 'cause it sounded more British. And a friend of mine would cover for me whenever I went to see him. Sandy hair he had, and blue eyes with nice dark lashes. Nice teeth too, thank goodness, 'cause in those days I wouldn't even look at a boy who didn't have a decent set of teeth. After five months or so, Tommy was called up for military service, just like my brother Jan. And that bastard Jan told my parents I was seeing Tommy and that he worked in a factory that made coat hangers. Tommy lived in a poky terraced house with his mother. She was from Amsterdam and his father was dead and buried. No brothers or sisters. The factory was his uncle's. My parents looked down on Tommy for making coat hangers – thought he wasn't good enough. I didn't care what they thought and I kept on seeing him. By then he had his uniform and he was stationed at the barracks, same rank as Our Jan, but still not good enough for my parents. Whenever Tommy got off on leave, we dreamed of a future together and he was already talking about emigrating to New Zealand or Australia. Lots of folk went there after the war: they married, got a job, got rich, built a house, bought a big car and had children in a paradise where the sun always shone, even in winter. That's what Tommy wanted too. My mother thought it was all a pipedream. "How's things with your coat hanger?" she used to say when I got home. "And keep your knickers on or you'll end up in the family way!" That was all she said. Not much of a talker, my mother.'

'I can't say I remember anything much your mother said. Apart from that one time. We were staying with Gran during the summer holidays and they took us swimming in the lake at De Peel. Gran was soaking her feet at the water's edge. She slipped and as she fell backwards into the water she shouted, "Ooh, there goes Granny! Ooh, there goes Granny!" The only words I ever remember her saying. "Ooh, there goes Granny!" And your father barely said a word. In the workshop he would tell me what to do sometimes, but the rest of his life was one big mime. Every morning he'd grin and tap a boiled egg on his forehead. The rest of the time he'd look at us like we were strange because we couldn't see the funny side of his gags. Or maybe 'cause we looked too foreign.'

'Ah, but on his deathbed he said to me: "Where are the children?" He asked after you. You especially.'

'Well, I never saw the good man again after our last visit, not at our house, and certainly not at the children's home. Did he have an emotional bone in his body?'

'Oh, don't ask me. He grew up in children's homes himself and I doubt anyone ever came to visit him. He was just a quiet man, a tradesman, always busy in the workshop. When Our Jan was sent off to the Indies, I had to take over from him and deliver the repaired shoes to the customers and extract money from the ones that hadn't paid. On market day I helped at the stall and my mother ran the shop. We loaded up the car at six in the morning, the market started at seven and it was done by two. If business was slack, he'd let me go home as long as I was back in time to load up the car again. Boxes full of heels, for ladies and gents, nails, glue and goodness knows what else. My parents were in a state when Our Jan had to go to the Indies, 'cause he was their only son. But they were happy as Larry when Tommy was shipped off. I didn't know what to do with myself, 'cause Tommy had to serve eighteen months to two years in that stinking place. I cursed the rotten war that lay behind us and now our boys were being sent off on the warpath themselves in that filthy, ape-infested country. A year we'd been going out together, when he set off with his big duffel bag one grey day in November. Me and a girlfriend of mine took the train to Roermond to see our boys off at the station. The place was packed with soldiers, some with a girl, some without. "Good-bye-ee, I have to leave you..." was the song at the time. Hugs, kisses, tears, the train comes, time to board and "Good-bye-ee, I'll be true..."'

'You didn't exactly hang about...'

'Oh, what do you know about life?'

'Don't mind me. Lugging coal is all I'm good for.'

'In the beginning you write to each other of course – passionate love letters. You stay at home moping and your mother keeps nagging you to go out to the dance hall with the other girls instead of sitting at home like an old widow waiting to die. And I'd say, "No, I'm saving myself for Tommy." "The coat hanger?" she'd say. "Where's the future in that?"'

'Did you ever hope he'd take a bullet to the head?'

'Oh, I don't know. I don't think so. Things like that don't cross your mind.'

'Or that his tank would hit a mine? The wouldn't be as bad, that's just providence. An Indonesian who blows your brains out is a bastard responsible for his own actions, but a landmine just lies and waits for the Almighty to point the finger. Isn't that how people think?'

'Well, if you think *that's* how people think then you've got more of a screw loose than I thought. That's not how people think. That's how *you* think! You think like that!'

'Okay, Ma. But if you didn't want me to bad-mouth the Almighty, you should never have sent me to that stupid church.'

'I didn't want to, not for a minute. That was your father. He insisted you were christened.'

'What a nightmare that was! Nana was still a baby, but I was six or seven and there we stood, all five of us with that Indo father of ours. It's a miracle he managed to brave the stony faces of those gruesome parishioners. Or at least act like he did… There was a photo. Did you know that? For some reason, I see that scene in 360-degree vision. I see us, the whole family gathered at the font or whatever it's called and at the same time I see those pews full of people in their starched Sunday best. Maybe there were two photos. Black-and-white. Enlarged. Burned to a crisp by that German wife of Pa's. What a nutjob she was. Pa used to give her a Nazi salute if she ordered him about. In the worst possible taste, of course, but he was clearly kidding. His *Hausfrau* begged to differ and planned her exit to perfection. Teutonic efficiency. First she went to a souvenir shop and bought one of those little Dutch flags. Then she arranged for a removal van to arrive as soon as Pa had gone to work. Before she closed the door of that twelfth-floor flat in Delft behind her one last time, she went to the toilet. She stuffed all the photos of him she could find down the toilet bowl and set them alight, including the negatives. Then she took a dump. And as a finishing touch, she planted that little Dutch flag in her turd. Part of the photographic record of my childhood ended up incinerated and covered in shit.'

'What the…?'

'I kid you not. That German matron fought back harder than you ever did.'

'Oh, so now you think I'm weak?'

'That's not what I'm saying.'

'Well, that's what it sounds like.'

'I wish things had been different, Ma. I remember a lot of the photos Pa took. Like the one in the church. Well, maybe he didn't take that one himself. But you saw the Christian hordes in those pews, their long faces looking down on that Indo family with a brown father and a white mother while the vicar sprinkled our foreheads with water. Poor Nana took a ducking. She was still a baby and the vicar held her under. That water was ice cold. The church was ice cold. The people were ice cold. I felt the cold, and being christened only made me feel colder.'

'Yes, and that father of yours was ice cold too.'

'Are you trying to tell me you were warm?'

'Oh, bugger off back to whatever planet you came from, you little prick.'

'Did your Tommy come back alive? The forgotten army – isn't that what they're called nowadays? The lads who came back from that forgotten war in the Indies? At least 6,000 died over there. The figures vary, depending on the latest publications. Did you know it's mainly Americans who write books about the Dutch colonial war these days? Why do you think that is? No one up to the task here in Holland? Anyway, back to Tommy.'

'Tommy. Yes, Tommy! Well, the trip back from seeing him off at Roermond station was sad. I remember thinking, that bloody war destroyed everything. Then came Liberation and we were happy for a while and now this. But life went on and Tommy and I wrote each other passionate letters. Then one day, after three months of having no fun at all, I thought to myself, "Am I going to spend two years waiting around like this?" I started going to the pictures again, and to dances and that kind of thing. I kept writing to Tommy – he was somewhere on Celebes I think. I had promised to be faithful and not to go out dancing 'cause he was over there in the jungle and couldn't stand the thought of me waltzing around in someone else's arms. Well, his cousin happened to see me at a dance and she wrote and told him I'd been dancing a lot with this one fella. Tommy was angry and disappointed over there in the jungle and my mother was pleased that, after six months of writing and writing and writing, I'd finally put Tommy behind me. I felt free again. And I got to know someone else. That was Nico. He was studying to be a councillor.'

'Studying to be councillor? Don't they get elected?'

'Well, something like that. In any case, he was handsome *and* he had brains. And he used to sing me love songs. In the park, mind, 'cause you could only bring a boyfriend home if there was an engagement in the offing.'

'And?'

'Oh, Nico only lasted a month or two and then there was Jan, and then another Jan, and another Jan after that. I thought about Tommy sometimes, but he was still mad at me. In Holland we were rebuilding the country with a vengeance and over there they were still at war and of course that was another world to me. There were plenty of jobs going in those days and I started work at a bookbinder's and then at a place where they made stockings, as an assistant to the manager, one of those drippy bachelor types. That was 1948 and then Annie van Asseldonck comes to me and says, "Oh, An, I've got a bunch of lovely pictures of servicemen out in the Indies who want to correspond with Dutch girls. Anything here you fancy?" I took a look and that same evening I sat and wrote a letter to your father. He was a handsome man, best looking of the whole bunch! My parents found out and they were shocked at me writing to a coloured man. They thought people in the Indies lived in huts and ran around in grass skirts or with a fig leaf to cover their privates – yes, that's how people in Helmond thought back then. Even Amsterdam was a foreign country to them. My parents went once and once was enough. We had one Indo family in Helmond but they were very brown, they were *different*, and that's why my parents were against me writing. But I was interested in the Indies – to me it was all very exotic. And so I kept on writing. My parents found out that I was having his letters delivered to another address and then they said all right then, you might as well have them sent here… But Arto's letters became fewer and farther between. And some letters he'd sign Arto and others Arend and of course my parents thought that was fishy. When I was cleaning out the cupboard one day, I found a whole stack of letters my mother had intercepted and hidden away. I made a big scene about it – I was nearly twenty after all – but if only I had listened to her, 'cause my dear mother and my good father were very fond of me and if only I'd listened I could've had my Tommy back, but the more my parents were against it the more stubborn I became. And one day Tommy did come back from the Indies, alive and well. It was a Saturday evening and I was over at a girlfriend's house and I was very nervous about seeing Tommy again. Arto was in the Indies

– little did I know he'd come to Holland. And would you believe it, I saw Tommy again at the dance and it was just like before he went off to the Indies! He walked me home and he was all set to call and pick me up the following week. There was to be a big party for the soldiers who had returned from the Indies. I put on a lovely dress and sat there waiting for Tommy that evening. It was the first time a boy had come to the house to pick me up – quite something in those days! My mother thought it was better than me corresponding with that shady character from Surabaya, and my father was pleased too. So I waited and waited and waited but Tommy didn't turn up. And then Mies, my very own sister, the evil little cow, piped up and said she'd told Tommy that I'd been writing to a boy from the Indies for ages and that his name was Arto and that he was coming to Holland and that I'd probably leave Tommy in the lurch again. Nowadays the little bitch swears she can't remember a thing about it. Cool as you like. "Oh, I've forgotten all about that," she says. Well, my world just about caved in 'cause I really did love Tommy – I knew for certain as soon as I clapped eyes on him again! I never got to go to the party and after that I never saw Tommy ever again! And later I heard he'd emigrated to New Zealand with another woman. Broke my heart, that did. Can you imagine?'

'Would you really have gone to New Zealand with him? You didn't want to go to America with Pa.'

'Of course I would have gone away with Tommy!'

'To New Zealand? You? Don't make me laugh!'

'Love is blind! Not that you'd understand. And you don't know that song we always sang when we were sad. Always too busy listening to that jazz and pop rubbish of yours.'

The heffalump sings:

The war it came
And then it went
You walked into my life
We were oh so content!

Then you had to go
Love left on the tide
It took you so long
To return to my side

We found happiness again
Then came clouds, then the rain
And you left me forever
Alone

'Pa had his songs too, but they weren't nearly so sentimental. Remember this one?'

Her dear son sings:

Your dreams of the babu *are made to last*
Just lift up her sarong and ogle her ass

'Your Pa taught you those songs when you were barely out of nappies, that madman.'

'That one even features in his memoirs. You read them, didn't you? After the police threw him out of the house?'

'No, I didn't. He got Arti to sneak them out of that trunk of his, that big, ugly thing I kept banging my shins on when I did the housework. One ladder after another in my stockings.'

'In any case, they're back in circulation.'

'The memoirs of that filthy war of his? Never read a word of them. Willem did, though. He found the manuscript, read it from start to finish and told me all about it.'

'You let your boyfriend read your ex-husband's secret memoirs? Is nothing sacred?'

'You're a fine one to talk! Your father's holy scriptures were thick as a brick. Do you honestly think I was going to sit down and read all that? I was happy to be shot of that lunatic once and for all. Willem was curious. I sure as hell wasn't.'

'Not even now? Pa went through a war in his youth, just like you. Your country was occupied by Germans, his by the Japanese. To say nothing of what came next. Of course, you lot never want to hear about that.'

'What do you mean "you lot"?'

'You. The Belandas.'

'Oh, so now you're calling your own mother a Belanda?'

'Only because you act like one. You show no interest in the history of the young man from the tropics you ended up marrying. Like most Belandas, the Dutch who think the war started and ended with the German occupation. You're full of stories about being the first white girl to take a stroll through The Hague with a boy from the Indies but forty years later, with Nana on the tram to Scheveningen, you looked around and announced to everyone within earshot, "That's right! She's my daughter!" Nana was livid.'

'To this day I've no idea why she got so worked up about that.'

'Because you were apologizing for your daughter, your own flesh and blood, a woman in her thirties. Are you still stuck in the fifties? How often did you apologize for me and Phil when you were out with the pram? That's something I'd like to know. Didn't they all stare at you for having kids with some jungle bunny? Whose side were you on anyway?'

'Your side, of course!'

'Even so, Pa's stories never interested you at all. You were always telling him to shut up.'

'I did that for your sakes!'

'Fair enough, Mam. But his youth was about more than just the war.'

'He never spoke about that.'

'Yes he did. Shooting bats as a kid, that kind of stuff. Your father drove a Citroën Traction Avant and his father drove a Ford. In the 1930s! Now that was classy, don't you think?'

'Oh, don't be so daft.'

'I'll leave the first few pages here with you. Okay? Listen, your father grew up in an orphanage, my father was a bastard son. I grew up in a children's home, the same one your boyfriend Willem grew up in during the thirties. You're the only one who was raised in a decent family. Everyone around you has a dodgy past.'

'You don't.'

'Maybe you don't see it that way. But other people do. And Pa was a dodgy character even before the war broke out.'

From Baldy's memoirs (2)

Regarding my birth

I was born at around three o'clock in the afternoon of 28 September 1925, to be raised on the dark side of East Indies society. Much has been written about the well-to-do circles in this former Dutch colony, in particular the bygone days known as *tempo doeloe*, when life was said to be sweet. I barely knew those 'good old days'. And the history that surrounds them, a history the Dutch never tire of reading, is a lie.

Later in life, when I came to Holland, I made a point of avoiding social clubs and associations that celebrated the Indies. Their *tempo doeloe* nonsense sickened me. I was a warrior, a fighter, not some mollycoddled runt who attended the theatre with mummy and daddy.

When I was born, my parents lived at Koninginnelaan No. 3 in Surabaya. I enclose documentary evidence below:

Extract … [illegible] … certificates of Birth for the Chinese, issued in Surabaya in the year nineteen hundred and twenty-five

No. 726.

On this day, the first of October nineteen hundred and twenty-five, I, Alexander de Witt, deputy registrar of Births, Deaths and

Marriages in Surabaya, acting in the absence of the registrar, who is otherwise engaged, hereby record the declaration of Pieter Hendrik van Baak, aged fifty-three, a resident of Malang with no profession. Having been present at the birth, Mr Van Baak declares that at three o'clock in the afternoon on the twenty-eighth of September nineteen hundred and twenty-five, at the home of Willem Nolan, Master of Laws, in Surabaya, a child of the male sex was born to SIE SWAN NIO, a resident of Surabaya with no profession, and that the child has been named SIE AREND.

Present at this registration are Charles Guillaume Roerich, aged seventy-five, no profession, and Tan Tjhan Ing, aged twenty-eight, occupation tradesman, both residents of Surabaya.

To this end, a certificate has been drawn up which, having been read aloud and presented in the Malay language, has been signed by the declarant, both witnesses and myself.

Signed: P.H. van Baak; C.G. ~~Ror~~ Roerich; T. Tjhan Ing; de Witt.

Issued as a true certificate on the fifth of December nineteen hundred and twenty-five by the undersigned, Registrar of Births, Deaths and Marriages in Surabaya.

[stamp and signature illegible]

Seen for authentication of the signature of Bernard Benjamin Faber, Registrar of Births, Deaths and Marriages in Surabaya. The President of the Court of Justice in Surabaya.

[stamp: president etc. signature: illegible]

I am the illegitimate son of Willem Nolan, who was born as a European in Jember, East Java. He was raised in the Indies and went to the Netherlands to study law. The offices of his law firm were located on Rozenplein in Surabaya. His clients were people of means and my father preferred to handle cases that reeked of foul play, as these tended to be the most lucrative. He imported his own whisky from Scotland. Alongside his law firm, he ran a dry-cleaning business in the Simpang neighbourhood. He was also the owner of two cargo ships, which sailed from Surabaya to Makassar, Balikpapan and Banjarmasin, transporting coal, wood and the like.

My father married his cousin Aleida and had two children with her, a boy and a girl, who unfortunately cost a good deal of money, spoiled as they were. From the boy, my 'legitimate' half-brother, I received a large metal bedstead as a memento upon my return from Blitar, more of which later, as he left for the United States of America never to return. My brother Jacob later heard that our half-brother had considerable trouble finding work in America due to the dark colour of his skin.

My mother Sie Swan Nio was a Chinese housewife of simple means. By the light of a waxing moon, she made her own *kecap* in the back garden and sold it to the people of the neighbourhood. She was divorced from her Chinese husband named Djie Lian Hwa, by whom she had a daughter, called Nonnie for short. As I was not recognized by my father, the following epistles were sent to my mother:

Surabaya, 20 November 1925

To
Miss Sie Swan Nio
Koninginnelaan 3
in
Surabaya

The Orphans and Probate Court of Surabaya asks you to consider recognizing at the earliest opportunity the child by the name of Sie Arend, born on 28 September 1925. According to the notification given to the Registrar of Births, Deaths and Marriages in Surabaya, you are the child's mother. Recognition may take the form of a notarial deed or a declaration of your intention to the Registrar of Births, Deaths and Marriages. Without such recognition there can be no legal bond between you and said child, whereas recognizing the child has the following consequences:

a. You will have custody of the child and are therefore the child's legal guardian. If you refuse, the present Court will submit a request to the Court of Justice to appoint another person to be the child's guardian. (If, in the interim, the man who fathered the child decides to recognize or jointly recognize the child, a course of action which this Court deems highly advisable, he will then become the legal guardian.)

b. The child will require your consent in order to marry before reaching his majority.

c. The child is under the obligation to support you in a fitting manner should you find yourself in reduced circumstances.

d. You will be the child's legal beneficiary and the child will be yours (which without recognition will be out of the question).

Lastly you are informed that if this Court has received no notification of your having recognized your child within three months of the above date, immediate arrangements will be made for the Court of Justice to appoint a legal guardian.

The Orphans and Probate Court in Surabaya.

~~President~~
Secretary,
[signature illegible]

No. 38
RECOGNITION

Today, Wednesday the twenty-third of December nineteen hundred and twenty-five.

There appeared before me, JUST TOWNSEND, Notary in Surabaya, in the presence of the witnesses named below, whose identity is known to me:

Miss Sie Swan Nio, of no occupation, a resident of Surabaya, Koninginnelaan 3, by her own declaration thirty-five years of age and unmarried.

The party is known to me, the notary.

The party declared that she wishes to recognize as her natural son the child who according to the notification given to the Registrar of Births, Deaths and Marriages in Surabaya was born in Surabaya on the twenty-eighth of September nineteen hundred and twenty-five, to whom she is mother and to whom the names Sie Arend have been given.

THUS DULY NOTED

Drawn up in Surabaya on the above date in the presence of Loo Lam Twan and Sie Khwan Djioe, both notarial employees, resident in Surabaya, who immediately after the reading aloud of the certificate to the party and the witnesses by me, the notary, and interpretation in the Malay language for the party concerned, signed this certificate along with said party and me, the notary.

Drawn up with an appendix and a deletion without amendment.

(Signed) Sie Swan Nio, Loo Lam Twan, Sie Khwan Djioe, Townsend.

ISSUED AS A TRUE COPY

[stamp and signature of Townsend]

Horoscope

There's nothing remarkable about your birth certificate, of course. Its inclusion in your memoirs is the act of an illegitimate son, determined to prove he was ever born at all. Phil told me to pass on his regrets for the 'three o'clock' they scrawled on your birth certificate over there in Surabaya. An approximation, most likely, which makes your horoscope difficult to pin down. Half an hour's difference only affects the position of Pluto in your houses, but then Pluto is Mars squared: violence, terror, magic, compulsion, sadism. Three o'clock on the dot puts Pluto in your sixth house and spells trouble in your working life. Wind the clock back fifteen minutes and Pluto is in your seventh house – extreme relationships – which would account for the miserable marriage to that heffalump of yours. As if the Moon, Venus and Mars in your marriage house wasn't enough! Uranus doesn't do us kids any favours. Those with Uranus in their fifth house have trouble with their children. We were trouble, weren't we Pa? But my God, then there's the Sun, Mercury, Saturn and Neptune in your eighth house, the house of death, sex and the deepest recesses of the soul. In a single word, that spells war. In fact, only Jupiter is auspiciously positioned: in your second house, you old skin-flint. Always had more money than you let on… a Chinese trait, if you ask me. An experienced astrologer could only read this as the horoscope of a fascist, paranoid, mass murderer. A seasoned astrologer might see a bald eagle. And if he's a fool into the bargain, he might see a young Buddha. Was your father a fool by any chance, wielding those hair clippers of his? I mean, did he see a baldy little Buddha in you? But there I go poking fun again. Not at all noble of me.

One phrase from that last document piqued my interest: *interpretation in the Malay language for the party concerned.* So your mother could not read Dutch, at least not well enough to know what she was signing. I'll refrain from calling her a *nyai*, for fear you might chuck stones at me.

From Baldy's memoirs (3)

Near death

I was a baby, ten months old, when a wound behind my right ear began to fester and I was soon at death's door. Prominent physicians and acquaintances of Papa's – Dr Markovitch, a Hungarian, and Dr De Vries, a Dutchman – gave me up for dead. My mother could not bear to see me die. She summoned her younger brother Sie Soen Thjwan, Uncle Soen for short, and told him to take me to her family in the country. Uncle Soen swaddled me in rags and an old sarong and took the train to Blitar. There he was to seek the help of Aunty Mien, his sister Sie Mien Nio, who would attempt to heal me with all kinds of wild herbs. If this failed, he was to bury me in a secret place deep in the jungle.

It took over two years, but I was cured and Uncle Soen brought me back to my mother in Surabaya. She spooned cod-liver oil into me three times a day. I loathed the stuff, but if I refused to take it she would beat me. On Papa's orders my head was shaved. He believed a bald head would make me a better scholar, though what is there for a child of three to learn? Until my twelfth birthday, I had to walk around bald headed. At school the other children threw stones at me.

My older brother Jacob was fourteen years my senior, my twin sisters Ella and Ina were twelve years older, and my brother Karel eight. Of the five of us, I had the darkest skin, and so my brothers and sisters often bullied and beat me. They liked to insinuate that I had been fathered by an Indian. Karel and both my sisters had a slight slant to their eyes that betrayed their Chinese blood; Jacob and I did not. Of course, they never dared treat Jacob the way they treated me, as he was the eldest and ruled the roost in our father's absence.

At that time my mother was a follower of the Kong Hu Cu, the teachings of Confucius. When my grandmother died – a woman straight out of Canton, who dressed like a classical Chinese doll and hobbled around on lotus feet – we attended her funeral with my mother and they rubbed chalk behind our ears to protect us from evil spirits. After the funeral, I sneaked some sweets from her grave and had myself a feast. This was at the cemetery, so my mother, brothers and sisters were not allowed to hit me. But as soon as we got home, the lash appeared and I received my deferred punishment. I was four years old.

The happiest times of my childhood were the Feast of Saint Nicholas, Christmas and my birthday. On these special occasions, I was spoiled with expensive toys and Mama, our *babu* Tenie and our *kokkie* Tas would make my favourite dishes: Cantonese fried rice and macaroni cheese.

On New Year's Eve, my father used to order an ox cart full of Chinese fireworks. My big brothers would festoon our front fence with firecrackers and the whole neighbourhood would turn out to watch. The tremendous din lasted a full hour and the streets around us disappeared in a cloud of smoke.

At the age of five I became an uncle of sorts, when my half-sister Nonnie gave birth to a daughter. Betty Tie was her name, but everyone called her Poppy. I watched the birth through a crack in the door and it made me feel very uneasy. Poppy refused to call me 'uncle'. To the family I was her half-brother and we grew up fighting like cat and dog. She had a big mouth and would never let me tell her what to do.

Wolf and Bear

I had two good friends in those days: Wolf, a watchful stray dog, and Bear, a little black bear my father had shipped back to Java from Banjarmasin on the island of Borneo.

One morning I was helping our driver Petro polish my father's 1929 Model T Ford in readiness for his daily trip to his offices on Rozenplein. In the mood for mischief, I sneaked onto the luggage rack below the spare wheel to hitch a ride. We set off with Wolf bounding along after us. When Petro hit a bump, I nearly fell off and was dragged along behind the car. Wolf barked at Petro, and he braked. Shocked to see me lying there in the road, Petro accosted a Javanese man and asked him to carry me home. He did not dare say anything to my father, who had been dozing in the front passenger seat throughout the incident. When my mother saw me in the arms of the Javanese stranger, she thanked him and gave him a bottle of her homemade *kecap* for his trouble. The man was barely out the door when my mother grabbed the cane and was ready to give me a beating, but Uncle Soen, who had just started feeding Bear, walked over and snatched the cane from his sister's hands. Our two *babus* took me to the bathroom, undressed me and washed the cuts and grazes on my knees and legs. My mother had calmed down by this time and made a paste from traditional herbs for the *babus* to rub on my wounds. I cried out in pain. As a punishment, I was sent to my room. Wolf stayed with me and bared his teeth at my mother whenever she popped her head round the door.

When my father came home at dinner time, he collapsed onto his bamboo chaise longue and called me to his side. Flanked by my twin sisters Ella and Ina, I was still dizzy from the pain in my legs. Without saying a word, my father sat up and lashed out with his fist. I fell to the floor and blacked out. When I came to, my sisters were standing there pleading and sobbing, and I had peed my pants.

> So you pissed yourself in fear too? Like we did when you came charging over to give us a thrashing. Even so I can't feel sorry for you, Pa. You're going to have to come up with a lot more misery to change that.

Ella and Ina took me back to my room. The *babus* washed me and laid me on my bed. When my father appeared in the doorway, Wolf bared his teeth again. My father vanished but returned with a rifle and took aim. Pointing the barrel at Wolf, he said coolly, 'Tie that dog to your bed, or I'll blow him to pieces and you along with him.'

My father had a wooden rack with six hunting rifles. It stood in the dining room, next to a cabinet that held all kinds of ammunition. His collection consisted of four double-barrelled shotguns, 16 and 12 calibre, a six-round Winchester repeating rifle and a small firearm known as a *tjies*. This last model was the smallest rifle among hunters in the Indies. Every boy had to learn to handle one as part of his upbringing. Once you could shoot straight with a *tjies*, you got to practise with the heavier firearms.

Baldy goes to European Public School

We moved to a house on the other side of Koninginnelaan. When I was nearly six, Mama had to submit a request to the Resident of Surabaya so that I could attend the European Public Primary School.

Extract from the Register of Decisions taken by
the Resident of Surabaya.
Surabaya, 29th July 1931

No. 367/31.
HAVING READ:
a. the petition dated Surabaya, 17 June 1931 made by Sie Swan Nio residing at Koninginnelaan No. 28 in the regional capital of Surabaya, requesting that her son named AREND, 6 years old, be admitted to Public European Primary School C in this city,

b. and further

In consideration of the fact that the applicant's elder children – full siblings of Arend – have been lawfully admitted to the above-mentioned educational institution and with a view to ensuring that the children from one and the same family receive a similar upbringing, this present request for admission should also be granted.

In light of the above

It has been decided that:

Arend, the son of Sie Swan Nio, who resides in Surabaya, be admitted to year one of the 1st European Public Primary School C in Surabaya

EXTRACT issued to the interested party for reference and information purposes.

In agreement with the pre-school Register, The Assistant-Resident Secretary.

[signature illegible]

And so my bald head and I began to attend European Public School. The other children knew that I was illegitimate, a bastard in common parlance. In colonial Java, parentage counted for much more than it does in the Netherlands. The schoolmistress was nice, but if I made the slightest mistake I was caned and made to stand in the corner. Despite the bullying, I advanced to second year and third year. At that age, I had to attend Sunday school every week. Under the regime of a teacher named Claproth, we had to learn Bible passages by heart and if we failed to do so, we would catch it with the cane. Mr Claproth also used to slap us with the back of his hand, a gold ring on almost every finger. I came home with lumps on my head and dried blood around my mouth. At first, my mother and my brothers shouted at me, assuming that I had deserved my punishment. But one Sunday my brothers came with me to Sunday school to see for themselves. When I emerged from the class with yet more lumps on my head, they waited until Mr Claproth appeared with his bag and his notorious cane in hand. My big brother Jacob strolled up to him and without saying a word let fly with his fist. The man fell to the floor and lay there dazed. He eventually got to his feet, only to find himself eye to eye with my brother Karel, who subjected him to an expert beating. Other teachers came running and they too made the acquaintance of Jacob's fists. My eldest brother demanded that they give me extra homework as a punishment instead of a beating. From that day on, I received no more abuse from my teachers.

Even so, my upbringing at home remained tough and ruthless. If I came home one minute after six, Jacob and Karel would be on hand to give me a good thrashing.

> Thank you for this insight, Pa. If I came home one minute after five, you would knock me from one end of the hall to the other. I also took a beating when my little brothers were late home, since I was the one charged with rounding them up and making sure they were in on time. If they were playing hide and seek and it took me too long to find them, I would thump them all the way home so that they would have no sympathy for me when I received their share of your blows.

At the back of the house, Ella and Ina were waiting to give me a hiding with the cane. Mama finished the job, wielding a branch. At the end of this calvary, it was up to the sobbing *babus* to comfort me. They would take me to the bathroom and wash me. Kokkie would abandon her pans on the stove for a while to fetch me clean clothes. I have often thought back on these humiliations, but I can find no reason for them.

> I can: backward eighteenth-century colonial ways. One Willem van Hogendorp raised the issue of the senseless beating in his novella *Kraspukol; Or the Dismal Consequences of Excessive Severity towards Slaves (An Edifying Tale)* from 1780. In his account the culprits were not Dutchmen or Chinese, but mestizos, people of mixed Portuguese and Javanese blood… Indos, if you will. It's tough to be an Indo, eh Pa?

On my eighth birthday I received a brand-new bicycle, made in Japan. I was over the moon and set out to explore the city. One Sunday I decided to go fishing near the port offices at Tanjung Perak. My brothers kitted me out with a bag of bait and a small bamboo fishing rod. On the way I bought a young coconut to quench my thirst in the heat of Surabaya.

Arriving at the port, I found myself a quiet spot by a narrow beach. I laid my bike on the ground, settled down and cast my line. After catching a few fish, I spotted one that seemed to be gasping for air. I jumped into the water and waded to where it was flapping about. Before I knew what was happening, I felt myself being sucked down into the mud. Quicksand! I was so paralysed with fear that I could not even cry for help. Deeper and deeper I sank, until I was in over my head. I swallowed seawater, reached for the surface, then everything went black. A strange but wonderful sensation came over me. Life no longer mattered, I was prepared to die, to be free of the beatings at home, the shame of my bald head and the stones the other children threw at me. Underwater, I saw a sudden, brilliant light and was overcome by feelings of bliss. Just as I was passing out, I felt myself being pulled up by the arms.

I woke to see faces swimming into focus above me. The faces of three white sailors. One of them made me stick my fingers down my throat so that I would throw up. To wash away the filthy taste of seawater, they gave me something sweet to drink.

Back home, I told my mother what had happened. To my amazement, there was no punishment. Instead, our *kokkie* cooked for me, serving up the fish I had caught with steamed rice and vegetables.

Karel teaches me to fight

I was skinny as a young boy, and when I turned ten my brother Karel decided it was time to toughen me up. He could no longer bear to see me coming home with my bald head covered in bumps and bruises. He started by making me get up every morning at six. After a quick wash and brush-up, I had to jog a couple of blocks wearing only my underpants. Karel jogged with me. As I ran, I had to feint and throw punches in the air, and when we got home, he made me lift barbells with heavy weights. At six-thirty I took a bath, followed by breakfast and a mad dash to school. When I came home in the afternoon, I had something to eat, took a short nap and then did chin-ups on the high bar in the garden. Next I had to take a shower and keep my eyes open as I looked up at the streaming water. That was the hardest test of all. For months all I could feel was pain and when the pain disappeared, Karel dripped lemon juice into my eyes to toughen me up even more. Six months later, I could see the drops of water coming towards me in the shower and my reaction time had become much faster.

Uncle Soen joined forces with Karel. They became my instructors in the garden, where Wolf was constantly on the alert for intruders and Bear, tethered by a long chain, rummaged around under the tamarind tree. My instructors pelted me with pebbles, which I had to fend off with the backs of my hands. They threw sticks for me to parry using classical Chinese martial arts techniques. I was fifteen before I learned to parry knives, a skill both Uncle Soen and Karel possessed.

Uncle Soen was a smallish man, five feet four at most, while my brother Jacob was over six feet tall. Jacob trained with barbells and had a naturally athletic build. Yet I saw Uncle Soen take hold of Jacob's wrist and paralyse him completely for five seconds. He did this to protect me when Jacob attacked me for the umpteenth time. Uncle Soen called him a 'filthy animal' and sent him to his room. My uncle walked with a limp, the result of a childhood bout of polio, but in his hands he had a kind of elemental strength. He often visited us and in his presence I felt safe. If he was not around, Aunty Kiep would come and look after me. Whenever Jacob turned nasty, she would stand between us and scream bloody murder at him in a language all her own, a mix of Dutch, Malay and Chinese not unlike my mother's.

Of course, we had neighbours on Koninginnelaan. A few doors down, there was Mr and Mrs Van Baak, an elderly couple who kept a beautiful collection of birds in their back garden. They were always pleased to see me and let me in so that I could marvel at the enormous aviaries and learn the birds' names off by heart. They had an elegant home, with rooms full of antiques, porcelain and glass.

A couple of houses further along lived the Van Geel family. They had a magnificent collection of antique Chinese and Japanese vases, and their daughter Ilse was a charming girl, who used to tell me Chinese and Japanese fairy tales.

Next to the Van Geels lived an Indo family by the name of Wetzel. Their daughter Lien was my age. She loved to stroke and kiss my shaved head. More used to cutting words and hard blows, this was something I detested. When Lien came and sat on my lap to lavish kisses on that bald head of mine, I would wrestle free and walk off. This made her angry and she would fire insults at me, and sometimes even scratch and hit and bite. I never hit her back. To hit a girl was cowardly in my eyes.

Another local family were the Zweerts, and I was good friends with their three sons. Across from the Zweerts lived the Perazzos, a Jewish family with a son and two daughters, very kind people.

Our next door neighbours on the left were a Japanese couple, both of whom worked at the Chiyoda department store on Tunjungan. Shortly before war broke out, it was revealed that they were Japanese spies with military ranks. But as a boy I was too naive to understand such things.

Our other next-door neighbours were the Altmanns. They were German and had two grown-up sons and a late arrival my own age. I didn't get on with the eldest son at all. In fact I disliked the whole family. Both of the older boys were bruisers, always shooting their mouths off. Their hobby was playing with four fully grown pythons, ten to fifteen feet long.

My twelfth birthday

On my twelfth birthday I screwed up all my courage and asked my father to let me grow my hair so that I would no longer be bullied at school. After a lengthy conclave with Mama, my brothers and sisters, my request was finally granted, on condition that I passed my secondary school entrance exam. As a lawyer, Papa wanted me to follow in his footsteps, but Jacob and Karel thought I should study engineering. I narrowly failed the exam and my family made me repeat my final year. Although Papa still saw the need for it, I no longer had to have my head shaved.

By this time a bitter conflict had developed between Papa and Jacob about Papa's refusal to recognize us as his children and to allow us to bear the surname Nolan. In protest, Jacob decided to change his name to Nolans. Karel took a more measured approach: he simply adopted Papa's surname, Nolan, regardless of whether it was legal or not. I understood very little of the background to this quarrel and followed Karel's example. But at school they continued to see me as a bastard. In so many words, I was and would remain Arend Sie, Sie Arend, or 'Arend Sie who goes by the name Nolan'. To my Indonesian friends, I was Si-Arend, but my father's wealthy background meant they often called me Si-Arto or Arto for short, a play on the word for 'money'. Indonesian names such as Soegiharto and Soeharto were often shortened to Harto or corrupted as Arto. Even my own family called me Arto sometimes.

It was mainly the Indo coterie – Eurasian families with a higher status – who looked down on me. Hollanders were less inclined to do so, and the Germans had no such airs and graces. Jacob, Karel, Ella and Ina had the good fortune to be born light-skinned, but I was as dark as my great grandmother Rabina, who prior to her marriage had been a lady-in-waiting at the sultanate of Pamekasan.

Where did you get that nonsense, Pa? Talk family history with any Indo and an abducted princess or the like is bound to pop up before long. The same way every Hollander can dredge up a family coat of arms. What do you mean 'lady-in-waiting'? And what was that grandfather of yours doing in that sultanate anyway? Give it a rest man, with your stupid Indo fairy tales. That's the colonial Indies in a nutshell: always casting back for some princess or courtier in your ancestry.

Tensions rose between Jacob and Papa. Jacob poured all his energy into boxing, a warning to Papa to forget any ideas he might have about hitting him. Jacob was a heavyweight. Karel was slender, as was I, and practised all kinds of martial arts such as judo, jujitsu, *pencak silat, kuntao* (a form of taekwondo) and wielded the three-pronged weapon known as the *sia*. Instead of deferring to Papa, my brothers began to take more family decisions themselves, one of which was to send me to Queen Emma School, a technical college, to study mechanical engineering. This was much to Papa's dismay.

Around that time, I began to go out with an Indo girl called Hermina, but when her mother found out that I was an illegitimate Nolan, she was strictly forbidden from seeing me. Hermina protested loudly, as did her brother and both her sisters, but in vain. In her mother's eyes, I was cursed, tarred and feathered. Standing on the porch of their house one day, my heart sank as I listened to the quarrels raging inside. The pain was too much, and I slunk away without a word to anyone.

The deaths of Bear and Wolf

Late one afternoon, Papa came home and was greeted as usual by Bear, who had grown as tall as Jacob. Papa was in the habit of feeding Bear a couple of sugar lumps but on this occasion he was in a foul mood and instead rapped him on the nose with his walking stick. Bear let out a ferocious growl, pulled his chain from its anchor and lunged at Papa. Uncle Soen picked up a branch that had fallen from the tamarind tree and began to beat Bear with it. Karel and Jacob heard the commotion and both grabbed a double-barrelled hunting rifle from the rack on the dining room wall. Quick as a flash, they loaded their weapons and fired two shots each. The animal fell dead at Papa's feet. Instead of thanking his sons for saving his life, Papa swore loudly and began to rant and rave.

I lay on the ground with my body pressed against Bear's for a long time. Indoors, the quarrels about the incident raged into the night. My brothers buried Bear in the garden by moonlight. Days later, I lost Wolf when he was run over by a car. I buried him beside Bear with my own hands.

Shooting practice

With primary school behind me, Jacob thought it was high time I learned to handle a gun. As stated previously, this was a tradition among boys in the Indies. It was my job to clean and grease the rifles, and, even though one of those weapons had killed Bear, holding them in my hands filled me with pride.

The roofs of our home on Koninginnelaan were pointed, and bats hung from the eaves. An old outbuilding behind the garage served as a scullery where Mama brewed and bottled her *kecap* to bring in a little extra money. It was a dirty little shack, crawling with rats and mice. At first, I practised on the bats. During the day, I shot them down from the eaves and burned the bodies in a pit at the bottom of the garden.

In the evenings, Karel and I would take up positions on the floor of the attic above the garage, equipped with a torch. Karel handled the Winchester and I had the *tjies*, a small 5.8 millimetre hunting rifle. We took turns shining the torch on the run-down scullery in search of mice and rats. Mice were the hardest to hit, especially with a *tjies*. But every Indo boy had to learn on that thing; it was tradition. We took turns: I aimed at the rats, Karel at the mice. If we got bored, we would line up empty tins in the garden and practise with the Winchester repeating rifle. Mama, Jacob and Uncle Soen looked on approvingly. I grew to love firing guns. It gave me confidence, even though I went to school unarmed.

Meanwhile Jacob never gave me a moment's rest. He no longer allowed me to take a siesta in the afternoon. The dusty attic above the garage was full of junk and Jacob tied thick ropes around a beam and hung rings from them so that Karel could teach me gymnastics. Jacob had me working with barbells of up to 45 pounds. With padding strapped to my body, I had to learn to fight Karel. Months passed before I was able to fend off his rapid-fire blows and kicks. Jacob also suspended a heavy jute sack from the beam, filled with sawdust and sand. When he hit it, that dead weight would dance around on the end of its rope; no matter how I pummelled away with my fists, it hung there still as could be.

The death of my father

Papa had already bowed out of the legal profession and he also began to withdraw from family life. He moved into the pavilion of a large club house somewhere on Embong Malang. That's how we lost our driver, Petro. Perhaps Papa found my mother's sharp criticism of his lifestyle hard to take. The man was addicted to alcohol and gambling. If I had an afternoon off school and went to visit him, he had to get out of bed first and brush his teeth. He rinsed his mouth with whisky.

> Oh, so my nocturnal tendencies run in the family… Atavism, huh? Except for the whisky. The hard stuff from Scotland brings out a strange aggression in me. In that respect, I take after you.

We had to find a smaller house and moved to 144 Arjuno Boulevard. There I made a lot of new friends: Dutch, German, Indo boys, Javanese and Ambonese, a right old mix. We shared the garden with another Indo family, who lived in a pavilion in the grounds. It was cramped and money was tight, but it was a warm and happy place to live. We had a Chinese lodger, Kwee Lian Bo. He studied architecture and was a great help to me with my mechanical engineering studies.

Little by little, Mama began to break it to me that Papa was going from bad to worse. It began with his business interests. The dry cleaner's on Simpang went bankrupt, and he had to sell off his cargo ships and eight of his cars to pay off his gambling debts. Even his stamp collection, worth millions of guilders, had to be auctioned off. The one thing he managed to hold onto was his Model T.

Papa's old ailment, diabetes, began to get the better of him. When he still lived with us, Mama used to patch him up with herbal remedies but over at the clubhouse pavilion he was at the mercy of his private doctors and those Westerners did little more than send him to hospital. Mama, Jacob, Karel, Ella, Ina and I became regular visitors at Darmo Infirmary.

One September afternoon, I found myself at Papa's bedside with George Nolan. 'Arend,' Papa said, 'this is your cousin George. From now on, he will be your guardian. I have made financial arrangements with him regarding your further studies. Listen carefully to what George has to say and follow his instructions to the letter. One day, when you are older, you will understand. You are the youngest of the five and the eyes of the Nolan family are upon you. Ella and Ina are useless – I've seen more brains in a pig's backside. Karel is not worth a farthing – he knows how to charm the ladies and nothing else. I have left those three nothing in my will. Jacob is brave and knows how to handle himself, and so I have put his financial affairs in order. But of course my primary concern is your mother.'

My visit over, I waited for my cousin George in the hall of the hospital's side pavilion. 'Arend,' he said when he came out of Papa's room, 'your father is not long for this world. A few weeks at most. He senses the end is near. At times he is lucid, but his mental faculties come and go. It is a blessing that he still remembers you. At times he doesn't even recognize your brothers and sisters! But all this aside, Arend, you have heard and understood your father's words. Do your level best at school. You will soon be fourteen and if, when you are sixteen, I can see that you have given the best possible account of yourself, you will receive a splendid motorcycle from me as a present.'

Cousin George – son of my uncle Louis Nolan, a wealthy planter – gave me a firm handshake. From under the brim of his white hat, he looked me deep in the eyes, a look of sympathy. I got on my bike and, feeling downhearted, I cycled home without calling in on my playmates.

One Monday, three days before my fourteenth birthday, I was working at the lathe in the school workshop when I clearly saw my father's face appear in the wire screen in front of me. He spoke to me, but I could not understand his words. I called out to him and my classmates stopped what they were doing and looked at me in surprise. At that moment our Chinese lodger Kwee Lian Bo came dashing into the workshop. He shouted over to me that my father had died and that my sisters were waiting for me in the headmaster's office. The teachers helped me out of my overalls and took me to the washrooms where I had to put on my Sunday best. I was given the rest of the week off school.

Three days later my father was buried in a solemn service at the European section of the General Cemetery on Kembang Kuning. Almost every Sunday I visited his grave, which was marked by a large headstone made of Italian Bianco Carrara marble. I filled the vases with fresh flowers and begged God to forgive my father for all the sins he had committed in his life. Mama was sometimes at her wits' end, as even after his death many of my father's possessions had to be auctioned off to settle his debts. Cousin George compensated Mama for all of the financial losses.

Jayabaya and Nostradamus

A year after Papa's death we had to move again. This time it was to a larger house, but without a garden, located on Pasar Besar Wetan Gang IV. Eventually, Mama also had to sell the hunting rifles and all our other valuables. But we were able to hang onto the twelve large Chinese vases we owned, and they came with us to our new address.

Unfortunately, I saw Cousin George less frequently than I would have liked and my brother Jacob took over as my guardian. It was a role he relished. One Saturday afternoon when I was fifteen, I came back from doing Swedish gymnastics at school: this consisted of exercises on the wall bars and the rings, vaulting and rope climbing. I had the *babu* fill a tub in the bathroom. Having locked the door, I soaped my body and lay soaking in the cold water. The heat was stifling that day and I fell asleep. Half an hour later, Jacob came home from the office and began hammering on the bathroom door. I jolted awake, climbed out of the tub, dried myself and pulled on my underpants. Again Jacob pounded on the door. I opened it and before I knew what was happening, my brother had grabbed me by the throat and dragged me outside. He hit me hard, again and again, then kicked me to the ground. I curled into a ball and asked him what in God's name was wrong with him.

'Shut your face, you filthy dog!' he yelled, landing kicks wherever he could. Mama, Ella and the *babus* came running to see what all the fuss was about and ordered him to stop.

'What has the boy done wrong?' my mother asked.

'That animal has been wanking off in the bathroom!' Jacob ranted. 'He was still in there when I got home. I will not stand for Arend wanking off. A good thrashing is what he needs.'

I scrambled to my feet and asked Jacob what 'wanking off' meant. Again he turned white with rage and punched me full in the face. Unable to bear it any longer, Mama came and stood between us, and Jacob relented at last. Everything went black and I fainted. Babu Tenie fetched wet cloths and wiped the blood from my face, while Kokkie Tas held my head in her lap.

'Why did you hit me so hard?'

'Because you won't stop lying!' Jacob screamed.

That evening he came to my room, dragged me across the hall and made me sit at his desk. He pulled a thick volume from his bookcase and shoved it under my nose. 'This is a book about venereal diseases, written in the American language,' he said. 'And here is a dictionary. Take a good long look. The photos of the diseases are in colour. When I said "wanking" I meant playing with your dick. If something comes out, you can end up with a nasty disease. It will sap you of all your strength and you will become a mollusc, a shrimp! Sit here and keep reading till I tell you to stop. Understand?'

From that day on, I had to report to him twice a week to read that book on venereal diseases. He never told me how to behave with girls or women. All I knew was that Karel played guitar for them, which made me think I should learn to play guitar too. Luckily, Jacob also had books about planes in his room. He had bought Hutchinson's *War Pictorial*, while I saved my pennies to buy second-hand copies of magazines like *Flight* and *The Aeroplane*. Jacob also bought new magazines so that we could follow the war in Europe. Karel listened to the radio. We knew the Germans had occupied the Netherlands and that Japan was threatening to do the same to the Indies.

One day I read a newspaper ad placed by the Dutch Royal Navy, calling on boys aged fourteen and over to sign up for military service. Like many of my friends, I was eager to enlist. But Mama refused to give her permission and had Jacob put me right.

'Arend, if you join the Navy, you are going to have to fight. And that would break Mama's heart. You are her *anak mas* remember, the apple of her eye. She needs you by her side and that is why I cannot give you permission. Mama wants you to be an engineer when you grow up. And less of your whining about how she hits you. It's how all of us were raised, your brothers too. The lash toughens us up. Would you rather be spineless? Well then, stop making a big deal of it! You are a boy of fifteen, do you honestly think you can take on the Japs? Don't make me laugh, man. You have a Chinese mother and we are registered as Chinese. That is all there is to it! If our father had recognized us as his own, we would have been European and it would have been our war too. But he didn't and it's not! So you, me and Karel are going to keep our heads down if those Japs invade. Understand?'

For the sake of keeping the peace, I nodded.

'You know the story of King Jayabaya, don't you?' he continued. 'No? Sometimes I wonder why we waste good money on that school of yours. Jayabaya was Java's own Nostradamus. You must know who Nostradamus was… no? Thick as two short planks, you are! Nostradamus was a French chemist who had the gift of second sight. He foretold Napoleon, Communism, Hitler and the World Wars. Around the year 900, our Jayabaya ruled one of the Hindu kingdoms here on Java and he had the gift of prophecy too. Using seven dishes of food as an allegory, he predicted the seven ages in which seven great kingdoms would succeed one another. The last of these were the seafaring nations, first the Belandas and then the Japanese, who will plunge Java into ruin. Both nations will eventually be driven out, after which the kings of Java will take power once again. Every Javanese knows this. And, since we live among the Javanese, we need to know it too. *Sudah al!* End of story! There is no sense in fighting, all we have to do is wait. The only fighting you need to do is on Karel's battlefield.'

By Karel's battlefield, Jacob meant the patch of waste ground by Queen Emma School, where people fought to settle their differences. There, Karel demonstrated his lightning-fast technique with the *sia* and I saw him break the wrists of fearsome opponents. There were tough fighters among those boys and they came from all races: Indos, Madurese, Javanese, Bugis, Makassar, Manadonese, Ambonese and Timorese. Among them was one Radèn Soekaton, a Madurese boy of noble birth. He was an expert in *pencak silat* and could leap clean over his opponents, both forwards and backwards. He later became one of my closest allies. If he was around when I got into a fight, he would throw himself into the fray to help me. But it didn't take much to make him *mata gelap* and, blinded by the dark mist of rage, he could easily pick a fight with the wrong guy.

If I came home a loser, I could expect a thrashing from Karel and Jacob, who would then make me pound away at the punchbag. If I won, they would give me a guilder each. My mother would give me a guilder too, and Ella and Ina would give me fifty cents apiece. Despite all the beatings and humiliations, I had a wonderful childhood in the Indies. Until the war began.

II

SAMURAI

From Baldy's memoirs

Bombs land on our house

I was a schoolboy in class 2D of the Architecture department when the Japanese Air Force attacked Pearl Harbor. It was December 1941. The United States declared war on Japan, and the Netherlands followed suit. The Dutch declaration was read out to us by the headmaster. Needless to say, this pretty much put an end to our studies. All citizens of German and Japanese origin, including any mixed blood descendants, were arrested and carted off to internment camps. Among them were German and Japanese classmates I never saw again. A Dutch boy from our school was called up to serve with the Dutch Royal Navy and became a gunner on the *Surabaya*, a coastal defence ship. He was killed when Japanese planes bombed Surabaya's docks at Tanjung Perak.

Through the school governors, I signed up for the Air Defence Service. Equipped with transmitters and receivers, I was regularly posted in the airport district of Darmo with orders to report back by radio and telephone. Thanks to Jacob's books and magazines, I was adept at recognizing aircraft. Air Defence supplied me with binoculars and a .36 calibre Colt revolver, and I wore a green khaki uniform and beret. The Royal Netherlands East Indies Army, known to everyone as the KNIL, was not exactly a force to be reckoned with and reinforcements came in the shape of Australian soldiers, who showed far greater bravery in taking on the Japanese invaders.

Ads appeared in the local papers calling for youngsters aged fourteen and over to train as aircraft engineers with the KNIL's air force. My mother and my self-appointed guardian Jacob refused to let me join up. At the time Willem Nolan, a cousin and my father's namesake, came to see us occasionally. On his final visit he turned to me and said, 'Arend, I am now serving with the KNIL and soon I will be fighting the Japanese. Be thankful that you have not been recognized as a Nolan and that you bear your mother's name. Lay low here, under her roof. I do not think I will survive this war.' He embraced me and I never saw him again. He died as a prisoner of war working on the Burma Railway and his body lies buried in Thailand.

In early February 1942, the sirens on the school roof began to wail. Through my binoculars, I saw nine Japanese Zero fighters coming in low. Above them were fifteen Mitsubishi Bettys on a bombing run. I was sent to the forge and told to open a valve that would release the carbide gas from the boiler and cause a massive explosion if the fighters sprayed the place with bullets. I heard the rattle of machine-gun fire and 110-pound anti-personnel bombs began to fall. Before I could get the job done, the roof of the boiler house was blown clean off. Everyone dived for cover and when the all-clear sounded we began shifting rubble. We had to dig out students trapped in makeshift shelters and pinned by fallen trees.

Classes were cancelled and as I was getting on my bike to cycle home, a Javanese neighbour called to me from outside the gate. He told me that our house on Pasar Besar Wetan Gang IV, close to the power company buildings, had been hit. The front of the house had been reduced to rubble and police were patrolling to prevent looting. They let me through. Our antique Chinese vases, each one over three feet tall, lay in pieces. My room was wrecked and the bomb blast had ripped through the kitchen. The interior of the dining room was gutted and the back walls were riddled with machine-gun bullets.

I cried out for revenge. A policeman calmed me and told me to go to the Central Civic Hospital on Simpang, but the chaos in the streets made it impossible to get there. A Javanese neighbour, whose home was also in ruins, let me stay with his family on Baliwerti, around half a mile from our house. There I was given a warm welcome and a small room with a *balai-balai*, a simple bed made of bamboo. In the courtyard was a well where I was able to wash.

The next day I cycled to the hospital in search of my family. My mother and Ella were in a mild state of shock. Ina had injuries to her right arm and her left leg. One of our *babus* had suffered a head wound. When they were discharged after a stay of several days, Ina joined my brother Karel in temporary accommodation in Surabaya. Jacob arranged for me to be evacuated along with Mama, Ella, Poppy, Kokkie Tas and Babu Tenie. We were to go to Blitar, around 80 miles south, the place where I had been nursed back to health as a baby. I packed my wicker suitcase, took my leave of the Javanese family on Baliwerti, and left my bike behind. My mother waited for me at the hospital and from there we walked to Gubeng station. The train was full to overflowing, the day hot, the journey long.

In Blitar we were met by Aunty Mien and other members of Mama's family. I was confounded by the loving embraces I received from those Chinese women: a far cry from the beatings and punishing garden training sessions I was used to, not to mention the endless fights with my brothers and sisters. I was given a room at the back with a *balai-balai*, and a rickety table and chair. I wandered out of Aunty Mien's *kampong* house to the end of the street and found myself looking into a deep ravine. I wondered how Karel and Ina were doing, for we knew that the Betty bombers – 'flying cigars' us schoolboys called them – were continuing their raids on Surabaya. I had only one thought: to fight for Queen and Country.

The next morning I decided to explore the neighbourhood. Invading Japanese troops were flooding into Blitar and were hailed with loud cheers by the Indonesian population. Indos were nowhere to be seen. They stayed indoors. Uncle Soen warned me not to confide in anyone. The Indonesians saw the Japanese as liberators from their Dutch oppressors, and Indonesian political parties were quick to seek Japanese support. Uncle Soen told me the Japanese were arresting every Dutch citizen they could find – men, women and children – and putting them in internment camps, but Indos were still being allowed to work and move freely. The Indonesians spat at the white Dutch internees when they were marched from their camp to their workplace and back. The Japanese looked on and laughed.

To kill time, I took language lessons, arranged by an acquaintance of Aunty Mien's. A Chinese girl taught me Ching Iem, a local Cantonese dialect with characters to match.

One morning I went to the *pasar* with Ella and Poppy. Japanese soldiers with bayonets fixed to their rifles had rounded up a crowd of people in the town square. In their midst was a ten-year-old boy, all skin and bones, who had stolen from a market stall to still his hunger and was awaiting punishment. The boy was made to place the hand he had stolen with on a wooden block. The Japanese soldiers forced everyone to watch; I was hit with a rifle butt when I looked the other way. An officer drew his samurai sword and hacked off the boy's hand. Any Javanese onlookers who tried to help the boy were beaten senseless by the butts of Japanese guns. Through an interpreter, the officer made it clear that the same fate awaited anyone who was caught stealing. A buzz of contemptuous indignation ran through the crowd. Were they still so happy with their Japanese liberators? That evening I walked to the end of the street and spent hours staring across the ravine.

A portrait of the Queen

Early in May, Mama heard from Jacob that he had found a place to rent in the Undaan Kulon district of Surabaya. For me this was welcome news, as I was bored stiff in Blitar, though I did enjoy my Chinese lessons. We packed our suitcases, said our goodbyes to the family and set off for the station. The steam train that took us from the mountains to the plains left in the afternoon and pulled into Gubeng station late that evening. Every platform was swarming with Japanese soldiers. At the exit we were all checked by members of the notorious Kenpeitai, the Japanese secret police. I showed them my Chinese ID, was greeted with a short bark and allowed to pass. We found ourselves a *kossong*, a horse-drawn carriage that could carry six.

The streets of Undaan Kulon bore the names of Dutch naval heroes. Our new home was at No. 5 on a street named after Jacob van Heemskerk. The square where my brother Karel lived commemorated seafarer Piet Hein. And the street where my half-sister Nonnie lived with her husband Ang Soen Bing paid tribute to Maarten Tromp.

With the help of Javanese police officers and acquaintances, Jacob and Karel had managed to salvage much of the furniture from our bombed-out home on Pasar Besar Wetan Gang IV and had put it in storage until the official permit to occupy the new place on Heemskerkstraat was issued. Among our salvaged possessions were some of my textbooks from Queen Emma School, so I was able to continue studying at home. I was given a room of my own, ten feet by ten. It contained nothing but a wooden divan with a kapok mattress, a pillow and a mosquito net, a chair and a small table. To my surprise I found a large roll of paper among my scant belongings. I removed the wrapping to reveal a colour portrait of Queen Wilhelmina of the Netherlands, which a teacher had once presented to me. I pinned it to the wall above my bed.

'Arend, take that picture of Queen Wilhelmina down off the wall!' Mama ordered.

I refused.

'It will cause us no end of trouble if the Japs turn up to inspect the house!'

'Wilhelmina is our queen. Those bandy-legged bastards have their Tennō Heika, don't they? Besides, what do they know about our House of Orange far away in Holland? I don't give a damn about the Japs. They attacked my school, bombed our home on Pasar Besar Wetan and beat me when I refused to watch them mutilate that boy in Blitar.'

Mama flew into a rage. 'And where do you think that hostile attitude will get you? Are you planning to take on the whole bloody lot of them by yourself? Do what you want, only don't come crying to me!'

Bike, bricks and turtle meat

A few days later, Karel gave me an old bike. Knowing I would have to find myself a job, I did what I could to knock it into shape. But the first trip I made was to see Uncle Soen, who lived in a little house in a *kampong* near Peneleh. He informed me about the movement of Japanese troops in and around Croc City and explained how life was changing under the heel of the Japanese jackboot. He told me about the Kenpeitai's reign of terror and filled me in on how they operated. Uncle Soen was a member of two small-scale Chinese resistance movements and warned me once again not to confide in anyone. Dutch citizens had been herded into internment camps but Indos were still being allowed to work and move freely for the time being. Some Belandas had even smeared their faces with shoe polish in the hope of passing themselves off as Indos.

I cycled around aimlessly for days on end. From Undaan via Genteng, Tunjungan, Kaliasin and Tamarindelaan all the way to Darmo. From there I headed north, turning back when I reached Gresik. On one of these trips I stopped at Karang Pilang to watch a couple of Indo boys spearing turtles on the banks of Kali Brantas. I got off my bike and went over for a chat. They told me they were labourers in a brickworks across the road and asked me if I needed a job. In no time they had introduced me to the head foreman, a Dutchman by the name of Huitink. I was taken aback to see a Dutchman running the place when so many had been interned in the camps. Mr Huitink took me into his office, checked my ID and jotted down my details in a notebook. He looked up in surprise when I told him that I was in fact an illegitimate Nolan. The family's name was known far and wide, from Surabaya and the surrounding area to the far east of Java.

Huitink took me to the office of the *hanchō*, the Japanese chief inspector. He was dressed in a white uniform with the five petals of the *sakura* emblem on his left breast pocket. I had to bow low before this man, and felt deeply humiliated. In broken English he told me I was to start the next morning at a rate of two cents an hour.

Back home, I told Mama I would be starting work the next day. She was delighted, although she thought they were paying me a pittance. Every morning at six-thirty I set off for the brickworks in Karang Pilang, a trip of over 15 miles. First I learned to make bricks by pressing lumps of clay into moulds. As time went on, I helped out in the workshop occasionally, forging iron or working as a fitter and welder. We worked up to fifteen hours a day and when the bricks had to go into the furnace, we were on duty round the clock and left to snatch a nap whenever we could. The work was tough but at least I was earning a little money, which I used to buy food for Mama and the rest of the household. It was nowhere near enough, of course, but Karel and Jacob were also bringing in a wage.

Karel had married his childhood sweetheart Wiesje Muller and they had rented a pavilion on Krangganstraat. Wiesje's sister Erna was living with a Chinaman to avoid being sent off to an internment camp.

When I was on night shift, I would go down to the river with the Indo boys to catch turtles and iguanas. We killed the iguanas with spears we made ourselves, sliced open their bellies, gutted them and rubbed salt into the cavity. The turtles were more of a challenge, but those Indo boys knew exactly what they were doing. Once all the bricks had been stacked in the furnace, we stoked the furnace room, first with firewood, then with coal. The boys laid the dead creatures on top of the bricks, within reach of an opening, and we would use fire tongs and sticks to turn them until the flesh was tender. The resulting meal saw us through the night. There was a strange taste to the meat but we had appetite enough and it never made us sick.

I was cycling over thirty miles a day on bad roads to get to work and back, and one day the tyres on my bike gave out on me. Karel provided me with a set of solid crepe rubber tyres but all they did was turn the bike into a boneshaker, which meant an even earlier start in the morning.

By this time, a bond had developed between the Indo boys, Mr Huitink and me. We kept one another informed about the war in the Pacific. Before long, another Indo lad by the name of Fred Verhoef came to work for us, without applying through Huitink. I couldn't help but notice the preferential treatment he received from the *hanchō*, and I let Huitink and the others in on my suspicions.

Huitink took the next day off and did some investigating. He returned with the news that Fred Verhoef was an informer for the Kenpeitai. The blood drained from our faces, but Huitink advised us to act as if we were none the wiser.

In confidence I told my friends, 'That guy has to go, whatever it takes. Do nothing and one by one we will fall into the hands of the Kenpeitai. One wrong word and you're a goner.' They nodded, but none of us knew how and when we should settle the score with the spy in our midst. The brickworks ran on the Japanese calendar, so there were no Sundays off. We were only allowed an occasional day's leave when production targets for the building projects had been met.

On one of my mornings off, I went to Pasar Turi to buy fish for Mama and bumped into Soedjono, a Javanese friend from Queen Emma School. When I had run my errand at the market, we set off for his house in Krembangan district. Since long before the war, it had enjoyed a fearsome reputation as the part of town where the toughest, most ruthless hoodlums would hang out. On our way, we met more of our former school friends – among them Soenarjo, Soetopo, Soemarsono, Soetjipto and Soemarno – and the whole gang of us ended up at Soedjono's. We talked about the Japanese occupation and Soedjono told me that all the former members of the Destruction Corps at Queen Emma School were wanted by the Kenpeitai. A Chinese boy called Lim Tan Ko-Ko had turned out to be a Kenpeitai spy and had betrayed a bunch of former pupils, all Indo boys, who were then arrested, interrogated and tortured. The teachers in charge of the school's Destruction Corps – Mr Sonneville and the Trestorff brothers – had been arrested, tortured and beheaded. This could only mean that I was on the wanted list too.

The conversation with my Javanese friends soon turned to the matter of Indonesian independence. 'Nolan, we know that you are loyal to the Netherlands and the House of Orange,' Soenarjo said. 'We saw Mr Sonneville present you with a portrait of Queen Wilhelmina on behalf of the school governors, in appreciation of your patriotic spirit. Our loyalties lie elsewhere. Our goal is independence for Indonesia. This war with Japan will not last forever. One day this yellow peril will be driven from our soil. And then we will rise up to make sure that Dutch colonial rule does not return. It will be a bloody battle. But let us not get ahead of ourselves. We are here now to discuss ways of resisting the Japs. Are you prepared to join us, even though you are only a *peranakan*, Chinese of mixed blood?'

I looked long and hard at each boy in turn, and then agreed. Soenarjo was a close acquaintance of Uncle Soen's and he too had a good many contacts among the Chinese resistance.

'From now on I am willing to join you in resisting the Japs, but when the war is over I will not be part of your fight for independence. Indonesia is not my country. Although I was born here, this is not my *tanah air*. It is not my fatherland.'

'That is not true, Nolan!' Soetjipto exclaimed. 'You were born and raised in this country. Your mother is Chinese, but she too was born and raised here. You belong to this land and this people. We all accept you as our own.'

I was thrown into turmoil by Soetjipto's words. I thought of all the Indos who had looked down their noses at me because I was illegitimate, while this bunch of native friends accepted me as an equal, without question. It was a crisis of conscience that shook me to the core. My hatred of the Japs did not make things easier. I could team up with Indo boys to commit acts of resistance, but I knew that if they were arrested and tortured by the Kenpeitai, they would probably crack under the unbearable pain and betray everyone they knew. Even in those days I had little respect for the typical Indo's character, not least because they had no sense of solidarity. Always ready to look down on one family while bowing and scraping to another, Indos squabbled more among themselves than they did with the Dutch or the Javanese. Ever since childhood, I had been fighting Indo boys who mocked me as a baldy little bastard. In such matters, they were all too willing to form a pact, while in everything else they were at one another's throats. And yet there were Indo lads who gave me a strong sense that, as the son of a European father and an Asian mother, I belonged among them.

Soedjono and his gang gave me a mission: to keep tabs on the Chinese traitor Lim Tan Ko-Ko, along with his contact at the Kenpeitai's intelligence service, a Chinese detective by the name of Oei Boen Pong, formerly of the Political Intelligence Service. They warned me to steer clear of a red-haired Dutchman nicknamed Red Rose, a traitor who worked for the Kenpeitai. Highly skilled in espionage, Red Rose was known to be an exceptionally smooth operator who had already driven countless Dutchmen and Indo-Dutch into the hands of the Kenpeitai, where they had been tortured and beheaded.

I wanted something in return, and told my Javanese friends about Fred Verhoef, the traitor in our midst at the brickworks. I proposed a plan to kill him, knowing that the Indo group led by Mr Huitink were in a tight enough bind as it was. It was them or Verhoef. Soedjono gave me his immediate backing.

I began by keeping tabs on Fred Verhoef. He was in the habit of taking an East Java steam tram from the station at Pasar Turi to Karang Pilang. We set a date to dispose of the traitor. All I had was a penknife, while Soedjono was armed with a small razor-sharp dagger. I left home before sunrise, cycled to Soedjono's and we set off for Pasar Turi on foot. There we saw our target board the tram. Despite the morning crush of travellers, we managed to squeeze into the same compartment as Verhoef. We said hello and exchanged small talk.

By the time the tram approached Karang Pilang, we were the only three left in the compartment. Soedjono gave me the nod and I began to pick a fight with Verhoef, accusing him to his face of being a traitor and a spy. He turned white with rage and threatened to report me to the Kenpeitai. I grabbed Verhoef by his shirt, pulled him to his feet and laid into him with my fists. He hit back, but Soedjono attacked him from behind. I dragged him onto the gangway between the coaches and gave him a good kicking, while Soedjono threw open the safety barrier. Verhoef tried to struggle to his feet only to slip into the gap. I delivered the kick that finished him off. He fell onto the coupling between the coaches and let out a terrifying scream as his legs were torn off. We had already passed Karang Pilang and were heading for the next station. Soedjono took hold of me and together we leapt from the moving tram.

Soedjono and I walked the short distance from the tramway back to the brickworks. There I went straight to see Mr Huitink and told him I was quitting. He looked at me in surprise and asked why. I told Huitink I had sent Fred Verhoef to meet his maker and warned him not to say a word. Looking him in the eye, I shook his hand and returned to Surabaya with Soedjono.

'Allah, Nolan,' Soedjono said on the way, 'watching you give him that final kick made me feel sick to my stomach. I am starting to feel guilty. What about you?'

I told him the truth. 'Man, for as long as I can remember my father and my brothers beat me till I bled. If I lost a fight at school or out in the street, they made me go back the next day and fight on, for as long as it took to win. That is how I was raised. Now war has come and here we are, fighting for our lives. When I fight, I go *mata gelap*. That is why I feel no regret at all.'

Bamboo spears and Japanese lessons

In a matter of days, I found a job as a mandor in the packing department of the Lie Sin sweet factory on Undaan Kulon, by a canal near our house. As a boy of seventeen, I was in charge of a group of thirty native women and had to monitor their production. The factory board consisted of five Japanese, two of them army officers. Each day before lunch, we all had to take part in a military drill. The company supplied everyone with a *takeyari*, a Japanese bamboo spear, and the exercises for the male workers involved plenty of lunging and stabbing. The *takeyari* was a vicious weapon: it went in easily but took your victim's insides with it when you pulled it out.

It was a good time to join the company, as we were forced to stay after work and learn Japanese. The classes were taught in Malay by a cane-wielding army officer. Anyone caught slacking would feel its sting, whether they were male or female. I picked up Japanese with little difficulty; my lessons with the Chinese girl in Blitar had stood me in good stead. The characters were different and simpler, but the system was the same. After six months I passed the exam and was awarded my diploma in Japanese with considerable pomp and ceremony. In addition to katakana and hiragana, I also knew over two-hundred kanji characters, enough to read Japanese newspapers reasonably well.

Uncle Soen was delighted with this achievement, because it meant I could be deployed for espionage activities. He regularly supplied me with Japanese newspapers and messages from military operations in the Pacific and taught me how to interpret them. When the Japanese press wrote about heavy Allied losses, I was to assume they really meant losses suffered by the Japs.

One day I arrived home looking deathly pale and bathed in sweat after cycling home at full speed. Mama asked if I had been in another fight.

'No,' I answered, 'I was followed by an Indo girl. I don't know who. It was very creepy.'

Unable to contain herself, Mama burst out laughing. I failed to see the funny side and took offence. Mama mentioned the incident to Karel, who decided to investigate. He soon found out that it was his sister-in-law Emmy who had cycled after me. Mama advised Karel to fix me up with Emmy, so that I would have some experience with girls. Karel began to find excuses to invite me to his house on my days off, and drove me into Emmy's arms. She taught me how to make love to a girl but I didn't dare do anything sexual. Custom dictated that a girl had to remain a virgin until she married.

The Japs had banned us from listening to foreign stations but my Javanese friends kept their radios well hidden, so we were able to follow the progress of the war. We heard that the Japanese navy had suffered heavy losses at sea. Walking through the busy shopping streets of Tunjungan to Pasar Besar well before curfew, I picked up snatches of conversation between Japanese soldiers and could tell they were more than a little worried.

In addition to my Javanese pals, I also had Madurese, Bugis and Makassar friends in the resistance. Many of the latter were seamen and fishermen. One Makassar boy owned a seaworthy fishing boat with a secret compartment, where he hid a compact but powerful radio transmitter and receiver. He was the only member of the eight-man crew who could understand English. I passed messages to him through a *becak* driver called Jopie Reuben, who operated as a courier.

Betrayed by my family

Out of necessity, my sisters Ella and Ina took waitressing jobs at one of the big restaurants on Simpang. But I soon found out that, besides serving food and drink, they were working as hostesses for Japanese soldiers. I was outraged and complained to Mama about their scandalous behaviour. 'What has it got to do with you?' she replied furiously. 'Your sisters are years older than you. They need to earn money and you have no say in the matter! We all have to survive, whatever it takes.'

I took Ina aside and confronted her about what she was doing. She all but exploded and slapped me in the face. This sent me into such a rage that I punched her on the jaw, so hard that she reeled back and hit the wall. Blood began to pour from her mouth. Shaken, she found herself a chair, sat down and burst into tears.

'How could you hit me so hard?' she asked, dazed.

'Remember how you, Ella, Jacob and Karel beat me, kicked me and humiliated me since I was a child?' I answered. 'This is my revenge! I have been hit once too often and I am not a little boy any more. When the rage takes me, I no longer see the difference between a man and a woman. I hit back as hard as I can. You and Ella are collaborating with the Japs. And I will make you both pay!'

My family's behaviour filled me with shame. I noticed that Jacob and Karel were also going out of their way to be on friendly terms with influential Japs. A few months later, Ella even brought a Japanese airman home with her, an officer by the name of Kamei. It was all I could do to keep my animosity under control. But then I remembered the ancient Chinese wisdom passed on to me by my own mother: 'In certain cases, treat your enemy as a friend. Let him feel victorious. Wait for his moments of weakness, then strike.'

I played along with the Jap and before long I was holding entire conversations with him about his role as a bomber pilot and his acts of so-called heroism in his 'flying cigar'. All the while I was wondering how this path of feigned friendship might lead my sister's slant-eyed lover straight to hell.

One evening I was cycling near the *pasar* at Kembang Kuning. From the direction of the Chinese cemetery in Simo Kwagean, I saw a long column of trucks approaching. It turned onto Kembang Kuning heading for the docks. The trucks were loaded with cylindrical rattan baskets used to transport pigs, but these baskets held prisoners of war. Out of curiosity, I cycled in the direction the column had come from and discovered a POW camp on the other side of the cemetery. I rode on to Aunty Kiep's house and asked her if I could stay the night. By this time it was eleven o'clock and the curfew had begun.

Aunty Kiep told me that the prisoners held at the camp beyond the cemetery were Australian soldiers who had fought at Wonokromo Bridge during the Japanese invasion. Some had already been beheaded with samurai swords and lay buried nearby.

'Arend, if you saw a column of trucks loaded with pig baskets, it means the soldiers are being transported to the docks. If you want to know more, go and see Uncle Soen first thing in the morning and he will give you the addresses of his Chinese friends at the docks. They might be able to tell you what is happening to those poor Australian soldiers. But your aunty is afraid that they will be thrown into the sea, baskets and all, for the sharks to eat.'

I cycled over to Uncle Soen's the next morning. He sent me to see a friend of his, a Chinese ferryman who lived in the neighbourhood of Ujung and belonged to the same Chinese political organization as my uncle. 'What your aunt told you is true,' the ferryman said. 'For two nights now I have seen columns of trucks, piled high with pig baskets here in Ujung. The baskets are opened on the quayside and the prisoners are thrown into the sea. As you know, these waters are swarming with tiger sharks. These atrocities are committed after curfew to keep them from the locals, but everyone in these parts knows what is going on. In the morning, the sea where they dump the prisoners is still red with blood. Sometimes swollen limbs float to the surface, for even the sharks cannot dispose of so many bodies. Fear and hatred of the Japs runs deep among the people here. Almost all of us long for the Belandas to return or the Allied troops to arrive.'

Dutch prisoners of war were also falling foul of the Japanese *bushidō*. Another POW camp was located on the former fairground on Cannaplein, near the district of Tambaksari. One day, a dozen prisoners – most of them sailors with the Dutch Royal Navy – were found guilty of passive resistance and sentenced to be beheaded. Another dozen were tied to posts and bayonetted to death by Japanese soldiers. Among them was Hendrik Karssen, a sailor who died with a cry of 'Long live the Queen!' When the war was over, a minesweeper was named in honour of that brave Indo boy.

At night, far past the curfew, many Indonesians who still sympathized with the Belandas managed to sneak past the Japanese patrols and throw food parcels over the barbed-wire fence that surrounded the camp.

It was at this time that I met Mrs Thea Bürer, whose husband was a prisoner of war in Burma. She lived on Trompstraat, opposite my half-sister Nonnie and her family. As she was part German, Thea Bürer had been spared the internment camp. She had three children to take care of and also gave refuge to Olga Wetzel and her sister. These two ladies taught me to dance. We soundproofed the dining room windows with rags, cranked up the old gramophone and played foxtrots on ebonite discs.

Women 'fortunate' enough to stay out of the camps had trouble finding work. Many felt compelled to sell their favours to Japanese officers now and then. Like my sisters, Thea Bürer began working as a waitress but soon became a call girl. My neighbour Mary Scheffer met the same fate. Her husband, who worked for Royal Dutch Indies Airways, had been evacuated to Australia and she had been left to take care of her two young daughters alone.

I was a boy of seventeen and fell madly in love with Olga Wetzel, who was six years my elder. Much to the annoyance of Thea Bürer and my family, Olga strung me along for a while and expected me to spoil her with all kinds of treats and the loving ways I had learned from Emmy. But this soon made me feel like a gigolo and I gave her up. What I wanted was to be part of the resistance.

Torture

Karel warned me to keep a low profile and not to cycle around the city so much. He was worried that Lim Tan Ko-Ko and his boss Oei Boen Pong were on to me. His warning came too late. My Javanese friends had assigned me to keep watch on those two traitors, but in my heedlessness the tables had been turned: they now had me in their sights. One evening near Pasar Besar, I spotted Oei Boen Pong standing on the other side of the street, hands in pockets. He was staring straight at me and I failed to notice four Kenpeitai men closing in. They kicked me to the ground and dragged me off to their headquarters in the former Palace of Justice, across from the government building on Pasar Besar. There, in a blacked-out room, they tied a cable around my wrists and strung me up on a pulley until I was hanging with my feet ten inches off the floor. A thug with a baseball bat hit me in the stomach, then on my ribs, back and legs. I lost consciousness. When I came to, I was lying in a cell. The face of my brother Karel appeared before me. 'Scrap the words "fear" and "afraid" from your vocabulary,' I heard him say. 'They can beat you as hard as they want, it won't kill you.'

Two Japs laid me on a plank and bound me with lengths of thick rope. One shoved a funnel in my mouth and the other began to fill it with water from a bucket. I had no choice but to swallow and I could feel my stomach swell. Then they stamped hard on my stomach, forcing the water out through my ears, nose, mouth and anus. This torture was repeated four times until I was bleeding from the anus. Eventually they untied the ropes and booted me into a corner of the cell. 'Where have you hidden your weapons?' the interrogator asked, half in Japanese, half in Malay. 'Who are your friends? Who were you spying for?' Every question was delivered with a kick.

I was racked with pain. The whole room was spinning, but I said nothing.

I do not know how many days and nights I spent in that cell. It was so dark, I could not tell day from night. An officer came in with a tray of food. He made it clear that this was my last meal and that I was to be beheaded at half past one that afternoon. I could not eat, all I could do was groan from the pain. The door closed behind him and opened again later. Two Japs grabbed hold of me and helped me out to the duty officer's desk. I was overjoyed to see Uncle Soen sitting there.

'Arend, I have come for you,' he said. 'Your freedom has been bought. Do not ask me how.'

The duty officer apologized for any inconvenience I had suffered.

'*Bakeiro*,' I mumbled.

He was so angry I had called him an idiot that he immediately drew his samurai sword. Uncle Soen and another Jap stepped in to separate us. Muttering to himself, Uncle Soen dragged me outside. On Pasar Besar, he flagged down a *becak*, because I could hardly walk. He thought it better not to take me straight home, afraid Mama would break down when she saw the state I was in. I was caked in blood and thanks to the water torture I stank of piss and shit.

Uncle Soen took me to Aunty Kiep in the Chinese district of Simo Kwagean. She burst into tears when she saw me. Carefully she undressed me, washed me and rubbed me with herbal oil, while Uncle Soen went next door to fetch me some clean clothes. Aunty Kiep let me lie on the divan and, sobbing all the while, brewed up a herbal remedy for me. She suspected that I was suffering from internal bleeding. Her potion did me good almost as soon as I drank it.

My uncle explained that he had been told of my arrest by an acquaintance who had seen it happen. He had then called on all kinds of influential figures in the Chinese community until he had collected enough money to bribe a number of senior Kenpeitai officers. He told me I had been held in that building for four days.

Christened as a Protestant

Around six weeks later, I had more or less recovered from my ordeal, apart from severe pain in my guts every now and then. I played hide and seek from Mama, inventing one excuse after another, and occasionally visited Pah Tjillih on the sly. His healing powers were able to rid me of my pain for a while.

One day, Mama said, 'Arend, I have decided to have us all

christened in the Protestant church on Bubutan. We have an appointment with Reverend Laloe this coming Sunday. You, Ella, Poppy and I will be christened. My hope is that this will help you grow into a good, strong, God-fearing boy.'

Scenes from my Sunday school education ran through my mind like a film. The Protestant teachers who had caned or whipped me whenever I stuttered over a psalm, a hymn or a passage from the Bible. How my brothers had accompanied me to school to have a little word with those abusive teachers. How Jacob had let his fists do the talking and put an abrupt end to Mr Claproth's Protestant bullying. But Mama's word was law, and in mid-June 1943 we took our places in the front row of the Protestant church on Bubutan. During the service we had to go up one by one and kneel at the font so that Reverend Laloe could christen us. After the service, we were ushered into the vestry, where the minister gave us a long talk.

Reverend Laloe was a marvellous man, a Minahasan who hailed from Celebes. Strangely enough, I felt like a new man after the christening, as if God was closer to me than ever before. Mama impressed upon me that I should pray frequently, because it was only through God that I could expect miracles. She had always followed the teachings of Confucius, passed down from generation to generation as part of the Chinese tradition. But her dealings with Christians had led her to immerse herself in the Malay Bible, and what she read there had changed her mind. Her sister and brother, Aunty Kiep and Uncle Soen, respected her decision to follow a new path but they remained disciples of Confucius. Our family were never ones to waste words on matters of faith.

After the service and our talk with Reverend Laloe, I went for a walk and struck up conversations with Chinese and Indonesians about the latest news. The Allies seemed to be making headway in the Solomon Islands and in Burma. Mulling this over, I dropped in to see Karel on Jalan Kranggan. As a rule, my brother showed no interest at all in how the war was progressing. That afternoon, I found his wife Wiesje alone and I could see from her face that she had been crying. She called my brother a bastard and told me he was having an affair with a white Indo woman called Marietje Mertz, whose husband, an officer on a merchant ship, had been taken prisoner.

'Why hasn't she been interned, like all the other white Indo women?' I asked.

'I don't know,' she replied. 'Marietje lives near Pasar Besar. A nanny looks after her children, a blonde girl by the name of Ciska Wagner. She comes from a German family and must be about your age… Arend please, try to talk your brother round. Persuade him to come back to me.'

My Indonesian contacts gave me directions to Marietje Mertz's house. In the narrow side street off Pasar Besar, I knocked on her front door. A sweet blonde girl opened it. I asked to see my brother. The girl introduced herself and let me in, but not before she had given me a long, meaningful look. Karel was surprised to see me. I told him to go back to Wiesje. Tempers flared and Karel growled that his little brother should watch his big mouth.

A few evenings later, I found myself back at Pasar Besar. Out for a stroll, I wound up in a fight with two Japanese soldiers. They were blind drunk, bawling and slurring as they staggered around. One of them bumped into me and started yelling. I yelled back and they began to hit me. I kicked them to the ground and passers-by warned me to make myself scarce. I ran to Marietje's house and, when Ciska opened the door, I asked her if I could spend the night so that I could go and see my Madurese friends in Dapuan district the next day. No sooner had she let me in than Karel appeared and, without a word, began to beat me. Ciska tried to explain the situation but Karel would not stop. I exploded in fury and went *mata gelap*, punching and kicking him till he fell. Marietje came running in to separate us, but I knocked her to the ground as well. Ciska cried out that I would kill her if I didn't stop. 'The days when you could treat me as your little brother are gone for good,' I sneered at Karel. 'Never again will I let you humiliate me! *Senjata makan tuan!* From now on, I hit back!'

Soon after this, I fell out with Jacob too. He had married a girl called Ietje and came round to ask Mama for a kapok mattress for their spare bedroom. I was sitting there talking to Uncle Soen. Mama had already given me her spare mattress, but Jacob was having none of it.

'Give me Arend's mattress. What does he want with a mattress? Let him sleep on the wooden divan. That's good enough for him.'

No sooner had he said these words than he walked over and punched me in the face. I fell to the floor. His wedding ring had left a deep gash in my forehead. Half-dazed, I got to my feet and went to attack him, but Mama stopped me. I grabbed a teapot and hurled it at Jacob's head. It missed by a hair. Then I rushed into my bedroom and grabbed my father's old fighting knife. Uncle Soen came after me, took hold of my right hand and squeezed it with that mysterious power of his. I fell to one knee, almost unable to move. 'Arend,' he said, 'this is no way to act. Heed my words. Remember that you have me to thank for your life, twice over. If you harm your brother, God will punish you. Get a grip on yourself…' His embrace calmed me down.

'Why do my brothers keep hitting me?' I asked.

No one answered.

Resistance

Much to my delight, I ran into Ciska a couple of times on Pasar Besar, when she was out walking with Marietje's children. It turned out that Ciska and her sister lived in Dapuan too, albeit in wretched conditions. When she had a day off, I would invite her to our house and she was allowed to stay overnight. Mama doted on her, spoiling her with tasty meals and Chinese biscuits. Ciska was Catholic and always wore her rosary beads around her neck. Little did I know that her rosary would save my life one day.

Towards the end of the year, air-raid sirens in the night announced that the Allies were closing in. Their Flying Fortresses were caught in the searchlights but flew so high that the Japanese anti-aircraft shells could not reach them. By this time, I had been pressganged into sentry duty with a *tonarigumi* group, patrolling the local neighbourhood of Undaan Kulon to combat thieves, looters and the like. Anyone who refused duty was labelled a spy by the Kenpeitai. When curfew began, I had to pin on a white armband with Japanese characters and head out armed with a *takeyari*. My patrol consisted mainly of Indonesian lads roughly my own age. They came from the *kampong* of Undaan, beyond Heemskerkstraat and Trompstraat. Needless to say, they were always banging on about Merdeka, their dream of an independent Indonesia. Those boys hated Belandas with a vengeance, so even though they saw me as one of them I was in hostile company. My secret hope was that the Allies would make their presence felt and soon.

Christmas was ruined by the presence of that slant-eyed devil Kamei, who was even permitted to spend the night in Ella's room. As the youngest member of the family and the only one loyal to the House of Orange, I had no desire to get into a political argument with Jacob and Karel, so I told Mama that I was going to stay with Aunty Kiep. Instead I cycled on to Gubeng district, where my friend Ernst Motta lived.

Ernst and his mother had a house on the fringes of Gubeng, with a wonderful view of the southern railway. On nights when curfew was approaching and I was unable to make it home without being blown to bits by the Japs, I sometimes stayed at the Mottas'. Ernst's mother suspected that he and I were up to something but asked no questions, though I could tell she was often afraid. Their Italian papers had saved them from internment, just as my Chinese ID had saved me. The Mottas pinned the Italian tricolour to their clothing, just as I wore the badge of the Chinese flag given to me by Jacob.

Shortly after midnight, the sirens began to wail and the low drone of engines filled the air. Mrs Motta retired to her bedroom. Ernst and I went out into the garden and hid among the bushes with a pair of binoculars. We spotted three Consolidated-Vultee Liberator bombers, lit up by searchlight beams. The planes came under heavy fire but were out of range of the Japanese anti-aircraft guns. Small red, green and yellow fireballs suddenly shot up from various directions: tracer bullets. We had no idea what this meant. More bombers flew over and we clearly saw one or two making a bombing run. Flashes of light appeared on the southern horizon, followed by massive explosions from the direction of Wonokromo, where the Batavian Petroleum Company had its installations.

I took the *takeyari* from my bike, put on my armband and strapped the sheath of my fighting knife to my right leg. I told Ernst to put on a hat to cover his blond hair. He whined about not having a Japanese armband and not being a *tonarigumi* member, but that did not stop him running inside and returning with a hat, a knife and a revolver. Without an armband, he was forced to slink along the bushes that lined the streets and take cover in gardens from time to time. I was able to walk openly down the street brandishing my bamboo spear.

A few streets away we saw a white, fair-haired woman among the trees, firing red flares in the direction of Wonokromo and the industrial sites of Ngagel as a flight of four-engine bombers approached. Ernst walked on. Then I heard bellowing in Japanese. A Kenpeitai officer was charging towards the woman, samurai sword drawn. He ran her through with his blade and, when she collapsed on the ground, severed her head from her body with a single blow.

At first, I stood there in shock. Then I slowly began to walk in his direction. I no longer remember exactly what I was feeling. The officer shouted at me, citing the ancient *bushidō* on which he had acted. I understood most of what he said. 'The same fate awaits anyone who commits acts of resistance or treason against Nippon!'

He wiped his bloodied sword on the dead woman's clothes and, as he was sliding it back into its scabbard with a proud samurai flourish, I attacked. I was on him in seconds and drilled my *takeyari* deep into his side. The tip was so sharp, it pierced his body with ease. The officer grabbed the bamboo spear with both hands. I heard a rattling in his throat, saw him shake and then witnessed the terrifying death throes in his eyes. My stomach was churning like mad. I let go and the Japanese officer fell back slowly. My God, he took an age to die! Not daring to pull the spear from his side, I ran.

Ernst knew nothing of what I had done. All he had seen from his hiding place in the bushes was people firing flares into the night sky. It dawned on me that if he had been arrested and tortured, he would surely have mentioned my name. And then the Japs would have come for my head too.

Ella's lover is sent to hell

In mid-May 1944, Surabaya came under attack from large formations of Grumman Avenger and Douglas Dauntless dive bombers, escorted by Chance Vought Corsair and Grumann Hellcat fighter planes. Down at the Tanjung Perak docks, ships and buildings vital to the Japanese war effort were hit. The first raid targeted the port, the second the oil installations at Wonokromo. I was near Pasar Turi and looked on with satisfaction as the aircraft went about their deadly mission. They met with hardly any resistance, as the enemy had been weakened considerably. But in the days that followed, a swarm of Japanese planes landed at Morokrembangan airfield, among them a large number of 'flying cigars'. One of those bloody machines was being manned by Kamei, my sister Ella's so-called sweetheart.

In the meantime, I had heard from Uncle Soen that formidable Allied naval units with aircraft carriers were heading for the waters near the Philippines.

One evening Kamei came to our house to say his goodbyes to Ella. Afterwards he took me out to Shanghai Restaurant on Palmenlaan. When we arrived, I saw my pal Jopie Reuben with his *becak* and went over to see him while Kamei was paying our driver. Keeping my voice low, I told Jopie to come back in an hour to take me down to the port. He listened in silence and nodded.

Kamei had organized an *inkai*, a farewell dinner with five of his fellow pilots. We took off our shoes at the door to a side room and sat down on carpets which had been laid specially. Each of us was assigned a hostess. A whole range of Japanese dishes were served, washed down with plenty of alcohol. I pretended to drink but was careful to down no more than one jug of sake. The more they drank, the more talkative the Japanese pilots became, letting details slip about their targets, their weapons and the bombload of their aircraft. Soon they were undressing the hostesses and gradually shedding their own clothes. My hostess was offended by my lack of attention. I apologized for my behaviour, gave her a peck on the cheek and told her I needed to go to the toilet first. Creeping out of our side room, I put on my shoes and hurried outside.

Jopie was ready and waiting. I had him take me to Soedjono's house in Krembangan, since he knew the whereabouts of our Makassar friend and his boat. We rode there together and when we arrived I told them everything I had heard from the drunken pilots. The Makassar boy transmitted the details to his contacts. We thanked each other and Jopie cycled us back home.

Two days later, a Japanese serviceman came to our home. Partly in Japanese, partly in English, he announced that Kamei had been killed in action. Tears welled up in Ella's eyes. I went to my room and gave thanks to God.

And forty years on, your first-born son would travel to Java in search of his roots. There, at Aunty Ella's house, I made the acquaintance of Kamei's grandson. Kamei's daughter, born to Ella after his death, was living there too. The boy was called Jongky and had a calendar full of Japanese girls pinned to the wall above his bed. He dreamed of marrying a Japanese beauty one day, dreamed of walking the streets of Tokyo, where his grandfather had walked as a young man. I understood my little cousin's yearning for Japan. I kept your secret from that boy, half-hoping you had made it all up. War between countries is one thing, but war within the family… What the hell is a human being supposed to make of that?

A few days later, on Tunjungan, I bumped into a friend of Kamei's, a fellow bomber pilot. We went to a Chinese restaurant that served Japanese food and he told me how Kamei had met his end. On a mission to Luzon, the largest island in the Philippines, his squadron of bombers and fighter-plane escorts had come under attack from US aircraft. The entire squadron had been shot down. I feigned compassion in polite Japanese but inside I felt only contentment. I nearly gave myself away by tucking into our meal with too much gusto, washing it down with the occasional swig of warm sake. The Japanese pilot was knocking back the sake far quicker than I was. He boasted of missions to come and a glint of fighting spirit returned to his eyes. Leaving the restaurant after our meal, the pilot threw an arm around my shoulder. Swaying drunkenly, we walked along and bumped into more pilots, to whom I was introduced. We were joined by a bunch of Japanese nurses and all twelve of us went to another restaurant.

One of the nurses turned out to be a girl I had gone to school with. She had clearly sided with the Japanese. When she came and sat next to me, I whispered sweet nothings in her ear in the hope of extracting some new information. The sake was flowing and once again my fellow diners began to say more than they should. I excused myself and left their company. Again I took a *becak* to Soedjono's and we went in search of our Makassar friend and his transmitter.

On his boat, surrounded by crates of stinking fish, the three of us sat and pored over a map of the Indonesian Archipelago and the Philippines. I passed on all the information I could remember about the bomber squadrons, their fighter escorts, and possible dates and times. As soon as I told them what I knew, I left. I did not need to know how the messages were sent and the last thing I wanted was to be arrested and endure more torture. I later found out that the pilots I shared a meal with had been shot down in action. Every last one of them.

My Indonesian friends

Many of my good friends during the Japanese occupation were Indos. But any resistance put up by Indo boys tended to be passive. They were caught in the middle, between the Dutch, the Japs and the Indonesians. When it came to active resistance, I could rely on my Javanese and Madurese friends from Queen Emma School: Soedjono, Soenarjo, Soetopo, Soemarsono, Soetjipto and Soemarno. Knowing they had an entire people behind them, they were more inclined to risk acts of violence. I often went down to the port with them, armed with knuckledusters and fighting knives. With the curfew approaching, we would roam the docks in groups of four and pick a fight with Japanese soldiers on their way back to barracks. As soon as the Japs drew their swords in anger, we pounced. The Madurese among us slit their throats with crooked little knives. When the fighting was over, we would scatter and regroup at a secret address in Krembangan or Dapuan. There we tuned into the radios we had stashed away and caught up on events in the Pacific. News of Allied victories made us rowdy and we would head out again to hunt down any lone Japanese soldiers we could find.

When the Kenpeitai began to raid our neighbourhoods, we became more careful, dragging our victims' bodies off to rubbish tips or burying them in places no Kenpeitai thug would think to look.

Sabotage at the bicycle factory

Towards the end of 1944, I was put to work in the welding shop of a large bicycle factory on Pasar Besar. The chief welder was a shady character called Liem, a bootlicker on very good terms with some of the Japanese foremen and the directors. It was my job to make bike frames to Japanese specifications. The storeroom behind the welding shop was piled high with old, half-rusted European frames and I had to loosen the couplings and saw the tubes down to size so that Liem could weld them into new frames. We worked with carbide blowtorches, copper welding rods and borax powder with a petroleum burner. This massive job was left to the pair of us, and sometimes we swapped duties. Liem and I were not exactly a winning team. In fact, I loathed the man.

A handful of Indo lads worked on the assembly line, but most of the workforce was Indonesian, every last one of them a nationalist with an undying hatred of anything that smacked of Holland. This included the Indo colleagues they were forced to put up with. They often eyed me with suspicion too, not sure what to make of my Indo looks and my Chinese ID card. I showed the necessary tact and diplomacy in my dealings with that Indonesian rabble, and avoided talking war and politics whenever I could.

I began a one-man sabotage operation, deliberately overdoing the blowtorch when I welded the tubes into the couplings; this made the joints brittle and ensured the frames wouldn't last long, certainly not on bumpy roads. The bikes were intended for Japanese infantrymen and *heihos*, Indonesian auxiliaries sent into battle against Allied forces in Malacca and Burma. The frames went from the welding shop straight to the paint shop, where they were painted by hand, a time-consuming process. Even so, dozens of those rickety bikes were loaded onto trucks every other day and transported to the docks at Tanjung Perak. From there, they were shipped to Malaysia and Burma. For at least six months, my scheme went without a hitch.

Never miss a chance to big yourself up, do you Pa? I have another take on this story. If you ask me, you were just a lousy welder…

One fateful day, Liem and I were summoned to the boardroom. We walked in to find an army officer and a big shot from the Kenpeitai standing there. Both factory directors were sitting behind their desk, sporting the *sakura* – the cherry blossom emblem – on their shirts. In a mixture of Indonesian and Japanese, we were told that soldiers on their way to combat zones in Burma had seen their bikes collapse under them. The army officer lambasted us for doing a poor welding job on the crankshaft and the steering, and began to slap us in the face. Since Liem was on good terms with the bosses, he got off lightly with a slap or two and a barrage of insults. But the Kenpeitai bruiser grabbed a truncheon and started to beat me mercilessly. He hit me hard on my lower back, still painful from the torture I had already endured. In agony, my legs buckled under me. I was ordered to stand up and lay my hands flat on the desk. He brought his truncheon down hard. By some miracle no bones were broken, but in no time my hands were severely swollen. The pain was excruciating.

I can't help wondering when you wrote this episode, Pa. Was it before or after what you did to me that day? I was seven years old and you decided it was time I learned to tie my own shoelaces instead of getting Ma or Phil to do it for me. It was Easter Sunday. The previous day, I had volunteered to run to the shops just before closing time to buy a bottle of sweet white wine so that we could raise a family toast to Easter. You even promised me an extra glass by way of a thank you. That Easter morning, we were all going out for a walk. I was in the kitchen fumbling with my laces. Ma and Phil were ready to help me while you stood seething in the hall. You came storming in, sent Ma and Phil out of the room, and ordered me to tie my laces. I made a few more clumsy attempts. Then you went to the hall cupboard and came back with a bamboo cane, the thin end of a three-part fishing rod that made a wonderful swishing sound.

'Have you tied your laces?'

'Not yet, Papa.'

'Get up. Lay your hands flat on the kitchen counter.'

The counter was granite. I curled my fingers around the raised edge to soften the slashing blows. The granite cooled the sting. You gave me a second chance. I was even less able to tie a decent bow.

'Get up.'

I tried to curl my fingers tighter around the counter's edge. The granite lost its coolness, the pain grew fiercer, welts appeared. You gave me another chance. My swollen fingers trembled and it was all I could do to hold the ends of my laces. How do you tie a bow? How on earth did my brother do it? My swollen fingers could no longer claw the edge of the counter. I clenched my teeth, bowed my head and stared helplessly at the stupid kitchen lino. It was yellow, dirty yellow, with an orange pattern. You walked out of the kitchen saying, 'By the time I come back, you will have tied your laces. Understood?'

You left the door ajar. Phil slipped into the kitchen and tied two quick bows. Minutes later you were back, nodding your approval. You had given my brother the chance to help me. It was either that or chop my fingers off, right Pa?

'No walk for you. And no wine tonight. Understood?'

I nodded, lowered my head and looked at the miraculous bows on my shoes.

Who did you see, that Easter Sunday in the kitchen with your first-born son? Was it that Japanese thug?

Our punishment over, we were sent back to work in the welding shop. Hands badly swollen, I tried to operate the torch. I bit my lips till the tears rolled down my cheeks, but I did not utter a word of complaint.

Nor did I. In case you've forgotten, Pa. No tears either, come to that. I wouldn't give you the satisfaction.

Liem looked me up and down, then asked, 'Hey, did you really mess with those frames?'

A moment's silence, then I snapped, 'Shut your face, you filthy traitor! The Japs will be driven out of this country before long. And when that time comes, I will murder you and every last one of your family. Understood, Liem?'

The bootlicker turned pale and held his tongue.

I wasn't finished. 'Liem, I know all about your pro-Japanese tendencies. Traitors like you will get no mercy from me. Say one wrong word to the bosses or the Kenpeitai and I will cut you down on the spot.'

Redjo, the foreman and chief mechanic, had been watching us. He had a formidable reputation as a *pendekar*, a first-class *pencak* fighter. Not only that, but he headed a section of the notorious Indonesian political movement led by Sutomo, also known as Bung Tomo, who would go on to lead a bloody campaign in Surabaya during the Indonesian Revolution. Once Liem had slunk off with his tail between his legs, Redjo called me over.

'Hey, Si-Arto, I know that your real name is Nolan and that you are an Indo-Peranakan, but don't worry, I can keep a secret. Many of my Javanese friends are your friends too, and have worked with you against the Japs. That is why I am warning you about chief welder Liem and his forked tongue. Watch your step and never talk politics with him. The bosses have spies everywhere, even here in the workshop.'

I studied Redjo's face and replied, 'All well and good, Redjo, but how do I know I can trust you? This is bound to offend you, but first I need to contact my Javanese and Madurese friends from the resistance.'

'You do that, Si-Arto,' Redjo snorted. 'Ask around about me. You'll soon see how right I am. You count Soedjono, Soetjipto, Soenarjo, Soetopo, Soemarsono, Soemarno and Soekaton among your friends. They live in the neighbourhoods of Krembangan, Dapuan, Pacar Keling, Bubutan and Baliwerti. Isn't that right?'

All I could do was nod.

Another round of torture

Despite my threats, Liem went to straight to the bosses the next day and told them I had deliberately tampered with the bicycle frames. I was tipped off by Soedjarwo, Redjo's assistant and close friend. I managed to hide my anxiety and fear, but I knew what was coming. This did not stop me using the blowtorch to weaken the ends of the tubes.

It was high noon and the burning sun beat down mercilessly on Croc City. A pair of Kenpeitai officers came into the workshop and ordered me to accompany them. I left my welding for what it was, stole a glance at Soedjarwo and Redjo and followed the two thugs to the boss's office. Soedjarwo and Redjo gave me a thumbs up to wish me courage.

In the office, the boss asked me, 'Did you really tamper with the welding on those frames?'

I looked that shifty Sakura Jap in the eye and shook my head. He flew into a rage and barked one order after another at the Kenpeitai officers. I was taken down to the courtyard of the office complex and made to strip to my underpants. One of the Kenpeitai officers unfastened the metal scabbard from his belt, drew his samurai sword and laid it on a table. Then he raised the scabbard and began to beat me with it. Blows rained down on my whole body: my head, shoulders, arms and legs, my stomach, my ribs and my chest. The pain was so intense that tears poured down my cheeks, but I bit my lips to stop myself crying out. I was not about to give my torturers the satisfaction. Everything went black and I passed out. I came to when a bucket of water was thrown over me. The clerks and kitchen workers were made to watch. Anyone who turned away took a beating of their own. Here and there I could hear cries of sympathy, women sobbing and begging them to take pity on me. I was ordered to stand up. They placed a thick wooden beam on my shoulders and bound my arms to it. A broomstick was tied across the backs of my knees.

I was soon exhausted from bearing the heavy weight on my shoulders in the full glare of the sun, so exhausted that my legs gave way beneath me. But when my knees started to bend, the pressure from the broomstick was agony. The only way to ease the pain was to straighten up and lift the dead weight of the beam. Whenever I moved, the Japs beat my ribs, my back and my stomach with sticks. I lost all sense of time and could think only of death coming as a release. Then I went out cold.

I woke up to find myself lying on a thin layer of coal in a box that was around six feet by three feet by two feet; wooden planks on all sides, sheets of corrugated iron above me. The sun was still shining and the air in the coal box was stifling and getting hotter by the minute. Sweat poured from my body, and my mouth was dry as sand. Again I lost consciousness. Later I woke up shivering and saw through the cracks between the planks that evening had come. I tried to get up and banged my head on the iron sheeting. I tried to lift it but could not find the strength. I collapsed onto the coal and fell asleep.

The following afternoon I was dragged from the box and given another beating. Then two Javanese women who worked in the kitchen were ordered to wash me as the grinning Kenpeitai thugs looked on. With tears in their eyes, the women wiped me clean of dirt and blood. When they were done, I was sent back to the welding shop to continue my work. In all that time I had been given nothing to eat or drink.

Chaos

August 1945. The streets of Surabaya were full of Japanese soldiers looking worried and disheartened. Uncle Soen told me that the Japs had lost control of New Guinea and that Allied troops had landed at Balikpapan. Not only that, but the Americans had occupied the Philippines. Uncle Soen spoke of a shift in the Indonesians' attitude to the Belandas and those who sympathized with them, and made me promise to watch my words whenever I was in Indonesian company.

Around this time, I struck up a bit of a friendship with a sympathetic chap of around twenty from the *kampong* behind our house in Undaan Kulon. Soedarsono was his name and I regularly used to drop in to see him and his family. He and his father were members of the Indonesian National Party. Soedarsono was honest with me. He knew about my loyalty to the Dutch and my love for the House of Orange. Like Uncle Soen, he warned me to keep these feelings to myself. Soedarsono told me that if Japan capitulated, the Indonesian people would never again allow themselves to be colonized by the Dutch. Instead, Sukarno would declare an independent Republic of Indonesia. I did not know who Sukarno was, and Soedarsono told me a few things about him. Such was my ignorance of all things political.

Among the workforce at the bicycle factory, relations between the Indos and the Indonesians had taken a serious turn for the worse. The situation was explosive. I sided with the Indos. Before long, heated exchanges flared into fighting and of course the Indos were very much in the minority.

As tensions ran high, I found myself squaring up to Redjo, the workshop foreman. A notorious *pendekar* fighter, he went as if to walk away but in fact he was gathering himself for a jumping scissor kick that could break my neck. I saw what he was up to and grabbed a big, rough file in my left hand and a sledgehammer in my right. I leapt to the side to dodge his attack and spun round in a flash to bring the hammer down hard on his back. He fell forwards. I jumped on his back and stamped his face into the ground. I heard bones break. His friend Soedjarwo jumped me from behind. I hit him hard with the file and just about ripped his face open. When the other Javanese saw this, they made themselves scarce.

In the meantime, fights had broken out with the other Indo boys. I called on them to make a move. We quickly formed a group, lashing out with anything that came to hand, and ran out onto the main road. There we scattered in all directions and fled for home.

As the sixteenth of August dawned, I was walking through Pasar Besar armed with a fighting knife. On the roof of the government building, I saw the Japanese flag being lowered and, a little later, the red, white and blue of the Netherlands was flying proudly. From the windows of apartments above the shops, I heard the strains of the Dutch national anthem blaring from the radio. I cried out with joy, but before long I was surrounded by a bunch of hostile Javanese, bellowing their cry of independence. 'Merdeka!' As they bore down on me, I drew my knife and struck the first man in the face. When the others saw the blood, they shrank back and warned each other. 'Watch out for that boy. He is a dangerous fighter!'

The next day I pinned my badge with the flag of Nationalist China to my shirt and, armed with my knife, I walked from Undaan Kulon to Jagalan and on to Contong Square, where I had a good view of the government building. To my amazement I saw the red, white and blue sliding down the flagpole and the red and white flag of Indonesia being raised in its place. The Indonesian people who crowded the streets were beside themselves with joy. The cry of 'Merdeka!' rang out everywhere. The few Japanese soldiers on the streets with a rifle slung over their shoulder looked on in bitter resignation.

The terror against the Japs began that same day, across from the Luxor cinema on the main square. I saw a Javanese boy attack an unsuspecting Japanese soldier from behind with a *takeyari*. He drove the spear right through the soldier's body, shouting '*Senjata makan tuan!*' Their own weapons were being turned against them.

A deafening roar burst from the crowd and in no time every Japanese soldier on the street had been speared to death. Even after they were dead, people continued to hack at them with *klewang*. Those Japs were maimed and mutilated by the raging crowd of Javanese, their guns and equipment seized. It was a terrifying, sickening sight.

I was surrounded by a group of screaming, bloodthirsty Javanese. 'For over three hundred years we were colonized and trampled underfoot by the Belandas. Then the Japs did the same. Now we are the boss! We want independence! That is what President Sukarno has promised us. We heard his declaration on the radio. Once the Japs have gone, it will be the Belandas' turn. Death to the lot of them!'

I nodded and slipped away from the massacre. I walked in the direction of Sulung viaduct to get a view of what was happening around the government building. What I saw was total chaos. The police had lost all control. Young rebels had even seized the policemen's weapons. They forced Japanese soldiers to hand over their guns and then shot them in cold blood. Even a handful of Indo men fell victim to the frantic mob. I felt panic rising and hurried back to Pasar Besar and on to Baliwerti. There too, I witnessed murder and mayhem. The crowd had taken leave of their senses.

Out of nowhere I was seized by a group of five bloodthirsty rebels. They wanted to know if I had any NICA money on me. I did not know what they were talking about and swore on my life that I had none. I pulled out my ID and when they saw I was Chinese they let me go. On the way home from Baliwerti I thought to myself, 'I am a *peranakan*, armed with a fighting knife. I can take any side, join any movement. Yet there is only one path open to me.'

I think I'll spare Ma these tales of yours, Pa. Leave her in peace with the crap she watches on TV. Too much cruelty could rip the lid off the cesspit of her memories, and I've been hard enough on her already. Perhaps I should ask Phil what he makes of it all. He severed all ties with you a while back. Even smashed one of Grandma Sie's Chinese vases to smithereens in a fit of rage one New Year's Eve in Geneva. But that was long ago.

III

SHADOW ON THE WALL

Snow

Surabaya Papa has found himself a bargain: a second-hand sled. But he will not come outside with us. He feels the cold. He comes from a country so warm it never snows. I share the sled with my twin brother. We have to share everything, right down to the mandatory bottle of school milk. We take turns pulling each other along, argue about whose turn it is and peer into the distance, down a lane that is fading to white. The snow over in Zuider Park must be thick as pillows.

A man in a grey hat and a Loden overcoat passes us by and tells us we need a good wash. We nearly rub our little brown eyes out of our little brown heads and stare after him in amazement.

'Oh, let those folk say what they like,' says Mama Helmond without looking up from her granite kitchen counter.

We were too young to understand the narrow-minded quip of a man born and bred in The Hague, let alone Mama's dismissive response. To us it was all deadly serious, like the snowflakes turning to powder, the runners on our sled scraping over bare paving stones. A polar expedition turning intractable, boring and wet.

We sat back to back on the slats of our sled and swore we would wait as long as it took for the snow to start falling again. The thickest snow was always over yonder, a place where you never had to lug your sled over rasping pavements, where you could sledge on and on and on. What would it be like to get there at last?

One day, dragging our sled behind us, we walked to the very end of Melis Stokelaan, all the way past Zuider Park. Walked until we could no longer see the block of flats where we lived.

Another man in a grey hat and a Loden overcoat asked us where we were going. We told him we were lost. He was friendly and, hoisting our sled on his shoulder, he walked us all the way back to our little tenement flat. A place where war was raging, mostly at night, when the shadow of Surabaya Papa and his dagger played on our bedroom wall as he fought an enemy we could not see.

'He sees ghosts, that father of yours,' was Mama Helmond's daily refrain. 'He thinks those ploppers from Indonesia are coming to kill him, and us along with him.'

'What are they, Mama? Ploppers?'

'Bandits. That's what they are. They fight in camouflage so you can't spot them in the jungle. They chased your father out of Indonesia. He won't even let me say the word Indonesia. All he can talk about is that precious Indies of his. But your father's from Java, and Java is still Java. Now go to your room and leave me in peace. Can't you see I'm busy in the kitchen?'

'Hey, we should have told the nice man in the grey hat that we didn't have a home to go to. We could've said the ploppers kidnapped Papa and took him back to Java. Maybe he would have taken us to church. That's where the nice people go, the ones that help children. The church gave us blankets. Those warm, prickly ones, they're from the church.'

'Yes, and the nice man in the grey hat's big footprints would have confused everyone. He was carrying the sled, so it left no tracks. They would never have found us.'

'But then what about Mama? And the others?'

If only it would keep snowing, on and on, then maybe the miracle might come, the one that will take us far beyond the end of the lane. Away from the war on the bedroom wall, forever and ever and never again.

Aquarium

A black-and-white photo from the late 1950s. Wavy edges, yellowing, but without the haze of nostalgia. A small aquarium on a rickety table draped with a checked tablecloth. *Still Life with German Torpedo*. The torpedo being the cylindrical light fitting on the glass lid. Mama Helmond curses the aquarium. It stinks, she says, with its filthy plants, its filthy snails, its filthy algae and the filthy worms crawling through the sludge at the bottom. The filthy worms have a name: tubifex. The madman opens a jam jar full of worms and shoves it under the noses of his wife and all his children so they know what tubifex is supposed to smell like. The jar is left on the windowsill too long and everyone becomes acquainted with that smell too. The worms turn green and brown. Death and decay, the madman calls it. His children need to learn what death and decay smell like, God help us!

'It's the stink of the Indies, if you ask me!'

Mama Helmond complains the whole day long. She wants a bit of peace and quiet but finds none. What a life, cooped up with her Indo family in a miserable little council flat in a miserable post-war neighbourhood of The Hague.

One day Surabaya Papa makes a clumsy move and electrocutes the fish with the heating element. He gets rid of the small tank and enlists two of his Dutch colleagues to carry a bigger tank up to our flat on their Saturday afternoon off. Mama Helmond retreats to the kitchen and puffs her way through half a pack of Miss Blanche, but us kids are enthralled. The hulking great thing is half-rusted and layers of putty have been pressed into service to shore up the glass sides, which are scratched in places. The tank is mounted on a steel rack and can hold over fifty gallons of water. The next day we cycle from our cramped little home on Melis Stokelaan to Kijkduin and spend a day at the beach, fuelled by thermos flasks of cold, sweet tea and white bread slathered in jam. A poor family with a brown father, a white mother and five children ranging in colour from dark to light brown. I am the eldest and darkest, little Nana is the lightest. The dilution of the Indies: a profligate culture born of colonialism can be read in the skin of its children, you might say. We sit on a flowery tablecloth in our ill-fitting shorts, Surabaya Papa's hand-me-downs stitched to fit our scrawny backsides. The Dutch bathers eye us up with the same deadpan expressions as those hypocrites at church.

That's what Surabaya Papa calls them: hypocrites.

At close of day we cycle home with saddlebags full of sand from the dunes. Surabaya Papa thinks he can rinse away the sea salt. He fetches the big tin bath Mama Helmond uses to wash the bedsheets and bathe the little ones, and empties the saddle bags into it. He pushes a garden hose in among the sand and the water flows abundantly, like the old days in the Indies, a place of waterfalls. Here there is no such thing. Life in Holland is dull as ditches.

'If only you'd stayed there!' Mama Helmond's daily mantra.

Why can't she keep her trap shut? Much more of that and he'll beat her senseless again.

Surabaya Papa has painted the back pane of the aquarium the colours of a guerrilla uniform and plugged the leaky corners with yet more putty. He spreads a layer of potting soil on the bottom of the tank so the water plants will grow and dumps the sand on top. Lugging buckets of water, we fill the aquarium to the brim. From the ditch that skirts the playing fields across from our flat we fetch waterweed, which Surabaya Papa says grows almost as fast as bamboo. Almost. In Holland everything is almost.

Surabaya Papa is impatient and gives his budding paradise no chance to take root. He insists on seeing fish swim in the water. We are sent to the ditch with our little fishing nets and return with a couple of sticklebacks. Next day we find them floating belly up in the brackish water. Surabaya Papa shrugs indifferently, but we give them a solemn burial in the communal back garden while Mama Helmond looks on behind her newly cleaned windows, fiddling with her hairdo.

One Sunday afternoon I have to accompany Surabaya Papa to an obscure address somewhere on Hengelolaan, where a man does a shady trade in tropical fish from his top-floor flat. Wall-to-wall shelves groan under the weight of aquariums. Air pumps sing. There are plenty of young Indos among the customers. Indos don't dress like the Dutch. They wear bomber jackets and stroll around with one hand in their trouser pocket. My father only puts his hands in his pockets when he stands still. When he's on the move, he's on his guard, arms swinging close to his sides, ready to defend himself at every second. The Indo boys in their jackets are quick to mix English words with *petjo*, their blend of Dutch and Malay. In that respect they are a good twenty years ahead of the urban rebels who will pepper their conversation with English hippie-speak in the seventies, while the Dutch mainstream will only catch up decades later.

Surabaya Papa selects his fish by the pair. He buys two zebra fish, which only thrive in shoals, not in pairs, and later has to invest in another ten. All the while Mama Helmond wonders out loud how on earth we are going to make it through the week when half his pay packet is going straight into the pocket of the tropical fish dealer.

'What good are those stupid fish if we have nothing to eat? It's all right for you, swanning off with your scumbag friends, gobbling down your filthy fried rice and noodles and treating yourself to a salted herring on your way home. Wasting good money on sausage rolls for lunch, while I'm sending the kids to school with dry bread and dishing up half an egg each for their dinner. All because you had to bring that stinking aquarium into the house for me to trip over all bloody day.'

'Ah, but just look how those fish brighten up the place. Beautiful, especially after dark.'

But when it gets dark she watches films, peering through the snow on a black-and-white TV that only shows one channel. We sit and stare at the aquarium, where life is beautiful and death is never far away.

'I think the water's poisoned,' says Joop Stokkermans, a Dutch acquaintance from Westland, an ex-marine never mentioned by name in Surabaya Papa's war stories. He plunges his arm into the tank and scoops sand from the bottom. 'Look, the previous owner covered up the rusted bottom with a lick of paint. That's what's killing the fish.'

'So why do the gouramis survive?' Surabaya Papa asks, and we share his wonderment.

Gouramis. Indonesian fish. Indonesians were once the enemy to Surabaya Papa and Joop Stokkermans. Dutchmen fighting Indonesians we could understand. After all, we always had to be the Indians when we played cowboys with our Dutch friends. But Indos fighting Indonesians was something my twin brother and I could never fathom, however hard we tried. President Sukarno of Indonesia, whose face we saw on postage stamps, looked far more like our father than anyone we saw on the street. The Indonesians had won the war. Surabaya Papa and his fellow marines might as well not have bothered torching all those houses in the *desa*.

When his old marine chum Stokkermans has left, Surabaya Papa spends a long time staring at the gouramis. If the toxic water doesn't kill off the guppies, they are eaten by those blasted gouramis. There are five of them, the biggest fish in the aquarium. Those gouramis are *pelopors*, extremists, enemies of Queen and Country. The fish visit Surabaya Papa in the night, growing into huge monsters that swim through his blood-soaked dreams. Images of hate, fear and destruction congeal into a gourami *batik*.

Aunty Lieke

There was an air of distinction about Aunty Lieke, so much so, I used to think her name was spelled with a *q*: Lique. She lived on Regentesselaan, or was it Valkenboslaan? Two wide avenues that cut a swathe through the neighbourhood. I never could tell them apart. It was as if she lived in a shop window, complete with matt glass decorations bought from a defunct colonial shop that dealt in 'knick-knacks from the Indies'. Why we called her 'Aunty' I have no idea. She wasn't family, although there was some mysterious link to second cousins of my father's, veiled in cryptic references to missed inheritances, loss of capital and unfathomable goings on between Holland and Indonesia. Aunty Lique's skin was white but she came from Indonesia. From Surabaya, I assume, like my father.

She called round to see us until I was seven or eight. After that she stayed away, grew old and unsteady on her feet. It always took her an age to shed the many garments piled on to protect her from the Dutch cold: a see-through plastic rain bonnet, a raincoat with a fur coat underneath, a long scarf – her entrance was nothing short of majestic. Even my mother would attend on her by the coat rack.

In her shop-window house stood the trunk from her voyage from Indonesia to Holland, along with a wardrobe, a divan, a sideboard and a whatnot. The rest of the room was stacked with books and a variety of suitcases. Still packed, my father said, so she could high-tail it back to Indonesia, if ever the occasion arose.

'And when will that be?' I asked.

'Never, numbskull! How many times do I have to tell you? That sleazeball Sukarno has grabbed the lot.'

I kept quiet. I knew who Sukarno was, but not what a sleazeball was. He used to call me and my brother Phil 'a pair of sleazeballs' too sometimes. I also knew that the war had made people come to Holland even though they didn't want to. My mother told me my father had come because he had 'done things during the war.' But what could Aunty Lique have done?

Aunty Lique performed her ablutions at a washbasin, and always washed with cold water. Nothing odd about that, my father said, it was the custom in the tropics. We, his children, had to wash with cold water too, even if the temperature outside was ten below freezing. To toughen us up. It was a tradition he himself had broken with, and he liked to boast about the long, hot showers he took.

'He's a waster, that father of yours,' my mother muttered. 'Wallows in luxury like it's his God-given right. How am I supposed to keep the gas meter running on the weekly pittance he hands me?'

In those days, the shower was heated by the kitchen boiler, which only worked if you fed the gas meter with tokens, special coins with a square hole in the middle. My mother would always complain when she was down to her last token and had to cut back on her Miss Blanche cigarettes. She suspected my father of slipping them into the satchel he took to work, as every now and then he would rummage around in it and find a stray token when he wanted to 'have a soak'. That's what he called it: soaking. He used to have a soak after a bowel movement too. He soaked himself silly, while the rest of us had to make do with one tub of water on a Saturday morning.

Sometimes I had to accompany my father on his visits to Aunty Lique's. Perched on the back of his bike, I would feel his tread on the pedals, strong and steady, the little luggage rack above the back wheel tugging me along by the seat of my pants. He rode a bike like he was riding a horse.

I never knew what to say to Aunty. My father didn't seem to know either. In her company, he was far less gregarious than he was at home. Was it because they shared a secret they didn't want me to know about?

One day he sent my mother in his place. Protesting furiously and with a face like thunder, she set off on her bike with me on the luggage rack. Her pedal strokes were irregular and apt to make me doze, but her non-stop yammering kept me awake enough to stop me falling off.

It was a good day. Aunty Lique took a colossal jar out of her whatnot, full of delicious biscuits, a kind I had never seen before. They had a waffle pattern, some kind of filling and they were sprinkled with the finest icing sugar. And Aunty Lique's orange squash was the sweetest I had ever tasted.

Unlike my father, my mother always had plenty to say to Aunty Lique, who complained of chilblains and was always filling earthenware hot water bottles to warm her toes. My mother liked a good natter about ailments and every other misfortune that can befall a person, especially varicose veins and other indispositions reserved solely for womankind. I did my best to sympathize, but the biscuits grabbed my attention that little bit more. Aunty had urged me to eat as many as I liked. The conversation faded into the background as I loomed over the jar at regular intervals to take another one.

When we got home, my mother gave a full account of our visit, complaining to my father about 'the filthy foreign smell' that filled Aunty Lique's house and how everything – the table, the chairs, even the ashtray – was sticky to the touch. She insisted he could pay his own house calls from now. What business did she have visiting some old relic from the Indies? They were *his* people, *his* kind, and that was all there was to it. There was a single ray of sunshine. As we said goodbye, Aunty Lique had whispered in her ear that I was such a good boy: I hadn't eaten all the biscuits but had left one in the jar. My father didn't see the sunny side. He thumped me all the way to the bedroom I shared with my brothers and sent my mother out the next day to buy a box of the exact same biscuits. They weren't cheap.

On his next Saturday afternoon off, my father cycled over to Aunty Lique's with me in tow. In my hands, the brand-new box of biscuits. It was cold, freezing in fact, and I wondered if Aunty would be wearing those creepy long brown stockings again.

Instead of stopping outside her front door, my father dropped me off at the corner and waited there. I walked the rest of the way alone and rang the doorbell of Aunty Lique's peculiar shop-window house. Her gloomy curtains were drawn.

She opened the door. Delighted by my unexpected visit, she invited me in. I told her I had only come to deliver the biscuits. She took the box and I registered surprise in her old grey eyes. Then I ran away as fast as I could.

My father had been standing out of sight at the corner of the street. He poked me in the ribs and repeated the commandment he had already drilled into me: for the sake of decency, I was allowed to take one – and only one – biscuit. That was the way in Holland.

'Understood?'

'Yes.'

'Yes what?'

'Yes, Papa.'

It wasn't as cold when Aunty Lique died. It was raining, though. I had to go to the funeral parlour with my father and my two brothers. It was in a dark, brick building with a massive carved wooden door somewhere on Van Boetzelaerlaan, not far from Scheveningen harbour. The room was full of old people in long, dark overcoats. Women with folded, dripping umbrellas, men clutching their damp hats, all standing in a wide circle around the coffin, keeping as much distance as they could. No one cried. I didn't know what I was supposed to do, except look straight ahead and keep a straight face.

'Do you want to see a dead body?' my father whispered. He was bending down and his voice sounded oddly nervous in my ear. I had never heard him like this.

I quickly shook my head.

'Follow your brothers over to the coffin. You have to see her corpse.' His eyes lit up, and he became even stranger to me than he already was.

I refused to budge, but he pushed me in the direction of the coffin. I looked around. The people in the circle were staring into space, looking at nothing, not even at me. I was alone, and just tall enough to peer over the edge. Aunty Lique lay there, dead. She did not look frightening but she was certainly dead. Stone dead, white as a sheet. I only took a quick look, the briefest of glances, but it was long enough to fuel my nightmares for years to come.

'Why did you have to make the boy do that?' my mother asked.

'He's a wimp. His little brothers didn't even bat an eyelid. He has never seen a war, he has never had to fight. The boy needs to know what a corpse looks like.'

'But it was his Aunty Lique!'

'So what? A corpse is a corpse.'

'Oh, so when my time comes, I'll be nothing but a corpse too?'

'Of course! All the life will have gone out of you.'

'And what good is that to a boy his age?'

'Death. Now he knows what death looks like.'

My mother turned to me and asked me what death looked like.

I said death was something to do with hats and umbrellas and people looking at nothing. She congratulated my father on my answer, adding tartly that now I was almost as mad as he was.

Guinea pigs

On one of his Saturday afternoons off, our fickle father surprised Philip, Arti and me by bringing us home two guinea pigs. The little brown creatures came in a hutch as big as the bunk bed in our shabby bedroom. For Mama Helmond, a highly strung housewife prone to volcanic bouts of housework, the flat was already several times too small. She yearned for her parents' home in Brabant, where her father kept his cobbler's workshop so spick and span that they'd never had need of a cat to keep the mice away.

'I bet one of his slick city colleagues conned him into buying that stinking hutch and those shitty little animals for way too much money,' she grumbled to the gleaming tiles by the kitchen sink.

The hutch was a rodent penthouse, with a little ladder that led up to a second floor with private bedroom. The guinea pigs were cuddly and communicative, a stark contrast to the inscrutable fish in Surabaya Papa's aquarium. The sounds they made at night chased the nightmares from our dark bedroom, where the air could churn with ghosts, especially when Surabaya Papa had told us yet more tales of wartime atrocities on Java. His photograph album showed us the endless rows of white crosses that marked the graves of his fallen comrades.

After school we plundered sawmills for miles around in search of shavings and sawdust to keep the hutch clean. The guinea pigs gave us something to care for and made us less likely to be at each other's throats when we played together.

Arti pointed out that the belly of one of the guinea pigs was getting bigger.

'They're going to have babies!'

Early one morning they arrived, nine of them. They lay snuggled up against one another, quivering gently. None of us said a word as we stared at them, experiencing for the first time the awe of nature we had been taught at school. We ran home faster than ever that afternoon, impatient to gaze upon the miracle again.

Miracle? What miracle? There was nothing to see but mummy and daddy guinea pig rummaging around as usual.

'Huh? Were we dreaming?'

'No way! We all saw them lying there!'

Mama Helmond was in no mood to talk. She had no time and other things on her mind: washing, ironing, polishing, scrubbing, dusting, more ironing, shopping, cooking, washing up and gossiping with the next-door neighbours out on the balcony. We had no choice but to wait for Surabaya Papa, due home at five.

By this time we understood and all we wanted to know was what Mama Helmond had done with the little ones.

'Did you bury them?'

'Bury them? What kind of fool do you think I am? As if I'd have time for that!'

'Well, where are they? Out in the garden?'

Her answer was a mumble.

In shock, we rushed to the toilet and stared into the bowl for a long time, in the hope that one of them might resurface.

'We can give it the kiss of life. At least then we'll have saved one little guinea pig.'

'And we'll make sure nothing ever happens to him.'

'Forever and ever. Amen.'

'They'd never do that in China.' Surabaya Papa grinned at the dinner table that evening. 'They eat new-born guinea pigs over there. Dip them in boiling water one by one, while they're still alive. Dunk them in soy sauce and then… down the hatch! Ha ha ha!'

'Oh, don't be disgusting,' said Mama Helmond. 'Now eat up your cabbage.'

After dinner, Surabaya Papa retired to his bedroom to hammer away at his Remington. We never thought to ask what he was typing. We assumed it had something to do with his engineering studies. We were fond of his rat-tat-tat. As long as he was at his typewriter, he kept a low profile, kept his hands to himself and no skirmishes broke out in the living room.

Broese

(1)

Broese. The name alone… Mama Helmond often said it with a harsh inflection, as if she were spitting out an obscenity. 'Oh God, if it isn't him again. Broo-sss-ugh! There's a lovely musical on the telly tonight! And I'll be stuck listening to him drone on while that father of yours is holed up in his room again, banging away at that typewriter. I wish he'd put more money on the table so we'd have more bread and bacon in the cupboard. All he can think of is the stinking Indies and that bloody war of his. And Broese's just as bad. Indies this, Indies that, there's no end to it. If only I'd never written to that father of yours. How was I supposed to know the war had sent him cuckoo? I'm telling you, all those Indos have had the sense knocked out of them. They were used to servants bowing and scraping and doing everything for them, and now they're over here and there's not a servant in sight, all they can do is moan, moan, moan. They're too idle to wash up after themselves – leave their dirty dishes till the next day caked in that muck they eat so the smell can work its way into every nook and cranny. They all act like they never left the Indies. If only they hadn't! I mean, look at the stamps on those bloody letters your father's family send him from that Indonesian stinkhole of theirs. Do you see a difference between your father and Sukarno? No? Me neither! All they did was fight their own neighbours, their own flesh and blood. Where's the sense in that? Those Indos are nothing but traitors, your father among them. Oh yes, your father was a traitor! So now you know! Now open the door for Broese and tell him to hang that motorcycle gear of his on the coat rack before he comes marching in here stinking up the place with his dirty leathers and the smell of motor oil. There goes my peace and quiet…'

Broese. A name worthy of a pioneering motorcycle prototype. But the man rode an old Jawa with an odd egg-shaped fuel tank, a Broese-type Jawa you might say. He was a curious character, with the hapless mystery of a woebegone clown. Did Broese ride a Jawa because it was one letter removed from Java? Did he want a bike that embodied his nostalgia for that island? Java was his native soil, but I don't think Broese had a drop of Asian blood. His parents might have been teachers who made the voyage to the Indies around 1920, only to perish there years later in a Japanese internment camp.

Broese had an extremely high-pitched voice for a man. Mama Helmond rolled her eyes at his corny jokes, but ever since he had whispered mischievously to us that we should call our father 'the Eagle', Broese could do no wrong in our eyes. Calling your father by his first name was out of the question, but nicknames were allowed. When we shared our astonishment at Broese's squeaky voice with the Eagle, he was quick to explain. 'The Japs lopped his balls off. How? With their samurai swords, of course!'

(2)

A boy in an old man's body, Broese rode around on his Jawa in his faded brown leather biker's jacket and matching leather helmet, which he only took off indoors. Purple birthmarks blotched the clearing on his head, ringed by flattened wisps of *alang-alang*, prostrate in lamentation.

Alang-alang was the tall grass in which Broese and the Eagle had played together as little boys. Broese loved to talk about those days, the Eagle did not. Broese was keen to conjure up scenes from their boyhood years before the war, but those years lay clotted on the blood-soaked, muddy battlefield of the Eagle's memory.

Tigers prowled through the *alang-alang* in Broese's recollection. Venomous snakes napped in the afternoon shade – 'Don't tread on their tails, or you'll be in for it, ha ha!' There was always a light-heartedness to Broese's stories, and if you didn't laugh at them then he would, in that unnaturally high voice of his.

In the Eagle's memory, the *alang-alang* fields are dark. The moon is new. Something is hovering in mid-air up ahead; it looks like a firefly. That's what the Dutch marines think, but not the Eagle. He creeps towards it like a tiger, plunges his bayonet into the back of a Javanese freedom fighter, pulls it out and, in a single movement, slits the throat of a crumpled young man who has just smoked his last roll-up. Leaves him lying there for the ants to find.

Broese sang his refrain. 'Won't you forget these things? We are here now, in Holland.'

The Eagle would not forget. And if Broese would not listen, then the keys of his typewriter would have to do.

Mama Helmond is bored to tears by Broese's stories, by the old boy and his shrill laughter. I lie in bed and tune into the dogged hammering of the Eagle at his Remington. There is a rhythm to his rat-tat-tat; at times it sounds like music. He goes through a typewriter ribbon a month. And although we do not know that he is punching his wartime memories onto those sheets of paper, my nights fill up with the ghosts of those he sent to their death. They come to visit me, to choke the life out of me, for I am a son of the Eagle, a man who went by many names back in the Indies, if Mama Helmond is to be believed. Some nights I am in luck: Broese outstays his welcome and his high, boyish laugh chases the ghosts away. I stay awake until I hear him drive off on his Jawa. Then the shadows pour back into the house, the shadows of that stinking war, as Mama Helmond calls it. I wonder if Broese sometimes burst into song as he roared home past Zuider Park on his Jawa. An old *kroncong* song perhaps? After all, a castrato can hardly bellow his loneliness at the top of his lungs.

(3)

Broese was an old orphan. Yet we called him Uncle Broese, just like we called that other solitary soul Aunty Lique. He had no one but his former school chum the Eagle for company. But the Eagle did not go easy on his old friend.

'You graduated from college, but you do the work of a coolie!'

'I like it this way! It's quiet at night. Gives me a chance to think.'

'Think? What about?'

'Let my thoughts run free, you know?'

'So you let your thoughts run free… You should be putting your mind to good use, man! I work for the government, the Civil Engineering department. And you? All your qualifications and the best you can do is night-watchman!'

Sometimes Broese watched by day. Crouching by the water's edge, he would keep a desultory eye on us kids while we splashed around. Lozerlaan, around 1960, rough terrain on which the city has run aground, strewn with the skeletons of new homes under construction. In the photograph, I am standing close to Broese, and even as a little lad there's an air of nostalgia about me, as if I am sharing Broese's memory of the *kali* from his youth somewhere in Surabaya. If I was unable to sleep at the end of such a day, I used to picture him making his nightly rounds of ghostly construction sites, carrying a torch, killing time by hunting rats and talking to them. Sometimes he came out with a story I only half understood, about a pair of lovers caught in the act. Did he ever regret growing old as a boy because the Japanese had castrated him?

On a Sunday afternoon, the Eagle took me with him on the back of his moped. The old boy with wisps of hair on his round, stained head lived somewhere on Loosduinseweg, in a ground floor flat with windows so dirty you could barely see through them.

The doorbell wasn't working.

The Eagle took out his hanky and tried to wipe a clean spot on the window, but the dirt was on the inside. He knocked. It took a long time for Broese to open the door. Perhaps we had roused the night-watchman from his sleep. Awkwardly, he let us in, flustered by these sudden guests. His flat was all but empty. The trunk from his voyage from the Indies was in use as a coffee table. The only chair was assigned to me.

'So, this is where you live…' the Eagle said.

He paced restlessly through the empty rooms, hands thrust casually in the pockets of his Terylene trousers, muttering, sneering, poking fun. Broese clumsily handed me a smudged tumbler of orange squash, hairs clinging to the glass. He kept apologizing to the Eagle for not having anything better to offer us. Yes, his flat was certainly due for sprucing up. He was planning to buy new furniture, some decent crockery and yes… curtains.

If all you can do is apologize for your life, why would death take the trouble to come and get you?

Castrol Oil

The Eagle had an uncontrollable urge to bring home cans of Castrol Oil, as if he were buying *kecap* for an Indo family with a whole slew of cousins, aunts and uncles to feed. He seemed to be addicted to the thick motor oil in those round green cans that bore the name Castrol – red letters on an L-shaped banner encircled in white. Mama Helmond detested the stuff, hated anything that left a stain. One drop of Castrol Oil on her scrubbed lino was enough to send her into a cleaning frenzy. Given half a chance, she would have tidied us out of the way too. Back in 1961, her mother had done exactly that in the house above Grandad's cobbler's workshop in Helmond, rounding up me, Phil and our younger brother Arti and locking each of us in a different attic cupboard.

Castrol Oil. Only one letter removed from the infamous castor oil, the remedy for all manner of ills in the Indies of yore. Parents used to threaten their kids with castor oil if they didn't clear their plate. As a boy, the Eagle must have been plagued by that spectre too. Following in his mother's footsteps, he would spoon cod-liver oil into us every autumn and winter, a surrogate for the potions she used to brew in her own back yard.

The Castrol Oil was for his moped: Zündapp, a German make, and cobalt blue, the colour favoured by Indos of his generation. Every Saturday afternoon he was hard at work to keep his most treasured possession ticking over. The Eagle saved the empty oil cans and when he had a pair he filled them with plaster and stuck them on either end of a pole to make barbells. First thing in the morning and last thing at night we had to build up our muscles by lifting them. When they got too light for us, he made new ones, mixing scrap iron with the plaster. If he was in a playful mood, he would lay our mattresses on the floor and we'd practise basic judo throws. Later we advanced to jujitsu and he taught us to parry attacks using knives from Mama Helmond's kitchen drawer. If he was in a rotten mood, he would scream at everyone till they let him be. No martial art offered a defence against that onslaught.

One day, Mama Helmond once again felt the urge to test his limits, though she knew damn well where they lay. She went too far. The Eagle – thug, madman, twisted and deranged devil that he was – threatened her with one of the barbells we lifted to punish our bodies. And still she wouldn't shut up. In the hall, on the coconut matting under the bare lightbulb that hung from the ceiling, he slammed one of the barbells into her arm. For weeks she was unable to wring out the sheets she had boiled in the washtub, so the Eagle bought her a second-hand wringer and persuaded us that she had a bad case of thrombosis. Only Phil refused to believe him. When we started quarrelling, Mama Helmond soon reached the end of her tether and used her good arm to whack us on the shoulder with a wooden coat hanger. She broke one coat hanger after another, till we got a fit of the giggles. This was nothing compared to the beatings we took from her thug of a husband and before long she was laughing right along with us.

Ghosts in the hall

They say us humans cannot decide to hate, just as we cannot decide to love. But then my mother always swore my twin brother wasn't human. Nor was I, for that matter. We were from another planet.

I witnessed the moment when my twin brother decided to hate the Eagle. It was in the hall of number 1394, our flat on an endless post-war avenue that was supposed to lead to happier places as yet unknown. I saw it from our bedroom, the boys' bedroom. The hall was a strip of hell you had to negotiate to reach another place: the kitchen, the living room, the shower, another bedroom, the front door… When evening came, the hall fell under the leering gaze of the Wheel-a-Wheel, who watched from the dark corners. None of us had ever seen the Wheel-a-Wheel, yet we knew that this ghost not only moved on wheels at lightning speed but was itself a wheel. Even so, it was possible to escape the Wheel-a-Wheel's clutches. If you ran and jumped fast enough, you could make it from bedroom to toilet before the Wheel-a-Wheel grabbed you.

The hall floor was covered in thin yellow lino decorated with a sorry-looking pattern of orange flowers under a long, rough stretch of coconut matting that curled at the edges. It was easy to trip if you didn't watch out. The matting hurt your knees when you played there during the day. There was something wrong in that hall, day or night. A place where things always seemed to happen.

I shared a room with my twin Phil and Arti, who was two years younger. We had a single bed next to a bunk bed, and always argued about who should get the top bunk. We scared each other witless by summoning the Wheel-a-Wheel whenever one of us had to go to the toilet. Our little brother got so scared he would pee his pants sometimes, and then we would have a go at him for having to sleep in a room that smelled of piss. If Mama came in to see what all the noise was about, we kept quiet. We knew she could report us to the Eagle if she was in a bad mood or if there was a film or a musical on TV, and he would come in and give us another thrashing. This gave her the chance to play her role, trying to hold him back like one of those swooning heroines of hers, acting the victim. When she became his target, she could be incredibly stupid: the more aggressive he became, the more she would needle him, till he went completely *mata gelap*. Perhaps part of her kept wanting to see it, spurred on by a fascination with the incomprehensible.

At the age of eight, I could sense the ghosts. Hours in advance I would feel them gathering around the paranoid ex-marine stalking through the house, the man with the black photo albums full of war graves and portraits of comrades who had been killed or who had killed themselves. Once a fight broke out in my parents' bedroom. Mama fled into the hall and even the Wheel-a-Wheel made itself scarce. The Eagle came after her, beat both her shoulders black and blue with a barbell. The next day he ordered us twins to do the washing. Mama was back in bed, he said. Another attack of thrombosis.

We washed the sheets by hand in the washtub, ran them through the wringer three times and hung them out to dry. Curious housewives peered at us from behind their curtains. Why didn't they come and rescue us from that house full of beatings, ghosts and war stories? A week later, Mama regained the use of her arms and the Wheel-a-Wheel was back at its post.

On his days off, the Eagle would use the hall as a workshop and suspend our bikes there on hooks and pulleys. Then the Wheel-a-Wheel would make way for a ghost that was even more terrifying. The Tultuh. Only us twins knew about the Tultuh. We kept Arti in the dark, for fear he would piss his pants even more. The Tultuh was invisible and could fill the hall all at once, paralysing you with fear. Unlike the Wheel-a-Wheel, he had no need of movement. You never knew when he would come. He could stay away for ages and appear again out of nowhere. That was the nature of the Tultuh.

One Saturday evening my twin brother stood paralysed in the hall, in the grip of the Tultuh. The Eagle came out of his bedroom and growled at him, asking what the matter was. My twin could only stammer, fragments of words. The presence of the Tultuh could not be explained; only we knew he existed. The Eagle was angered by the stammering, suspicious at the lack of an answer. He picked up something that had been left lying in the hall after a Saturday afternoon of oil, grease, benzine and polish. A thick steel cable. He lashed out at Phil, who turned away, groaning, doubled up with pain. God only knows who the Eagle saw in front of him – some enemy from the war in Indonesia, or a vision of his own back lacerated by stick, cane or whip, depending on whether the punisher was a Japanese soldier, his father or his mother.

Back on Java his father wielded the cane, his mother the whip. His father never counted the blows but beat him as long as he pleased. With his mother it was different. She pronounced a sentence and stuck to it. Ten lashes. Done. You knew when it would stop. The Eagle hit you until he was gasping for breath. I saw my brother's pyjama top rip open and welts appear on his back. And at that moment my brave twin turned and shot a look of intense hatred at the thug. All at once, he dared to conceive hatred for the Eagle and to let it show. That is what made it a decision. An irrational decision, but even so: he dared to do something forbidden by God through the agency of the church minister and the Bible studies teacher. I had never seen my twin look at anyone that way and would never see him do so again. A look of hatred, intense and irrevocable enough to last beyond the grave of the man who had booted us into this world for the sake of a valid Dutch passport.

The Eagle lashed out again with the steel cable: once, twice, three times. Then he stopped, surprised almost, now that my twin brother had ceased cowering and stood there looking at him in utter contempt.

Mama used to tell us about the ghosts in the Eagle's head. Ghosts that sometimes possessed him until he no longer knew who he was or who we were. He did not beat us as a father, but as a wartime marine. The beating was not meant for us but for someone else: an Indonesian freedom fighter who had refused to talk to the multilingual Indo interpreter typing up his interrogation report for the Dutch. At least that was the story he told her, and she told us. He had been nothing but an interpreter, hammering away at a typewriter while the Dutch laid into the Indonesians.

The silent Dutchman

Of all the names in my father's address book, Stokkermans was the most ordinary. A name that fitted like a glove. Many of Pa's friends from my boyhood in The Hague had European names that were out of step with their Indo appearance. The only one whose name was written on his face was Matagora. But then he was Ambonese, not Indo. It was the *a*'s that did it: long, open sounds. A world away from the congestion of Stokkermans, every vowel bunged up tight.

The notion of 'the silent Indo father' is a myth: a dubious literary motif, a hollow cliché drawn from the Romantic Western ideal of the wise Oriental as a smiling, modest man of few words. Fatalities aside, young men go to war and return from war. One man comes home silent, the other tells stories. My father told stories, spun yarns. He screamed his war, committed it to paper. But Stokkermans, a white man from Westland, held his tongue. He looked as if his lips had been welded shut. No less than 100,000 silent Dutchmen were conscripted to defend 'their Indies'. Stokkermans belonged to the other contingent of silent Dutchmen that included the marines. And, to my knowledge, Stokkermans opened his mouth about the war in the Indies only once.

I don't recall Stokkermans ever coming to visit us. But he did receive visitors. The Eagle often went to see him alone and once he took me with him. Stokkermans lived in 's-Gravenzande, in a house so spotless it was unsettling. The floors were scrubbed, the Dutch tablecloths free of dust and there was not a single dry or wilting leaf on the plants by the snow-white net curtains that hung in perfect symmetry at the painstakingly polished windows. It must have been spring or early summer because his wife cooked asparagus. I had never seen asparagus before and did my best not to pull a face when I tasted it. Stokkermans, the Silent Dutch Father, looked at me impassively with his drawn face and thin lips clamped together, while my own father urged me to eat the bitter stalks dripping with butter because he could see I didn't like them. Not a word was spoken at the dinner table presided over by the Silent Man and his wife. When you eat, you don't talk. How different to the homes of my father's Indo acquaintances, where everyone chatted incessantly about what they were eating: the *rijsttafel* as a twofold motive for moving your mouth.

The Eagle held Stokkermans in high esteem. For Stokkermans had been a true marine, a soldier who had made sure he was transferred to the Indies in order to restore peace and order. Had he burned down villages in the name of the Queen? He did not speak about such things. Had he mowed down Indonesian freedom fighters?

The Dutchman held his tongue.

Many years later, when I began to look into the story of my father's war, my mother told me the one thing 'that stuffed shirt Stokkermans' had said about the war.

'Well? What did he say?'

'He said your father was a coward.'

The Dutchman had spoken.

Not what a son wants to hear about his father. But, in hindsight, perhaps it is. Could that be why the Eagle went to see Stokkermans so often? To see the hero he himself so badly wanted to be? Had he fled in the heat of battle? Was it remorse that drove him back to Stokkermans' brooding presence time and time again? I never came across the name Stokkermans in my father's writings. Was his absence a deliberate act of omission?

Amerindo

Sundahl was not our uncle but, in a way, he was the younger brother my father never had: a wave of jet-black hair slick with brilliantine and combed back, a sharp crease in his Terylene slacks, gleaming black shoes, laces immaculately tied. Like my father, Sundahl detested jackets. They often wore pullovers with the same pattern: black with a broad yellow V-neck. I was given Sundahl's pullover as a hand-me-down, tailored to fit by my mother on her Singer treadle sewing machine.

I always assumed Sundahl was his surname, one that betrayed a Nordic ancestor on his father's side: a Swede or Norwegian who had once dreamed of building a future on Java. Like my father, Sundahl had sailed to Holland in 1950 after the war in Indonesia, without his family. That was unusual. Most young Indos who made the voyage were former KNIL soldiers and brought their whole family with them to Holland. And then there were a handful of Indonesians who, for their own murky reasons, had stowed away on the ships that sailed between Holland and Indonesia.

Indos without brothers, sisters, father, mother, aunts, uncles, grandfathers and, lest we forget, the grandmothers around whom these families revolved – such Indos were orphans of a kind, desperados some of them or, at worst, pariahs. They must have been childhood friends back in Surabaya, my father and Sundahl. Perhaps they had shared the same girls.

Sundahl seemed to be the eternal bachelor. Like a couple of overexcited kids, he and my father could talk motorbikes, planes and wristwatches for hours on end. Style was what they admired most: 'streamlined' and 'gleaming' were the Indo's watchwords.

I don't know whether Sundahl served as an interpreter with the Dutch Marine Corps and was forced to flee the Indonesians. Unlike my father, he never spoke of the war, at least not when I was around. Yet there was a nervous energy about him. He too would look up quickly or glance over his shoulder whenever he heard a noise. He was one of those switched-on Indos who could assess a situation in the blink of an eye and spring into action if need be. A slight, wiry young man who could almost certainly leap over you in a fight and break your neck with a scissor kick.

Sundahl always talked about emigrating to America. And I do mean always. He tried to persuade my father to go with him. Surely he hadn't given his kids American names for no reason? There was nothing doing here in Holland: too cold, too boring, too few opportunities to climb the ladder. 'Sponsor' was the magic word. You needed a sponsor to enter America as an immigrant. Sundahl went looking for a sponsor. Sundahl found a sponsor. And in the early sixties, Sundahl left. I have no idea why I missed him so much. Perhaps because his energy brought a lustre to our drab living room on that relentless post-war avenue that ran past Zuider Park.

My father wanted to follow him, with his wife and five children in tow. But my mother and I did not want to go. My father spoke of a life in the sun, a job as a paperboy after school, cycling on the sidewalk and tossing newspapers onto sun-drenched lawns – you didn't even have to stick them in the letterbox. My little brothers were sold on the idea. I was afraid of the unknown, though every day at school was grim and Zuider Park was all too often enveloped in mist and rain. Years later I felt like a coward for siding with my mother and refusing to budge. But how did we ever manage to block the move? Father's word was law. Had he simply been unable to obtain the immigration papers? Had I been spared even more misery in America or had I missed the chance of a lifetime? What would America have made of me? A cook in an Indo restaurant somewhere in Los Angeles? A Professor of Literature at a university? A TV scriptwriter? Or a guitar teacher who gets the occasional gig, same as in Holland?

Sundahl sent letters from California. Later they were accompanied by photos of Sundahl's toothy grin at the wheel of a Chevrolet Convertible. One blonde in the passenger seat, another two on the bonnet. A guitar in back. A Gibson, a genuine American Gibson, the favourite make of every Indo of that generation. The guitar my father once had, until its neck was snapped by a passing convoy. Sundahl's Chevy girls wore tight, quarter-length jeans with a checked pattern. Spotless white blouses with turned-up collars and two buttons open. Sundahl later sent us the very same denims by post. But they were too small. For Sundahl we remained the little boys from way back when.

'Oh, what a pity!' my mother wailed. 'You would have looked so American!'

Guitar Indo (2)

The Hague Southwest. Late fifties, early sixties. Long avenues of endless tenements, lined with rows of weedy saplings. A sorry sight compared to the jungle of which my father speaks. Us kids criss-cross our way through our own brick-and-mortar jungle, playing tig and hide-and-seek in the side streets. On the avenues you can't help but bump into one another. Dutch boys are big and strong, but relatively harmless. They give chase but they're easy to outrun. Indos are often smaller but they are a danger: they all know how to fight. Even worse, they all play guitar. And the same question is always burning on their lips.

'Hey, do you play?'

Some random Indo, a boy I barely know, asks the feared question and calls me over.

'Yeah, 'course I do,' I answer.

He scrutinizes my fingers. 'How many songs can you play? What about "Hello Mary Lou"?'

'No, not yet.'

'You have to play A-D-E, you know.'

'Yes, I know.'

'My uncle plays C-F-G. Barre chords, tricky stuff. He's in a band. Hey, is your dad in a band?'

'No, he plays alone.'

'Alone? Where's the fun in that? Hey, I live on Zwartsluisstraat. Come over Wednesday afternoon and bring your guitar, okay? Number 9.'

He saunters off. I watch him go and I can tell by his walk that he really can play guitar. That's what I want my body to say. That's how I want to walk down the street from now on.

First, I have to run all the way home, where my mother opens the door and nearly bites my head off. It's nice weather, I should be playing outside. I make up some excuse, wait for my chance and sneak into the forbidden bedroom. I feel my way across the fretboard on the neck of the guitar and wonder how long I'd need to practise before I can hold down the strings without hurting my fingertips.

'Leave that guitar alone! Your father will kill you!'

Zwartsluisstraat, a street to avoid from now on. If I don't watch out, that Indo will be calling me to come in. I have to steer clear of Indos until I can at least play 'Hello Mary Lou'.

There's no escape. On a Sunday afternoon, my father takes me to visit the Van Mouriks, a big, friendly family who live on Erasmusweg. Their house smells of fried tofu and *ikan teri*, dried anchovies. The playing cards on the coffee table are greasy to the touch, the windows fogged by cooking. I think I'm in luck when my father sends me through to the bedroom to play with the other kids. They are all crammed onto a bunk bed, and one of them has a guitar on her lap. They open their mouths and a song rings out in three-part harmony. I steal glances at the fingers of the girl who is leading the company.

The final chord sounds and she hands the guitar to me.

'Your turn.'

I grin and wave an apologetic refusal.

'Wah!' somebody shouts. 'He don't know how!'

'Course he does,' the girl says. 'Every Indo knows how. *Itu malu.* He's shy, that's all.'

Hey, Ma!

Hey, Ma... Mam! Maa-maa!! Maa-aaa-aam!!! I get it now, Mama. I heard it, felt it, perhaps I understood it all along. Suddenly there she was, Mam, singing the song you always sang at the washtub or in the kitchen. Young and haunting, she danced on the tightrope of despair and expectation, like you when you had a moment to yourself in the kitchen that smelled of mopped floors, detergent and cigarette smoke. All that granite made it a fine place to sing, eh Ma? 'Stranger in Paradise'. 1960. I can still hum the tune, picked up mostly from you. I carry it with me, deep in my memory. Just the other day, a Belgian radio station played the version you were so fond of, announced it in good old-fashioned, deferential style. Caterina Valente was the singer's name, and yes, I remember, she was a favourite of yours. She sang the song with an accent, a vague mix of German and French, betraying her background on the international variety circuit. Perhaps off stage she really did feel like a stranger in some paradise or other. How much did Caterina Valente identify with the prayer for love that warmed the valve of our Bakelite radio? Did she fall prey to that unattainable angel whose praises she sang? Did you understand the words or was the melody enough for you? For me as a little boy, music promised a future as lovely as your voice and the voice of Caterina Valente. Perhaps that's why an old woman's rasping cough can bring me to the verge of tears.

Guitar Indo (3)

On Sunday mornings, the radio played Dixieland from the Dutch polder. It was hard to find a foreign station that showcased the guitar in all its glory, something my father was apt to complain about. He wanted to hear *kroncong* and, above all, Hawaiian music. He told us about his brother Karel – our uncle, a man we had never met and would never meet – about Karel winning second prize in a Hawaiian steel guitar contest in Surabaya. The Hague was home to a couple of Hawaiian dance bands, often with a woman taking centre stage, the guitar laid across her knee, pressing a lipstick tube to the strings if there was no bottle neck or metal bar to hand. I never got to see those bands live, but whenever I heard a Hawaiian song on the radio, I listened open-mouthed to the beautiful things a guitar could do. I had a toy car with a wonky wheel and I dreamed of a guitar. My father had a guitar he barely touched and he still dreamed of America. Or was it Mexico by then? My father was no guitarist. My father was a drummer, banging out a rhythm on his Remington.

Operation Gourami

The Eagle's aquarium was undoubtedly inspired by his nostalgia for the Indies. He made a point of calling it his 'tropical' aquarium. A cold-water tank would never have been colourful enough for him: why settle for sticklebacks when you could have angelfish? Besides, you needed a tropical tank to pit two Siamese fighting fish against each other. We cut out cardboard coins and placed bets on the red or the blue fighting fish, one of which was bound to die. A cruel and objectionable Indo pastime in the eyes of Mama Helmond, not to mention a waste of money: the fish cost one guilder twenty-five a pair.

The object of our headmaster's nostalgia was a mystery to me. Though he was hewn from the clay of Holland, he too kept a tropical aquarium in the hall of his wretched school. It was a beautiful tank, a very beautiful tank, a tank of unparalleled beauty. Our grubby little home aquarium was unsightly by comparison, and one fish after another departed this life for the endless fields of tubifex. Gouramis were the only fish that survived our tank, creatures from the country that had emerged victorious in the colonial war.

As luck would have it, our headmaster had a deep loathing of children from an Indo background. Once a week a small group of pupils would learn English, a lesson taught by the headmaster in person. When I was handed my umpteenth eight out of ten for a faultless English assignment, the Eagle, still dreaming of America, reckoned it was time to take revenge on this Indo-hater. His aquarium might be impressive, but that wouldn't stop our Indonesian ploppers chomping their way through its residents within a week.

And so, with due pomp and ceremony, we presented the headmaster with a gift: a jar containing five gouramis. This made him so happy that the following week he gave me a nine for an error-free English dictation, still one mark short in the Eagle's eyes.

To our dismay, the gouramis failed in their secret mission. They seemed to shrink and fade into the vastness of the grey dictator's school aquarium. But then my twin brother and I were summoned to the headmaster's office. Had our tropical death squad sprung into action after all?

No, the headmaster had got wind of our artistic endeavours: flogging portraits of our favourite cartoon character Wilma Flintstone to our fellow pupils for five cents apiece. Saucy, topless portraits. We spent evening after evening producing these drawings, much to the hilarity of our father and the exasperation of our mother, who had no time for his roguish take on sex education and was utterly bewildered by his unpredictable responses to the conduct of his offspring. The desks at school were soon full of soft porn of our making, and although these masterpieces went unsigned, the headmaster soon suspected us as the artists. We were both told to pack our bags and leave. We trudged home with lead in our boots, convinced that the Eagle would knock lumps out of us, hit us so hard that for weeks we wouldn't be able to show our bruised and battered faces.

How wrong we were. By coincidence, the Eagle had come home from work early that day and he sent us straight back to school to fetch the rest of his children. The headmaster didn't lift a finger to stop us.

We stood there in the hall waiting for Arti and Mil – Nana was still at nursery school – and watched our gouramis make lethargic circuits of the school aquarium.

'Typical Javanese,' the Eagle grumbled that evening. 'Not to be trusted. No good to anyone.'

As kids we were happy enough to believe his words, which is not to say we understood them. He came from Java himself, didn't he? But a topless Wilma Flintstone inflicting more damage on the headmaster than a jam jar of tropical fish was something we definitely grasped.

Thanks to this episode, we wound up at three different schools. The Eagle did not see this as a bad omen.

Dudok's *kali*

He must have been a cold man, Willem Dudok. Only a cold man could have conceived a place as grim as The Hague Southwest. He began his career in the army, he knew barracks life, a bad start if ever there was one. The Eagle too once had 'something to do with the army', to use Mama Helmond's words, so he too was a wrong 'un. Sometimes I was made to accompany the Eagle on his walks through Dudok's brick-and-mortar jungle. My only pleasant memory of these outings is learning to eat salted herring at a little stall on the corner of Leyweg. Herring with raw onion. After lowering the herring into my mouth and chewing off a piece, I would dip it in a big bowl of diced raw onion and repeat, till the friendly Dutch fishmonger pointed out that his other customers might object on the grounds of hygiene and handed me my own portion of onions on a square of greaseproof paper. He corrected me with a smile, something the Eagle would never have done. My father was itching to give me a clip round the ear, but with the cheery fishmonger looking on he held back. Wonderful folk, the Dutch. Every lesson from an Indo who had been in the war was hammered home by physical contact. This had many variations:

a thump: a heavy blow with the fist to the shoulder, chest or stomach;

a clip: a blow to the cheek with the back of the hand;

a whack: a blow with a cane, ruler or similar;

a swipe: a slap to the side of the head with the palm of the hand;

a clout: an unexpected blow, one you don't see coming;

a boot: a direct kick to the stomach or the backside, so hard it sends you flying down the hall or across the room;

a good hiding: the thug pulls you towards him by the hair, plants his knee in your stomach, then pummels you into a corner till you fall to the floor and finishes you off with a kick;

a thrashing: an indeterminate series of blows with a belt, steel cable or length of rope;

a slam: your head is smashed against the wall or, as described in an earlier chapter, against the head of a sibling;

an endurance punishment: being forced to do press-ups, counting out loud until you reach one hundred, followed by one hundred squats; failure to reach that number will result in a thrashing (see above).

The whip wielded by Grandma Sie in Surabaya was outlawed in Holland, which was some consolation. Unfortunately, the belts that held up the Eagle's trousers had buckles that left welts on your back. The traditional Dutch spanking had no place among Indos. We laughed ourselves silly when a friend told us he had been put across his father's knee to have his backside slapped. That was nothing, nothing at all.

A gym teacher asks you how you got those red marks on your back.

You tell him there are lads in your judo class who don't cut their nails.

The gym teacher gives you an understanding nod.

Willem Dudok must have learned to eat herring too, but in his home town of Amsterdam, where they chop up the fish and fork the chunks into their mouth with a cocktail stick. Letting an Amsterdammer loose on The Hague was always asking for trouble. Dudok was a child of musical parents. By the age of thirteen he knew every Beethoven symphony off by heart. Later, he must have sat at his drawing board with a head full of bombast, picked up the pencil he had sharpened compulsively and dashed off a straight line from north to south and another from east to west. Look at a map of The Hague Southwest and it's the only logical conclusion.

Endless rows of identical tenements, as forbidding as a Beethoven symphony. To a former marine like the Eagle, they must have brought back a familiar sense of the barracks. For us kids, they were blocks of boring stairwells but thrilling cellars. Luckily there were a few bigger blocks of flats, with lifts to play in and gangways that let you charge past dozens of front doors while a gaggle of washed-out housewives hurled the worst kind of abuse at you. Terraced houses, in even shorter supply, were the mansions of Dudok's ghetto, complete with guard dogs and Indo-haters ensconced behind net curtains.

Those houses were the stuff of Mama Helmond's dreams. A TV in the living room, the children upstairs in their bedrooms and that madman from the tropics out at work. She wallowed in musicals and figure skating. Documentaries got her down. History had been and gone. The here and now was all that mattered. The past was something to be left behind.

'What is it with you two? I swear you're from another planet.'

'If only you'd left us there.'

'Don't talk daft! I'm your mother!'

'That's impossible. You're terrestrial.'

'Even back when you were little I thought you were different from everyone else. Now I know for certain.'

'Way back when is here and now, Mam.'

'Now you're talking rubbish! Leave the past behind you! Now is now! Do you hear me?'

'No, Mam. Now is the sum total of all the memories you carry with you.'

More than anything, she would have liked to see that bloke of hers go back to where he came from. But that was impossible. What a let-down it must have been, living with a brown-skinned man who fed his sons raw, salted rock-bass fished from the ditches of The Hague.

Those ditches had been dug around Dudok's playing fields and were the focus of our boyhood games. In spring, my brothers and I would catch tadpoles with our fishing nets, and sticklebacks in the summer. We used to plead with the anglers to give us a rock-bass, silent Dutchmen who could spend hours staring at their floats.

Most of them shook their heads and tossed the rock-bass back into the water after a few hours' captivity in the keepnet. But now and then an angler would relent and mutter, 'Go on, take 'em.'

'What you gonna do with 'em?' they asked, but always too late. By that time the water's edge was far behind us and we were sprinting home with our catch.

Rock-bass brought out the Eagle's tropical ways. He washed the fish, sliced open their bellies and gutted them. Laying them out on the granite counter, newly scrubbed by his disgruntled skivvy, he rubbed them with salt. In the land of his birth, the scorching sun would have dried such tiddlers in no time, but in Dudok's brick-and-mortar jungle it was a far lengthier process, even at the height of summer.

Summer holidays were hell for Mama Helmond. It was a blessed relief when her brown husband would take her brown children off her hands for an afternoon. And her brown husband, happy that the damp chill of Holland had let up for a month or so, was even cheerful sometimes. Something that could never be said of 'that fishwife', our mother.

With another brisk stroke of his pencil, Willem Dudok set the boundary of The Hague Southwest at Lozerlaan. A portacabin stands on the untamed strip of grassland through which water flows to the dunes of Loosduinen. A distant steamroller appears to have seized up in the burning sun. The one rounded element drawn by Dudok's hairy hands is the flight of steps leading down to the water at Lozerlaan. It resembles the paintings of terraced *sawahs* the Eagle's Indo friends hang on their walls. A symbolic, sympathetic gesture by the architect perhaps? If so, it's an awkward one: didn't he know that Indos seek out shade when it's hot? Even the sun-starved Eagle is sweltering, and rolls up his trouser legs. He has brought his camera with him. He likes to send photographs of smiling faces to Java, where his entire family stayed behind. Will they believe that life here in Holland is so cheerful? The fishwife is back home in her kitchen, free to smoke a half pack of cigarettes in perfect peace and bemoan a life that bears not even the faintest resemblance to the films she watched as a girl. That brown husband of hers has gone out wearing yet another set of clean clothes – it's enough to drive her to despair. And as soon as he gets home he'll take another nice long shower and put on clean underpants. If he's off sick and home from work, he changes them three times a day. All she ever does is wash and wear out her wringer and her clothes pegs. He still insists on calling them *pendeks*, those underpants of his. Once he's done with them, she has to adjust them for the children. There's no money for new underwear.

'That father of yours is a selfish git. Buys fancy clothes for himself and leaves you lot to run around in rags and plastic sandals, summer and winter. Refuses to take a packed lunch to work. He'd rather pay over the odds for his sausage rolls. And if we're lucky he has a few left over so I can cut them up and divide them among you, with a drop of Worcester sauce.'

'Worse chester.'

'Huh?'

'That's what Papa calls it. "Worse chester".'

'Oh, you can't teach that man anything. It's Wooster! Wooster!'

That's not entirely true. The Eagle *has* adapted to the world around him. He has learned that sunshine in Holland means you go out instead of staying in. It's Sunday in the photograph; I can tell by the clothes the passers-by are wearing. Building debris is scattered around the last of the grand architect's housing blocks. They are still vacant and the lampposts are not yet in place, only a portacabin so that Uncle Broese can watch over them by night.

We have walked all the way to Lozerlaan. My little brothers are brandishing fishing rods, and I am carrying a bucket for the rock-bass to swim in, assuming we manage to catch any. The wide, round steps are hot beneath my feet and I scoop water out of the channel to keep them wet. My twin brother is standing up to his baggy *pendek* in the water, a stick in his hand, as if trying to gauge the depth. Our younger brother is two steps higher. He looks like a young warrior, holding his bamboo fishing rod like a lance in front of his chest. A few steps above him, a couple of well-dressed children are making themselves scarce…

The Eagle took this black-and-white photo. There is nothing to suggest that we chased the well-dressed children away. We never chase anyone away. If it comes to the crunch, we are the ones who get chased. Most likely the children's mother has called them over in haste to help her fold the picnic blanket. Did she call them because a dissolute Indo family had turned up and taken possession of Dudok's *kali*? Or was she mindful of the leeches the Eagle had warned us about? Of course, those bloodsuckers were nothing compared to the crocodiles that swam in the real *kali* when he was a boy. In the real heat. In a real city, not this no man's land: Surabaya was a metropolis, The Hague is a hamlet.

Yet even in a hamlet like The Hague, you can indulge your urge to roam. His first stop was Parallelweg, board and lodgings with a money-grabbing Indo landlady. Then it was on to Alexander Barracks, living off whatever military pay was left. Then to Bilderdijkstraat with a heffalump from Helmond in tow. And then with twin boys to Schermerstraat, a place I barely recall.

A couple of photos survive from that time, kept in my mother's shoebox. One shows me and my twin brother learning to ride our tricycles. Another shows the pair of us on our mother's bike, my twin in a kiddie seat attached to the handlebars, me on the back with my feet in the saddlebags. Now there's a memory that's stuck: how safe I felt with my feet buried deep in the double pannier. I wanted the safety of those saddlebags. My twin wanted a view of the open road and would go on to get his driver's licence ten years before I got mine. A third photo shows us sitting on a picnic blanket with our maternal grandmother somewhere in Zuider Park. She came to call once in a while. Grandad never did. He despised his son-in-law and wanted nothing to do with brown people.

Two years later we move to the joyless, endless Melis Stokelaan, where the air is so thick with ghosts that I begin to see what the Eagle sees. Corpses rise from the mud and take on fearsome shapes that swamp me in my dreams. When I wake up screaming from a nightmare, my father comes in and gives me a slap to send me back to sleep. Screams night after night, what must the neighbours have thought? Time to move on. Time to pack up the shame that hangs around us in the stairwell.

'Why don't the neighbours go to the police and report that man?' my mother wonders out loud.

'Why doesn't she do it herself?' Phil and I wonder in turn.

'Are you talking about me? About your own mother? Don't you fucking well know that the fucking police will just send your mother straight back to that fuck of a father of yours?'

On to our next stop: the heffalump's dream come true. An honest-to-goodness terraced house on Hoogveen, the best house we ever lived in, even if it was the work of Dudok. Friends around every corner. Not just boring old streets but 'clearings' and 'gardens' and 'sidings' and 'fens'. Well, what do you expect with a writer on the planning committee? Het Oord has a bad reputation. You can't pass through it without getting into a punch-up. A detour along Hengelolaan is one solution, but that means having to run to school. The sidings are home to sweet girls, while the gardens are vast underground passageways full of mystery.

From Hoogveen it's not far to Meppelweg, which is home to 'the rocks': a giant caterpillar of massive boulders plonked down at random. Our mothers forbid us to play there; all too often we come home looking like the walking wounded.

Past the rocks are the meadows, where we form a pact with the lads from Het Oord against the yokel boys from Loosduinen. Jumping over ditches, we march to a wide canal and raft across. The water is almost black, so dark it's scary. Up ahead, the Loosduinen yokels are waiting for us in their dirty overalls, pitchforks in hand. We turn and paddle back the way we came.

One day we arrive home with armfuls of wild rhubarb, harvested from behind the rocks. Our mothers immediately suspend the play ban and send us back to collect bags of the stuff. It's a rhubarb feast for the whole block, until a bunch of workmen in blue smocks appear with a police escort and mow down the illegal crop with scythes.

Surabaya

Grainy footage. A chanteuse in a fluttering robe, singing her heart out in a decor that must have been shored up to withstand the blast of the wind machine. *Surabaya Johnny*. I didn't know whether the title song was about a real boy from Surabaya, nor did my musical-mad mother. Chomping cigarettes in front of the black-and-white TV, a dangling slipper danced on the tip of her big toe. Wallowing in romance was a tall order when you shared a house with an oddball who could come storming out of the bedroom any second, screaming at everyone to give him some peace. The strains of 'Surabaya Johnny' were not enough to lure him from the bedroom to which he retreated night after night to commit his war to paper. But when another song came waltzing out of the television set one day – 'Surabaya' minus Johnny – he did appear. We called the Eagle to come downstairs, away from his desk. A unique moment: we would never have dared call him otherwise. He appeared at the doorway in his striped pyjamas and stood there hanging on every *r* that rolled off the tongue of Indo songstress Anneke Grönloh. Halfway through the lilting final chorus he turned to go and we heard him mumble his way back upstairs. 'God, yes, my native soil.'

He began to discover the popular song as a balm for his overpopulated memories. But the time had yet to come when he could go out and buy a record player. Still too many mouths to feed.

At No. 168 Hoogveen, I had my own room for the very first time, a place where I could do my homework like a good little boy. Until, blind with rage at my brothers, I smashed my foot through a glass door. I hobbled through the summer holidays with my leg in plaster but this episode – my one and only attack of *mata gelap* – saved my life. Or someone else's. I never let myself go like that again. To this day I keep control, no matter how furious I am.

Just our luck: the tormented ex-marine with eternal blood on his hands could only bear the house for a year and the whole family ended up back by Zuider Park – Loevesteinlaan this time – in a flat that was way too small and where you could hear the spectators roar when local heroes ADO Den Haag scored. Beautiful, the way the stadium floodlights lit up the park in the evening. In the space of twelve years, the Eagle had made his round through Dudok's asphalt jungle. And it was there, by Zuider Park, that the interpreter from Java would meet his Waterloo.

What possessed the man to swap that roomy terraced house for a cramped four-room tenement flat? The fishwife from Helmond loses her rag over a birds' nest on our little balcony overlooking the wonderful park and sweeps the whole thing over the edge: mummy sparrow, daddy sparrow and all the baby sparrows, along with every twig us kids had watched them weave with their busy little beaks. An animal killer, that mother of ours. With her cold father and her cold family. A cold province, Brabant.

A stray tabby cat wanders into our home and warms us as we fall asleep. But one evening the creature is carried off. No place for guinea pigs, no place for birds, no place for cats. We never find out who is responsible for deporting our cuddly ball of fur. For the first time we see our parents form a united front, a married couple wearing the same sanctimonious expressions. She stares out of the front window at the treetops of Zuider Park, he stares out of the side window at the grim brick-and-mortar blocks that surround us.

'What in God's name has become of me?' the Eagle must have wondered. But I never heard him say those words out loud. What the lonely madman did do was ram it through our thick skulls on a daily basis that our childhood was nothing compared to his, nothing. And it was no good talking to that wife of his either. What did she know? Glued to her clueless television comedies, whining that she should have been an actress, not a skivvy. The news means nothing to her. The whole world mourns the death of the first president made for television, but Kennedy's death leaves her cold. She can't even cook, none of them can, the girls here in Holland. They can gut a herring and dice an onion. But they put milk in their coffee and look at you in blank disbelief when you tell them coffee comes from Indonesia. And when you go for a walk in Zuider Park with your white wife and your five children, everyone stares.

'Well, they're your kids. You shouldn't have brought them into this world,' the fishwife snapped in her worst moods. 'I never asked for them.'

'Ha ha ha!'

'Are you lot listening? That father of yours thinks it's funny. Get the joke? I'm off to the kitchen. At least there I'll get some peace.'

'Ha ha ha!'

The headlight

The Eagle must have been in one of his restless moods. He seldom took anyone with him but me, the eldest. That day he hopped on his bike and let me cycle next to him on the inside of the bicycle lane, giving me pointers all the way. We cycled to the end of Zuider Park and wove our way through a dizzying jumble of streets to reach the city centre.

Among the crowds, we walked our bikes to the narrowest of streets, Achterom. We parked them there and headed back to Grote Marktstraat. It was a strange sight: men of all shapes and sizes standing stock still in the middle of the street watching the news roll by on the electronic ticker at the Bijenkorf department store. The Eagle only glanced up to read the temperature that flashed between the headlines, too low as always. He swore that even the nights in Surabaya were warmer than the hottest days in The Hague. Well, most of them.

Near the swanky department store, in which he never set foot, was HEMA, the store for the common man. The Eagle bought a chunk of their famous smoked sausage for me, steaming in a leaky cone of greaseproof paper and slathered in mustard. My mother would have been livid, screeching that mustard was bad for my nerves. I was a jittery child, too easily unsettled by creepy films, scared of the dark, wary in traffic, always longing for the radio. Hustle and bustle were what my father was after; he missed the street life of Surabaya.

This was his Saturday afternoon off; in those days people still worked on Saturday morning. We retraced our steps to Achterom, that little old backstreet in the age-old city centre. It was quiet there, as if no one dared set foot on the cobbles between the blind walls of buildings so decrepit that bricks might conceivably come crashing down at any minute. The Eagle had just slid the key into his rear wheel lock when he looked up and saw someone standing there. A man roughly his age, same build, black hair almost dripping with brilliantine. He could have been a relative or at least an old friend from the Indies.

The man looked at the Eagle and his jaw dropped.

'You, here?' the Eagle erupted. 'Damn you to hell, you bastard!'

The man turned and ran.

'Watch my bike,' the Eagle ordered. 'Wait here.'

He grabbed his Marine dagger from his pannier, slid it into his pocket and set off in pursuit. Were enemies from Indonesia roaming the streets of The Hague, or was this man the only one? Babysitting a bike while the Eagle might be stabbing someone to death in a side street over by the Passage made me sick with worry. Knees trembling, I stood there hoping the 'bastard' would escape down a seedy back alley. But what if the Eagle failed to return? What if that bastard emerged victorious and came back to finish me off too? I looked around for an escape route. Was a human life worth less than this bike? It was a Raleigh with Sturmey Archer gears and drum brakes. It had been delivered as a self-assembly kit and the Eagle had put it together himself, no welding required. His ropes, pulleys and ceiling hooks were now installed in the cellar of our flat on Zuider Park. We knew the story of his sabotage at the bicycle factory in the steaming heat of Croc City. He had shown us the scars on his back.

Now, sixteen years later in a much colder city, had the Eagle gone tearing after the man he thought had betrayed him? Or was this about something else entirely? The Eagle told us so many war stories that just thinking about everything he had been through made my head spin.

'I'll get him yet, that damned Javanese weasel,' the Eagle muttered when he came back, slipping his Marine dagger back into his pannier.

I thanked my lucky stars he hadn't caught the man. But why call him a 'Javanese weasel'? The Eagle was from Java himself. It made no sense to me.

The Eagle might have a workshop in the cellar, but he's no handyman. I am almost thirteen and I have my own bike. He sends me out one evening to deliver a letter to acquaintances of ours. There is not a breath of wind and the night sky is turning bluish black. On my way back home, I see a giant meteor streak across the sky above Zuider Park. A dragon-tailed diamond, snuffed out high above the treetops. I step on my brakes and absorb the memory of this cosmic miracle.

I go to cycle on, but my headlight refuses to work. I stop, check my dynamo and inspect the rear light. That's still working. I start fiddling with the headlight and the whole thing comes away in my hand.

The Eagle explodes when he goes down to the cellar the next day and discovers my broken headlight. Of course he discovers it. He spends every moment of every day scrutinizing every inch of the world around him. Nothing escapes him.

Another Saturday – Saturdays are eventful, weekdays less so – he comes home tired from work, complaining about the pain in his back. Sometimes the pain is rooted in the torture he suffered at the hands of the Japanese, sometimes in the whippings his mother gave him, and at other times in the landmine that threw him clear of an armoured vehicle and sent him plunging into a ravine. Perhaps the pain felt different each time, like my head hitting the wall was different from my head hitting my brother's head, or a straightforward thrashing with the belt.

A belt across your back leaves welts, that's all. Your head hitting the wall makes you so groggy that you can't keep up with the lessons at school for a few days. Strangely, your head hitting your brother's head makes you believe that an enemy lives inside your brother. We were always arguing, Phil and I. Or else it was me against Phil and Arti. Or Arti against Mil. Nana was still too little to pick a fight.

I have to go down to the cellar, where the bikes are. The Eagle is wielding a soldering iron, Phil is holding the handlebars steady, and I have to hold the lamp casing against the bracket it was mounted on. I expect a quick fix. Soldering is a matter of seconds; it's not supposed to take longer. But the Eagle doesn't know what he's doing and starts to swear. The lamp is so hot against my bare hands that I have to let go.

'Hold that fucking lamp still, you spineless little prick!'

He tries again while the casing scorches my fingertips. I grit my teeth. My brother knows you can't solder tin to a steel bracket, you need a blowtorch for a job like that. The bike-factory saboteur ought to know that too. Phil looks on helpless. He has no choice but to keep his mouth shut, like the kitchen staff made to stand in the factory courtyard and watch as the Eagle, a young Indo of nineteen, was beaten senseless by two Japanese officers.

The dagger

The Eagle took the cool metal of his bloodthirsty friend with him everywhere, except to work. A heavy, black dagger with a blood groove to lighten the blade. It looked like it could stop a tiger in its tracks. Etched into it was the name NOLAN, one letter short of our surname: Noland. My father always made a great mystery of that final *d*.

It was an American fighting knife, given to him by a marine in Indonesia in exchange for two Japanese samurai swords. Phil and I used to think he'd cut a lousy deal, but later I read that the swords issued to Japanese soldiers were rudimentary affairs, not a patch on the legendary weapons forged by Japan's foremost blacksmiths. The soldiers' mass-produced swords were rusty and cumbersome. They lacked the beauty, the extraordinarily keen edge and cult status of the classic Japanese longsword, the *katana*. How the Eagle got his hands on two samurai swords was never explained. Philip and I decided that Gurkha soldiers fighting for the Brits had crept up on two Japanese soldiers in the dead of night, slit their throats with their curved blades and robbed them of their factory-made weapons. The Gurkhas must have given the swords to the Eagle as a souvenir and, idolizing all things American, he swapped them for a marine's fighting knife.

'Hey Mam, do you know if Pa still has that dagger of his?'

'That bloody Marine dagger? No, he tossed it. Told me in a letter once.'

'Tossed it? Why would he do that?'

'Conscience got the better of him, if you ask me. That thing could be lying at the bottom of any canal or ditch in The Hague. Damned if I know.'

Had the dagger begun to haunt him? Sometimes you would hear tales of people from the Indies who were plagued by an ornamental *kris* that rattled on its fixtures. Or a copper lizard that crept off the wall when the moon was full and stood on the rug in the middle of the living room. One thing was sure: everyone who fled the Indies was haunted by memories of the war.

Of all the first-generation Indos I have spoken to in my life – men who sided with the Dutch during the war of independence – not one admitted firing a single shot at an Indonesian. No one except the Eagle. One of his more graphic accounts was how, at a railway station, he fired a round from his carbine straight through a mother and the child in her arms, to take out an Indonesian freedom-fighter who was using them as a human shield.

'You really did that?'

'Yes. What else was I supposed to do? Let that *pelopor* blow my brains out?'

'And your bullets went right through that kid?'

'Of course they did! How else could I have hit the bastard hiding behind them? Numbskull! Now, get those dishes washed! Go and help your mother! Don't forget your apron! And wear a dress to school tomorrow! You sound like some pathetic little *nona* from the *kampong*!'

The dagger was always by his bed at night, within easy reach. Some nights I saw the outline of that murder weapon in the Eagle's hand slide across my bedroom wall, a shadow cast by the bare lightbulb that hung in the hallway. Then I would shrink into the corner and call out to him from my bed, tell him who I was so that he would not mistake me for an old enemy. It was said that some Indonesians had stowed away on the countless ships that brought throngs of Indos to Holland. But those Indonesian stowaways could hardly be called anti-Dutch. For a long time I – like my white mother and your average Dutchman – could not tell the difference between an Indo and an Indonesian. Or between Ambonese and Indo.

'That's the first and last time you call your father an Indonesian, understood?'

He points his Marine dagger in my direction. A threat of sorts, though it's still in its sheath. He only bares the blade when he threatens my mother. Or when paranoia takes hold.

One day I was home alone with my kid sister. My mother was out at the shops and my sister was sleeping. She was much younger than the rest of us, almost an afterthought. She brought joy to our home. No one ever yelled at her. When the Eagle worked himself into a lather with his war stories, we kept her as far away from him as we could.

When the bullets from my father's gun ripped through that mother at the station, was the child in her arms the same age as my peaceful, sleeping sister?

A soft afternoon light shone through the window, a rare moment of quiet in our household. I crept into the bedroom and picked up my father's dagger. It was still in its sheath. A restless feeling took hold of me. What if my mother were to come in and catch me? But I wanted to try to feel what goes through a man when he murders someone.

Standing by my little sister's bed, I broke into a sweat. I ran a fingertip over her soft cheek. She was sound asleep and did not stir.

And then I did it. I took the dagger from its sheath and held the blade to her throat. Not across her larynx but directly above it. Very carefully, I brought the point down. For a moment, it touched her soft skin. I did not understand. How could anyone kill a child like this? I slid the dagger into its sheath and, bathed in sweat, dashed back to my parents' bedroom to put it back exactly as I had found it, knowing my father hardly ever missed a trick.

I was twelve years old and still believed in God. I kneeled beside my sister's bed and prayed. When my mother came home, she asked me what I had been up to and sent me out to play.

I walked over to Zuider Park, but I could not find my brothers. There was a bench by a stretch of water. I sat down and imagined I was an old man with war crimes on my conscience. When I realized that such a man might never be caught, I wondered if he might have to punish himself and my gaze drifted up to the branches, in search of a hanging body.

Herring in tomato sauce

Bickering over a granite countertop in a kitchen in The Hague. A clash of cultures. The madman wants rice, the fishwife wants potatoes. They find each other in their love of herring in tomato sauce. Soaked herring conserved in a slimy bloodbath, broken by their long wait in the half-rusted oval tin and spooned straight into hungry mouths. I can't get enough of them; same goes for my brothers and sisters. Delicious on white bread greased with margarine. And at Christmas, the madman serves fruit wine in sticky glasses left to him by our old Aunty Lique from the Indies.

Herring in tomato sauce vanished from my life when the fishwife hatched a plan against the madman, in cahoots with a local GP, Aunty Fien and a band of accomplices. The Eagle's paranoia had taken on such grotesque proportions that living with him had become impossible. Life-threatening even, though it was unclear whose life was under threat. When one of the Eagle's beatings winded me so badly I nearly choked, my brave twin brother Phil exploded with rage and shouted after him, 'Next time you'll get a knife between the ribs!'

I don't know if the Eagle only pretended not to hear him. He marched out of our bedroom, perhaps with a vague realization that this time he had gone too far. A few days later, Aunty Riek came up from Helmond to stay for a while. One evening, she and my mother found me in the kitchen, sobbing and shaking uncontrollably. I had run from my bed with a nightmare snapping at my heels. They gave me a drink of water but I was in such a panic that I bit down and broke the glass. Later they told me that every time the Eagle popped his head round the kitchen door, I began to scream hysterically. Aunty Riek alerted the GP and they decided to let me stay with a kind Indo woman who lived around the corner. She had the radio playing softly all day, grew chilli on her balcony, kept a little pet monkey in a cage in her living room and flung herself joyfully into her husband's arms when he returned from his tour of duty in the merchant navy. Her husband was an Indo too, a quiet man with a moustache, who took me to see ADO play and made me sneak in under the turnstile – the old rascal – so he wouldn't have to pay my ticket.

When I came back home, the Eagle kept a low profile around me. I didn't know then that my brother was sleeping with a knife under his pillow. Nor did my father. My mother found the knife when she was making our beds one day and knew that she had waited far too long.

26 November 1964

A mild autumn day. I cycled to school that morning, a small makeshift building I would never be able to find my way back to. Long since demolished, probably. What was it about that little school that made me so happy? I can't remember exactly. It was half the size of my previous school, the teachers were stricter and my form teacher had a terrifying gift for noticing every last detail. He took an unaccountable dislike to my brother Phil, but reckoned I was 'all right for an Indo'. Occasionally he took me aside in the corridor, when my classmates were already seated at their desks. Fixing me with his piercing blue eyes, he asked me how I got those lumps on my head. Or those scratches on my face. Or that black eye, swollen purple and green at the edges. I stammered that I had got into a fight with a bunch of local lads. I could tell from his face that he didn't believe me. He knew I was no fighter and I sensed that he could see my father's shadow at my shoulder. He had spoken to my mother at a parents' evening and must have heard that my father hit me often and hit me hard. I was ashamed of the beatings he gave me. Ashamed of a shame that was his to bear. Ashamed of things that, as a boy of twelve, I could not even name.

Our tenement flat opposite Zuider Park was too small for a family of seven and my father had placed a little desk at the end of the hall where I had to do my homework. Every time he passed, he would lean over my shoulder and quiz me. Every wrong answer met with a sardonic Indo sneer. 'Tell the school I want my money back!'

My brother Phil was smarter. He had no trouble with algebra, my father's favourite subject and one which, as it later turned out, he barely understood. The interpreter's only flair was for languages. Mathematical formulas were meaningless to me. I could see nothing in them, no playfulness, no poetry. And how the hell was I supposed to concentrate with the Eagle looming over me?

Thanks to our screaming, fighting parents, Phil and I both had to repeat a year. Unlike me, Phil struggled with languages. The omnipresent slave driver in our house wrecked his nerves too.

After one failed year of secondary school, my father declared me stupid and sent me to a vocational school to spend three years training to be an office clerk. I was far from unhappy there. Blessed be the dimwits! The school was a tonic! Phil and I, the eternal twins, were separated at last and no longer had to endure endless comparisons, which spared us all kinds of mutual aggro. My grades went through the roof and I was all set to don a smart suit, shirt and tie, start work at a posh office at sixteen, meet a nice girl at eighteen, get married at twenty-one, leave home, start a nice family of my own and finally shake off the terror of my father. I loved the little makeshift wooden building with its handful of classes. A place safe enough to dream of a bright future, a school where you could do nearly all your homework on the premises. The man who taught me English and bookkeeping was a good-natured Indo with horn-rimmed glasses, the kind of man I would have loved to have as a father. Mr Van Engelenburg was his name. *Engel* means angel, and that's what he was.

The morning of 26 November 1964 was glorious. A gentle sun low in the sky. Autumn leaves lining the curb. A windless calm. I breathed in the fresh air and seemed to grow taller. My classmates were the docile kind; we were well-behaved pupils. I was only ever goaded into one fight. Luckily, my first blow missed my opponent by a whisker, and he made a show of falling and stayed down. In those days, that was that: you stayed down and it was over. Now they kick each other half to death. I have no idea why we were so determined to fight each other. Friction between Hollanders and Indos no doubt. The cheeseheads versus the wogs. Nothing racist about it. Rivalry is all about equality, racism is the opposite.

At school we all had to share an old-fashioned wooden desk with a fellow pupil. My deskmate was a mild-mannered Indo boy called

Ricky. We hit it off immediately. His lean face and troubled eyes are etched into my brain. It was almost ten in the morning. At ten past, the school bell would announce a twenty-minute playground break. There was an unexpected knock, the classroom door inched open and Mr Van Engelenburg was summoned in a whisper. We looked up from our textbooks in momentary surprise and then went back to work. Less than a minute later, Mr Van Engelenburg returned and came straight to my desk. He leaned over me, told me to pack my bag and report to the headmaster.

Without a backward glance, I slunk out of the classroom with my schoolbag over my shoulder. The headmaster was waiting in the corridor and told me I was to fetch my little sister Nana and take her over to Arti's school. I left the building, walked to the bicycle racks and carefully strapped my bag to the back of my bike. The school bell rang just as I was about to cycle off. I looked back and saw my friend Ricky come charging out of the building only to stand at the top of the steps looking lost. Despite the distance, he held out his hand and stood there as if paralysed. He wanted to call out, but nothing came. I wanted to call out to him, but nothing came. Classmates began to crowd around him and the strange thing was, no one came down those few steps towards me. They just stood there, looking in my direction without saying a word. I could think of nothing else to do but cycle away. I waved to Ricky and he waved back hesitantly. And though I had never said goodbye to anyone for life before, I felt that I was leaving him, leaving the others and that safe school building behind, and that I would never see them again.

When I reached Nana's school, she was already standing outside holding a teacher's hand. I couldn't sit her on the back of my bike. She was only six and my schoolbag was too heavy for her to hold. But the autumn day was pleasant, so I wheeled my bike along and she walked beside me. She kept looking up shyly and asking me where we were going. I told her it was a surprise.

Behind us a police car was driving at a snail's pace, stopping now and again to scan the surrounding streets.

The slave driver once punished me by making me run to and

from school every day, four times a day for three weeks: from Hoogveen to Genemuidenstraat in the morning, home again on the lunchbreak – where my mother was waiting with a sandwich for me to gobble down – then straight back to school and a final jog home at the end of the day. Some days he patrolled the route on his moped to make sure Phil hadn't secretly given me a lift on his bike. He rode past at an agonizingly slow pace without a glance in my direction, just to let me know he could appear anywhere at any moment, and he did, taking up concealed positions down side streets as if it was wartime. The police must have been tipped off, by my mother no doubt, that the Eagle was capable of showing up out of nowhere. Now, with my six-year-old sister at my side, I had no time to be afraid. I acted cheerful and she felt safe, even though I was constantly on the look-out and glancing back at the police car.

At the entrance to Arti's school, a teacher stood waiting with Aunty Fien, the same aunt who had opposed my parents' marriage from the start and who never came to visit, probably because my father could not stand her. We were led to a small meeting room that smelled of teachers, teachers and more teachers. Someone from the school was there to meet us, along with two police officers. Their caps were on the table. My mother, Phil and Arti were already there and my mother cried out in panic when she saw Mil was missing. Phil was ordered to go and fetch her. When all five kids were finally assembled, it was decided we would go into hiding at Aunty Fien's for the rest of the day and see what happened next.

I don't recall how we got to Aunty Fien's, all I remember is how beautiful she was. It struck me when we were in the living room at her house. In one supple movement, she reached down to take something out of her handbag on the floor without bending her knees. Through the veil of her long blonde hair I saw her breasts jiggle and a strange excitement came over me. Aunty Fien talked women's talk with my mother and together they puffed away at one cigarette after another. Ma told us we would be going to a safe-house for three weeks and then we would be able to come back home. The Eagle was to be thrown out of the flat, she said. I don't know if any of us felt sorry for him. I don't think we did. Perhaps Mil, his favourite, felt a secret pang, not of love but of regret: she had always been able to wind the Eagle round her little finger. We all sat there quietly, barely speaking a word to one another. There was no telephone and in those days there was nothing on TV during the day. More than anything, I would have liked to sit with one ear glued to the radio but I didn't dare ask Aunty Fien to turn it on. She kept us quiet with cakes and orange squash. Evening came and a taxi pulled up at the door. I had never been in a taxi before and I enjoyed the drive to a small town outside The Hague, a place I had never even heard of.

Voorschoten

My mother sat in front with the girls on her lap. The three of us were in the back. Just as I began to make out the shape of a spire, the driver said it was the Reformed Church in Voorschoten. It seemed a long way from The Hague, as if we had driven into an old Dutch picture book. The town was quiet and dark. We turned off Leidseweg and drove through the gates of a huge manor house with a driveway, a playing field and clumps of trees and bushes. The gravel crunched under the wheels of the black Mercedes. We pulled up at the bottom of a flight of wide steps and were welcomed by the head of the children's home, with a female teacher at his side.

The girls burst into tears when we found out the taxi was taking my mother straight back into hiding at Aunty Fien's. The teacher did her best to calm them. The three of us held it together, even when it became clear that the boys were to be separated from the girls.

In the boys' wing, Phil and I were shown to a common room full of older lads. Arti was sent to a room at the back of the building with boys our age. I assumed this unfortunate arrangement was down to lack of space. Either that or they didn't want three brothers sticking together. The lads surrounding Phil and I all looked years older, and some of them were even smoking. The oldest eyed us with suspicion and disdain. It was after eight and coffee was being served. I had never drunk coffee before but didn't dare refuse the plastic cup that was handed to me.

The group leader, a man of around forty, asked us if we'd had anything to eat.

Phil and I looked at each other.

That told the group leader all he needed to know and he had sandwiches brought over from the kitchen in the girls' wing. White bread sandwiches. They tasted good. The other boys protested because they had been made to eat brown bread at breakfast and they called over to us that from tomorrow it would be a different story. Phil and I took a timid look around at the ten boys we would be sharing a dorm with. At nine o'clock, orders were barked and the seventeen and eighteen-year-olds grumbled that it was too early for bed. Everyone took off their shoes and lined them up against the wall. We climbed the granite stairs on our stocking feet, past dorms where other boys were already sleeping.

Phil and I were issued with a flannel, a toothbrush, a tube of toothpaste, a small bar of soap and two towels, one of which we were only to use for our feet. The group leader showed us to our beds, where two pairs of pyjamas were waiting. Phil was given wash number 99, mine was 173. We would remember those stupid numbers our whole lives. When it came time to undress, we turned shyly to the wall, much to the amusement of the others, who showed no shame at being naked.

We still had a lot to learn, so we were told. The light went out and there was silence. The group leader disappeared into a little corner office at a diagonal to the rest of the room. A soothing glow filtered through a red curtain in the fanlight above the door. I lay awake for a long time wondering if, two chairs' width away, Phil was awake too. And if he, like me, was crying silently to himself.

Pleased to meet you

At five to seven in the morning, a small bulb nudges the dorm into half-light. At seven on the dot, the two big ceiling lights snap on and you are expected to be up on your feet immediately. Anyone still in bed is landed with extra chores. You strip your bed, wash at one of a dozen taps above two troughs in the washroom, get dressed and take your place at the breakfast table at twenty past – no sooner, no later. Most of the boys keep quiet, but the oldest are in a foul mood and they show it: moaning about the dense brown bread and having nothing but rosehip jam to spread on it, about the meagre slices of sweaty cheese and the lukewarm milk we drink from mugs stained brown by our afternoon tea and our evening coffee. The grouches mutter that they can't wait to finally see the back of this prison. Phil and I are stunned by their insolence. Our father would have knocked them from one end of the room to the other. But no one takes a beating in this place. Punishment here is different.

Four from our dorm, including Phil and I, attend the secondary school in Voorschoten, a twenty-minute walk away. The other eight bike to the technical college in Leiden and look down their noses at the 'four little piggies', as they mockingly call us. The school lacks the warmth of my modest clerical school in The Hague, but the pupils are nice enough and keen to get to know us. These are small-town kids, not city slickers. Phil and I are put in different classes. A girl in my class is the spitting image of French chanteuse Françoise Hardy. She inks her thighs with mathematical formulas come exam time and hides them under her miniskirt. No teacher dares inspect the evidence. She visits us all in our dreams.

One Friday evening, the head of the children's home drives us to Leiden, where the owner of a gents' outfitters opens his shop specially, locking the door behind us. With no other customers around, he is free to give us a hefty discount. He measures us up for Sunday suits. The next day, a female group leader takes us into town to buy a pair of weekday shoes and a smart pair for Sundays.

We are delighted, but the older boys scoff and tell us we should have insisted on something more fashionable, the winkle-pickers all the rock stars are wearing. Their rebellious streak is lost on us and, proud as peacocks, we put on our Sunday best to attend the ten o'clock service. We are all given two five-cent coins for the collection. I see two Ambonese brothers from school put two-and-a-half guilder notes into the collection bags, looking around to make sure the godly Dutch parishioners have taken note of their generosity.

In church, the girls from the home sit in the pews to the left of the aisle and the boys to the right. The girls are not allowed to wear the miniskirts worn by the girls from my class, girls who avoid church like the plague and spend their Sunday mornings in bed. We sit in pairs, just as we walk through the streets two by two. Gone are the days when hordes of orphans dressed in black were herded through the streets, marked out by an emblem on their chest. Thanks to endless pleading by the oldest boys, our morning and evening prayers have been curtailed and the punishment for swearing has been reduced to being sent to the dorm or, if that's already occupied, to the shower room. Time was when swearing would have got you sent to borstal, a place called Valkenheide. The name strikes fear into all of us. One mention accompanied by the wag of a warning finger is enough to bring us into line. Someone even convinces us the place is named after a falcon that circles above the grounds, keeping a beady eye on every inmate.

The children's home is a place of rules, written and unwritten. Most of the unwritten rules have been instituted by the boys themselves. Never ask why someone's in the home. There's a standard answer: 'Did I ever ask you that? Well, then…' Never grass on someone, even if it's you they're picking on. One day, they'll get you back. Never comment on an older boy's taste in music. Don't use fancy words when you talk to simpler lads from working-class backgrounds. If you hear someone wanking off in bed, play possum and ignore their heavy breathing. If someone sneaks over to the office door to spy on a female group leader, keep your mouth shut. If you're sent to the kitchen on an errand and someone gives you a note for one of the girls, don't come back with the news that you failed as a go-between. No one will believe you and, worse still, they'll think you read the message and suspect you of all sorts. If you check out another lad's dick in the showers, do it as surreptitiously as possible or you're 'bent as a corkscrew'. And so on and so forth.

It takes us a while to get used to showering in one of the eight open alcoves of the granite shower room and, looking back, there's something farcical about female group leaders in their early twenties walking around with a shampoo bottle and squeezing out the prescribed amount on your head. There are boys who swear out loud when a female group leader walks in, unless she's a looker… in which case there are those who will happily greet her with a full erection, provoking a curt command to turn around.

Our mother, sick with nerves, told us on arrival we would spend three weeks at this country estate. When she turns up for Sunday visiting three weeks later, Phil and I are waiting for her in the vestibule that separates the boys' wing from the girls' wing and functions as the only communal space. We are neatly dressed, in complete accordance with institutional guidelines: dark suit, immaculately starched white shirt, tie, Sunday socks and shoes. After church in the morning, it's compulsory to wear your tie all day on Sunday.

Our mother enters and holds out her hand.

'Hello there, how are you doing?'

This is odd. I have never shaken my mother's hand before. It's as if she's introducing herself to us. She tells us how handsome we look in our Sunday suits and asks if we knotted our ties ourselves. And even before Arti and the girls have joined us in our day room, she asks us if we'd mind staying at the home a while longer. Three months at most.

Phil and I shake our heads, happy to be free of the Eagle's brutal regime. I can barely stand the thought of seeing our flat on Zuider Park again. But Arti and Mil start to whimper when they find out. Nana doesn't make a sound. Our mother puffs on a cigarette and takes a look around. She strikes up a conversation with the young woman on duty as group leader, just as she always used to make conversation with the next-door neighbours out on the balcony. To us, she doesn't have much to say.

What we don't know is that our crazy father rides past her house every night on his moped. Early on the evening of 26 November, detectives removed him from our home but not before he smashed the place up. He has lost all rights to his property, but he insists that the trunk that accompanied him on his voyage from Java to Holland is sent on.

The chain-smoking woman racked by nerves stares out at the bare treetops during the darkest days of the year. She sees him again, at the other side of the road, riding slowly past Doornenbos hill in Zuider Park, and ducks out of sight below the windowsill. A short time later she hears him ride up the street in front of the flat. He stops but does not ring the doorbell. The next morning she finds an envelope in the letterbox. It contains a drawing in East Indian ink; he must have drawn it at work. A burial mound bearing six crosses, one for each of us and one for him. That leaves one person in an unmarked grave beneath the soil, our mother, in a coffin or then again perhaps not. The madman's creative juices are flowing; he returns every day with a variation on the same theme. Our mother keeps the drawings and hands them to her social worker, who puts them in a file. The idiot has no idea that with each drawing he is digging his own grave, undermining his ongoing battle with Child Services and the endless series of court cases he will bring against his former heffalump. Perhaps he doesn't care. Or is this a course of action they would have understood back in Surabaya, a clumsy attempt at *guna-guna*? The fishwife believes the madman is trying to drive her insane, to convince her that she does not belong with 'us'.

The raven's tale

No one from the neighbourhood or from our schools knew where we were. At most there were whispers that we had been taken to a secret address, off the Eagle's radar. He had lost all rights to his former home and for him it was the start of a nomadic existence, moving from one dingy boarding house to the next.

A hypnotic silence enveloped the tenement flat on Zuider Park. Migrating birds ushered in a new, lonely winter for Mama Helmond, who spent days, weeks, months, seasons in a chair by the window puffing on one cigarette after another, only leaving the house for her daily shop. Should she see the lengthy divorce proceedings through or work towards a reconciliation? She continued to find drawings of six crosses on a burial mound in the letterbox, committed to paper ever more adeptly in East Indian ink by the Eagle. It made her think of his strange world of hocus pocus, of all those exotic letters in Malay and mysterious parcels of herbs that no longer found their way from Java to her front door.

The portrait of her Chinese mother-in-law from overseas no longer hung at the foot of the bed but had been taken away by a friend of the Eagle's, sent over to inquire after his trunk and a few personal items that were most dear to him.

Could that friend have been Matagora?

The outline of the picture frame was still clearly visible, a patch on the faded wallpaper, and the old woman's piercing eyes seemed to shine right through it. Until Mama Helmond was roused one night by a hint of a breeze and saw a raven swoop through the bedroom. A raven. She sat bolt upright, clicked on the light, stared at the patch on the wall and instinctively understood that the Chinese sorceress confined to her sickbed in distant Java had departed this life.

> I reminded Ma of this story, Pa. At first she said she didn't remember it at all. Then she thought for a moment and gave a different version. Weeks before she planned her escape

with the doctor and Aunty Fien, you had told it to her as a dream you'd had. So it was you, not her, who saw the raven fly through your bedroom. But that's not all… your mother didn't die until one year later, devastated by the collapse of our family according to my sister Nana, who heard it from Ma. So the raven was not a harbinger of your mother's death but of your own divorce. Or the bird brought tidings of your mother's illness. Ma, every bit as superstitious as you are, must have seen your mother's weakness as a sign that she no longer had to remain spellbound and married to you. That's what she had always believed: that some magic power emanating from your mother kept holding her back from divorcing you. Now I want to know once and for all which of you saw the raven flying through your bedroom. Ma's memory is a fickle thing. Lying comes easily to her, I'm afraid, a complaint that regularly escaped your lips.

'The woman's lying!'

Maybe so, but in your universe everyone's a liar. I think it's time I finally came to visit you, so we can put that raven to rest. If that won't do, I'll settle for a discussion on racism, that eternal bugbear of yours. And if that doesn't cut it, we can listen to those old gramophone records you took with you to Spain.

No warning. I'll turn up on your doorstep unannounced. Perhaps then you'll be as happy to see me as you were that very last time in Haarlem, when I appeared out of nowhere and you welcomed me with open arms.

Liberated from the sorceress by a raven, our mother pulls up at the gates to the children's home in a Volkswagen camper van one Sunday afternoon in spring. She marches cheerily up the driveway, turns right and flounces along the pavement by the canal that leads to the vestibule. I stay behind in the day room and Phil goes to meet her. Through the matt windows, I watch their shapes disappear into the girls' wing. It's a good fifteen minutes before Phil returns and whispers in my ear that she has a boyfriend and that the head has given her permission to take us for a ride through the countryside of South Holland. A Sunday drive is an unheard-of luxury. Elated, we sprint down to the Volkswagen camper at the gate. There's a bed in the back, a gas stove and a big water bottle. The jovial man at the wheel introduces himself as 'Willem'. Our mother says we can call him 'Uncle Willem' if we like.

In walks a Chinaman...

It was like seeing him for the very first time. The way the average Dutchman saw him, no doubt: an Asian chap with a peculiar gait, slightly bent at the knees and crooked at the arm. Not upright but a little hunched, the weight of a mournful soul combined with the awareness of a fighter ready to spring into combat mode at any second, to lash out with speed and precision. Three months it had taken for the authorities to grant him permission to visit his children. We had been sounded out on more than one occasion by the head of the children's home in all his earnestness – a man who displayed an endless admiration for psychologists and did his best to imitate them. Surrounded by so many people and with the police station only a playing field away, we felt safe enough for a reunion.

First, my father went to see the head in his office. Then we were summoned from our respective day rooms for a reunion that took place in the long, dimly lit corridor in the girls' wing. He did not know whether to shake us by the hand or hug us, so he patted us awkwardly on the shoulder, stammering sentences he could not finish, close to tears. It transpired that the thug had missed us terribly, in contrast to his victim and her formal handshake.

The thug has lost something, lost touch with something. He is a boxer who stands defeated in the ring. No need for him to introduce himself to anyone at the children's home: everyone can see he is our father. And everyone nods at him with remarkable courtesy. Is it because the boys think Indos of his generation are indomitable fighters? Or do they simply see nothing unhinged behind his charming façade, his madness unseen by almost everyone who meets him for the first time?

'Such a charming fellow.'

'Handsome chap, that father of yours.'

'What a nice father you have!'

Our day room, Phil's and mine, is earmarked for what my father will call 'the reunification'. It is not a genuine reunion, nor will it ever be. For years he will fight court case after court case to get his children back and lose every last one of them. That day, the day we see him again, is a day without fear. We feel protected by a platoon of social workers behind the scenes, and by the proximity of the people who keep the home running, the folk we call group leaders, though to them we are nothing more than a job. Men and women with whom we will never form a bond because they can disappear from one month to the next and never work more than five days in a row or a weekend. And so later, when you go in search of yourself, there is no one who can tell you what you were like back then.

It must have been a Saturday. I glean this from one of the few photos to survive the vengeful farewell of my father's second wife, Eva. We are wearing our weekday clothes. My father has obtained permission to see us outside the traditional Sunday visiting hours so that he and my mother can keep out of each other's way. Many of the kids spend the weekend with one of their parents, so the dayroom is quiet. My father must have handed his camera to someone else, because all six of us are in the photo. Who would that have been? Another leftover boy with a talent for photography?

In the corner of the day room is a storage bin we chuck our bags into when we come home from school. A couple of benches have been nailed to the front, facing each other at a ninety-degree angle. The rectangular cushions are made of foam rubber and covered in grey plastic. When it's quiet in the day room, I put the radio on the storage bin, nestle in a corner with my legs tucked under me and listen to the Top 40 from two till four. I barely have any competition: none of the others can keep still long enough to listen to two solid hours of radio. The rest of the lads would rather be playing snooker, shuffleboard or ping-pong.

My father spoils my fun with his first visit. In the photo, the radio is nowhere to be seen. Arti is sitting on the spot it would have occupied. He has one leg pulled up in front of him, hands clasped around his knee. He is sitting upright, his left foot on the bench where I am sitting, my elbows resting on my knees, chin cupped in my hands. My father is sitting on the other bench, slightly hunched under the weight of Mil, who is perched on the storage bin with her legs hanging over his shoulders. Little Nana is on the floor between the legs of the man whose wrath she alone escaped. Next to my father, on the far right, sits Phil.

I am looking straight into the lens with an expression that blends surprise with dreamy disillusion. Arti's sad face belies his princely pose. Mil has her arms crossed and gives a cheeky little smirk. Nana's gaze is inscrutable. Phil is flaunting the house rules with a cigarette in his left hand, blowing smoke through his nostrils and raising his eyebrows defiantly at the cameraman. The only one avoiding the lens is our father. He gazes pensively across the black lino towards an uncertain future or a ghost-ridden past. Out of all of us, he has the greatest flair for drama, no doubt about it.

I am wearing jeans and a baggy shirt from the clothing depot at the home, cuffs unfastened, sleeves drooping. Arti is wearing jeans, a shirt and a pullover, Mil a Norwegian jumper and tight trousers. Nana has a white hairband. Phil is wearing a shirt under a sweatshirt. Our father is dressed to the nines, in a white shirt, tie and jacket. A version of him we have never seen before.

A snow-covered street peeps through the corner window behind Arti and Mil. Three months have passed, give or take, since 26 November 1964. It must be the fag end of February 1965, the year in which our father will turn forty. We have found our feet at the children's home. We have made friends and learned to give our enemies a wide berth though we occupy the same space. I do not think much was said that afternoon. What is there to say about something so broken?

Abode unknown

Hey, Pa, at the time we had no idea where you were living. We forgot to ask, or it never even occurred to us. All we knew was that you'd ended up in a bedsit somewhere. You sent us a letter, a censored version of which was read out to us by the head, who then cut it into snippets and tossed it in the waste paper basket. Enclosed were two copies of a colour photo of you: one for the girls and one for the boys. Taken with a self-timer, it shows you sitting in that typical Indo or Indonesian squat, wearing pyjamas of course like all Indos of your generation did around the house, a habit inevitably misunderstood by those prissy Hollanders, especially the ladies. In the foreground, the metal frame of a hospital bed edges into the photo. I hate those beds; to this day, they make me think of death. An Airfix kit, still in its box, sits on the windowsill in the background of your messy room. Behind your hunched, resigned figure is a stack of cases with a soup bowl on top, which you insisted on calling a 'mug'. A handful of books are piled on cheap shelves hanging from nails on the wall. On the top shelf, there's a radio and on the radio is a picture frame turned away from the lens. Your mother's portrait, most likely. She had less than six months left to live and would die in October of a broken heart, at least that's how you put it. It was Nana who came up to me in the corridor of the boys' wing and told me she had passed away, news I greeted with indifference… To the right of the photo are the contours of a wooden rack. And there's a chair. That's all. Your striped pyjamas make you look like a convict. I can't remember if I thought you deserved to be pitied. But looking at your image now, that was the impression you wanted to give.

With palpable reluctance, the head dipped his fingers into the envelope that had contained the letter deemed largely unsuitable for us, fished out your photo and handed it over. I still have it and no… I still cannot pity you.

The days, the weeks, the months

My parents squabble via lawyers and an agreement is reached. My father is allowed to come and see us every third Saturday afternoon and my mother every Sunday afternoon. Not only does this ensure that they never meet but also that my father, as the main culprit, takes second place. On the Saturdays when the Eagle does not come to call, I keep myself amused in the company of the other leftover weekend kids. There aren't many of us. We hang out in the hobby room, which is off the day room and next to the washing-up room. This den of ours isn't as squeaky clean as the day room. It is home to a workbench with a vice and a toolbox for doing woodwork, but mostly we just spin records there. Sometimes Phil livens things up: we pinch roof slates from the carpenter's shed and he breaks them down the middle with his forehead. He wins bets by performing this trick on ever thicker stacks of slates and earns the respect of the older boys.

The portable record player has two speeds, but the clapped-out belt drive slows our 45s till our idols' voices slide down a notch and fray at the edges. With the aid of a rubber band, I manage to get them spinning at something like the right speed. Some weekends we're out of luck and one of the older lads sticks around, which means he rules the roost and decides which records do and don't get played. Phil takes no interest in music, so he is no help at times like this.

The last of his cohort, the older lad is big and strong and brooks no contradiction. He is also the proud owner of two drumsticks, which he wallops off the workbench for hours on end to gormless tracks by The Spotnicks, René and His Alligators and a slew of guitar bands who try to emulate The Shadows and fail miserably. His all-time favourite is 'Wipe Out' by The Ventures, a pale imitation of Indonesian rock pioneers The Tielman Brothers. His drumming drives us out of the den and into the day room, with its books by Simenon, Ian Fleming and a guy called Franz Kafka. Much of what he writes is lost on me, but I'm gripped by the way his stories chime with our black lino, the bunches of keys on the group leaders' belts and the countless doors that may not be opened without permission.

My favourite door is the one on the first-floor toilet, where the dorms of the two younger groups are located. That toilet is for group leaders only and it's always clean. Sometimes a leader forgets to lock the door and I can sneak in and sit on the wooden toilet seat at my leisure. Not that I have a chance to read. Ten minutes' absence is usually enough to get you on the missing list. There are lads who have a go at me for reading books, though boys who read *Donald Duck* or *Panorama* are left in peace. The bullies all know a guy outside the home who sneaks a look at *De Lach*. When I admit I don't know what it is, they have a good laugh at my expense. In hushed tones, one boy lets me know it's a car magazine with a topless centrefold. 'Guys say they buy it for the cars but the first thing they do is take out the middle pages, pin them on the wall and wank off staring up at those titties. *De Lach* says 36-24-36 are the perfect measurements. That's bust, waist and hips. But you're still too young for all that stuff.'

The powers that be also reckon I'm too young to opt out of one of the home's annual traditions: Drenthe Time, a three-week summer outing. The school holidays are just around the corner and since I won't be fourteen until the end of the dog days, I am one of a hundred or so kids packed off on the train to the sleepy province of Drenthe. Arti goes too, so do the girls. For some reason Phil is exempted. Perhaps it's to do with his weekly sessions with the psychologist in an octagonal room in the girls' wing, a bid to temper his aggressive outbursts.

Each with our own suitcase, we travel to The Hague and board a green train reserved especially for us. The girls and the younger kids pile into the front carriages, most of them happy and excited. Us lads are less enthusiastic and occupy the rear of the train. Arti and I stare dreamily out of the window and hardly say a word as the Dutch landscape races past. Once or twice we gauge each other's curiosity about our host families. The train speeds along without stopping until we hit Drenthe, where it calls at every station. Children alight and are picked up by their host families. Arti gets off in Meppel, and a few stops down the line I wave my sisters goodbye from the open window and travel on, all the way to Assen. There I am met by a couple who have a son my own age. The boy is called Jochem. I've never met a Jochem in Voorschoten or The Hague and I decide it's a yokel name. I introduce myself politely and take my place on the back seat next to Jochem. I answer his parents' perfunctory questions in simple sentences and look out at a landscape of woods and low hills. Happily, the car radio is on, but just as The Rolling Stones come crackling through the speaker with '(I Can't Get No) Satisfaction', my host switches it off and leaves me bereft.

We arrive in a little town called Gieten and pull up outside a neat house with a neat front and back garden. Jochem's dad does me the honour of carrying my case from the boot of his shiny car. Inside, the house smells of furniture polish and the potted plants are gleaming. My neater than neat bedroom on the first floor is as big as the living room of our flat on Zuider Park, where my mother now lives alone, and where, as I find out later, she receives regular visits from her lover Willem, who then returns to his wife, a housebound schizophrenic living in constant fear of another German invasion.

The food dished up at the Drenthe family home takes some getting used to, not to mention the deathly silence at the dinner table and the gleaming radio, which sounds great but is only ever turned on when it's time for the news. Jochem does his best to keep me entertained. We play badminton in the back garden and take a walk through the town where he introduces me to his friends, who eye me suspiciously. When they slip into their local accent, I can't understand a word they're saying. One evening the master of the house takes me and Jochem for a drive to the Hondsrug nature reserve, stopping along the way to enjoy the view. Night falls and we turn back. Our headlights illuminate the asphalt road, deserted as far as the eye can see. All I want is to drive on aimlessly for hours, days, weeks, months, to drive for the sake of driving, till you don't know where you came from or where you are going.

Out of nowhere, a giant bird swoops down from the treetops and into the beam of the headlights, flying straight at us. Before it shoots upwards, its wide-open eyes look straight through me.

An owl, Jochem and his father note drily. But for me that encounter is up there with the meteor I saw whizzing across the night sky above Zuider Park and disappearing into nothingness.

When we get home, brand-new underwear is waiting for me on my bed, a string vest and pants, expensive and fashionable. I put them on the next morning and they feel wonderful. Jochem has a wardrobe full of clothes like that, but his life is boring. He doesn't have much to say for himself. I have plenty to say but not the kind of thing you tell anyone. You can tell them about the owl that almost grazed your car and looked you straight in the eye. You can tell them about the huge meteor glowing white above Zuider Park, but you can't tell them about the father who beat you. And Jochem's not a boy you can talk girls with. He's a year younger than me and for him too a summer excursion is on the horizon. He is going to a camp in his own province and I get to go with him for a holiday within a holiday.

It's a camp for boys and girls. We stay at a youth hostel, take long walks, have picnics in the meadow, toast French bread on sticks above the campfire and play asinine games. I am more interested in the youth leaders who keep an eye on us, the men and the women. I seek out their company so that I can talk about life. When I unexpectedly ask one of the guys if he's in love with one of his female colleagues, he answers with an astounded 'yes'. He calls her over, they hug each other and announce that they are planning to get engaged. They ask me about my life in Voorschoten.

The following day, something odd happens. We are out on a walk when the boys and girls suddenly pick up the pace until everyone is walking ahead of me. One by one they turn to face me, give me a look of utter contempt and walk on, laughing and whispering to each other. Jochem is among them. He does not come back and join me. The prettiest girl of the bunch seems to be the ringleader and that's what hurts the most. A little while later, all thirty of them turn and look at me again, that blonde, proud, beautiful girl at their centre. I stop in my tracks and have no idea what to do with myself. All I know is that I have been banished from the group.

The fiancés-to-be come to my rescue, reminding the whole company of the importance of comradeship, even with the 'strangers' among them. The boys and girls look ashamed, lower their eyes and as the walk continues they gradually allow me back into their midst. The pretty blonde girl even comes and walks beside me, though she doesn't say anything. Is their exclusion perfunctory? Is it because I'm too friendly with the group leaders? Because I'm a city boy? Surely it can't be because I'm the only one with black hair and brown eyes? This is a culture that's unknown to me. At home we always spoke the truth, no matter if it led to a fight. At the children's home, the talk is even tougher. Speaking your mind is not hurtful. At most, it's annoying for the other person. But silently excluding someone from the group with a stare and without a single word, strips them of the right to defend themselves.

Back in Gieten, I return to the monotony of breakfast, lunch, dinner and time spent hanging around with boys I can barely understand. I yearn for the end of Drenthe Time.

On the last day I am given another new set of underwear to take with me. And an invitation for next year. But I won't be back. Even if they drag me kicking and screaming into that train, I'll force open the doors and make a run for it. No longer a sad little care home boy, but a hero.

Guitar Indo (4)

The Eagle has plans, spends night after night writing letters to the authorities. He is none too happy about our mother extending our stay in Voorschoten. Phil and I have a secret: we are glad we don't have to go home. Without fully realizing it, we have freed ourselves from both our parents. The other three are still too young to take that inner step.

One day my father turns up with a brand-new guitar for my forthcoming birthday. Red with black trim. I hang it above my bed with pride. On my birthday I am sent upstairs for punishment, I forget why. It must have been some sarky comment about the way things are done, the 'guidelines' we have to live by. One of the oldest boys sticks up for me and has a go at the female group leader who exerted her authority. He says it's a disgrace to banish a guy to the dorm on his birthday. I'm not even allowed to play my guitar, not that I can play much. The boy feels sorry for me and sneaks upstairs to take a few snapshots. We push open the door to the fire escape. It's glorious summer weather and I sit down at the top of the aluminium staircase with my guitar, my first guitar, between my legs, hands cupped around the headstock. I look every inch the birthday boy – white trousers, shirt and waistcoat – but there's no smile for the camera. Smiling is for posers. None of my favourite rock stars crack a smile, they look out into the world like it can go fuck itself. I act like I don't give a flying fuck about my birthday. And it's true, I honestly don't give a fuck. I have a guitar. At last.

I had to hang my guitar on the wall above my bed in the dorm to keep it out of the clutches of the barbarians in our group. But guitars don't belong on walls: they wilt, dry out, turn into a castrato who's had his tongue pulled out for good measure. The rules on homework and domestic duties were so strict that I barely had the chance to strum my childhood dream on a daily basis. And for every half-hour practice session in the dorm I had to submit a request to the head through the group leader on duty, and they couldn't always leave the day room unattended to deliver my request to the head's office over in the girls' wing.

One evening, Danny paid us a visit. He was a long-haired Indo boy from the town, who wore frayed jeans and a denim jacket with a Union Jack sewn on the back. This was a special occasion. Hardly any boys or girls from Voorschoten called in to see us. Most parents assumed we were in the home because we were no good. But Danny treated us with respect and played exceptionally good guitar, so good that even the head came over to hear him play.

Danny could sing too. He knew whole Dylan songs off by heart, played The Beatles' hits better than they did and even managed to get a tune out of my guitar when two of the strings snapped. After he came to call, my guitar sang like a harp. Danny was my hero, a cut above any rock star you could name.

When I asked him how he was able to play on four strings, he told me it was a matter of tuning. He fiddled with the pegs till the guitar was in Hawaiian tuning.

'You know *kroncong*, right?' he asked with a grin, a sly one because it was a style that had long since gone out of fashion.

I dodged the question and asked if he could play Indo rock.

'Sure,' he said. 'The old Indos play like *this*... But nowadays we play like *this*...'

Danny's preferred mode of communication was the guitar. He was fifteen when his band laid down their first track and made the local papers. But the real challenge was making sure the band, two Indos and two Hollanders, stayed together. The bands that followed all went the same way. His bandmates couldn't understand him. His musicality knew no bounds, he became harder and harder to keep up with, till eventually he left everyone behind.

Care home boy

Like all the others, I have found my place among the lads in Voorschoten. I have become a care home boy, unfit for family life forevermore. We are brought up by group leaders, male and female, most of whom move on after a year. We meet. We say goodbye. The people who raise us are legion. Boys come and go. Girls appear, girls disappear. There are pupils – that's our official title – who are sent packing after only a week, who do not fit our care home culture. They are too aggressive, gifted or disturbed, there's too much of the Amsterdammer or the homosexual in them. We have no idea where they might feel at home or where they are sent.

On Fridays, we take fifteen cents and go down to the evening market in the town to buy waffle crumbs. One night, the oldest boys get into a fight with a bunch of locals who call them 'scum from the kids home'. Punches fly. I steer clear of trouble and keep my mouth shut when we are interrogated on our return.

They line up the twelve of us under a stark ceiling light in the day room. The head in his standard-issue blue suit paces to and fro, repeating the same question: which of us troublemakers were involved in the punch-up at the market? The interrogation lasts for half an hour. Then sentence is passed. All weekend leave is cancelled.

The next day we are sent out into the grounds with rakes, to the town square with brooms, and up and down the corridors with mops. The television is unplugged and we are packed off to bed at the weekday time of nine o'clock. Then all hell breaks loose. One lad curses another for not keeping his hands to himself at the market. The fighter tells his accuser to shut his gob. A scrap breaks out in the washroom. Everyone flees the scene and heads for the dorm, knowing these lads are too big and strong to be held back. Even the head, summoned by our cries for help, can't separate them. By the time a hastily mustered troop of male staff arrives, the washroom is red with blood. The brawlers are overpowered, trussed up and dragged off, one to solitary confinement, the other to the shower room.

Two days later, both have disappeared. Without a sound. It's eerie the speed at which boys can vanish from our midst, gone before we know it. Weeks pass before we find out they've been dispatched to the place we all fear: the borstal at Valkenheide. The following week it's quiet at the dinner table. Order and discipline have been restored with a vengeance.

But we learn to forget quickly. With October comes a local holiday and we head to Leiden without a penny in our pockets to watch other people celebrate what we don't have the means to celebrate ourselves. The autumn break is a drag. Trysts with girls from the other wing fall through when the group leaders catch on and take it in turns to patrol the woods. My fingers hurt from mastering my first guitar chords. The strings are too far from the fingerboard, but at the time I have no idea that more expensive guitars are far easier to handle.

The best times are to be had at school, beyond the gates of the home. I swap guitar chords from chart hits with the local boys. The Christmas holidays are lonely, but at least it's quiet in the den and I get to play my first LP over and over, a birthday present from the home. I am mesmerized by The Kinks' hollow guitar sounds. The muffled strains of Gene Pitney and Roy Orbison filter through from the girls' wing.

On New Year's Eve, Phil, Arti and I join a few other leftover boys to watch a pathetic firework display light up the sky above the steeples of the churches we hate so much. There are three in all: Dutch Reformed, Presbyterian and Catholic. The canals and ditches have frozen over, and the rink over by the Vliet is open. We take to the ice on our Frisian skates – wooden blades that keep slipping out from under our shoes – while the prettiest girls pirouette on immaculate white figure skates and the local toughs race around on hockey skates. Then the rain sets in. Not a drop of wine to be had. Back at the home, we shake one another by the hand and it's 'Happy New Year!' and off to bed. I lie awake until the church clock strikes two and the group leader on duty, a blonde of 23, returns from The Club, a cosy lounge for senior leaders over in the girls' wing. I creep over the cold lino to the duty office and spy on her through the keyhole. The glimpses of her breasts are fleeting and cherished. When I think of them, my bed gets warm and there's not a mother in the whole wide world I miss. Only the beautiful woman who is not lying next to me. I've heard there are children's homes where everyone has their own room and even a key or a bolt to lock it with. Where you can lie down for a while when you get in from school.

Weekend in The Hague

One weekend, we, the boys, all three of us, are allowed out to visit our mother. Every time we see her, she continues to greet us with an outstretched hand.

'Well boys, how are you all doing?'

Can we expect a handshake this time, too? What reason could she have for coming over all ladylike?

'Hey, boys! How's life treating you? Ha ha ha!'

That question comes courtesy of Uncle Willem. A decent bloke who knows a bit about life. All my mother knows is her clean kitchen counter. And the abuse she took, that too.

With a heavy heart, I climb onto the bus behind Phil and Arti. In The Hague, we take Tram 9 to the far edge of Zuider Park. It takes ages to get there, a long ride back into a dismal past. This time our mother doesn't introduce herself at all but greets us with the news that she's just cleaned the house so we'd better not make a mess. We barely recognize our room, so much of our stuff has disappeared. The mantelpiece has been painted white, as if memories can be blotted out by a thick coat of emulsion. Our mother shoos us out to play with our old neighbourhood friends again. Phil and

Arti don't hesitate, but I settle down in the basket chair by the window, overlooking Zuider Park. I am fourteen but I feel old. My exasperated mother exclaims that I'm turning into a recluse, she won't stop banging on about it. Why can't she just leave me in peace?

'Where's my radio, Mam?'

'Sold it. I needed the money.'

But my drawings from school are gone too. Nor do I see anything that belonged to Phil or Arti.

'What do I want with that junk of yours?' she snaps.

She sold it all off, dirt cheap. Even my stamp collection, my precious stamps with postmarks from the war years, the one hobby I shared with my father. It's as if she was determined to tidy us away as well. She doesn't feel like cooking and come dinner time she sends us to the chippy.

I look into my mother's eyes and feel a strange, sudden fear. I no longer recognize her, it's someone else I see. It is different to the fear my father instilled in me. I see traces of another madness in her eyes, or years of revulsion that have finally surfaced. Perhaps it's the worst thing that can live inside my mother: a heartfelt loathing of her own Indo children. I panic and run for the door, down the stairwell, across the road and into the park. God knows where I'm heading – anywhere as long as it's away from that wretched flat where Phil slept with a knife under his pillow in the days before we were taken away.

My brothers find me on an old wooden bridge in Zuider Park, one of our boyhood haunts. I tell them I'm not going back inside, that they'll have to call the home. Our mother gives them twenty-five cents and we go in search of a phone box. Phil does the talking. Late that afternoon, the head turns up in person to collect me in his own car. Phil and Arti wave me off and my mother looks on desperately from the balcony she once swept clean of our beloved birds' nest.

The head is a stern man, strait-laced and averse to personal questions. The one thing he says as he drives me back to Voorschoten is that we are under no obligation to visit our parents. And vice versa.

Island

When the summer holidays arrive, the head summons me to his office. The lanky figure in the blue suit, red tie and black shoes picks up the receiver of his Bakelite telephone and starts calling around to find me a job. Peeling flower bulbs on the outskirts of Voorschoten? No. Working at the paint factory on the other side of the railway tracks? No. He doggedly continues his search and finally gets a 'yes'. From a dog food factory in Valkenburg. It means getting up at six in the morning. I cycle to the factory with another boy from my group, where we are paid to do all kinds of odd jobs. The cycling is the best part. On the way there, at least, when the world is still sleeping. On the way back, we're worn out and car after car zooms past us. It's so late by the time we get home that we're stuck with the leftovers from dinner.

There's a girl who works in the packing department at the dog food factory, an Indo girl who is nearly sixteen. I am nearly fifteen. She's pretty and she's nice. What does she see in me? A little brother or a guy she could fancy? A lad from a good school works there too. Tall, smart and well-read, he makes a big impression on me, with his deep voice and his mop of sandy curls. If only he were in the children's home with us. At least then I'd have someone to talk to about books and music. When I return to work after a day off sick, Curly says to me, 'I missed your dynamic presence around here yesterday…'

I'm pleased to hear it, but I have no idea how I come across to other people. All I know is that beyond the home and beyond Voorschoten, the world is a different place. No place for me. The early starts wear me down and after two weeks I throw in the towel. The only thing I really miss is the Indo girl from packing. She kisses me to sleep each night with those beautiful lips of hers, until she fails to materialize one night, then two, then three… then a whole week… What was her name again? Where does she live? There's no point wondering. The very idea of a girlfriend from outside the home, from outside Voorschoten, is absurd.

I manage to save up enough money to spend a week at a youth hostel on the sleepy little island of Ameland, a trip arranged by the head. Train and bus take me as far as Holwerd, where I board a boat along with a bunch of other kids my age from all over the country. I get seasick on the short crossing and feel like a wimp. What follows is a long, sunless week on a cold, deserted, wet and windswept island. There's nothing to do but walk and walk and walk. And, circling the island on foot, there's nothing to see but dunes, grass and birds that don't interest me in the slightest. The islanders are friendly enough but not in the least curious. It's like they live on a reservation. We spend our evenings at the youth hostel in thrall to a blond chap with a Christian look about him, a gifted guitarist with the entire Top 40 at his fingertips. We sing along. With him around, I hardly miss the radio and the record player but he's not an easy man to access. He gets so much attention from the girls that I never get the chance to ask him for guitar tips. The evening rambles suit me better than our outings in the mornings or afternoons. We carry torches and move through the landscape like figures in a shadow play. A blonde girl from Haarlem walks beside me for a while. She introduces herself as Kristel and has a sharp, witty way about her. She wears glasses and sports one of those cool sixties hairdos with symmetrical locks that curl towards the corners of her mouth. I am reminded of the female teachers back in Voorschoten. It's the summer of '66, but we are all bundled up in jumpers and anoraks. One night, a couple of pals and I are caught by the hostel warden trying to sneak back in after a disastrous hunt for a decent pub. It's past midnight and, brandishing a pitchfork, he chases us into his barn, where we get to spend the night among the hay and the rats by way of punishment. Kristel listens to my tale of woe the next day and asks me schoolmarmish questions about my conduct. During one of the evening walks, she slows right down until she's at the tail end of the group, where I've been strolling along waiting for her. 'I don't do tongues,' she says, just so I know. My first kiss with her is the same as my first ever kiss, in the bushes round the back of the home with a leggy girl who was a year older than me. Kristel has twice the brains of that care home girl and is doubtless on her way to straight As at the grammar school she attends. The letters she writes me in the weeks that follow come without spelling mistakes and sometimes require the aid of a dictionary, which means I have to knock on the door of the governor's house over by the lake. The man limps over to his bookcase, pats me on the shoulder and limps me to the door to show me out. His dog limps too. They say he had polio and that he once served in the police force.

Years later, during a reunion at the home, the governor tells me that he used to work as an immigration official, charged with arranging the reception of repatriates from the Indies. That he sat at a desk somewhere in The Hague stamping forms. That among the repatriates were people with no passport and no proof of where they came from. On rare occasions, there were people who couldn't speak a word of Dutch.

'So what did you do with them?'

'We issued them with a residence permit and after that we gave them a passport. No point kicking up a fuss about that kind of thing. Didn't have the time. No one was ever sent back – it simply wasn't done.'

In other words, my father could well have run into Indonesian enemies in the back streets of The Hague. It wasn't just the stuff of nightmares…

In my letters to Kristel, I skirt around awkward questions prompted by the double house number in my address: 96–98 Leidseweg.

Eventually I have no choice but to tell her – to my shame – that I am a 'pupil' at a children's home. She writes back to tell me her father has no problem with that at all, that any shame lies with my parents and not with me, and that I am welcome to visit for the weekend. I don't dare ask the head, afraid he'll say no, but I set a date anyway, knowing that I won't be able to go through with it and I'm only making trouble for myself. One week later, Kristel sends me a letter listing all of her parents' preparations to make my stay a pleasant one. I can't bear to write back. I tear up all her letters and even her photo, afraid one of the other boys will find it. I curl up with the radio or kick a ball around the playing field, help the gardener and, when there's nothing left for me to do, I get permission to play my guitar up in the dorm. I am not allowed guitar lessons; the head is convinced that I won't stick at it. He doesn't like music, though he does like dancing. All a dancer needs is a beat, an endless loop of crash, bang, wallop. Melody is neither here nor there.

For the duration of the summer holidays, two groups are combined into one. That means Arti is in with us for a change. He too receives a guitar from our father, who continues to visit us faithfully, while Ma has gone off to Germany with Uncle Willem. The rough and ready man from Scheveningen is working on the construction of the Olympic stadium in Munich, and my mother makes coffee for the Dutch builders. The summer fades fast and for the first time we visit our father in Delft.

Weekend in Delft

Hey, Pa, I don't know how you remember this episode, but as I recall it went like this… After the arrival of a hefty German matron in your life – the first woman from your book of German contact ads to show willing – us boys were given permission to visit that flat of yours on Bosboom-Toussaintplein in Delft.

We set off in the afternoon and take a bus, then a train, then another bus and to top it all a lift to the twelfth floor. Despite the hair-raising heights, your flat is cosier than we could ever have expected, and you are astoundingly considerate and easy to get on with. Not that you have much choice. Lay one finger on us and there's every chance you'll never see us again. Frau Eva has two young kids from a previous marriage and an unfortunate habit of giving them a good hiding every now and then. But boy, can she cook. She serves up sandwiches as soon as we arrive: three slices of white bread piled with ham, cheese, tomato, lettuce, boiled egg, tomato ketchup and mayonnaise. An unbelievable treat compared to the dry brown bread at the home. You tell us that's all anyone eats in Germany, which is why Germans are all so fat. Frau Eva gets the gist and complains that you shouldn't talk about her countrymen like that. You grin, give her a Hitler salute and bark, '*Jawohl!*' We are familiar with your wicked sense of humour and remember all too well how little Ma appreciated it. I begin to doubt whether you and Eva are a match. Nevertheless, the three of us are happy with your matron, moaning non-stop about everything under the sun in her own peculiar mix of German and Dutch. She rivals Ma in the moaning stakes, but that's the only resemblance. Ma cannot cook. Ma has no desire to cook, none whatsoever. Ma hates cooking. She fries eggs with a dishcloth poised in one hand to wipe away the oil spatters. Frau Eva practically shoves those German goodies down our throats. Dinner consists of soup, fried potatoes, roast meat and all kinds of veg. Mayonnaise and ketchup, forbidden at the home, are staples on her table. Desert comes with lashings of cream. We spend at least two hours at the dinner table with the TV chattering non-stop in the background. At the home, television is restricted to Wednesday afternoons for the younger kids and Wednesday and Saturday evenings for us. The set is switched off at ten sharp by the head, who marches over from his office in the girls' wing to perform this task in person. There is no leeway. Even if the Wednesday whodunnit only has ten minutes left to run, we have to wait and find out the killer's identity from our classmates the next day. Your flat in Delft is a different world, Pa. The TV stays on till the final programme ends and the test card appears, accompanied by an ear-splitting whistle. Your turntable never stops spinning either. No one seems to mind that the record player and the TV are blaring away at the same time, not even you. Your typewriter no longer rattles through the evening and into the night. Your record collection is housed in special cases and even includes music I like to listen to: Manfred Mann, the Bee Gees, The Shadows. Your flat knows no official bedtime. While you are sound asleep, I sit with my feet up on the radiator listening to music and gazing out of the window. Far below, trains wind their way towards the lights of Rotterdam and I picture myself in one of those carriages, travelling far beyond the horizon to an unknown country, a place where I can dream like this, sitting and staring out of another window while my records play over and over. I sleep on the couch. The next day I stare out of the window at the trains again, listening to The Shadows and their melancholy guitars. Frau Eva is already busy in the kitchen and stuffs us so full of food that we can't help but laugh. Sunday flies by and you walk us to the bus stop, talking all the while about your battle with Child Services, your battle with Ma, your battle with the authorities, your battle with the head of the children's home, your battle against your alimony payments, against racism at work and a bunch of other stuff that means very little to us. Battles in which your dagger does not feature, thankfully. We will never see it in your hand again. Your weapon of choice is now your old pal the typewriter, which we will never hear again.

It's already dark by the time we get to Leiden. That's when things go wrong. We step aside politely to let an old lady board the bus ahead of us. Phil gets on after her and is still standing on the footboard as he drops the fare for our trip to Voorschoten into the tray. But the bus driver thinks our coins are the old lady's change. Phil begins to protest loudly, while the old lady insists the money is hers and takes her seat cool as you please. The dispute between Phil and the driver descends into slapstick: he jumps up, shoves the three of us off the bus and we end up flat on our backs on the pavement, Phil swearing blue murder as the bus roars off. Glum as can be, we stand there for half an hour waiting for the next bus to arrive. The extra pocket money Frau Eva slipped us as we left all goes on bus fare. We are already far too late when we come running through the gates to the home, and the head is standing there waiting for us in the vestibule.

No one believes our story and the head lets us know in no uncertain terms that it will be a good while before we get to spend another weekend in Delft.

You are a soldier at your typewriter. In his office, the head reads me censored versions of your letters, my privilege as your first-born child. I feel like a condemned man being read his sentence and can barely bring myself to listen – why can't you stop churning out these missives awash with venom, sarcasm and veiled self-pity? And it doesn't stop there: you stir things up so much that Eva – long patent leather boots, fur coat, lacquered hair piled high like candyfloss – ambushes Ma one Sunday afternoon and claws at her with those long, sharp nails of hers while you look on. Eva is furious at Ma for being such a bad mother: what kind of woman leaves her own children to rot in a cold, Calvinist children's home? But then what kind of ex-marine enlists his second wife to do battle with his first?

The intervals between Ma's visits grow longer and one day she turns up with Uncle Willem to take us out for another drive. Puffing on cigarettes in the passenger seat, Ma turns round every now and then to fire perfunctory questions at us. How are things at school? Have we been punished lately? Do we still have to go to church? Phil, Arti and Mil provide the answers. I say nothing. All I feel like doing is strumming my guitar, sitting on an upturned potato crate in the back of the van. Ma is only in a good mood when Uncle Willem is around, or so it seems. What your life is like, Pa, we have yet to discover. The weekends at your Delft high-rise are few and far between, but they continue to be one big party: we gorge on German sandwiches, red fruit wine, cakes, TV, LPs and the addictive view of the trains and the distant lights of Rotterdam, not to mention the complete absence of rules. I am always last to fall asleep so I can stare out of the window alone with no one to disturb my dreams of time creeping past in slow motion; with nothing happening, no one telling me what to do, what to think, what's expected of me; with no need to listen to someone else's opinion of me, how I behave, what I amount to.

I do not come to Delft for you. I come for Eva's cheese, ham and mayonnaise sandwiches, for her fried potatoes with sausage and ketchup, for your portable record player and the view of the railway tracks. And best of all: the chance to play your guitar. If only you had let me do that eight years earlier, man! You never ask us how we are, simply inform us that you have fired off epistle No. 125 or No. 133 to your umpteenth lawyer and that you will continue to fight the good fight until we are back home where we belong. But time rolls on like the trains far below the windows of your high-rise flat, which rocks gently when the gales blow. And not one of your three sons dares look you in the eye and tell you it's time you gave up on your letters and your court cases, because the last thing any of us want is to come back to you. Not that you would have listened.

The park

By the lake in the park in Voorschoten, there's a massive bench made of stone. The stone bench is where boys and girls meet after school. These rendezvous pass us 'four little piggies' by, because we have to stay for two hours after class to do our homework. Care home boys shower on Tuesday and Friday afternoons, and some teachers – either unthinkingly or for a laugh – call out halfway through the homework session, 'You lot can go home for your shower now.' Amid classroom sniggers, we pack up our shame in our schoolbags and make a hasty exit. The park is on our way home and we always make sure we take in the stone bench. It's usually deserted, but on the odd occasion we see older boys and girls hanging around, and God how we envy them: a room and a wardrobe of their own, the freedom to hang anything they like on their bedroom wall, parents who knock politely and don't just come barging in. Kids who can lie on their bed whenever they feel like it, a level of freedom unknown to us. Sometimes they sit there making out, look up for a second, then carry on right where they left off, while we blush and walk on by. I am fifteen, have yet to smoke my first cigarette, and do my homework like a good little boy. When I enter the day room, the lads from the technical college are already lounging around the coffee table slurping tea and munching on the crusts from the loaves the local baker delivers to our kitchen first thing in the morning. Those crusts are reserved for us and spread with butter and sugar as a surrogate for cakes or crackers. At five o'clock we are sent upstairs to get cleaned up, which we do at the long rows of taps above the troughs in the granite washroom, unless it's our turn to shower. Between five thirty and six we are left to cool our heels. We get bored easily and that's when most of the fights start. After dinner, if we're unlucky, there are household chores to be done. Exemptions are available to those who mop the corridors on Saturdays, sweep the square, clean the bike racks or rake the backyard. The best jobs are reserved for the gardener and the handyman. The gardener maintains the lake where the Maria House is situated: a separate building for foundlings. Some of those foundlings pass through every stage of the home: all three rooms as a young kid in the girls' wing, then two rooms in the boys' wing until they end up in the last room with us. By that time they've had dozens of carers and you can read it in their faces. I visit one of those boys years later, together with one of his former teachers, and he tells us bitterly how his father turned up on the doorstep on his twenty-first birthday – his first day of adulthood – to inquire how much money he had in his savings account.

*

No, given the choice, I'd rather have the Eagle, who turns up at the gate faithfully, promptly, and on his best behaviour. Now he even has permission to visit every other Saturday afternoon. One of the orphans, Rico, accompanies us on our outings. We buy beer, cola, crisps and cigarettes in the town and head over to the park. We give the stone bench a miss, whiling away the Saturday afternoons with our father on the three wooden benches on a mound that overlooks the lake. Frau Eva never joins him; in fact, we never see her again. Eventually we discover that she's done a runner and taken everything with her. The Eagle comes home from work one day to find the flat stripped bare, even the carpet and the lino gone, and, yes, when he opens the toilet door he finds the blackened bowl full of charred photos under a pile of her shit with a Dutch flag planted in it. One of those little flags from a souvenir shop. We have come to expect stories like this from him, but I cannot say that my father leads a strange life. No one at the home would say such a thing about their father or mother. It's our life that's strange.

In the world outside the home, divorce is taboo and a woman who works is pitied because her husband doesn't earn enough to put bread on the table. The head makes a weekly appearance to bore us senseless with talks on the workings of 'normal life', its rights and wrongs, and the etiquette that keeps everything ticking over as it should. What he means is that when we get out of this place we'd better not mess up like our parents did. His pearls of wisdom come straight from *Reader's Digest*. For our edification, he gets us to read *Het Parool*, an Amsterdam newspaper that says nothing about life in The Hague. We want to read about our own turf, about the battles between white gangs and Indo gangs, the Kikkers versus the Plu, rebels with girls in petticoats perched on the back of their souped-up mopeds. What do we care about wrinkly old Simon Carmiggelt and his wry sketches of life in the capital? Yes, the man can write and he was born in The Hague. But that only makes him a traitor for moving to Amsterdam, home to the head of our institution, a man who is a stranger to self-deprecation, and always determined to make someone else the butt of the joke.

One day he summons the family to his office, all five of us. He breaks the news as if he is reporting a crime: our father has had the temerity to rent a flat a mere fifteen-minute walk from the home. We take this announcement in our stride, not yet knowing it's the biggest blunder he could have made. In the eyes of Child Services, the Eagle had landed: a dodgy Chinaman with a shady past had infiltrated Voorschoten, a clear and present danger to peace and order at the home. Something would have to be done.

The band

It took a few years, but eventually I sussed out all the nooks and crannies of the children's home, knew exactly where and when I could give the group leaders the slip and have a sly smoke or enjoy a few stolen moments alone with a girl. The girls were housed in a converted eighteenth-century manor with a driveway long since buried beneath the playing field. In our day, a smaller gravel driveway led up from a green wrought iron gate on Leidseweg and stopped dead at a hidden square bordering on a grove behind which rose the steeple of the Catholic church so vilified by the head. The boys' wing was a perpendicular extension to the old manor and dated from the 1930s. The wings were linked by an asymmetric vestibule, which served as the main entrance for both the girls (to the left) and the boys (to the right). The broad stairs and marble foyer of the former entrance in the girls' wing were now reserved for distinguished visitors only. I had been a distinguished visitor once. It was through that entrance that I first set foot in this place on the 26th day of November in the year of our Lord 1964.

The stately main entrance gave way to a long, dingy granite corridor that ran past the kitchen, the scullery, the octagonal reception room, the three rooms for the girls and the boys under ten, and on to a courtyard at the back of the building. At the other end was the girls' cloakroom and around a corner to the left, a set of granite steps led down to the door between the wings, which was locked at nine every evening. Beyond that door lay the vestibule, with the boys' coat racks, a granite floor criss-crossed with cycle tracks, and the matt glass windows of my day room. A short hallway ran past a window on the left, overlooking a row of bike racks, then past the entrance to my day room on the right and arrived at the foot of the granite stairs to the boys' dormitories, before passing the storeroom entrance on the left and the second day room on the right to end at the day room to which Arti had been allocated. From the storeroom, a narrow passage led to the conservatory of the governor's house, which had its own driveway at the front and a lake at the back, teeming with fish. In winter, a fire crackled in his open hearth.

Older boys who had been at the home as long as they could remember never uttered the word 'storeroom' without pulling a face. True, the air there was stale and the shelves were piled high with bedclothes and hand-me-downs. The day after we arrived, Phil, Arti and I were sent to the storeroom for clothes to tide us over, handed out by two women in charge of sewing and laundry. We were happy enough with our new togs, but the older boys turned up their noses. If you went into town wearing storeroom clothes, they would refuse to walk down the street with you.

One year later, a new storeroom was created in the girls' wing when a plan was hatched to restore the old one to its former glory as a chapel. The chapel dated from a time when the children attended a service each morning before school. The governor rejected the name 'chapel' as old-fashioned and dubbed his new creation 'The Ark', a name as old as the Old Testament. It didn't catch on; to us it was always the chapel.

The restored chapel featured a stage, complete with wings and a sound system, but after an inaugural evening of songs and sketches, the place filled with dead air. The only sound heard there was the footsteps of the governor's wife as she traipsed back and forth between her office and the kitchen to draw up the menu for the day. The governor was never heard. He limped along in his slippers and seemed to be in a perpetual state of ennui. We wanted to start a band and asked him if we could use the sound system. He turned us down flat. The sound system was reserved for the word of God. But wasn't that covered by our trip to church on Sunday? This cut no ice with him: the sound system was for God's word and God's word alone. When a local band began rehearsing in the chapel, we felt betrayed. They brought their own equipment, played far better than we did and turfed us out of the room. We complained and the governor ruled that the band could only get rid of us if we disrupted their rehearsal. Eventually the band members, all at least five years our senior, got used to us and even asked us the odd question about the home and how we had ended up there. They would turn up every Saturday afternoon and trot out a repertoire that was dated but a damn sight more substantial than ours. While my bandmates drooled over their slick instruments and amplifiers, I studied the chords they were playing. We waged a war of attrition and were eventually allowed to rehearse in the chapel too, with our own crummy guitars and crappy equipment. The bass player had to be taught each song note by note, the second guitarist couldn't make it to the end of a break without losing the plot, and since none of us could sing, the vocals were left up to me. Our rare performances only came about thanks to equipment borrowed from lads at school and the help of a local drummer.

The lyrics we sang were rebellious and so I became a rebel, in the conviction that you should live what you sing. I railed against the church, our childish bedtimes, the restrictions on how we spent our clothing allowance, and soon we had a following among most of the older boys, my brothers in the vanguard.

Arti had now come of age and joined us in the senior dorm, supposedly the portal to something that resembled freedom. The group leaders had a tough time coping with three Nolands in one room and hardly a day went by without one of us being banished upstairs. Phil preferred to sit out his punishments in the dorm, while Arti usually opted for the shower room.

It had been a long time since anyone had been locked in solitary confinement. When they took me to the cell, they told me I'd been asking for it by stirring up trouble with my rebel songs.

Welcome

I spent only two days in solitary. The first was to cool me down and on the second I was to hear my sentence. On 1 May 1968 they fetched me from the cell and bundled me into my social worker's car. I was to be disciplined at a secure unit. I remembered all my trips by car, so few in number: the taxi to Voorschoten, my encounter with the owl in Drenthe and the head driving me back from my mother's, away from that gruesome flat by Zuider Park. This drive was my longest yet, to a town I would come to hate with every fibre of my being for the rest of my life. It had been built on a river and secreted in one of its dark, narrow, cobbled streets was a sombre building from 1900, a place called Welcome. It had begun life as a workhouse for the destitute, then became an orphanage and by the time I arrived it was a halfway house for juvenile delinquents. On the way, my social worker – a man who showed his face twice a year at most and whose role in my life I had never understood and would never understand – apologized that he had been unable to find me a place at Valkenheide. The borstal at Valkenheide was already the stuff of nightmares, and so I was left to conclude that an even worse fate awaited me at Welcome in the town of Arnhem.

The entrance was big enough to accommodate a lorry. Heavy gates clanged shut behind me, a sound I recognized from detective movies. A second gate lay ahead. It opened to reveal a dozen or so boys standing in a row. They had crewcuts and wore shorts, and looked for all the world like a troop of boy scouts from bygone days. A gym teacher was inspecting the ranks like a sergeant sizing up a bunch of new recruits. My social worker delivered me to the office and made a swift getaway.

I found myself eye-to-eye with a former officer of the Royal Netherlands East Indies Army, who looked me up and down suspiciously. He ordered me to turn out my pockets, cast a pitying glance over my empty wallet, diary and pen – all I had with me – and dropped them into a brown paper bag. Just to be sure, he had a second gym teacher frisk me from head to toe.

Once I had written my name on the paper bag, he looked at my handwriting and said, 'Are you at school?'

'Yes.'

'Yes what?'

'Yes, sir.'

'And what kind of school might that be?'

'Senior secondary.'

'Hmm. None of the lads here ever made it that far. Some can't even write their own name. What did you do to wind up here?'

'It's in the report from my social worker. I caused trouble in the group, that's all. I'm only here for two weeks.'

'Report? We know nothing about a report,' the man huffed. 'And as for two weeks, that's for us to decide. From this moment, you are under disciplinary orders. Dismissed!'

They locked me in a cell with a peephole in the door, a polished wooden floor, a bed I wasn't allowed to lie on during the day, and a wooden chair and desk without blotter, paper, pen or ink. I read the ten rules to be obeyed by inmates in their cell and began to cry, then scream. I pounded on the door but no one came. After a while, I calmed down. A small noticeboard above the desk was scribbled full of names. I wondered how those boys had managed to get hold of a pen. Or did those scribbles date from a time when writing in your cell had been permitted?

As evening fell, the door was unlocked and a boy with lips pressed firmly shut brought me something to eat while a gym teacher stood in the doorway to ensure that not a word passed between us. I was handed a green plastic dish of cabbage and a dollop of mash with a spoon planted in it. The milk came in a plastic beaker, but I was used to that. With plastic or a spoon you were less likely to harm yourself or someone else than with china or glass or a fork. What kind of boys were kept within the walls of this bleak institution?

At eight, I heard the other boys climb the stairs on stocking feet and I was called out of my cell to get cleaned up before bed. All I had been given was a towel. No toothbrush, no toothpaste, no soap. One of the boys gave me a squeeze of toothpaste, whispering that we had to work for our toiletries. A gym teacher stood in the washroom doorway, arms crossed, staring in our direction. Without soap, I washed myself silently with ice-cold water and returned to my cell. There I was given exact instructions on how to hang my clothes over the chair, without the slightest fold or crease. Once I had my pyjamas on – a striped cotton uniform worn by every inmate – I had to put my chair on the landing outside the cell, with my shoes beneath the seat and my socks folded inside them. The dustpan and brush, part of the cell's standard equipment, also had to be placed under the seat. Later I understood that this was to prevent you using the brush to smash the window, as if that were possible given the thickness of the matt glass and the gap-toothed grin of the bars beyond. Later still, I heard tell of four lads who had beaten two gym teachers unconscious with the brushes, grabbed their keys and made a run for it. They opened the main gates to find two police cars waiting for them.

The window slid open a fraction but was rigged to go no further. The cord was glued to the track. How could you ever escape from such a cell? And, supposing you did, where was there to run to in this gloomy river town? One inmate had managed to pull off a spectacular escape through the ventilation shafts and swim to the far bank, only to be caught in the beam of a police searchlight.

Such were the stories that had echoed round this place for years.

The nights were silent. For the first time in my life, I felt completely alone. I missed the snoring of the boys around me in the dorm, their mischievous whispers and sniggers, the soft light that filtered through the red curtain above the office door, where the leader on duty wrote their account of the day or updated the individual reports we constantly complained about because we never got to read what they said about us. It took me hours to fall asleep. The only sound was an occasional bang, perhaps the slamming of a pub door, followed by solitary footsteps that soon died away.

Freedom is being able to open a door and close it behind you. It's that simple.

At six in the morning I hear the key in the lock. The double security mechanism is disabled and the door swings open. The gym teacher at the door is tall, muscular and glowing with health. Anyone who isn't on their feet within a minute runs the risk of solitary confinement in an underground cell over by the playing field. I stand by my bed awaiting orders. Strip the bed. Sweep the floor with the dustpan and brush. Wait beneath the window at the back of the cell, not by the door. My pals at the home will never believe all this.

I am handed a PE kit and we are herded up to a gym on the top floor. We have to run circuits, do press ups, squats, vaults, hang from the wall bars… Gobs shut scumbags, filthy bunch of losers, you're in here for a reason and none of you, and I mean none of you, will ever amount to anything! Be thankful you're being looked after at all, you pack of weasels.

One gym teacher grins at the other one's patter.

After an hour of this, it's downstairs for a quick wash at the taps. Faster! Get a move on! The group file back down to the ground floor, I am sent to my cell. If I behave myself, I will be allowed into the common room.

I behave myself and, on the third day, I am released from solitary and sent straight to the barber, who shaves my hair to the wood. At a storeroom, I have to exchange my clothes for a pair of shorts and a short-sleeved shirt. I am now one of the pre-war boy scouts who shot me strange looks when I came walking through the gate in my fashionable gear.

There is no talking at the breakfast table. After breakfast, we are sent back to our rooms or our cells to make the bed. Then the floor is inspected. The gym teachers run their fingers along the skirting boards, show us the dust on their fingertips and order us to start over. I fail to make my bed properly, despite my reputation as champion bed-maker back in Voorschoten. Here in Arnhem, the top sheet has to be turned down exactly in line with the stripes painted on the bed frame, not a fraction more or less. The rigours of my father's domestic regime mean I can take this madness as it comes. I'm not stupid enough to play the rebel around here. I can't say I was stupid back at the home. What I can say is that they betrayed me, those group leaders who passed on their secret reports to a bunch of faceless officials in their government offices in The Hague. I step into line in a quadrangle hemmed in by high walls. Barbed wire snakes down the drainpipes. A vision from the countless war films that kept me awake at night. I look up to see a pigeon fly over. Where has that fat little bird come from? Where is it going? Does it have a ring around its leg? A place to call home? Is it welcome there? One of the gym teachers barks a command and we march to the workshop where a domineering foreman sets us to work.

I learn to put a hundred square inkpots on a wooden tray and fill them with ecoline using a funnel. You have to fill your funnel by hand from big bottles in the corner, watched over by one of the boys. Someone whispers that the boy has been here six months, a record for Welcome, which explains why he's the foreman's helper. His knuckles are caked in hard skin. Other boys whisper that he does karate and practises on the walls. That he likes to challenge each and every newcomer. Get into a fight with him and, win or lose, they'll add a month to your sentence. So watch out and keep your head down.

The boy beckons me over, pours ink into my funnel and tells me to watch out for the foreman. If the foreman calls 'crimson' and you deliver a hundred pots of ecoline crimson, there's nothing to stop him insisting it should have been ultramarine and docking you for the hundred pots it took you an hour to fill by the time you collected the pots, unscrewed the lids, filled the pots, screwed the lids back on and attached the labels. Got it, new boy? You make twelve cents a tray and if you work hard you'll end up with ninety-six cents a day. Got it, new boy? By the end of the week, that means you can buy a toothbrush, toothpaste, soap and a pouch of tobacco with cigarette papers. Got it, new boy?

At ten o'clock we break for coffee in the yard. Tobacco pouches, each one with a name scrawled on it, are removed from the cupboard. We are allowed to smoke and talk till twenty past, but our reasons for being here are off limits. The gym teachers eye us from behind their desk but every now and then we manage to escape their scrutiny and tell one another stories. Short and not so sweet. A succession of cliff-hangers. To be continued.

'One of the lads hanged himself in his underground cell. Over there – see the bars behind that matt glass? A social worker came to see him and I swear that guy must've had second sight or something. He was heading home but this feeling came over him between the first gate and the second. He ran back to the cell and found the kid. He'd used his clothes for a noose.'

'Was he still alive?'

'…'

'Hey, fucker, I asked you if he was still alive.'

'No swearing!'

One of the gym teachers looks me up and down. I avoid his eyes, look left, look right, look down at my feet. Don't come the fucking camp commandant with me, you bastard. If you ever cross my path out in the real world, I'll get my brother to kick your head in. Yes sir, that's right sir, I can't flatten you myself. I play the guitar, that's all I'm good for. What the fuck am I doing here? I miss my guitar.

The lunch break lasts an hour. We eat, have another smoke out in the yard and talk under our breath. Work continues till five, when they march us like soldiers in two groups to the cell block where we get cleaned up for the evening meal. Strange but true, there's no kitchen duty after dinner. Instead, we are all allowed to go to the common room in the building opposite the main gate, above the underground cells where the heating pipes converge. We play cards. I'm no good at cards, I hate cards. Card games are for idiots. I want to strum my guitar.

It's Sunday before we are allowed to write a letter. Our letters are read by the staff and, once they have been censored, rewritten and approved, we are allowed to buy an envelope and a postage stamp. I describe my circumstances as matter-of-factly as I can and my letter makes it through the censorship committee in one go. The price of the envelope and stamp are deducted from the wages of my forced labour.

A letter from my father is kept from me. In the office of the former KNIL officer, I am only allowed to see the address:

My Son Alan Noland
"Willkommen" Internment Camp
Weerdjesstraat numero 26-29
Arnheim
Belanda

'Did your father see combat over in the Indies, by any chance?' the former KNIL officer asks me.

'Yes, sir,' I reply.

'We cannot allow you to read this letter. Its content is not suitable for a youngster. Some passages are unsuited for a man my age.'

He looks me straight in the eye and rips my father's letter to shreds. No matter. I know what it says, what all his letters say. That he will go on fighting until he has rescued his children from the clutches of those 'filthy racists at Child Services' and that one day we will be reunited and start a new life together, without 'that fishwife of a mother of yours'.

When my two weeks are up, they hand me the brown paper bag with my things. 'You know, it's funny,' the former KNIL officer remarks to one of the gym teachers, 'but you can pick them out just like that, the kids of ex-marines who fought in the Indies. The kids of our lads from the KNIL never sink this low.'

Yesterday don't matter if it's gone

It feels like a long time since I got into the car with my social worker. I look around me, surprised by all these people free to come and go, by the cars on the motorway, the trees, the fields, the cows, the shifting sky. I am free again. But when we drive through the gate and the home looms up ahead, it's like arriving for the very first time. I am not returning. No, I am new, I come from another world. The boys have a good laugh at my shaved head, and ask what it was like, the food, the regime and the rest of it. I don't answer any of them. The group leaders give me concerned looks. I look away.

One sunny evening after dinner, when the boys go down to the yard to play volleyball with the girls, I stay put in my chair by the window. I light up a cigarette and look outside.

'Shouldn't you be out playing with the others?' the group leader on duty asks. Martha is her name.

I shake my head.

Martha usually takes care of the younger kids but she has been called in to cover for a sick colleague. In her John Lennon glasses, jeans and baggy jumper, she sits with me for a while, an English book in her hand. The cover is a jumble of multicoloured pills and the title is a riddle to me. I get up, stand behind her and read a few sentences over her shoulder. Pointing to words I don't know, I ask her what they mean and she gives me the Dutch translation with a smile. Three words later I know enough and have no idea what to say or do. It doesn't even dawn on me that she's the first person I've spoken to since I got back. I hope she can read minds. How could they have sent me to that hellhole? One of the inmates had tied his own mother to the bed and raped her, not once but five times. Another boy was in for attempted murder, two for attacking and mutilating young girls in the woods around Arnhem. I taught a boy to write his name; he turned out to be the one who had tried to kill somebody. The boys there told me Valkenheide was a walk in the park compared to Welcome. That only Het Poortje up in Groningen was worse. That no one from Arnhem was ever transferred to an 'open institution'. No way, couldn't happen. 'You're talking shit, man. You're being sent to borstal. Don't act like you've done nothing wrong, you stuck-up little prick. You don't come from an open institution and you sure as fuck don't go to school. No fucking way.'

Girls from my class stroked my hair and tried to comfort me. When they could find me that was, skulking around the bike sheds at break time. If a teacher asked me a question, they got no answer. My silence went unpunished. I got out of the homework sessions and sat on a bench in the park waiting for the other three little piggies to come past. Then I would join them and tag along back to the home. I sat down to do my homework straight after dinner and everyone left me in peace. After a week or two, the head called me in to ask me if I thought I might have outgrown the home.

I said nothing.

Weeks came and went, and arriving back at the home one day I was met by my sister Mil, screaming hysterically that Nana had been taken away while we were at school. They had packed her bag, put her in a car and driven her off to a foster family in Ede. Mil would not stop screaming and cursing the group leaders and the social workers. I did not comfort her, said nothing, listened impassively. When my father came to visit on Saturday and my mother on Sunday, I was nowhere to be found. There was always a hideout in the woods where you could vanish for a while, provided you made it to the trees unseen. I would find girls there smoking in secret, working-class girls from The Hague, tough talkers but kind-hearted. They cursed the 'scum' who had sent me to that 'shithole' and said if anyone ever threatened to send them to Arnhem, they would run away to The Hague. They knew guys who would look out for them, guys armed with stilettos and pistols, who drove American cars and who would take them under their wing till they turned twenty-one.

Twenty-one, the age of adulthood.

One night after dinner, the boy next to me at the table yelled, 'Hey guys, don't you think it's time monkey nut here opened his mouth?'

A second was all it took. Two perhaps. I shot out of my chair and cracked my left elbow against his temple. He fell off his chair and lay unconscious on the floor. The other boys and the group leaders – one male, one female – jumped to their feet in disbelief. I walked over to the window, leaned against the windowsill and lit a cigarette.

It wasn't long before the head responded to the alarm. He came in, motioned to me to follow him upstairs and locked me in the solitary confinement cell. As soon as the door shut behind me, I felt calmer. Here I was as much a prisoner as I had been at Welcome, only without bars on the windows and with a view of the girls' wing. One of the bolder girls got undressed at her window in the evening and waved at me. I waved back. Phil came at intervals to slide cigarettes and flattened matchboxes under the door. My food was brought by one of the younger boys. No one from my group was allowed to have any contact with me.

After a week of confinement, they let me out to go to school, where I told everyone I had been ill. When I got home, it was back to the cell. In the dead of night, I heard a key in the lock. The door opened to reveal the shape of a woman, who turned and locked the door behind her. It was Martha, with her round glasses, jeans and baggy jumper. She sat down beside me on the bed and put her finger to her lips. Then she lay down. We shared a cigarette. The following night she appeared again, this time wearing only her dressing gown. We smoked. She took my hand and guided it across her skin. The next night, we lay there naked and she taught me to explore her body. In the second week, I cautiously learned to make love and by the third week I was a man. She held a pillow to her face so that her cries could not be heard outside the cell.

When they let me out of solitary, I was taken to the head's office. He told me I was to see a psychologist one hour a week and a psychiatrist once a month. Luckily for me, the boy I attacked had since been allowed back home, somewhere in Twente. Otherwise I would have ended up in Valkenheide. The other boys kept their distance, which was fine by me. I had Martha.

Around the corner from the cell, in an extension beyond the washrooms, was a small corridor with three rooms for staff who stayed over. I would lie awake until the group leader on duty made their way back from The Club and went to bed, usually around eleven or twelve, though at the weekend it could be as late as one thirty. Unless I had drifted off to sleep, I would sneak out of bed, cross the landing and tap lightly on Martha's door. She liked to be on top and ride me while she smoked a cigarette. Lack of sleep meant I would sometimes doze off in class and I scraped into my final year at school with a report card full of C minuses.

One night I sneaked over to Martha's door to find it locked. Same the next night. I couldn't ask after her for fear of attracting attention. I heard rumours that she was on holiday and some of the boys began speculating about her replacement. Others said she had quit. We had barely exchanged a word. Apart from how to make love in silence, all she had taught me were three words, translated with a smile from the book with the multicoloured pills on the cover: 'horny', 'nipples', 'climax'.

At the psychologist's instigation, I was allowed to visit a bunch friends from the town during the summer holidays. They made music together in a rehearsal space and let me play with their band. I learned to sing two- and three-part harmonies and slowly began to open up a little more around the home. Girls would hang around the rehearsal room, younger and prettier than Martha, but not as mysterious. Where had she gone? Where had she come from?

Where was she living now? How old was she exactly? Would she find herself another boy at another home? Could the lads from the band sense a change in me? When we covered 'Ruby Tuesday' by The Stones they let me sing:

She would never say where she came from
Yesterday don't matter if it's gone
While the sun is bright
Or in the darkest night
No one knows
She comes and goes

The dispersal

Though my father's flat was within walking distance, the authorities never caught him making impromptu visits or stalking the grounds. Not that it mattered: in the eyes of Child Services he was still the dodgy Oriental with a horrific wartime past that at any moment could make him go *mata gelap* – an expression with which they were familiar. Nana was first to be sent away, to the care of a foster family in Ede. Mil left one year later, transferred to a home in a remote area not far from the German border. After sitting our final school exams, Phil and I left to board with an Indo family in The Hague, while Arti was dispatched to a boys' home in Delft. We were scattered across the country, as had been the way with Indos who had been kicked out of Indonesia.

Our father became the only one left to visit in the dreary town of Voorschoten.

I didn't last long at that boarding house with the Indo family and their sickening colonial ways. We and another Indo lodger were treated like servants and given cold leftovers to eat once the family had left the table. Their eldest daughter was so spoiled that she screamed blue murder when one of us inadvertently dug his knife into her butter. I began to skip classes at our new school, a vocational college, cycling over to the promenade instead, where I spent hours looking out to sea, much to my brother's disgust. My listless ways were really beginning to piss him off. Five years after the police had come to fetch us from school that day, I found myself standing forlornly with my guitar strapped to my back outside a messy four-room flat on the fringes of Voorschoten, home to a solitary Indo. He opened the front door with the bearing of a fighter who suspected an ambush any second, and greeted me with the words:

'Why did you forsake me?'

An accusation I took so much to heart that I spent years thinking it was justified.

In the beginning, the solitary Indo left five guilders on the aluminium kitchen counter each morning before he went to work. He was a draughtsman for a US oil company in The Hague. I did the shopping and learned to make noodle soup. After three days the pan was empty and I made more. Apart from that, we munched on Ryvita with cheese and snacked on peanuts, washed down with sweet unfiltered *kopi tubruk*. One evening he took me to The Hague to see a movie. It was strange travelling back on the bus to Voorschoten with him, a place where I was more at home than he was. Miniature bombers and fighter planes hung from his living room ceiling, model tanks lined the windowsills and the bookcase was brimming over with war books. I couldn't help wondering where he had stashed his Marine dagger. On the wall was a framed official letter from the US State Department thanking him for his application to join their forces in Vietnam.

'Look...' he said with a devilish glint in his eye. 'They rejected your father on the grounds of his age, but I still feel young enough to fight those filthy commies!'

When he discovered I was buying tobacco from the household allowance, the five guilders he left for me became two-fifty. This was no longer enough to make noodle soup, so I skimped on the ingredients. He did not believe me and suspected me of buying marijuana. Before long I woke up to find one guilder on the kitchen counter.

I went into his bedroom one day when he was out and found a stash of food in his wardrobe, including a tin of herring in tomato sauce. I took it back to the spare room with a few crackers and ate the whole thing. Sneaking back into his bedroom, I cautiously poked around his bed. Under his mattress, I found the dagger.

There would be no sleep that night. Getting up for a piss, I noticed his bedroom door was ajar. In the faint glow of the toilet light I saw him sleeping, saw my father sleeping for the first time in my life. To my horror, his eyes were half open. I knew he could not be awake or he would have growled, 'What are you up to out there?'

It dawned on me that ex-marines who sleep with their eyes half open in peacetime are as vulnerable as every other human being. But another day passed and I found the door to his room locked and no money on the kitchen counter. I made an evening meal from what was left in the fridge. My father ate in silence. The next day when I got up, the living room door was locked too and the fridge and the kitchen cupboards had been cleared out completely. In fear, I left the house key on the kitchen counter and, yes, that is when I finally forsook him.

After a nomadic existence sleeping at the homes of former schoolfriends in Voorschoten and squats in Leiden, I ran out of options. One winter's day I took the train to The Hague and walked all the way from Staatsspoor station to Scheveningen. I headed for the Circus Theatre and from there I found the street where Uncle Willem lived. I spotted his blue-and-white Volkswagen camper van parked by the kerb, went down the steps to his basement flat and knocked on the door.

I cannot remember ever being welcomed as warmly as I was by Uncle Willem that day. The man from Scheveningen yanked me into his shabby flat, sat me down with a smile and gave me fresh herring to eat. Then he stuffed me full of soup and fried egg butties.

He referred to this feast as a 'quick bite', proving himself a man to rival Frau Eva. He let me doss down on a spare bed in his room. The rumbling snores of the man who smoked full-strength tobacco made me feel safe. When my mother dropped by the next day, she brought a tin of herring in tomato sauce and did not hold out her hand when she asked me how I was doing. I stared down at the tin for a very long time. The oval stood for endless memory. For my father's hermetic hostility. The label for a mother I could not read.

Willem

When the Germans invaded in 1940, young Willem was put on a barge that left from Brouwersgracht and shipped off to Germany with other lads his age. He wound up operating a lathe, making the missiles that obliterated London in Hitler's dreams. In exchange for his labour, Willem was fed and watered. But there was no herring. He escaped and made it back to Holland, where he was arrested and put behind bars in Scheveningen, a condemned man. His childhood sweetheart Corrie secured his release, perhaps by putting her body at the disposal of some officer or other. It was not a story she could tell now, even if she wanted to, as she sat in her chair all day poring over the Bible, under the yoke of Jehovah's Witnesses who called round once a week and appeared to be unfamiliar with the concept of laughter. Corrie took pills for depression and anxiety and suffered bouts of incontinence which left the whole room reeking of urine. A wartime photo on the mantelpiece showed a pretty young Scheveningen girl. Without her, Willem would have been dragged off to the dunes to face a firing squad. After his death-row reprieve from the notorious German jail they dubbed the 'Orange Hotel', he had beaten a man to a pulp for a hunk of bread among those same dunes.

'Him or me,' he said with an apologetic chuckle.

Willem was a restless, good-humoured man, unable to sit still for five minutes, born under Gemini. He had one of those typically

Dutch noses that bloomed red at the end, an old-fashioned conk. A Scheveninger to his very bones, he bore a surname we all thought was hilarious: Toot. His wife Corrie was a Toot too. The custom of the time dictated that a widow or widower should add their deceased partner's surname to their own. So if death did them part, one of them would live out their days as a Toot-Toot. I once saw that very surname on a front door in Scheveningen.

After the war, Willem spent a year in prison. He never told me why. By the time of his release, he had read the Bible twice from start to finish, pronounced God a figment of the collective imagination and knocked together a refectory table with a top made of burned-out matches, which now stood in his living room.

Long before the war, Willem had himself been a care home boy in Voorschoten, or the orphanage as it was then. In his day, the boys had to wear a black uniform with a yellow emblem when they went to church or school, while the girls stayed indoors learning how to be good little housewives. The summer holiday was short and sweet: a day trip to the seaside at Scheveningen. Willem didn't have a single qualification to his name, not even a swimming certificate, but he brandished his driving licence proudly.

'Listen, kid, this scrap of pink linen is a driving licence! And a driving licence sets you on the road to freedom!'

Willem never planned a single day in advance. After breakfast he would pace up and down for a bit, sucking on a roll-up and asking himself out loud what the day might have in store. One of his activities was driving from hotel to hotel buying up reject bath towels to sell at the street market. Before he left for the day, he would ask me to keep an eye on Corrie. 'I'm off to hunt down some merchandise. A man's got to make a living somehow, right, kid?'

Sometimes he would stay away for days. Working at the docks in Rotterdam, he said. Or bedding down in a caravan at a breaker's yard in Leidschendam, looking after the place for a small fee as a favour to a friend. As my mother told it, he had married his life-saver Corrie, divorced her and then married her again, probably because she had begun to show signs of schizophrenia, living in constant fear that the German occupiers, long since gone, might come marching down Dirk Hoogenraadstraat any minute. When Holland converted to natural gas en masse, Willem went door-to-door as a gas fitter, adapting the boilers. By the time he turned up on the doorstep of our flat by Zuider Park, we were in the children's home, the police had escorted my father off the premises and my mother was a bag of nerves living on her own. That was her story. The cheery gas fitter returned the same evening to see how that lonely woman was doing and the next night he was back again, bearing a meal of soup and herring. From then on, he visited whenever he was able to leave Corrie alone for a spell.

Now that I had found a roof over my head at Willem's, the fifty-six-year-old Scheveninger was able to spend more time with his lover, my mother. I was around to keep Corrie company, calm her down every now and again, and play guitar for her if she asked me to.

My father had his own version of events, in which Willem and my mother had met long before the boiler needed adapting. In the days when all seven of us were still crammed into that cursed Zuider Park tenement, she worked as a cleaner from seven to nine at the V&D department store on Leyweg. And it was there, in one of the toilets, that the two of them first started pawing at each other, or so Pa claimed. Phil, Arti and I sometimes wondered which account was true, but we absolved Willem of all blame regardless. We were so fond of him that Arti even began to look on him as his stepdad.

Oddly, when I attended a reunion at the children's home in Voorschoten many years later, not one of our carers could recall a single thing about my mother or Willem. Some didn't even know I had a mother. It was my father they remembered, every last one of them. Though he only had half the visiting rights, his appearances had made an indelible impression. Only then did I start to remember how my mother used to skip her visits. She later confessed that she and Willem toured around Europe, but only when Corrie was 'on good form' and able to make the beds and wash the sheets of the migrant workers who boarded with her. Ma and Willem drove to Germany and sometimes down to France and so there was no way she could get back in time to visit us. It was an admission that disappointed me. My father never missed a visit, not one. My social worker said it was to show our carers how loyal he was to us.

The trunk in the basement

A short flight of whitewashed steps led down from the street to Willem's small front garden, with its assortment of dying trees, loose paving stones and car tyres. I would sit at a little table in his kitchen writing lyrics in colourful notebooks, reading books by the Russian masters or playing guitar. The kitchen window afforded a view of paint peeling off the wooden façade of the living room where Corrie sat and read her Bible, unless electric currents were coursing through her limbs, an affliction she insisted was the work of the Germans. Each morning, Willem put a fresh square of lino under her seat to stop the urine rotting the wood of her chair. She had her good weeks, when she was able to do the housework and wash the sheets of their migrant lodgers. The room the six of them shared contained three bunk beds and was at the end of a long hallway accessed through the kitchen. They came from Tunisia, Algeria and Morocco, and adored Corrie for taking such good care of them. When she was ill and unable to clean up after them, they prayed for her. If it was a bad week, they would each give me a guilder to take their sheets to the laundrette.

Willem's room, where I slept, was next to the migrants' room. I never once heard them leave for work at the crack of dawn; Willem liked his sleep and the man of the house was not to be disturbed. They looked tired when they came home in the evening. After a cold shower, they would come into the kitchen wearing grey-and-white striped caftans and take it in turns to cook an enormous pot of food: mutton usually, with potatoes, tomatoes and veg. Sometimes they invited me to their room to share a meal. No knife and fork; they ate with their hands. They taught me how to break bread and use it to lift potatoes and chunks of meat from the pot. They barely spoke to one another. All they did was work, cook, sleep, work and send money home to their wives and children every week. But if they came and joined me at the kitchen table, they were more talkative. One had a little book in which he kept a record of how often he had made love to his wife whenever he spent a couple of weeks in his homeland. Another taught me to write my name in Arabic. And another taught me an Islamic prayer. They told me they had worked in Germany too, but that conditions there were lousy. Life was good in Switzerland, they said, but they weren't allowed to stay long. None of them had a residence permit and to me their lives seemed sad.

My favourite was the quietest of the six. The others whispered that he sent every spare penny to his family and permitted himself no luxuries at all. He liked to listen to me play guitar, until nine, when he would thank me and turn in for the night. When Corrie went to bed an hour later, I would wait a while and then go out and find a bench on the promenade, look out to sea and listen. Scheveningen was old, quiet and deserted back then.

One day Willem said to me, 'Hey, did you know your dad's name isn't Noland at all? He's called Sie, after his mother. Your father is a Chinaman. He typed up his life story and kept it in a thick file.'

I looked at him in surprise. Was *that* what my father had been doing at his typewriter all those years?

Willem led me to a room off the kitchen, where he stockpiled sacks of rice and tins of food ready for the outbreak of World War Three. I helped him drag the heavy sacks aside. Behind them stood the trunk from my father's voyage to Holland.

'What's that doing here?'

'The trunk makes your mother nervous. She asked me to look

after it. I should really take it over to your father's but… well, we'd have to do it together, you know?'

'I wouldn't if I were you. My dad can get pretty riled up.'

'I know. I'm sure it'll all work out one day. Go on, open it…'

I lifted the lid of the trunk and saw nothing but papers: books, documents, letters, photos and files. Willem pointed to the file in question and asked me if I wanted to read it. I hesitated, then nodded.

'Have you read the whole thing?' I asked.

'Yeah, from start to finish. Just like the Bible.' He chuckled. 'You're going to need nerves of steel my boy, ha ha! If you can't stomach it, just give it back to me. We'll keep it here behind the sacks of rice. And don't let those migrant workers see it. Not that they'd be able to read it but, you know… it's still an exceptional document.'

'Didn't my dad ever ask after it?'

'You bet he did! But your mother told him she'd set fire to the lot. I'd have handled things differently, but your mother does things her way. Hey, you wouldn't mind looking after Corrie tonight, would you? It'd give me a chance to go and see your mother. She's all alone over there, you know?'

It took me one week to read the first instalment about his youth and the second instalment about the Japanese occupation. After that, I found myself putting it aside more often, taking aimless walks over the promenade night after night, wondering if I would be able to make myself read the whole thing. Some passages terrified me. In the end, I took the pages out of the file and divided them into three equal parts, taking care not to damage the photos and official documents he had pasted in. I tied the three parcels with string and put them back among the sacks of rice.

One evening, I put the parcels in a shopping bag and took the bus to Voorschoten. I walked down my father's street and looked up at his flat. There was a light in the window and I could make out the shadows of his model warplanes on the ceiling. It didn't feel like I was coming home; I couldn't ring the doorbell. But for the manuscript, at least, it was a homecoming of sorts. I slid the three parcels through the letterbox, tossed the bag into the bushes and took the next bus back to The Hague. It was his war, not mine. Not yet it wasn't.

IV

THE INTERPRETER FROM SURABAYA

From Baldy's memoirs

Merdeka

When, on 17 August 1945, Sukarno declared an independent Republic of Indonesia, a cry went up for revenge against the Belandas. It was an evening of celebration and killings. I stood alone, the only member of my family to pledge allegiance to the Netherlands. Amid the chaos and violence of this new time known as Bersiap, I was sickened by the actions of my own flesh and blood, who showed themselves to be as spineless as they had been during the Japanese occupation. My elder brothers Jacob and Karel derided my loyalty to a Dutch queen I had never even seen. I paid them no heed and went out into the city the next day, armed with my fighting knife. At Genteng Bridge I spotted Harry Tjong. He showed me his knuckledusters and called me over to the Red Cross building opposite the Oranje Hotel, where fighting had broken out between Indos and Hollanders on one side and *pelopors* on the other. We rushed over to Tunjungan. The traffic was in chaos and policemen and Japanese soldiers were running towards the Oranje Hotel, where a brave young Indo had raised the Dutch tricolour on the roof. A couple of *pemudas* armed with bamboo spears had climbed up after him, clutching the red-and-white flag of Indonesia. They skewered the Indo, along with a Dutchman who tried to defend him. We found ourselves among a bunch of Indos, outnumbered by bloodthirsty *pemudas* and *pelopors* armed with samurai swords, revolvers, *klewang* and all kinds of weapons seized from the Japanese. I drew my knife and plunged it into the throat of the first *pemuda* I encountered. A stone struck my head and I ran for the cover of a shopping arcade on Embong Malang, then crossed Simpang to reach Ketabang. I had hoped to stop and catch my breath but everywhere I looked I was surrounded by Javanese, killing, fighting and looting. Even women and children were not safe. Cars were sprayed with bullets and set alight before their occupants could escape. As I staggered down the street – head pounding, clothes stained with blood – a couple of *pemudas* came up to me. Seeing my Chinese badge, one of them took out a handkerchief and wiped the blood from my face. They asked me where I had been fighting. I came up with some lie or other and walked on. 'Merdeka!' they cried after me, and continued in the opposite direction. Sticking to the side streets, I avoided the fighting and reached our house in Undaan Kulon.

Mama was shocked to see me walk through the door with my head wounded and my clothes covered in blood. Wide-eyed with fear, our *babu* and *kokkie* took one look at me and began to sob. I grabbed clean underwear and slippers, took a cool bath and then slumped onto my bed. My whole body was shaking. Mama came in demanding to know exactly what had happened. I gave her a vague account of the fighting and she all but collapsed in a fit of nerves.

The next day my former sweetheart Ciska Wagner came to see us, in a terrible state. I took her in my arms and comforted her. She lived in Dapuan district, not far from the notorious Werfstraat prison, but was too afraid of the rioting *pemudas* to go home. It was already late in the afternoon. I fastened my knife to my belt and we ducked into the *kampong* behind Undaan Kulon in search of a friend of mine by the name of Soetardjo. I asked him to use his Javanese contacts to get hold of a looted car to drive Ciska home. Soetardjo rounded up his pals and around twelve of us set off for Peneleh, armed with bamboo spears, rifles and pistols.

At a police guardhouse we came across two *pemudas* sitting on a looted truck that had belonged to some Chinese merchant. Soetardjo had a quiet word in their ear and we all climbed aboard. Ciska was white with fear, but she held herself well. With Soetardjo at my side, those bastards took me for a friend.

From Peneleh we drove down Jagalan to Contong Square, then through Pasar Besar via Sulung to downtown Surabaya. Armed Indonesian freedom fighters were everywhere. As we drove, Soetardjo spoke. 'For over 350 years, the Belandas have exploited and humiliated the Indonesians, trampled us underfoot. All that is over. Now that Japan has capitulated, we will not accept a new Dutch government. We will fight for our independence under Sukarno. When I die, a brother-in-arms will take up my weapon. We hate the Belandas. And we hate those rich Indos who think they are better than us and treat us with contempt. We will kill them all. Make sure you are not among them when we do. I know you, but many of my comrades do not.'

After driving for half an hour through streets strewn with bodies and burned-out cars, we arrived in Dapuan. I thanked Soetardjo and his comrades for their help, and said farewell with a two-faced 'Merdeka!'

Ciska was shivering. I put my arm around her as we navigated the narrow side streets to her home. Her worried sister was waiting at the door and they fell weeping into each other's arms. I could not bear to watch and turned to go, but Ciska clung to me, terrified that I would be murdered if I left. It was already dark and I decided to spend the night with her. When I left the next morning, Ciska gave me her rosary beads and prayed to Our Lady to protect me. I arrived home safely to find Uncle Soen at our table. He told me about the revolutionary forces in and around Surabaya. In addition to the Indonesians' newly formed military, there were militia units of the BKR, fanatical Hizbullah fighters and Masyumi Islamic nationalists, all fighting for Merdeka.

Captured by *pemudas*

Days later, I set off on my bike to visit Aunty Kiep but when I reached Kedungdoro I was stopped by a bunch of hotheads armed with guns, knives and clubs. They made me get off and bow to each of them in turn. I bowed low in front of what looked like a ten-year-old boy brandishing a Japanese rifle, then straightened up and slapped him in the face. Rifle butts came at me from all sides. I went *mata gelap*, picked up my bike and swung it wildly, knocking my adversaries to the ground. I continued to ram them till I had no strength left, then threw the bike at a *pemuda* who was charging at me with a bayonet fixed to his rifle. More rebels came running over. I hit the ground, felt blows raining down on me and passed out.

When I came to, the stink of shit and urine filled my nostrils. It was daylight and I was locked in a toilet. A *pemuda* opened the door and handed me a bowl of tapioca. I asked him how long I had been there. He told me I had been locked up for over two days, and that I was to be taken out the next day at noon and killed by firing squad.

That evening, I took out Ciska's rosary beads and prayed to God. I was bathed in a cold sweat, but as I finished my prayers I felt a sudden rush of courage, hope and strength. High on the wall was a window with rusted bars. The cistern had come away from the wall and, by placing it on the toilet, I was able to climb up and loosen the corroded bars one by one. I heaved myself up, stuck my head through the opening and realized that my shoulders would fit through. Looking down, I saw a guard pacing the length of a narrow alley below. I waited until he reached the far end, then gripped the broken bars again, squeezed through the window and dropped to the ground. The moon was shining into the alley but I pressed myself to the wall and waited in the shadows for the guard to approach. When he was only a few feet away, I lunged and kicked him full in the stomach. He dropped his weapon. I grabbed it by the barrel and smashed his skull with the butt, then removed the bolt and tossed it in the gutter.

The alley led to a side street off Kedungdoro. Sticking to the shadows, I made my way to the main street. It was close to midnight and there were not many people about. My clothes were covered in blood and hung from my body in tatters. I crept along until I reached the junction with Kembang Kuning, where I headed for

Simo. Aunty Kiep was still awake when I turned up at her door and nearly had a fit when she saw the state I was in. She burst into tears and bundled me into the bathroom, where she made me undress and gently began to wash me. She dried me with great patience, for every part of my body was badly hurt. I was covered in lumps, scratches and cuts, and shaking with tension and emotion. Aunty Kiep gave me a sarong to put on and let me lie on the divan. She washed my underpants, the only item of my clothing still in one piece, and hung them by the kitchen fire to dry. Then she made a paste from medicinal herbs, smeared it on plantain leaves she had cut into patches and applied them to my wounds, binding them in place with strips of cloth. The poultice felt cool against my skin and gradually the pain ebbed away. I fell into a deep sleep but woke the next morning groaning because my arms and legs hurt so much. I staggered to the kitchen and Aunty Kiep gave me a plate of *kacang ijo* mashed with brown sugar. I stayed with her for a few days, until my wounds had healed a little.

Aunty Kiep received a visit from Pah Tjillih. He beckoned me into Aunty's bedroom and closed the door behind him, so that we were alone. Pah Tjillih began to pray and told me to spit on his palms. Then he loosened my bandages and began to run his hands over the wounds on my arms and legs, murmuring all the while. A miracle occurred. Every last one of my wounds healed. The pain disappeared and I felt the strength return to my muscles. I clasped Pah Tjillih's hands and thanked him with all my heart.

'No need for thanks, my boy,' Pah Tjillih replied. 'I am happy to help. My love for you is strong. Yours will be a long, hard struggle. But you will survive.'

Meanwhile, Aunty Kiep had found me a change of clothes. Kneeling before Pah Tjillih to show the depth of my respect, I asked this saintly man for a fighting knife and begged him to bless it for me. He took me to his home. There I first had to sit quietly and drink coffee with him. Then he went to his bedroom to pray and returned with an impressive blade. 'I have infused this dagger with magic powers,' he said. 'Wherever you go, the enemy will avoid you.

A vision has told me that you will return home along Kedungdoro. There you will find your lost bicycle leaning against a fence.'

I thanked Pah Tjillih and, following the route he had given me, found my bicycle in the place he had predicted. Astoundingly, it was still in one piece. When I arrived home, Mama asked me where I had been for days on end. When I told her I had been staying with Aunty Kiep, she heaved a sigh of relief.

I had no job, and therefore no money. The terror that had gripped Surabaya struck fear into everyone. Indonesia's revolution was becoming more ferocious by the day. The hatred towards Belandas and Indos grew. Slogans and rallying cries were daubed on the walls of public buildings, and even on the sides of buses and trams. *DUTCH GO HOME!*

One morning, Uncle Soen came to see me, his face creased with worry. 'Arto,' he said, 'I know what happened to you over the past few days. Take care! I saved your life when you were a child and have always treated you as my own son. When anything happens to you, I sense it strongly. I am a crippled man and unable to give you physical protection. The only protection I have to offer is spiritual and magical. Friends informed me that yesterday three trucks carrying Dutch and Indo women and children to Tanjung Perak were halted by mobs of *pemudas*. Every woman, every child was slaughtered on the spot and mutilated beyond recognition. The trucks were set ablaze. There are many who detest the colonialism of the Belandas, but these murders have nothing to do with the revolution declared by Sukarno. If you go wandering through the city again, Arto, for heaven's sake do not forget to pin your Chinese badge to your shirt!'

Cycling down Ngemplak on my way to Ketabang district a few days later, I heard someone call my name. Four heavily armed *pemudas* across the street beckoned me over. I cycled towards them slowly, feeling for the knife on my belt, but as I got closer, I recognized Radèn Soemarno, a classmate from Queen Emma School.

'Hey, Nolan! Remember me?' he shouted.

'Yes, of course I remember you. How are you doing?'

'I am well, as you can see,' Radèn Soemarno answered. 'Let me introduce you to my comrades. We have joined the Indonesian Army.'

I shook hands with the other three *pemudas* and studied their faces.

'I cannot understand why you side with the Belandas,' Radèn Soemarno continued. 'Your mother is Chinese. Your European father refused to recognize you. Like your mother, you are *peranakan*. Join us in our fight against the Belandas! You were born here, too. This is your native soil, your home. What is Holland to you? Everything you know of that country you learned from schoolbooks, just like us. You should be fighting alongside us, Nolan.'

'I respect your patriotism, Soemarno. But why sacrifice innocent women and children?'

Radèn Soemarno smiled but I could see the hatred in his face. 'You are an illegitimate child, Nolan,' he answered. 'In fact, you are not a Nolan at all. You bear your mother's name, Sie. We were friends for many years, got up to all kinds of mischief together. We fought, shared the bitter and the sweet. You are more than a friend to me – you are my brother. I saw how Indos humiliated and despised you, simply because you were born out of wedlock. In the Japanese time we were often together. You and I committed acts of resistance along with other young Indonesians. You think of yourself as an Indo, but where were those Indos when you needed them?'

Radèn Soemarno's words hit home. I had to admit he was right, and my convictions were shaken. He saw through me, as did his comrades. One by one they embraced me and told me they understood the problems I had faced in life. Yet somewhere deep in my soul, I did not feel at home in their world. Since my earliest childhood I had often felt that I did not belong in the Indies.

Our conversation at an end, we mounted our bikes and cycled to Simpang, where a large crowd of *pemudas* and other heavily armed freedom fighters were gathering. Gunshots rang out all around us, along with cries of 'Merdeka'. One of Radèn Soemarno's friends shouted above the din: 'Let's head over to the Holland Club! Terrible things are happening there!'

On the way I saw dead bodies in the streets, the corpses of Dutch people and Indos. Arriving at the Holland Club, formerly known as the Simpang Club, the streets were so crowded that we had to get off our bikes and walk. I crossed the street and cut through the garden of a dentist's surgery, bike and all. Radèn Soemarno and his friends followed. Portraits of Queen Wilhelmina, Princess Juliana and Prince Bernhard were being smashed and burned in the streets. The Dutch red, white and blue was set alight amid loud cheers and more cries of 'Merdeka'. What happened next will stay with me forever. A heavily pregnant woman was mercilessly attacked with a bamboo spear. Her unborn child came flailing into the world to be stabbed by another spear. A few yards further on, I saw a young girl beheaded with a samurai sword. Radèn Soemarno and his friends were sick at the sight. It was there by the Holland Club that I took my revenge.

As their faces turned chalk white, I glared at Radèn Soemarno and his friends in contempt. 'Is this how you want to achieve your Merdeka?' I asked them. 'Look at what these madmen are doing!'

'Nolan, I never expected this!' Radèn Soemarno whined.

I stood there, half-dazed by the atrocities around me, until dusk fell and I said goodbye to my Merdeka friends. I cycled home along Tunjungan and Genteng. The streets were littered with bodies, some in a state of decay, others charred because they had been set alight. Turning onto Trompstraat, I ran into Soetardjo. He signalled to me and I got off my bike. We walked together in the direction of his *kampong*.

'Where have you been?' Soetardjo asked.

'I have come from Simpang. I was with Radèn Soemarno, an old school friend who has joined the Indonesian Army. They were lynching people over there. Is that what this revolution of yours demands?'

Soetardjo grabbed my shoulder. 'Nolan, these vicious outbursts towards the Belandas have got completely out of hand,' he said. 'Those murdering fanatics belong to Bung Tomo's movement and to Hizbullah. Even as a BKR militiaman, I am powerless to stop them. It is barbaric, I agree, but when all is said and done the Belandas have it coming.'

'I understand their rage, Soetardjo, but surely you can negotiate with the Belandas?'

'Nolan, you were raised by your mother. She belongs to this country, even if she is *peranakan* Chinese. This soil is where you were born and raised. This is your home. How were you treated by the Belandas? They trampled you underfoot. We Indonesians are your friends. That is why you have to fight alongside us, even when the British forces dock in Tanjung Perak. I have heard that a British landing fleet is on its way from Singapore to occupy the entire region and pave the way for the restoration of Dutch rule. That is against the will of the Indonesian people. And so there will be war. Our military and political organizations are in the highest state of readiness. Guns and ammunition have been stockpiled, some taken from the Japanese forces, some smuggled in. I can make sure you are well-armed. Remember, you are already under orders to patrol the neighbourhood with a *takeyari*. To refuse is an act of treason and you know the punishment that awaits traitors. And before I forget, Sie-Nolan: never speak the name of Queen Wilhelmina in the company of other *pemudas*. They may be the last words you utter.'

Allied troops in Surabaya

My twentieth birthday on 28 September 1945 went by unnoticed. Tensions were running too high for celebration. Day in day out, I sat with my ear glued to the radio. At this time, I was forced to join the other men of Undaan Kulon on nightly neighbourhood watch patrols, armed with a bamboo spear.

The next day I went to Uncle Soen's house in Peneleh *kampong*, not far from where we lived. He told me that British and Indian troops had landed in Batavia. Their mission was to disarm Japanese soldiers and to free prisoners of war and those being held in the internment camps. Uncle Soen was aware of my pro-Dutch sentiments and believed that I did not belong here in the East. For Pah Tjillih too, this was no secret. That saintly man sometimes had dreams about me and shared his premonitions with Uncle Soen.

A few weeks later, I was back at my uncle's door. In his kitchen, he opened a newspaper and said, 'The Allies will be here soon, and when they come the entire population is being told to resist with every weapon they can lay their hands on – knives, sticks and stones, if need be.'

'But Uncle Soen, that is madness! Who can brave machine-gun fire armed with a knife?'

'Arto, people are willing to give everything for Merdeka, even their own lives. Hatred of the Belandas runs deep. But for you I have come up with an escape plan. That is, if you dare. I have persuaded my contacts to help you. Many of them know you, some even sympathize with your Western attitudes in this Eastern world. What do you say?'

'Uncle Soen, if I can cross over and join the British, I will turn against the *pemudas*.'

Early one morning at the end of October I heard Royal Navy cannon fire coming from the port of Tanjung Perak. It was music to my ears. Fires broke out everywhere in the centre of Surabaya. I had no appetite for breakfast and left the house, much to Mama's indignation. Behind our house, I slipped into the *kampong* to go to Uncle Soen's. On the way, I saw Soetardjo again. He was wearing the green uniform of the Indonesian Army and carrying a Lee Enfield rifle with bayonet and two cartridge boxes. Four hand grenades hung around his neck. He approached me and said, 'Nolan, beloved brother and comrade, I bid you farewell. I am going into battle against the British invaders. If I should die, remember that I have always been a good friend to you, in spite of the political divide between us.'

I saw tears in Soetardjo's eyes, embraced him and realized this might be the last time I would ever see him.

On the nights that followed, I patrolled the neighbourhood armed with my *takeyari*. On my belt, I carried the dagger Pah Tjillih had given me. I had more faith in a blade than a spear. At Piet Heinplein I climbed a tree and looked in the direction of the port. I saw the traces of flares in the distance and flashes of light caused by mortar shell impacts. I heard the guns roar.

From Uncle Soen I found out that the British troops had occupied and cordoned off the entire port area. The vanguard was now advancing towards the city. The roar of the guns came closer.

Walking down Undaan Kulon the next day, I saw armoured vehicles and jeeps driving up the other side of the canal. I ran over the pedestrian bridge to Undaan Wetan to take a closer look. As I thought, they were British military vehicles. One of the trucks, manned by Indian soldiers, stopped close to where I was standing. A Punjabi officer got out and waved me over.

'Are you Indonesian?' he asked.

'No, sir,' I answered, 'I am Chinese, half-caste Chinese.'

I then explained to him in English where he could expect resistance from *pemudas*. He took a notebook from his shoulder bag and made a record of the intelligence I supplied. He seemed extremely grateful. I asked the Punjabi lieutenant if he would let me accompany them as a guide, but he refused. The resistance they expected to encounter would be much too fierce, he said.

Disillusioned, I returned to my neighbourhood and saw thick columns of smoke rising above Ngemplak. The next morning I walked over Genteng Bridge to Ngemplak. The decapitated bodies of British and Indian soldiers were floating in the water. The streets were strewn with corpses, among them Indonesians. In the tropical heat, the stench was appalling.

A few days later, the fighting in the city subsided. Uncle Soen reported that the Indian infantry's Fighting Cock Brigade had suffered huge losses. Sukarno even had to come to Surabaya in person to force a ceasefire between the warring parties.

At the beginning of November, I found myself walking down Jagalan over Pasar Besar, past toppled lampposts and buildings and homes that had been shot to pieces. People were wandering the streets, searching desperately for victims and possessions. With 'Merdeka' as my password, I negotiated my way past groups of *pemudas*. Arriving at Contong Square, I met a number of my schoolfriend Soedjono's brothers-in-arms. They told me that a British brigadier had been killed by a civilian militia the previous evening, his mutilated body thrown from the Red Bridge into Kali Mas, fodder for the ravenous crocodiles, iguanas and giant river turtles that lived in the city's waterways.

One morning at dawn, the drone of a Mitchell bomber was heard and pamphlets were scattered over the city. Hungry for news, people ran out to pick them up. Partly in English and partly in Malay, the pamphlets said all of Indonesia's combat forces had forty-eight hours to surrender their arms at designated collection points in the city centre and the port districts of Tanjung Perak and Ujung. Unless this Allied demand was met, there would be another bloodbath on the streets of Surabaya.

The demand was ignored. People were prepared to fight to the last breath. The *pemudas* began reinforcing their positions and building new barricades armed with all kinds of smuggled military equipment.

On my visits to Uncle Soen, I often encountered boys who fought alongside Soetardjo. They too were armed to the teeth. When I asked after him, I was told that he was helping to man the positions near Westerbuitenweg. I began to pity him, for I believed that he and his ragtag bunch of schoolboy fanatics did not stand a chance. The 5th Indian Division would be their next adversary. Newly arrived in Tanjung Perak, it consisted of British colonial army units: Gurkhas, Dogras, Punjabis and Sikhs, all with formidable combat experience.

'Be careful, Arto,' Uncle Soen warned me. 'Lay low during the coming hostilities. If you still want to escape this place, wait for a sign from me and say nothing to your mother, brothers and sisters.'

He gave me a red-and-white insignia to replace the Chinese badge I had been wearing. The colours of Indonesia on my shirt would make it easier to cross *pemuda* lines. He also gave me the *pemudas'* new password: 'Sudara – Merdeka'.

Waking at the crack of dawn one day, I was unable to doze off again. A peaceful night's sleep was something I had not known since the Japanese invasion. I picked up on vibrations in the air that told me when fighting was about to break out. Around ten I heard the first artillery fire from the direction of the port, building steadily. After thirty minutes, the intensity decreased and Royal Navy Mosquito and Thunderbolt fighter-bombers appeared in the skies above the city. I watched them dive and fire. The Mosquito engines were so quiet that, by the time you heard them, they were already overhead, spitting fire from their noses. The *pemudas'* positions were blown to pieces.

I went to see Uncle Soen again late that afternoon. He had visitors: a couple of *pemudas* who had just been relieved of their post among the fighting in the port district. As was the Javanese custom, I sat on the floor beside them. From their garbled accounts, I made out that they had fought a desperate battle against Indian infantry units and had gained a profound respect for their enemy with their shaved heads and their pony tails. These were Gurkha and Dogra soldiers who had seen intensive combat not only on the Burma front, but also in southern and western Europe. To a man they carried a *kukri* strapped to the back of their belt, and used its curved blade to slit the enemy's throat. The *pemudas* said they had met overwhelming resistance and had been forced to pull back to the start of the long Sulung viaduct near Pasar Turi.

That night as usual I joined a handful of neighbours to patrol the streets of Undaan. We started at two and finished at four. The gun battles and artillery fire continued throughout the night.

On my way to Uncle Soen's the next morning, I met Soetardjo's mother. Sobbing, she told me that her son had been killed. I felt for Soetardjo but I was happy to hear that the *pemudas* were losing ground. Poker-faced, I offered the poor woman a few words of comfort and continued on my way. Arriving at Uncle Soen's, I asked him when I would be able to make my escape. He said I would have to wait until British troops controlled the full length of the Sulung viaduct.

I showed him the dagger Pah Tjillih had given me and asked him to treat it with poison. After some hesitation, he set to work in his small kitchen. Uncle Soen selected poisonous herbs to make a deadly arsenic compound, which he mixed with a powerful prussic acid solution. He smeared the mixture on my dagger and let it work its way into the metal. Within the hour, the entire blade had rusted.

'Graze your enemy's skin and he will die within minutes,' he said, handing me the dagger. 'Be careful not to cut your own hands. As I smeared the blade, I uttered a terrible curse that will protect you and bring death upon your enemy.'

Tears appeared in my uncle's eyes. 'Arto, I am forced to acknowledge that you have grown into a cold-blooded killer. During the Japanese occupation, I sensed that you had killed Japanese soldiers near Genteng Kali. As a child, you were shown no love by your parents, your brothers or your sisters. Now you are twenty, a grown man, yet your eyes are kind and your face is soft as a girl's. Every adversary will underestimate you and pay dearly for their mistake. Arto, promise me one thing… If you find yourself in conflict with your brothers and sisters, do not kill them! They are your own flesh and blood! It was with pain in my heart that I turned your dagger into a highly poisonous weapon. Remember that not all Indonesians are your enemy. Few among them have done you harm. But you are torn between two worlds, and revenge and hatred have clouded your heart.'

I embraced Uncle Soen and left. That night I took my dagger with me. And of course, I strapped that cursed *takeyari* to my back. I hated that bamboo spear, just as I hated everything that smacked of the Japanese and their atrocities. Taking the footbridge across the narrow canal, I walked from Undaan Kulon to Undaan Wetan. After exchanging the necessary passwords and greetings with the *pemudas* who manned the barricades, I slipped past them into the *kampong*, taking care to stick to narrow alleys and dead-end paths. I spotted a solitary *pemuda* urinating against a wall, drew my dagger and slid it between his ribs. With a muted cry, he collapsed in a heap. I took his Mannlicher rifle, removed the bolt and hurled it far over the wall. I wiped my bloodied blade on the *pemuda's* clothes, slid my trusty friend back into its sheath and moved on without making a sound. A few alleyways along, I saw another *pemuda*. He was sitting on the ground dozing, his weapon lying thoughtlessly beside him. I crept up on him and thrust my dagger deep into his neck. The poison did its work swiftly and thoroughly. I wiped the blood from my blade on his uniform.

Visions of the innocent women and children slaughtered in front of the former Simpang Club flashed through my mind. I felt a surge of revulsion but forced myself to go on. My body turned cold, then warm. The more men I killed, the fewer there would be to resist the British. A few yards along, snores alerted me to the presence of a third *pemuda*. I plunged my dagger deep into his throat.

Cautiously I made my way back to Undaan Kulon and, wielding my *takeyari*, joined the neighbourhood patrol. From the sound of the artillery barrage, I concluded that the battle for Surabaya was nearing the city centre.

At four in the morning, when my watch ended, it was still dark. Instead of going home, I walked to Jagalan to assess the situation. There I saw groups of young nationalists, men and women, advancing through Pasar Besar to Sulung district. The British front-line units had nearly advanced as far as Pasar Turi and the fighting there was fierce.

The banks of Kali Peneleh

From Jagalan, I walked back to Undaan past the banks of Kali Peneleh. All along the way, I saw lepers who were facing certain death. Grubbing around among the iguanas and crocodiles, some had been reduced to cannibalism. With no other food to be found, they ate the flesh of corpses. The stench was unbearable. Such was the state of every river that flowed through the city to the sea. If I was to break through and reach the British lines, my only chance would be to follow these waterways, to wade through this water. The thought turned my stomach. What brought these wretches to seek out a final resting place by the rivers? I suspected there were *rōmusha* among them, people who had been sentenced to hard labour by the Japanese and who, after the capitulation, had returned to Surabaya utterly destitute. With no family left in this ravaged city, they had been unable to find food, work or shelter, and were too weak to join the ranks of the *pemudas* and *pelopors*. Plagued by hunger, disease and other hardships, they had settled on the river banks. In desperation and then resignation, they waited for death.

Guide

Around 20 November, news reached me that the Indian 5th Infantry Division had occupied the entire area north of the Sulung viaduct. That evening I locked my bedroom door and made my preparations. I kneeled before the portrait of Queen Wilhelmina that hung above my divan bed, and gazed up in veneration. 'Your Majesty,' I murmured, 'I will fight for you and, if I should die, know that I died defending Your honour.'

Before going to bed, I asked God on bended knee for his protection and his blessing. I woke at two, dressed and, grabbing my cursed *takeyari*, set off on my nightly patrol. From the flares and the crackle of gunfire, I could tell that the battle was coming closer. As a precaution, I steered clear of Undaan Kulon that night. The street was full of posts manned by heavily armed *pemudas*.

The night for breaking through to the British lines came at last. Early that evening, I told Mama that I had been called away on patrol for a few days and that she was not to worry. I called at Uncle Soen's and gave him my *takeyari*, my poisonous dagger and my pocket knife for safe keeping. I was dressed in nothing but a white short-sleeved shirt and a worn pair of khaki shorts. I made sure not to wear any insignia. However, I did take my wallet, which contained photographs of my parents and a document stating that my status was equivalent to that of a European.

Uncle Soen told me that the government building was under fire. The Kenpeitai headquarters in the former Palace of Justice had been reduced to rubble, the Werfstraat prison had been overrun by Punjabi and Gurkha combat troops and most of the Dutch and Indo prisoners had been freed, narrowly escaping death at the hands of the Indonesian guards, who had poisoned their food. Every single guard had been killed. The British had also taken control of the entire Chinese district on the far side of the Red Bridge.

'Here is your escape route. Follow my instructions to the letter! Go directly to Kali Peneleh, follow the river bank and, once you have passed under Jagalan Bridge, head straight for the railway crossing at Sulung viaduct. Pass under the viaduct to the shunting yard and there you will come to a British outpost. Approach with your hands above your head and speak English. Ask the guard to take you to his commanding officer. Tell the commander all about yourself and offer your services as a guide. As soon as you leave, I will burn incense and entreat Allah to help you. I already have a feeling that you will make it through safely. The blessing of Allah be with you, my boy. Pah Tjillih will also pray for you. We are in touch by courier.'

Uncle Soen took me by the shoulders and pressed me to his chest. Midnight was not far off. I crossed Undaan *kampong* to Kali Peneleh. I encountered many *pemudas* along the way. They appeared to be on edge and I read dejection or sorrow in their faces. Fortunately none of them paid me the least attention. I saw vehicles carrying the wounded, and the sight of trucks piled with the bodies of dead *pemudas* filled me with satisfaction. Reaching Kali Peneleh, I went down to the riverbank, which was littered with the corpses of *rōmusha* and lepers. Countless iguanas and dwarf crocodiles were rooting around. The water stank terribly. I found a long stick and used it to hit out at the reptiles in my path. Here and there I had to wade up to my knees in the stinking water. I staggered under Jagalan Bridge and headed for the viaduct. It was a clear, moonless night but the sky was full of stars. Thankfully I had no trouble seeing in the dark, even at some distance. As salvos rang out between the warring parties, I walked straight through hell to the shunting yard, where a Gurkha sentry was standing guard. Not far from him, I saw clusters of soldiers firing mortar shells. I walked up to the sentry. He saw me coming from a long way off and pointed his Sten gun at me. I raised my hands and shouted, 'I am a Dutchman! A friend!'

'Come over here!' he shouted back, keeping his gun trained on me all the while.

I did as he asked. Without a sound, two soldiers came up and frisked me. I showed them the photographs of my parents and asked to speak to their commander. They looked at me in surprise and said, 'We thought you were an Indonesian.'

The two soldiers kept their distance, trying not to breathe in the stink of the river mud that clung to me. We arrived at a small building but they did not let me follow them in. After a brief interval, a British officer came out and greeted me. I showed him the photographs of my parents and told him the salient facts about myself. He ordered the two soldiers to put me in a bath and then thoroughly disinfect me. I took off my clothes, which were immediately disposed of by the soldiers.

An improvised bathing cabin had been set up at the edge of the shunting yard. I was handed a bar of soap and a towel. After a refreshing bath, I had to stand naked in a cold storage truck while one of the soldiers sprayed me with DDT. Then I was handed a set of military underwear, a British uniform with beret, a pair of woollen socks and black combat boots with ankle straps. Everything fitted me perfectly and I immediately felt like a whole new man. I slipped my wallet into one of the many pockets of my uniform and followed a couple of Punjabi soldiers back to the building I had been led to before.

This time I was granted entry. The officer handed me a mug of strong coffee and a cigarette. He offered me a seat and then questioned me. I asked to see a map of Surabaya. With the help of two NCOs he unfolded a giant, detailed map of the city and showed me the lines being held by the 5th Infantry Division. I pointed out almost all of the key *pemuda* contingents as far as Darmo district, relying on intelligence I had received from Uncle Soen. Then I offered my services as a guide to accompany his troops. The officer took me to the commanding officers' quarters, where he introduced me to his direct superior.

That same night I was roaming the city streets, guiding Allied troops towards Darmo and Wonokromo. I pointed out the key positions and Gurkha soldiers gunned down at least a dozen *pemudas*.

When I took my leave of the Gurkha soldiers in Wonokromo, an army captain gave me a lift to Tunjungan, Surabaya's main shopping street. There too, shops and other buildings had been reduced to rubble. Overhead tram lines lay across the road and looters were clambering over the ruins. At the crossroads with Genteng, close to what was left of the famous Whiteaway Laidlaw department store, I leapt out of the jeep, saluted and thanked the captain. He thanked me in turn for acting as their guide.

Feeling happy and fulfilled, I walked home dressed in a brown-green belted uniform with no insignia. My mother was surprised and asked where I had been all this time. I told her I had been staying with friends over in Darmo. When she asked me how I came by my uniform, I shrugged and headed for my bedroom. I undressed and lay down on my divan. Trembling with emotion and excitement, it was a long time before I fell asleep.

In the service of the AMA Police Forces

Early one morning at the start of December, I once again said goodbye to my mother. This time I put her mind at ease by telling her I was off to join the police. Dressed in a shirt and a pair of white trousers, I slipped my wallet into my back pocket and set off down Undaan Kulon past Genteng Kali to Tunjungan and then on to Embong Malang. I stopped outside the headquarters of the Allied Military Administration Police Forces – AMA for short – and stated my intention to the guard on duty. An officer came out and escorted me to the inspector's office. He got up from behind his desk, shook my hand and offered me a seat, before asking me all kinds of questions. Of course, I had to tell him that I was the illegitimate son of a Nolan. Though he could hardly hold that against me, he did think it tragic.

Once the paperwork was out of the way, I was issued with a police uniform and assorted equipment. My only weapon was to be a truncheon. I thought this was a joke, but kept my opinion to myself. I then walked from AMA HQ to Kaliasin, where I was given a room at the illustrious Hotel Brunet, sharing with a policeman by the name of Albert Toorop, a fair-haired Indo with a sturdy build and a retiring nature.

The next morning we lined up in front of the hotel and were marched to a field near the telephone exchange at the back of AMA HQ. Having been put through our paces by a drill instructor, we 'native police constables' were addressed in English by the major and chief commissioner of the British expeditionary force. A week of training in various police duties ensued, after which we were assigned to our various groups. On patrol we were accompanied by soldiers armed with Lee Enfield rifles and bayonets. But as a constable first class with the AMA Police Forces, that ridiculous truncheon was my only protection. Not surprisingly, I walked the streets feeling very uneasy indeed.

Our patrol group was assigned to southern Surabaya and environs. It was a large area and we were tasked with ridding it of subversive elements within a short period. This mainly involved nightly patrols. Our first weeks were marked by night-time gun battles with extremist groups offering stubborn resistance to the enormous firepower of the 5th Infantry Division. Occasionally, 'native policemen' had to accompany the Indian troops. I sometimes found myself assigned to a Gurkha platoon, at other times to a platoon made up of Punjabis and Sikhs. The Gurkhas fascinated me most. They were remarkable chaps, masters at sneaking up on the enemy and finishing them off with their *kukris*.

I was put on guard duty at the edge of the Chinese cemetery on Kembang Kuning, where the Punjabi regiment was stationed. I found Punjabi food strange at first, but gradually developed a taste for their odd pancakes filled with goat's meat and hot curry sauce. Guard duty was dull and I soon began to get fed up with it.

On evenings when I was not required to stand guard, I wandered around the encampment keeping my eyes and ears peeled. I saw Punjabi soldiers secretly handing over Lee Enfield rifles, Bren guns and hand grenades to the locals in exchange for sexual favours from the local women. I reported this to a number of inspectors, who in turn filed a complaint with Major Tanner, our commander-in-chief. No action was taken, and I was left baffled.

I found myself in the back of beyond one night, on patrol with three Punjabis. The moon was new and the cloudless sky glittered with stars. In the dim light, those Punjabis could spot *pelopors* up to 300 yards away. They gave me their firearms for safe keeping, drew their foot-long *kukris* and crept up on the enemy. I strained to see them pounce but my eyesight was no match for the darkness and the distance. Minutes later they came back and whispered, 'It is done!'

Hotel Brunet

The police barracks at Hotel Brunet, where I shared a room with the taciturn Albert Toorop, had a front garden with a paved section adjacent to the street. Benches for police personnel and their families had been placed in the shade of a few tall trees. I had only been staying at the hotel for a short while when a number of police inspectors and their families moved in, newly liberated from Indonesian concentration camps by British troops. Ironically, such camps were often guarded by Japanese soldiers awaiting repatriation. All of these former internees were wearing clothes handed out by the Red Cross, and the deprivation and emotional uncertainty they had endured were still etched on their faces. On the evening of their arrival, I was sipping a lager at the bar in the magnificent hotel salon when one of these inspectors came and stood next to me.

'Good evening. Van Meeuwen's the name. How's life in these parts?'

I shook his outstretched hand and answered, 'My name is Nolan, a humble constable first class. I have been here since 7 December 1945. You and your family will be safe here. The entire area as far as Surabaya's southern boundary has been cleared of *pelopors* and looters. The hotel is a pleasant place to stay. The food is excellent and the service is good. A simple man could wish for no more in these troubled times.'

'Nolan, you said? The next drink is on me.'

I had only just emptied my glass when two girls walked up to Inspector Van Meeuwen and kissed him on the cheek. They turned out to be his daughters, Truusje and Lotje. Their mother had died in the internment camp.

I made the girls' acquaintance and expressed my condolences to Van Meeuwen for the loss of his wife.

'Thank you, Nolan. I say, boy and girls, why don't we sit down somewhere for a quiet chat? Enjoy each other's company in a little more comfort.'

We found a charming spot in the corner, overlooking the garden, and had only just settled down when a young man joined us. Van Meeuwen introduced him as the fiancé of his younger daughter, Lotje. I shook his hand and sat back down.

They spoke at great length about camp life and the many hardships they had experienced. All the while, Truusje hardly took her beautiful eyes off me. This fairly rattled my nerves. When I got up to order another beer, she placed her hand on mine for a moment and said she would get it for me. She refused to let me pay and served me my drink so attentively that I was left completely flustered. Her father laughed sheepishly, well aware of his daughter's advances.

It came as a relief when time wore on and the family retired to their rooms. I wished them good night and we shook hands. But Truusje held my hand for a long time and looked deep into my eyes. I broke into a cold sweat.

The next morning, my truncheon and I were back on patrol with a number of other policemen in a Dodge truck. I also had a fighting knife attached to my belt. A soldier accompanied us on every patrol, carrying a Lee Enfield rifle with bayonet. To us it seemed like madness to be patrolling without guns while the enemy were armed to the teeth.

The police inspectors acknowledged our objections and we were given permission to scavenge for firearms and ammunition. When searching a number of fire-blasted *kampong* houses, I had the good fortune to come across a .38 calibre Smith & Wesson revolver hidden in a drain, with six bullets left in the cylinder. In another house in Kedung Anyar *kampong*, I happened across a charred body strung up on a roof beam. The place was swarming with flies and the stench was unbearable, but I still managed to track down a Mannlicher rifle concealed in a drainpipe. It was badly rusted but intact.

Before long, all us 'native policemen' had found ourselves a weapon and in our spare time we were permitted to clean them of dirt and rust. The barracks at Hotel Brunet had a weapons room that housed large quantities of ammunition. One of the inspectors supplied me with cartridges and I was allowed to get the range of my Mannlicher rifle by practising on the drill ground behind the nearby telephone exchange. Having handled my father's rifles as a boy, I soon got to grips with my new weapon.

Sitting on a stool outside my room, dressed only in my shorts, I was busy cleaning the weapons I had found when Van Meeuwen came up to me and stood there watching.

'I say, Nolan,' he said out of nowhere, 'can't you see the way my daughter Truusje looks at you? Why not pay her more attention? The girl no longer has a mother and she's already at an age where she has to think seriously about her future. She can see how happy her sister Lotje is with Lothar. So Nolan… show her a little understanding…' I stopped cleaning my rifle and looked up at him, dumbfounded.

Not long after this encounter, Truusje began to inquire about my service roster and soon I had no way of avoiding her. Every time I returned from patrol, she came looking for me so that I could join her on the hotel veranda. But whenever I looked at her legs, she would cover them with her skirt or shield my face with her hands. When I asked her why, she declined to answer. Eventually I put the question to Lotje and she showed me her own legs, which were covered in boils.

'Truusje's legs are the same as mine. We suffered from malnutrition in the camps. That is what killed our mother,' Lotje explained, 'and so many women her age.'

I looked at both sisters, gave the matter some thought and then said, 'Perhaps my mother can cure you of this ailment. Let me ask her. Will you come with me?'

Their father gave his permission and asked me if I had ever driven a jeep. I shook my head. He taught me to handle his jeep on the hotel grounds and I set off that afternoon, with Lotje and Lothar on the back seat, and Truusje beside me up front.

We arrived at the family home and I introduced the three of them to Mama. She examined the girls' legs, thought for a while and then went looking for the right medicinal herbs from her store. In her potpourri of broken Dutch, Malay, Javanese and Chinese she said, 'Arto, I will give you a supply of these herbs to take with you, along with some prussic acid. Those grains are highly poisonous, so be very careful. Take a bucket of boiling water, add a small quantity of the herbs and a few grains of prussic acid. When the water has cooled to lukewarm, the girls must put one leg at a time into the water. You will wash them and repeat this treatment every morning and every evening. Their legs will heal within a week. Wash your hands thoroughly with soap after every treatment. Do not get a single drop of water in your mouth, or you will be dead within minutes.'

Van Meeuwen was allocated a house on Arjuno Boulevard, a street I had known well as a child. Once the family had settled into their staff residence, he drove to the hotel personally to pick me up after my shift. In addition to a jeep, he owned a Harley Davidson motorcycle, which he lent me to make visiting his family easier. The force provided petrol free of charge. When I was not on night shift, the Van Meeuwens insisted that I stay with them. I treated the sisters' legs patiently. The skin of my hands became chapped and painful to the touch, but after one week the boils had indeed disappeared. My mother instructed me to rub their legs with soothing Purol ointment and, three weeks later, every last scar had all but vanished. From then on, the girls were able to show their legs without a trace of embarrassment.

Meanwhile, Truusje's tender feelings towards me grew ever more serious. Unless I was working, she insisted that I spend the night with her. She slept under a mosquito net, and I slept on a rush mat on the floor at the foot of her bed. Truusje was unable to sleep without me there, and so I acceded to her wishes.

A little while later, a cousin moved into the house with them. We got along well. The idea of spending every night off watching over Truusje struck me as excessive, so one evening I left the house and set off on my borrowed Harley. On Palmenlaan I ran into an old pal of mine. He was riding a Harley too and we went to a bar together. When both of us were half-drunk, we mounted our machines and powered down Simpang to Tunjungan and on to Pasar Besar. On the way, I let my legs rest on the highway bars, let go of the steering and crossed my arms. I rode down the street like this doing around thirty miles an hour. My pal rode behind me and followed suit. We had the time of our lives. As the night wore on, we slowed things down and headed for Waru, where we hung around the *kampong* for a while. My pal visited a prostitute and was gone for quite some time, while I watched over our bikes. It was the early hours of the morning by the time we got back to Surabaya. My friend headed for his home downtown and I returned to Hotel Brunet. At last I was able to sleep in my own bed again, instead of curled up on a mat at the foot of Truusje's bed like a manservant from the olden days. Little did I know that Truusje had been awake all night, worried sick about me.

The next day I worked an extra shift, on patrol in the *kampongs*. Here and there the stink was unbearable and led us to the badly decomposed bodies of civilians. Some of the corpses were half-burned. By now I was armed with the Mannlicher rifle I had found, and my superiors turned a blind eye. I fired shots in the air when I saw looters, as there were women and children among them. In the evening, I joined a team of ten other policemen and we headed for another area to sweep the *kampongs* clean. Looting was rife in the Chinese district on the other side of the Red Bridge, where the streets were still swarming with the remnants of fanatical *pemuda* units. Wherever we encountered the enemy, we leapt from the truck and hit the ground running and shooting.

One day, Inspector Van Meeuwen came storming into my room. 'I say, Nolan,' he burst out, 'we haven't heard from you for days. Truusje is driving me to distraction. She worries about you constantly. As soon as you have some time off, get on that motorbike and go and see her. Stay with her until your next shift. Understood?'

'Mr Van Meeuwen,' I replied, 'I have been working extra shifts all this time.'

Face flushed with anger, Van Meeuwen.

My roommate Albert Toorop had heard everything. 'Who in blazes does that chap think he is?' he said. 'Anyone would think you are his son-in-law. If I were you, I would watch myself with that girl. Before you know it, the whole family will have you under their thumb and your life will no longer be your own. And another thing… do you think he would have spoken to you that way if you had been a Belanda and not an Indo? I may be white, but I am an Indo too. I know how they think, how they talk about us. The colonial airs they put on with us will never change, not now, not ever. In their own minds, those Belandas are always reliving the glory days of the Dutch East India Company. The more I see, the less I understand what business they have being here.'

'You know what you need…'

The ranks of the AMA Police Forces included intellectuals, planters from companies in East Java, civil servants, railway officials and prominent members of the business community – all survivors of the internment camps and seething with hatred of anything that smacked of Japan or Merdeka. But by April 1946, conditions in and around Surabaya had stabilized to the point where many constables returned home and, where possible, tried to pick up the thread of their old lives. This left the force so short of manpower that even Indonesians were recruited as part of the reorganization. The fact that they were restricted to the traffic division didn't stop me viewing them with suspicion.

When the AMA Police Forces became the Municipal Police and fell under strict Dutch command, it spelled the end of the old free-and-easy approach. Each shift had to go by the book: every last bullet had to be accounted for and every incident, however minor, had to be reported in interminable detail. Before long, I was sick to the back teeth of it. One day they had me on patrol, the next I was on guard duty and they even had me directing traffic in the blazing sun.

I was popular with the girls but, with no sex to be had, frustration began to get the better of me. For months I suffered from a pounding headache above my right eye. I called in sick and the chief inspector sent me to see the police doctor, whose surgery was in a wing of Hotel Sarkies on Embong Malang.

The doctor examined me and asked, 'What kind of exercise do you take?'

'I lift weights now and again, do gymnastics on the high bar, I box and I go running.'

'You know what you need, Nolan?'

'And… what would that be, doctor?'

'You need to get married!' he said, with a deadpan expression.

'Get married? But I am much too green for that. I don't turn twenty-one until September. My mother would never allow it. I have no idea how to treat a girl or a woman.'

'Calm down boy, I am not talking about *marriage* marriage. I mean you need to start seeing women. Going to bed with women. What you need is… a good fuck! Once you have done that and done it on a regular basis, your headache will disappear all by itself.'

I looked at him in bewilderment and he asked, 'Don't you have a girlfriend?'

'Why yes, doctor, I am in love with one of Inspector Van Meeuwen's daughters. Do you know who I mean?'

'Ah, you must mean his elder daughter… Truusje, I believe? She bears a striking resemblance to her late mother.'

I nodded.

'If I were you Nolan, I would not put her off too long. She would make a good match for a boy like you. Give it some thought.'

I left the doctor's surgery with mixed feelings, but carried on doing my shifts with a fanatical devotion that left me little time to go and see my girl.

It was late in the year when I heard that the Dutch Marines were taking over the occupation of Surabaya and the surrounding area. I had seen them on shore leave in the city and, full of admiration for their modern weapons, I hatched a plan to work for them. In our intimate moments, I shared these thoughts with Truusje but they did not go down well, triggering wave after wave of protest and prompting many a tear. Lotje and her fiancé Lothar were equally vocal in their disapproval. But their father's comments were the final straw. In the presence of his daughters, he accused me of practising *guna-guna* on them. And while he had no qualms about my using black magic to cure their skin, he lambasted me for bringing Truusje under my spell.

These accusations really got my goat. Not only did I believe that using *guna-guna* to get a girl was the most cowardly thing a man could do, but I also had absolutely no idea how to go about it. Furthermore, I had not set out to charm anyone; it was Truusje's father who had charmed me. From then on, my relationship with the family cooled and, alone in my room, I took to brooding and worrying. I loved Truusje deeply, but I had no idea what to do about her.

Regarding my background

It was September 1946, my twenty-first birthday, and we celebrated at home with a modest party. The whole family was there, except Ella and Ina, who had been interned in women's camps somewhere near Malang. My brothers Jacob and Karel, my half-sister Nonnie, her husband Ang Soen Bing and their children, and Uncle Soen and Aunty Kiep all wished me every happiness and presented me with small gifts. Mama, Babu Tenie and Kokkie Tas had prepared my favourite meals: fried rice Cantonese style and macaroni cheese.

Before the festivities, the family gathered in the dining room. The table was only partially set. At its head sat Jacob, as the eldest son and Mama's right hand. Before him lay a large folder containing a number of documents. Mama sat to Jacob's right, with Karel beside her, and Uncle Soen and Aunty Kiep sat to his left. I took my place opposite Jacob at the far end of the table.

When we were all seated, Jacob began his speech. 'Arto, today you have reached the age of twenty-one. You are now an adult. Ever since your cousin George died in a Japanese prison camp near Bandung in 1943, I have fulfilled the role of your guardian. Today my guardianship comes to an end. As you know, Papa was not officially married to Mama. All five of us were fathered by him but never recognized. That is why we bear the name Sie with the name "Nolan" in quotation marks, in full "Sie, goes by the name of Nolan". But all five of us have been recognized to the extent that we have been granted equivalent status with Europeans. Here in this folder, I have an extract from the Government Gazette in question. You no doubt remember my many quarrels with Papa. Before war broke out, I had my name changed to "Nolans", and for this reason it is not listed in the Government Gazette. It is of course a despicable thing for Papa to inflict on the five of us. It makes us pariahs in Indies society. But Papa has more to answer for. Before he met Mama, he fathered another child by a Chinese woman. Only she came from a powerful and influential family who threatened Papa with all manner of retribution if he failed to take responsibility for his offspring. As you know, Papa was a lawyer at the time, so the last thing he wanted was a scandal. That Chinese woman gave birth to a son named Jonas Chen. At Papa's expense, the boy was given an outstanding education. After school, he attended a Dutch university, graduating in economics from Leiden. He then went on to settle in Jember, where he was appointed chief administrator of the Nolan estates under the supervision of his cousin Alfred Nolan and Alfred's father, David Nolan. He also enjoyed the confidence of others, including his cousin George Nolan, your former guardian. Before Papa died, he made cousin George your guardian and reserved a large sum of money in his will for your further education. Papa wanted you to obtain a degree in engineering or to become a Master of Laws. Unfortunately the war has dashed many hopes and I no longer know where to find Papa's will. I suspect the document is in Jonas Chen's possession. I aim to recover it, because we are determined that you should resume your studies. My first priority, therefore, is to discover the whereabouts of Jonas Chen.'

'Thank you, Jacob,' I said, 'for resolving to help track down

Papa's will. But there can be no question of my studying at present. I have to earn money because no one is looking after Mama.'

Jacob handed me the folder. My mood was one of dismay as I accepted these documents on my background. It was time for me to have my say. 'Mama, having heard all this, I – like Jacob – wish to change my surname so that later I too can found my own family tree and above all lead my own life. I now know that I will never legally bear the name of Nolan and so I wish to purchase the name "Noland" with a *d* and to live out the rest of my life under that name. Will you give me the money I need to change my name?'

'Arto,' Mama answered, in tears, 'I understand your reasons. You are still my *anak mas*. Tomorrow I will go out and sell a little of my jewellery. Come here, Arto, and kneel before your mother. I will pray for you and give you my maternal blessing.'

I kneeled before her and laid my head in her lap. She clasped her hands above my head and began to pray. Everyone stood up and joined her in prayer. Now and then, I could hear a gentle sob and even I shed tears of disappointment. How could my father, a man of the law, have acted so lawlessly? How could he have done this to me?

It was time for the party to begin but I could do little more than stare vacantly into space. A few days later, Mama gave me my twenty-first birthday present: the 250 guilders I needed to change my name. Because of the war, I was required to wait. Mama kept the money until such times as I would be allowed to submit my petition. To alter my personal details, I would have to apply to the chief representative of the Crown in Batavia. Changing my name to Noland was a symbolic act. I wanted to distance myself from the colonial taint of the Eurasians and the fair-skinned Dutch Indo elite. It was a name that would make a new man of me: a Dutchman born of the Indies, loyal to the House of Orange of my own free will.

Interpreter with the Dutch Marine Brigade

December 1946. I was still a constable first class with the Municipal Police, deployed with Section 2 at Kaliasin. The work bored me. Relations between Truusje and I had cooled, but I still had the use of Inspector Van Meeuwen's police motorcycle: the Harley Davidson with its 1500 cc two-cylinder engine.

I was out for a ride one day on Arjuno Boulevard, when I met my old pal Nono Sloesen, dressed in the khaki uniform of the Dutch Marine Corps. He talked at great length about the special forces intelligence work he was doing for the Marine Brigade Security Service. I asked him how to join up and he advised me to report to a man named Mulder, a captain in the Marine Corps and also an Indo.

The next morning I donned my police uniform, jumped on the Harley and rode to Firefly Barracks on Porongstraat in Wonokromo district. At the barrier, I asked the marine on duty if I could speak to the captain about enlisting. My request was granted and I parked my motorcycle next to the command building. A marine took me to see the captain. I saluted, he offered me a seat and proceeded to question me about my police duties. It did not take him long to find me wanting. He thought my appearance was too feminine and believed I had no place in a corps of hardened soldiers. I saluted and left his office.

My hopes crushed, I got back on the Harley and rode straight to Nono Sloesen's house on Arjuno Boulevard. He assured me that a change of command was due soon and told me to try again when the new commander was installed in January 1947.

At the end of a night shift in late January, I went to the family home in the early hours of the morning, took a refreshing bath and changed into fresh clothes. Babu Tenie made me breakfast. Mama had woken and came to ask me what I was up to. When I told her I was planning to join the Marines, she protested. 'I won't have it! The school has reopened – go back and finish your studies. You have a future to think of.'

I let Mama say her piece and went down to Firefly Barracks a second time. Again I reported to the guard on duty and this time I was taken to see the new commander, Captain Rob Groeneveld of the Marine Corps. I stood to attention and saluted him. The captain held out his hand and introduced himself. He struck me as a friendly chap and asked me all kinds of questions about my past under the Japanese occupation and during the Bersiap period at the start of the Indonesian revolution. A first lieutenant of the Marine Corps was present throughout. We spoke for an hour, after which I was introduced to the senior interpreters Piet Dikotta and Bert Hermelijn. Piet Dikotta I already knew from the AMA Police Forces under British command. Captain Groeneveld decided that I could start work immediately. He summoned his senior NCO, Sergeant Major Vestdijk of the Marine Corps, to sort out the contracts. Proud as a peacock, I saluted the gentlemen of the staff, jumped on the Harley and rode back home.

The next morning I handed in my resignation to the Chief Commissioner of the Municipal Police. After a considerable show of reluctance, he finally relented and I said farewell to my superior officers and fellow constables. That same evening I rode that mighty Harley over to Arjuno Boulevard to return it to Inspector Van Meeuwen with my thanks. Surprised, he asked me what this was all about. His daughters appeared on the porch behind him, and Truusje flew into my arms and kissed me. I looked at the three of them in triumph and said, 'I have signed up with the Marine Brigade and will continue to fight as hard as I can against those *pelopor* savages. I will take revenge for what they have inflicted on me and on so many others. I will sacrifice myself for Queen and Country! If I should die, then so be it. And as for you, Mr Van Meeuwen, you have falsely accused me of practising *guna-guna*. A more serious accusation is barely conceivable and for this reason I will now take my leave of you.'

Inspector Van Meeuwen froze. Truusje burst into tears and tried to throw herself into my arms again, but I shunned her and walked away without a word of goodbye.

Halfway down the boulevard, I hailed a *becak* and asked the driver to take me home. My mind was a jumble of thoughts – ugly, mournful and happy. My love for Truusje was strong, but I still felt far too young and restless to marry her. The closer I came to Undaan Kulon, the more relieved I felt. I wanted to be free, to feel no love for any girl. I had to stay tough; this was war, after all. Arriving home, I grabbed Mama by the shoulders and said proudly, 'Mama, from tomorrow I will be a marine and fight the enemy with renewed vigour. My salary will be much higher, so I will be able to give you more financial support.'

'But I do not want you to be a soldier!' Mama whimpered. 'You might be killed! Look at what happened to your cousin Willem. Are you out of your mind?'

'Mama, I am duty bound to take care of you. Jacob and Karel do not want to support you financially. I am the only one who can do anything for you. The police paid me a pittance for those long, demanding shifts, and they were dangerous too.'

Early in the morning I said farewell to Mama and walked to Undaan Kulon, where I took a *becak* to Firefly Barracks. The duty officer sent me to see Sergeant Major Vestdijk of the Marine Corps, who took me to the quartermaster's store, where I was fully kitted out as a marine. Vestdijk then summoned the head of household services to escort me to the interpreters' dormitory. There I met a few boyhood friends, including Nono Sloesen and Harry Tjong. Two ammunition chests piled one on top of the other served as my bedside table. I hung my M1 Garand rifle from the straps on my folding bed and placed my bayonet belt at the foot.

After downing a mug of coffee, I went to see Piet Dikotta in his office. He was head of Espionage and Documentation. I got better acquainted with Bert Hermelijn, chief interpreter with the Interrogation Department. Between them, these two men would be responsible for my training. Interrogation of political prisoners and POWs was to be my primary duty. Training was to take two weeks. In the meantime I underwent general military training alongside many other interpreters. This consisted of daily marches in full combat gear to the golf course at Wonokromo, where I was able to let rip on the rifle range.

Back at barracks, we were instructed on how to maintain an assortment of infantry weapons. Each interpreter harboured his own feelings of hatred and revenge against the barbaric Indonesian freedom fighters. Our number included Indos, Chinese, Javanese, Ambonese and Manadonese and we trained with a grim fanaticism. There were Indo boys who had seen family members raped, tortured and killed before their eyes. They, more than any of us, were champing at the bit to be sent to the front line. I waited my turn to be allotted a frontline posting. First I had to complete further training in prisoner interrogation, writing up interrogation reports, and the appraisal and transmission of details of military importance. I also learned to process the entire administration of prisoners from capture to arraignment. My duties were both extensive and important.

One morning I and four other interpreters were ordered to interrogate five *pemudas* who had been taken prisoner, members of a fanatical guerrilla movement called the Indonesian People's Revolutionary Front. The charges brought against them included the murder of Reverend Laloe on the town square in Porong. Another three of their group were still at large. The captives' confessions revealed how the pastor had met his end. I told my fellow interpreters I had known Laloe well, that this kind-hearted Manadonese clergyman had christened me, my mother, my sister and my half-sister at the Protestant church on Bubutan during the Japanese occupation. The five killers sat patiently on the ground, staring indifferently into space. I ordered them to get up quickly and we proceeded to kick them to the ground. They writhed in pain. Then I asked them who had tied Reverend Laloe to the tow hook of the truck. Two of the *pemudas* confessed. I kicked them until they passed out. When they came to, I asked them who had been driving the truck that dragged Reverend Laloe across the square until he died. No one said a word. I stamped on their chests until their ribs cracked. The other interpreters sat at their typewriters and hammered out the interrogation reports.

Every day, alongside our military exercises, I had to interrogate prisoners with my fellow interpreters. Every interrogation involved the use of severe force and each time the torture I had suffered flashed before my eyes.

When I was home on leave one weekend, Mama handed me a letter from the Military Service department of the General Staff of the Royal Netherlands East Indies Army. On my return to Firefly Barracks, I reported to Captain Groeneveld with the letter and he provided me with a cover letter stating that I was already in active service with the Marines. I was given permission to visit the KNIL's Military Service office, not far from the Red Bridge. I turned up in my utility uniform and the guard sent me to see a lieutenant. I tried to explain that I was unable to fulfil my military service with the KNIL because I was already in active service with the Marines, but he was having none of it and sent me to see the general. The man just about exploded.

'I will not accept this, Nolan!' he screamed at me. 'You will rue the day! I can assure you of that!'

'I will rue the day as a marine, Sir, when I am sent to the front.'

'Out of my sight! Dismissed!' he barked. 'And never let me lay eyes on you again!'

I sprang to attention, saluted, turned on my heels and marched out of his office feeling relieved. Even then, I had little respect for the KNIL's fighting power. I had seen them run as the Japs advanced on Surabaya. Back at barracks, I informed my senior officers that the matter had been resolved and I was free to resume training.

The marines I encountered could be divided into three main categories. First there were the Sixteen Sixty-Fivers, who took their name from 1665, the year the Dutch Marine Corps was founded. They were professional marines with a six-year contract that was up for automatic renewal until they retired. I soon realized that most of them were the kind of soldier I needed to watch out for:

often petty, all too ready to open their big mouths, adept at sucking up to their superiors and shitting on those below them.

The second category consisted of war volunteers on a three-year mutual contract. Trained in the United States, they were a cheerful bunch on the whole, though aggressive and often spoiling for a fight. On paper, this was my category too, though I was on a one-year 'local' contract that was extended automatically. Needless to say, it was also the category to which most of my good friends belonged.

No provisions whatsoever were made for us interpreters. We were handed our pay and that was that. It barely occurred to us at the time, but if you were married with children and killed in action, your dependents had to dry their tears on nothing but an additional one month's wages. Many a dead interpreter's family must have been reduced to begging in the streets.

The third category of marine were the conscripts. They had undergone a brief spell of conventional battle training in the Netherlands, before being marched onto a boat to the Indies to face the rigours of guerrilla warfare. These poorly prepared young lads accounted for most of our fatalities in later battles.

On patrol with the Marine Brigade Security Service

On completing my intelligence training, I was assigned to Krembung as additional manpower for Marine Brigade Security Service, Detachment III. The quartermaster issued me with a camp bed, two blankets, a poncho, four hand grenades and four types of cartridge for my M1 rifle. After an early breakfast, I loaded my gear onto a truck stacked with food crates and we set off. The pals I had trained with were stationed elsewhere.

It was a dusty ride over bad roads from Wonokromo to Krembung, around twenty-five miles south of Surabaya, in the Porong Delta. On arrival, I reported to Detachment III, which was based in a governor's residence near the sugar factory. The commander was Sergeant Cornelissen of the Marine Corps, a white Indo born and raised in Holland. He showed me to my room, which I was to share with an Ambonese soldier by the name of Ben de Lima. I folded out my camp bed and attached my mosquito net to poles at each corner. Then I took a refreshing bath.

At the base, we had a couple of *babus* and a house boy to attend to all the household chores. When night fell, the *babus* were kept otherwise occupied by the Dutch marines. This appeared to be standard practice. Ben de Lima and I were indifferent to their physical charms.

The road to the sugar factory was blocked by a barbed-wire barricade and an access barrier guarded by a handful of infantrymen from A Company. Every day around dinnertime, the poor from the *kampong* would come to the barrier and beg for leftovers. We fetched the occasional sack of sugar from the factory warehouse and struck up a lively trade with the locals. A cup of sugar would get us an egg, a saucepan of sugar a whole chicken.

A ceasefire was in place but it was being violated by both sides. We were lucky that the *pemudas* were poor marksmen, so poor in fact that not one of us was wounded, never mind killed. That said, many of the Dutch lads succumbed to the usual tropical diseases: everything from malaria, dysentery and diarrhoea to ringworm and nasty rashes. We patrolled night and day, and under cover of darkness we often came close to the demarcation line. Now and then we encountered small bands of Indonesian Army infiltrators. Brief skirmishes took place, generally resulting in the deaths of a few *pelopors* and the rest being taken prisoner. For every dead *pelopor*, I carved a notch in the butt of my M1 rifle.

Every *pelopor* we captured underwent tough interrogation. They were guilty of massacres on simple villagers and Chinese merchants and their families. But that was not all: they took a perverse pleasure in carving up bodies. Some Chinese women and children had their limbs severed before being buried alive. After questioning, the culprits pointed out the graves and we got them to dig up the bodies. We had little patience with those savages. If they refused to confess, Ben de Lima and I threatened to make them eat paper and drink their own urine. These threats worked. Once interrogation was over and the reports were drawn up, prisoners were transported by way of General Headquarters at Firefly Barracks to Surabaya's notorious Werfstraat prison.

In mid-March, A Company was put on high alert throughout Krembung district. Ten-tonners loaded with ammunition and equipment shuttled back and forth. I had to bid Ben de Lima farewell, as I was the sole interpreter from Detachment III to be assigned to the first platoon, which was to accompany a platoon of assault troops through Mojosari to Mojokerto, a short distance inland. Ben de Lima and I had shared some good times during those weeks in Krembung.

At the crack of dawn, I filled my knapsack with ammunition, hand grenades and K rations. The rest, including my mosquito net and folded camp bed, went into my duffel bag. My baggage was then labelled with name, registration number and unit. Over my shirt, I hung two slings each with six clips of .30-cartridges. My fighting knife for man-to-man combat was strapped to my right calf, the sheath tucked in my legging. I sharpened the blade on a whetstone with a little water till the edge was keen enough to shave the hair from my legs.

I joined the assault troops and the lads from the Demolition Group in the first truck. Sergeant Cornelissen shook me firmly by the hand and wished me luck. Both groups rode to Porong first and then across Porong Bridge into hostile territory. We met with little resistance. Not far from Mojosari, the tanks and armoured vehicles stopped at a river, where a bunch of amtracs stood waiting as planned. We leapt out of the trucks and marched aboard. When the ramp slammed shut behind us, we felt the full heat of the exhaust pipes, which ran through the body of the vehicle and out the top to keep it watertight. Pouring with sweat, we cursed like devils.

The amtracs drifted slowly to the other side of the river. The ramps creaked open and we were left to make our way to Mojosari on foot, straight through the jungle at times. We avoided the roads whenever we could for fear of landmines. Trees had been felled to form roadblocks, and booby-trapped barricades meant dangerous work for the Demolition Group.

We made decent progress, encountering sporadic light artillery fire along the way, but the enemy stood no chance against our modern weapons. As we marched, other marines swept the area clean. Here and there I saw the bodies of dead *pemudas*. Approaching a rice-husking plant, we came under heavy fire. *Pemudas* had set up machine-gun posts in two abandoned KNIL pillboxes close to the factory building, each gun manned by three fighters. We called back for bazookas. Marksmen with Browning Automatic Rifles provided cover and before long the pillboxes had been blown to kingdom come, *pemudas* and all. There was no time for celebration: we needed all our wits about us to take the plant itself. A bazooka rocket slammed into the main entrance and I ran into the factory with a handful of assault troops, guns blazing. I had to be quick reloading my M1. One of my reserve slings was already empty and I could see *pelopors* skulking among the heavy machinery. With a tight group of marines, I headed for the machine rooms, where we fanned out, surrounding the *pelopors* and picking them off one by one. We were lucky: they had been planting explosives under the machines. Outside, marines were hunting down *pelopors* as they ran. Not one of them escaped with his life.

We marched into Mojosari to find the place deserted. Almost all the villagers had fled. A few old men and women were the only ones left, wandering around with nothing but dogs and chickens for company. A good place to rest. We sat down by a dry ditch with a few lads from the Demolition Group. I slid the knapsack from my shoulder, took out two tins of K rations and pulled my water bottle from my belt to swig leftover tea from our early breakfast.

After resting a while, the entire column moved on in the direction of Mojokerto to join the main force. Above us flew a number of Fairey Firefly strike fighters belonging to the KNIL air force. Every now and then the planes dived to fire rockets. Reunited with the other units, we made rapid progress. Arriving in the centre of Mojokerto, we all had to jump off the trucks and advance on foot to the market square. There I saw three of our Sherman tanks, one firing its mighty gun at the mosque, where a clutch of fanatical Hizbullah units were thought to be holed up.

There was a *pasar* that day. With the assault troops I ran across the square and opened fire. Market vendors and customers scattered in all directions. I picked out soldiers among the crowd and gunned them down. Running alongside me was a Dutch corporal, a good-hearted lad from Limburg. He spotted a Jap lying on the ground. After the capitulation, many Japanese soldiers without an exit plan wound up fighting alongside the Indonesians. This one was bleeding heavily, lying face down with his right hand under his belly, an odd position for a fallen soldier. The corporal wanted the Jap's insignia for his collection and went over to him. 'Stick him with your bayonet first,' I yelled. 'The bastard is still alive and reaching for his gun!'

The corporal was too cocky to listen. Suddenly the Jap rolled onto his back, drew his Nambu pistol and fired two shots at my comrade in rapid succession. Fatally wounded, he collapsed in a heap. His last words were, 'Oh mother, what have I done?'

In anger, I blasted my entire clip of eight rounds into that Jap bastard.

There was no time to dwell on the dead boy from Limburg. Fierce fighting had broken out across the town. With a few lads from the assault platoon, I charged down a side street and was amazed to find Indonesian policemen directing traffic amid the chaos. They were trying to wave through a couple of heavy tanks. I recognized them as Japanese tanks from the time of the occupation, only now their gun turrets were painted with the red-and-white of Sukarno's Indonesia. I signalled to a corporal rifleman to load his M1 with anti-tank rounds. I led by example and fired four shots at the turret, which immediately stopped turning. I had taken out the gunner. The others took care of the second and third tanks.

No sooner had the marines wiped out the Indonesian policemen than hordes of Hizbullah fanatics came charging at us wielding bamboo spears and machetes in all shapes and sizes. I let loose with one clip after another, exhausting my slings of back-up ammo, and ran with a small troop of marines to the veranda of a house that had been shot to pieces. There we pulled our knapsacks from our shoulders, grabbed our hand grenades and lobbed them among the advancing hordes. BAR and tommy gunners came to our aid. At last the enemy turned and ran. Little did we suspect how much fight those fanatics had left in them.

Night had fallen and my combat pack was pretty much empty. But I still had clips of phosphorus rounds on my belt. If I suspected *pelopors* might be hiding in one of the *kampong* houses, I fired one or two of those tracer bullets into the roof. In no time the *attap* thatching would catch fire and the walls of bamboo matting would start to burn. Those bastards would come running out soon enough and we were waiting to gun them down one by one.

Head of Prisoner Interrogation at Surabaya HQ-II

When Mojokerto was fully under our control, I was sent to Mojosari, where Surabaya Headquarters II of the Marine Brigade Security Service was located, SHQ-II for short. There I was made Head of Prisoner Interrogation under the command of First Lieutenant Lichtenberg of the Marine Corps. My main task was to gather as much intelligence as possible regarding the enemy's overall military situation in the areas around Pacet and Trawas. Before the war, both had been popular holiday resorts for colonial families.

With a team of five interpreters at my disposal, I interrogated dozens of prisoners a day and had no qualms about the use of force. After a week of grinding out counterintelligence and combat intelligence reports based on these interrogations, I began to suffer from acute insomnia and Lieutenant Lichtenberg sent me to Surabaya for a few days' leave. I travelled by food truck and took a *becak* through the city to our home in Undaan Kulon.

As soon as I arrived, I took an invigorating bath, after which Mama treated me to a delicious meal. While we ate, Mama asked me to recount my experiences. Curious to hear more, Babu Tenie and Kokkie Tas hovered close by until I ordered them to join us at the table. Though taken aback, they both obeyed. It was unheard of for servants to sit at the family table and they did not know quite what to do with themselves, but I reassured them and soon they were eating with us. Mama laughed and did not seem to mind. Of course, I gave them only the sketchiest account of my exploits. The meal over, I retired to my room, collapsed on the divan and fell into a deep sleep.

In the tropics, night falls within ten minutes at around six in the evening and that was when Babu Tenie woke me. I took a bath, put on my khaki dress uniform and strolled over to the Marines Club on Tunjungan, a thirty-minute walk. There I ordered a tray of stiff drinks and found myself a quiet spot at the back of the dance hall. The atmosphere was good. They were spinning tunes by Glenn Miller and Benny Goodman on the gramophone. I steadily drained one shot glass after another.

After a few days, I reported to Firefly Barracks and was duly dispatched to Mojosari. 'Good break, Nolan?' Lieutenant Lichtenberg asked on my arrival. 'You look rested at least. Preparations are under way for the big push to Pacet and Trawas. Make sure you have sufficient ammunition and grenades, then help the others pack up the intelligence records and prepare them for transport.'

The day came when all Marine units, including the Security Service, were ready for action. I was once again ordered to join the vanguard and climbed onto the first truck of the column, already full of lads from the assault platoon. 'Welcome aboard, Intel!' they said and broke into the battle song of the US Marine Corps.

We were led off by three Greyhound armoured cars and two Sherman tanks from the Heavy Artillery Company. Then came the first truck, with me on board, followed by the Marine Brigade's second infantry battalion. As we headed south in the early morning and left Mojosari behind us, the road began to rise beneath our wheels. The mountainous terrain was magnificent but with it came the danger of snipers. We passed deep ravines and walls of sheer rock. No one said much. Some of the men smoked nervously. I maintained an icy calm and kept a sharp lookout in all directions. My M1 rifle was primed and loaded with anti-tank rounds, which could pass through walls and the trunks of young trees.

A couple of Fairey Firefly fighter-bombers escorted us on the way to our objectives in Pacet and Trawas. They launched rockets at enemy positions here and there, after which our Demolition Group had to spring into action to make sure they did not pose a threat: a time-consuming process. Those boys usually had to perform this dangerous work under sniper fire. When the bullets began to fly, we leapt out of the truck and fanned out on both sides of the road to provide cover. By chance, I spotted a sniper in a tree at the edge of a ravine some 200 yards away, his carbine aimed at one of our mine disposal squad. Without a second's hesitation I pulled the trigger of my M1 and fired three shots in quick succession. The carbine fell from the tree first, then the *pemuda*.

'Good shot!' someone behind me shouted.

Then all hell broke loose. From behind rocks on the slopes around us, the enemy let rip with light artillery and small mortar shells. Almost to a man we jumped from the trucks, ran for cover and began returning fire. A single BAR gunner per truck stayed behind. Everywhere on the mountainside and against rocks I saw *pemudas* being blown to bits. Latching onto the assault troops, I pressed ahead of the column, scouting deeper into hostile territory. We stumbled upon a nest of *pemuda* resistance, one of them armed with a Japanese Taisho machine gun. We dispersed rapidly and gunned all five of them down.

After a mile of walking and shooting, we reached a ramshackle bridge that spanned a deep ravine. The railing had been knocked away. The town of Pacet was already visible on the other side.

'There lies our first objective,' I said to a few of the lads in the platoon.

The sergeant came and stood next to me. 'Damn it,' he said, 'that bridge is in bad shape. Wait here. I'll go back to the column alone and put this to the commander.'

Thirty minutes later, the column arrived. Assisted by the boys from the Engineering Corps, the commander examined the construction and the state of the bridge. After weighing up our options for a while, it was decided that a single Sherman tank should cross first. When it reached the other side safely, two more followed. I jumped aboard the second tank. All the way across I could feel the bridge swaying under the heavy weight. The remainder of the column followed. Only the drivers remained in the trucks, while the rest crossed on foot.

The hills of Pacet were studded with splendid bungalows, once the property of wealthy colonials and the Indo elite. Now they stood abandoned and shot to pieces. I searched each building for military documents and translated the few I found for the column commander. This yielded some information on where to expect pockets of resistance as we advanced towards Trawas.

In great haste, a sick bay for wounded marines was set up in one of the larger bungalows and a detachment of marines stayed behind, occupying the buildings that were relatively intact. The main force advanced the extra mile to Trawas, which was already taking a pounding from our Fairey Fireflies. As we approached the town, our party – which included a number of journalists and one or two representatives of the UN Committee of Good Offices – came under intense fire from Japanese knee mortars and machine-gun posts in the *sawahs*, well camouflaged among the plantain trees.

I was among the dozens of marines who leapt from the road into the *sawahs* below and opened fire on the enemy. A likeable Frisian lad was running not far from me. I caught sight of a gunman hiding behind a couple of plantain trees some two hundred yards away and, raising my M1 in a reflex, shot him in the head. Not quickly enough: my Frisian comrade fell face down without so much as a whimper. Blood and brains spilled out as I pulled him from the mud and laid him on his back. I wiped the dirt from his face with my handkerchief. A dumdum bullet had hit him square in the forehead. His skull was cracked and stuck to the inside of his helmet.

Members of the UN Committee came over to take a look and a journalist snapped a few photos of the poor Frisian boy. I swore out loud and walked on, straight through the *sawahs*, in search of more extremists. One or two raised their hands in surrender, but I did not trust them and shot them dead. Further along I spotted another machine gunner and his helper, hidden behind plantains and tall reeds. He was a lousy shot and I eliminated him in seconds. Before his helper could even take aim, one of my mates had blown him to bits with his tommy gun. The Frisian boy was our only fatality that day, though several men were injured, some of them seriously.

The main street in Trawas led up to a grand hotel with a beautiful swimming pool. It turned out to be the *pemuda* headquarters. Ten marines stormed the building. Resistance was weak and in no time we had seized control of the entire complex and immediately began putting things in order for the staff of the second infantry battalion.

In Pacet and Trawas, we all went in search of decent accommodation among the abandoned holiday bungalows. Sentries were stationed at strategic points. A bunch of us from the Marine Brigade Security Service settled into a bungalow beside a waterfall. I stripped off and showered in the wonderfully cool water. The Dutch lads followed suit.

Events took an unfortunate turn. It transpired that we had advanced much too far into hostile territory and put the government in an awkward spot, politically speaking. The order came down from on high to relinquish our newly won positions in and around Pacet and Trawas. This meant pulling all the way back to the boundary between Mojosari and Mojokerto. It felt as if our hard-earned victory had been for nothing and most of us refused to comply. Colonel Roelofs, our senior commander, was obliged to travel all the way to the front from GHQ in Surabaya to address us in person. He too expressed regret at this state of affairs but insisted that retreating was not an act of cowardice. As marines, we had no choice but to follow orders. Grumbling, everyone prepared for the journey back. Out of revenge and frustration, we booby-trapped buildings, houses and even pianos. Mines were laid on the access roads and on the day of departure we dynamited all the sluice gates to drain the water from every single swimming pool.

In the lowest of spirits, we made our way back to Mojosari. At Surabaya HQ-II, I resumed my work as head of Prisoner Interrogations with Department III. In consultation with the head of Department IV, we selected a number of prisoners to conduct espionage operations in the areas we had abandoned. One week later, our informants returned with news that Pacet and Trawas were once again crawling with Indonesian Army units.

From Mojosari, I was transferred with another interpreter to the Marine Brigade Security detachment at Purwokerto, some fifty miles south. The entire area had to be purged of extremists, a mission that involved lengthy and exhausting daily patrols, and the occasional skirmish. Indonesian forces were waging a guerrilla war but though the US-trained marines had been primed for conventional warfare, they quickly mastered a range of guerrilla tactics. As local interpreters, we had all been born and raised in the country and spoke the language. Not only that, but we knew the mindset and habits of the Indonesians through and through. This made us invaluable to the Marine Brigade. When I manned the border control with a few marines and saw people heading to market early in the morning, I could pick out suspects among the hard-working locals with considerable accuracy. A look in their eyes or something in the way they moved their arms was often enough to tell me who I was dealing with. Searching market-goers at the checkpoint, I often surprised my Dutch comrades by discovering cunningly concealed hand grenades and landmines under a load of rice sheaves hanging from a trader's *pikolan*, or Sten guns and revolvers in the food baskets women carried on their heads. A tough round of interrogation would usually result in arrest and transport to Surabaya for trial. If the danger was more immediate, I shot the *pelopors* dead on the spot or had them shot. These were men whose sarongs were rolled up at the waist to conceal a knife, a revolver or a hand grenade, men out to kill marines in a surprise attack. Within a week, we had purged the entire Purwokerto area of extremists and other subversive elements, and I returned to Surabaya for a few days of heavy drinking, scheming Indo girls and an anxious mother.

Tinned cabbage and Bali

In mid-June 1947, I received a telephone call ordering me to report to Surabaya HQ-II in Mojosari. There my commander, Adjutant Mulder of the Marine Corps, told me to travel to Surabaya the next day with my full transport pack. On arrival, I was to report to Captain Groeneveld.

I travelled with a column of food trucks and asked to be dropped near Porongstraat. From there I walked to Firefly Barracks, where I made my presence known to the duty officer. A little later, I was knocking on Captain Groeneveld's door.

'Enter!'

I walked into the office, snapped to attention and saluted, awaiting further orders. Instead, Captain Groeneveld came up and shook me by the hand. He offered me a seat, then a cigarette and asked for news from the front. 'Nolan,' he said, 'we will soon be gearing up for a major military operation. Within a limited time frame, we have to capture East Java from the *pelopors* and occupy the entire area. But before we undertake this mission, I am sending you and a detachment from the Marine Brigade Security Service to Bali for three weeks' leave, departing in three days. Until then, you will continue your intelligence work here at the office and translate a number of military documents that have been seized. To date, your work at the front has been exceptional. I am extremely satisfied with you. Enjoy your leave.'

'Many thanks, Captain Groeneveld.' I rose to my feet, saluted and left.

I began sorting out my pack for the trip. Fortunately I was not required to bring a camp bed or mattress. Any unnecessary items I put in my duffel bag, which I deposited with the quartermaster. In the meantime, the chaplain had given me the addresses of a number of Dutch girls and writing to them struck me as a good way to spend my time, especially during the quieter moments at the front. There was a lively trade in photographs of female penfriends from Holland. There were Dutch girls here in the Indies too, of course, but they were mostly the daughters of civil servants with a colonial posting and were forbidden to have any contact with Indo men, let alone an illegitimate young man like me.

Soon I was heading for the port at Tanjung Perak along with my Security Services detachment and F Company of the Marine Brigade's second infantry battalion. At Firefly and Willemsoord barracks we boarded the local shuttle service nicknamed the Tapeworm Express and were waved off to the familiar strains of Vera Lynn's 'We'll Meet Again'. The burning sun beat down on our weary heads as we arrived at Ujung naval base to find the quayside swarming with people and a large colonial navy troop ship baking in the heat. Uniform soaked with sweat and shouldering my heavy transport pack, I walked up the gangway and headed straight for the cabins. I dumped my pack and weapons on a bunk that was to my liking, stripped to the waist and stepped out into the gentle breeze to pace the deck and inhale deep draughts of warm sea air.

Half an hour later we were lining up at the galley for food. Everyone was given a two-pound tin of cabbage, mash and sausage, a mug of orange squash and a portion of plantain. Cabbage and mash tasted foul in the heat, and the air turned blue with complaints and obscenities – a time-honoured Marine tradition. With a couple of other lads, I found a shady spot in one of the lifeboats beside the funnel. I opened the tin with my bayonet, fished out the sausage and gobbled it down. After a couple of mouthfuls of mash I chucked the rest overboard, tin and all. The waters around the ship were teeming with sharks and, in a fraction of a second, I saw the jaws of a greedy tiger shark close on the tin. My Dutch comrades did the same and gazed in awe at the creatures chomping on their tinned cabbage and mash.

The ship's horn sounded three times and our old tub sailed slowly out of the port. We were waved off and whistled at by the men who stayed behind and others on the quayside. The sound of Glenn Miller came over the speakers, chipper as ever.

Evening fell as we sailed through the Madura Strait. A stiff breeze got up and as the old tub began to buck and shudder, I felt a strange sensation in the pit of my stomach: my first ever bout of seasickness. Many a marine was already hanging over the railing. I stood among them and puked my guts up.

By morning, the sea was calm and the sickness had passed. We were sailing through the Bali Strait. Off the starboard side I could see the city of Banyuwangi in the distance, and on the port side the vague contours of Bali itself. I took in the magnificent view. We docked at Denpasar harbour early in the afternoon. Everyone grabbed their transport pack and their weapons, and we disembarked in an orderly fashion. Everywhere I looked, I saw soldiers from the Red Elephant Brigade of the East Indies Army. Since their release from the POW camps in Burma, they had been clearing Bali of extremist and subversive elements. I also saw servicemen with a White Elephant emblem on their sleeve.

When I disembarked, a corporal from the White Elephant Brigade came up to me. 'A warm welcome to you, my brown-skinned marine.' He smiled. I returned his greeting.

'Listen,' he continued, 'as an Indo like me, I expect you're not as cocksure as those Dutch lads when it comes to the ladies. So let me warn you about the women of easy virtue here on Bali. Most have "gone sour", if you know what I mean, so watch out! Avoid them! If you have to bed a woman, make sure she is from a remote mountain *kampong*, or stick to girls of fifteen if need be. That will mean a marriage of convenience but it's only for the sex. Those women are still pure. Only women from good families demand a serious marriage proposal, otherwise you will never get them into bed. By the way, those women are mad about Indos. You will be barracked in Klungkung but to have some fun on shore leave, Denpasar and the other big towns are the places to be. Steer clear of the brothels! The Lion's Den here in Denpasar has the worst reputation. The White House is another one. There is a serious lack of doctors and medicine for the islanders. In short, enjoy your leave but be careful! So long, marine!'

I thanked him for his warnings. We jumped aboard the waiting army trucks and set off for Klungkung. On the way, I finally found the peace of mind to enjoy my glorious surroundings and the beauty of the landscape. We were given a warm welcome at the White Elephant barracks and everyone wished us a good time on leave. The men there already knew about the preparations for the First Police Action.

There were excursions almost every day, with a few lads from the KNIL as our guides. We enjoyed the natural surroundings and the beautiful, shapely women. It was the custom among Balinese women to walk around with their breasts bared. For us marines that was something extraordinary. We gazed around hungrily.

One evening I was strolling across the busy marketplace in the centre of Denpasar with a couple of Dutch pals. I knew to keep my hands to myself or risk ending up at the sharp end of a *parang*, and I warned my pals accordingly. But of course one pig-headed chump had to play the big man. With a smirk on his face, he went up to one of those shapely Balinese women and pawed her breasts. Within seconds, her protector appeared, *parang* at the ready. In a flash, I kicked the long blade from his hand, then punched and kicked till he lay on the ground more dead than alive. More Balinese bore down on us, spoiling for a fight. The Dutchmen backed me up and we formed a circle so as not to be jumped from behind. I pulled out the fighting knife strapped to my right leg and lashed out at the first Balinese man who went for me, leaving a deep gash across his chest and stomach. Another man came at me with *parang* raised. I parried the blade and stabbed him till he fell. Two of my mates sustained knife wounds, but nothing serious.

Before long, the KNIL Military Police came to our aid. They spoke to the crowd in Balinese and tried to calm things down. The local police then turned up to arrest us but at the sight of our drawn bayonets, they soon backed off. They had never encountered marines before, but by the look on their faces they had heard all about us. Just as well firearms were not permitted on shore leave or someone would have been killed.

The fight over, my two wounded pals accompanied the Military Police to hospital for treatment. The rest of us went on our way as if nothing had happened. Many of the market-goers gawped at me, not least because I was the only brown soldier and was armed with a bayonet and a fighting knife. I also received many admiring looks from Balinese beauties but was wise enough to pay them no heed. A little further on, I sat down on a wooden bench by a satay vendor with two of my pals. In Malay I asked him what kind of meat he was roasting.

'Dog meat, *tuan*, and very tasty too!'

It did smell good. Each of us ordered around thirty of those little sticks with sauce and sambal, and beer to wash it all down. That dog meat was delicious. But one stall along, a vendor was roasting dog heads, complete with grinning teeth and lolling tongues. He dunked them in soy sauce over and over. A few Balinese locals were sitting by his stall, gnawing the meat off the bones and savouring every bite. I was nearly sick at the sight. I nudged my pals and pointed. It turned their stomachs too, and we took our satay and beer elsewhere.

The next morning I joined an excursion to Sanur, where there was a beautiful beach. A Belgian painter by the name of Adrien-Jean Le Mayeur lived nearby with his lovely Balinese wife. That afternoon, he invited a bunch of marines to his home. First, he showed us his work and I was greatly impressed by his talent as a painter. Close to sunset, a couple of gamelan players came to give a recital. The painter's wife retired to her room and changed into a dancer's costume. She emerged as a picture of elegance in a beautiful sarong, naked from the waist up. We stared speechless at her shapely breasts and hips. Embarrassed and aroused in equal measure, my pals and I exchanged glances. Our cheeks were burning. The Belgian painter's wife danced the *legong*, a courtly Balinese dance, to the strains of the gamelan music. It was a sight to behold.

We returned to Sanur beach the next day for a refreshing dip in the sea. There on the sand I got into a fight with a sergeant named Bitter. He mocked my brown skin and inferior background to the point where I lost control and beat him up. Sergeant Cornelissen – an Indo himself, though white and raised in the Netherlands – separated us and clearly took Sergeant Bitter's side. Both NCOs made no secret of their feelings of superiority and their hatred of coloureds. In my rage, I turned on Sergeant Cornelissen too. Other lads waded in to break up the fight. They advised me to forget all about it and settle the matter with a friendly handshake. Instead, I spat in the officers' faces. That was my answer to their delusions of grandeur and their Dutch brand of racial hatred. No wonder their breed of Dutchman was so reviled by the native population.

Almost every day brought another excursion with the KNIL boys, who showed us the most beautiful parts of the island. I enjoyed those three weeks on Bali intensely, soaking up the glorious and exotic natural surroundings. I even had a fling with a Balinese beauty or two.

*

Our holiday at an end, we once again had to board a waiting troop ship. As evening fell, the old tub sailed slowly out of Denpasar harbour and back through the Straits of Bali and Madura, with the port of Tanjung Perak as our final destination.

Early the next morning, we were piped up on deck for the mandatory prick parade. After leave on Bali, every marine had to strip down to his green vest and underpants and line up for a rubber-gloved medical officer followed by four orderlies bearing large trays of 606 syringes to combat venereal disease. They were followed by an admin sergeant major clutching a register and a fountain pen. Each man in turn was required to present his member to the doctor for inspection. As soon as the doctor uttered the word 'positive', the sergeant major took down name, rank, registration number and unit as the poor sod steeled himself for a painful jab in the buttock. Every man serving with a naval unit was required to report to the medical department for disinfection within twenty-four hours of sex with a woman of easy virtue. 'Paying their dues' we called it, as the cost of any such treatment was duly noted and deducted from the sailor's wages.

Late that afternoon, the ship sailed into port and was moored at Ujung docks. On disembarking, we lined up on the quayside and the transport commander ordered all those booked by the medics to step forward. A good forty per cent did just that. For them it was quick march to the waiting Tapeworm Express and a costly trip to the navy hospital at Karang Menjangan in Surabaya. The rest of us were driven to our respective barracks: Firefly Barracks on Porongstraat for us Marine Brigade Security lads and Willemsoord Barracks on Jambistraat for F Company. The holiday was over, the prelude to a tough assignment ahead.

First Police Action

17 July 1947. Shouts and whistles at six in the morning. Cries of 'Wakey-wakey! Marching orders!' from the corporals on duty rang through every dorm in the barracks. Still half asleep, I dragged myself out of my camp bed, folded down the mosquito net and staggered to the washrooms, towel and sponge bag in hand. The cold water did me good. I dressed in my utility uniform and headed for the mess. All through breakfast, the place was buzzing. At seven came the order: 'Fall in!'

Almost every man in the barracks was lined up. Captain Groeneveld and Lieutenant Brink took turns reading out the routine orders and then Captain Groeneveld addressed us. 'Men, in a matter of days a major campaign will get under way. Many of you have already had your own baptism of fire, so for you this will present few difficulties. But let me assure those of you fresh off the boat from Holland that all will be well provided you heed the guidance of your experienced fellow soldiers. As of this moment you are off duty. Go and say farewell to your family and friends. I expect to see you all back here tomorrow at noon, which will give you ample time to check your equipment and your weapons. Ask the quartermaster for extra ammunition and grenades. Look for your names on the notice boards tomorrow to find out which division you have been assigned to. Now go and enjoy this short spell of leave. Dismissed!'

Our brigade was to be divided into four columns charged with occupying Java's wild Eastern Salient and purging it of every last trace of terrorism. Our intelligence team, referred to simply as 'the interpreters', were spread across diverse battalions, companies and platoons. I was assigned to 3-INBAT: the 3rd infantry battalion, with orders to penetrate as far as Malang and the surrounding area. Back in the dorm, I thought of my sisters Ella and Ina, both of whom were being held in women's camps near Malang. I neatly made up my camp bed, folded away my mosquito net and checked through my equipment. Having grabbed my empty knapsack,

I signed out with the NCO on duty. I ducked under the barrier, walked to Darmo Boulevard, and took a *becak* home.

My mother looked troubled. 'When I see you like this,' she said, 'I can't help feeling that your life is in grave danger.'

'Mama,' I answered, 'in a few days' time I am going on a major campaign. I do not know whether I will come back alive. But perhaps I will be able to liberate Ina and Ella from Malang.'

My mother took me to her bedroom and sat down on a chair. I kneeled before her and laid my head in her lap. Mama prayed over me, pleading with God to stand by me in all things. I felt her tears fall on my head as I prayed with her. When she was finished, Mama stood up. 'God will bless you, Arto,' she said. 'My blessing and my prayers will be with you.'

With a sense of relief, I went to my bedroom and filled my knapsack with extra clothing, underwear and socks.

At eight thirty in the evening, Babu Tenie served dinner and we took our places at the table. Uncle Soen and Karel were there too. After dinner, I took Karel aside and told him, 'If you have not heard from me six weeks from today, you must assume that I have been killed.'

Karel turned pale, but nodded and said nothing.

Around ten, I took my leave of Mama, Uncle Soen, Karel, Poppy, Babu Tenie and Kokkie Tas. I walked to Undaan Kulon and took a *becak* back to barracks.

The next morning, I was told to report to Captain Groeneveld in the operations room. I entered, stood to attention, saluted and gave my name and rank. Other officers were also present.

'Nolan,' Captain Groeneveld said, 'there has been a change of assignment. I know you to be a bold soldier, always ready to show initiative. I therefore think it best to assign you to Lieutenant Colonel Aberson. You will join Blue Column and march with E Company under the command of Captain Willems. His men have suffered the heaviest losses to date and have need of experienced soldiers. He and Lieutenant Havik of the assault platoon will give you further orders and instructions. Following my address tomorrow, prepare to embark on LST-4, the *Pelican*. Captain Willems will send a jeep to pick you up at ten. Nolan, I wish you every success!'

I closed the door of the ops room behind me and swore bitterly. The reassignment had dashed my hopes of liberating Ina and Ella from the women's camps in Malang.

Early the next morning, fall-in was sounded. Every member of the Marine Brigade Security Service was present and correct. Captain Groeneveld, flanked by Lieutenant Brink and a number of other officers, gave a speech to end all speeches. 'Men, as you know, a major campaign awaits us. I assume that you have all now said farewell to family and friends. Our mission is to recapture the entire Eastern Salient of Java from Indonesia's armed forces. Be prepared to face huge resistance, so strong that half of you may not make it back alive. Give them hell! Shoot anyone who is carrying a weapon. I don't give a damn if it's a blade or a firearm – shoot, damn you! And shoot to kill! Remember, those bastards take no prisoners among marines who surrender… so make sure you are not taken. Save your last bullet for yourself! Never abandon a fallen comrade! Stand your ground till help arrives! Gather all the documentation you can and pass it on to the heads of Departments III and IV. Take as much ammo, as many grenades with you as possible. Now prepare for transport to your unit. You will find your names listed on the notice boards. Any questions, report to Sergeant Major Vestdijk. I wish you every success!'

As soon as we were dismissed, I returned to the dorm to check my weapons and equipment one last time. I folded up my camp bed and mosquito net, fastened my duffel bag and carried my things outside. I got my marching pack in order, strapping a long blanket roll around the knapsack, which contained spare socks, handkerchiefs, a belt and my K rations. I hung six slings around my neck, each with eight clips of eight cartridges for my M1 Garand rifle. My ammo included all kinds of cartridges and four hand grenades. The pack weighed a ton. My trusty friend the fighting knife was tucked in my right legging as ever. The barracks was a hive of disciplined activity. I saw troubled faces all around. The news that half of us might not be returning had hit home.

I lugged my belongings to the gate and waited to be picked up. The barrier was raised and a staff jeep came barrelling towards me. The driver got out. 'Are you Nolan of the Marine Brigade Security Service, awaiting pick-up under orders from Lieutenant Colonel Aberson?'

'Yes,' I replied, and hopped aboard.

'Smid's the name, driver, rookie 1st class.' The introductions over, I shook his hand. He went on talking as we drove. 'Heard a lot about you over at the Big Shit. You're in Colonel Roelofs' good books, and that's saying something. One wrong word from him and everyone's shitting themselves. Tiger of Gubeng barracks they used to call him.'

We rode to Coen Boulevard, where Captain Willems was waiting. He jumped into his jeep and we followed him to Willemsoord Barracks, on the other side of Darmo Boulevard. The roads along the way were lined with tanks, armoured vehicles and mobile artillery.

At the barracks, Captain Willems assigned me to the assault platoon under the command of Lieutenant Havik. I walked down the column and loaded my things into the farthest truck, which would be leading the way. Soon the whole column set off towards Surabaya's port district, bound for Ujung naval docks.

Landing ships were waiting at the quayside. We passed LST *Wundi* and arrived at LST-4 *Pelican*. Having shouldered our marching packs, we lined up and filed aboard, leaving the rest of our gear in the trucks. It was high noon and the heat was blistering. On deck I found a spot in the shade of an armour plate and a cannon, put down the dead weight of my pack and took off my shirt. Lunch consisted of a two-pound tin of sausage, cabbage and mash, a can of Pabst beer and a few slices of bread with cheese and jam. Once again, I fished the sausage from the tin and tossed the rest to the tiger sharks.

It was late afternoon before the *Pelican* was finally loaded with materiel and fighting men. The ship's whistle sounded and slowly we set sail. A little later, I saw the Wundi ease away from the quayside behind us. The cool sea breeze was a tonic.

The *Pelican* was carrying the men of Blue Column, the *Wundi* the men of Red Column. When we landed, Blue was to head east and push through to Jember and the rest of the Eastern Salient. Red was to head west to Probolinggo and Pasuruan.

On 20 July, our *Pelican* was making steady progress through the Madura Strait. The water was choppy and I began to feel seasick again. The atmosphere on board was tense. Some of the lads wrote letters to their loved ones back in Holland. A ship's chaplain for the Catholics and a pastor for the Protestants made their rounds, trying to boost morale. The pastor noted my personal details and asked me what I wanted to happen in the event of my death. I answered that I wanted my belongings to be given to my mother, Sie Swan Nio, and the band of the Royal Marines to play Glenn Miller's 'Moonlight Serenade' at my funeral.

That night I was unable to sleep below deck. I clambered out of my bunk and went looking for a quiet spot in the open air. Seeing a jeep that was lashed down, I climbed on the bonnet, set my heels against the ship's railing and leaned back against the raised windscreen. Scenes from my past flashed before my eyes. The beatings I took as a boy. The horrors of the Japanese occupation. The violence at the start of the Indonesian revolution. It did not matter much to me whether I lived or died.

I lit a cigarette and stared up at the countless stars in a cloudless sky. After a while, a marine from the Heavy Artillery Company appeared and kept me company. He was worried about what was in store for us and told me about his girl, his family and his life in Holland. Since I only knew Holland from my schoolbooks and a handful of movies, I was an eager listener. I had yet to write to a Dutch girl, though I was planning to. He told me brown lads like me were accepted as equals in Holland and were popular with the girls. This surprised me and piqued my curiosity about those girls, far away in Holland. Mama had always warned me that Indo girls were nothing but lazy two-timers. 'Marry an Indo girl, and I will curse you till the day you die. You deserve a better woman when you are older!'

The night drifted past. Dawn broke in the east to reveal the contours of the Wundi, the torpedo boat *Piet Hein* and other Navy vessels. Feeling sluggish, I left my spot on the jeep, went down to the washrooms and took a refreshing bath, perhaps the last of my short life.

Back at my bunk, I put on my utility uniform and buckled my belt. I got my marching pack ready for action and stowed the rest of my things in my transport pack. My comrades rubbed their sleepy eyes in astonishment at seeing me up so early. I returned to the deck and ambled over to the bridge. There I saluted Lieutenant Colonel Aberson of the Marine Corps, commander of 2-INBAT and of Blue Column, to which I now belonged. Directly on landing, I was to travel on with 2-INBAT's assault platoon.

Between six and half past it was 'up and at em', then off to the galley for a meagre Dutch breakfast of coffee and a few slices of bread with ham and cheese. As an Indo, I was used to starting the day with *nasi goreng*, but I found myself a quiet place on the footboard of a truck and made the best of things. I rinsed my mug in the washrooms, put it in its holder and carefully placed my water bottle on top, before attaching the whole thing to my combat belt. In the galley, I asked the cook to pour some coffee into my water bottle.

Between nine and ten in the morning, a Convair PBY Catalina flying boat belonging to the KNIL air force flew over, heading south towards the famous beach at Pasir Putih, where we were due to land. It was followed soon after by a couple of Fairey Firefly fighter-bombers. Before long, I saw them launch their deadly rockets at

Indonesian Army and Navy positions, and heard our naval artillery bombarding the beach.

After the barrage, the boys from 2-INBAT's assault platoon took their places for landing. Rope ladders were rolled out midships and the marines clambered down into the landing craft.

Just as I was about to join them, Lieutenant Havik grabbed me by the shoulders. 'Nolan,' he said, 'head straight for the lower deck. I need one man in the first truck, directly behind the Sherman tank. As soon as that truck hits the sand, your job will be to look out for enemy gunfire and warn the assault troops as they land.'

This effectively made me a sitting duck, drawing enemy fire by revealing my position. Not the most enviable assignment.

I rushed to my bunk, strapped on my marching pack, grabbed my M1 and my transport pack, and descended to the stifling heat of the lower deck, where the rolling stock were already warming up their engines. I glanced in the direction of the landing point and saw that the *Pelican* was heading straight for it at speed. I climbed aboard the truck behind the Sherman tank. The driver was bathed in sweat. My own uniform was sopping wet too.

Moments later, the *Pelican* scraped onto the burning sand. Its bow doors opened and a stiff breeze blew in. The tank rumbled down the heavy ramp onto to the beach and started up the slight incline towards the Panarukan road. Our truck was right behind. I stood up and began scanning for flashes of gunfire among the trees that lined the coast road above the beach. To my left a marine yelled, 'Look out, right above you! A *pelopor* in the trees!'

I spotted a shadow among the dense leaves and fired twice. Instead of a sniper, a big black monkey tumbled from the branches. I looked deflated, while every lad who saw it happen fell about laughing. For a moment they forgot the danger they were in.

Once the *Pelican* had disgorged its rolling stock, we formed a column on the road to Panarukan. The trucks were manned in no time and the tanks and armoured vehicles soon got the column moving. We met scant resistance and suffered only one casualty: a marine was shot in the chest and had to be carried back to the

Pelican. Even so, he was lucky: the bullet had passed through his rib cage and out the other side.

As we approached Panarukan, the leading tanks began firing. Every one of our trucks had a .50 calibre machine gun mounted on a pivot behind the driver's cabin. I shouted to the trucks behind, 'Up ahead! Two o'clock... enemy naval barracks, still manned!'

We found out later that many of those Indonesian marines were armed with nothing but wooden training rifles. Our gunners opened fire as we drove past and the trucks slowed to let us jump off. I ran to the barracks gates, while our assault troops spread out for a turkey shoot, targeting anything that moved. One of our armoured vehicles blew the gate off to give us access to the compound. Gun blazing, I sprinted across the parade ground, heading straight for the main building. With a couple of marines covering my back, I went through every office in search of military documents, yanking open desk drawers and filing cabinets, kicking in doors and blasting locks apart. It was rich pickings. Fellow marines helped me carry piles of military maps from the barracks. Lieutenant Colonel Aberson immediately began outlining the next phase of his strategy with the other commanders. Things moved so quickly that I did not get to interrogate a single prisoner of war. Every last Indonesian had been killed.

We jumped back on the trucks and made slow but steady progress towards Situbondo, one of the easternmost points of Java. Resistance grew and the column came under intense fire from heavily guarded buildings on either side of the road. Our tanks and armoured vehicles shot back. We had to leap off the trucks again, this time to storm the buildings. Enemy fire was so fierce at times that troops with bazookas and flamethrowers had to come forward while we gave them cover. The buildings were being defended by fanatical Revolutionary Front and Hizbullah units. Many were armed with only bamboo spears or machetes, while a few had hand grenades and rifles. Amid loud cries of 'Merdeka', those maniacs charged towards our tanks and armoured cars, running headlong to their deaths, completely *mata gelap*. Not one man surrendered. We blew them all to pieces.

When that massacre was behind us, we came across trenches and bunkers manned by the Indonesian Army. Our bazookas and flamethrowers came forward again, destroying one bunker after another. We lobbed hand grenades into the trenches and heard the sudden quiet that followed the blast. I crept over to size up the situation, a tactic I had learned from the Gurkha soldiers. But further on, resistance flared again and the column advanced at little more than walking pace.

We battled on through fierce fighting and reached Situbondo without losing a single man, though some had been wounded. Almost the entire company surged forwards as back-up for the assault troops as we searched every house in Situbondo for military documents of possible use to our commanders. Here and there we saw old people and children by the roadside. One old man told me there was an internment camp for women and children out towards Prajekan. I reported the existence of this camp to Lieutenant Havik and he ordered twenty lads from the assault platoon to board a truck and help me find it.

Sure enough, a few miles past Situbondo we spotted barbed-wire fences, patrolled by men armed with bamboo spears and machetes. We leapt from our truck and ran towards them in formation. I gunned down two of the guards and took out a third by the gate, which I proceeded to unlock with one of the keys from his belt. We walked in past the barracks and saw countless women and children: Indos, Dutch, Ambonese and Manadonese. Most lay on the ground, staring up at us in terror.

'We are Dutch marines! We are your friends!' I shouted in Malay. 'Collect your things and walk to the main road. Go on, leave this place. You have nothing to fear!'

Almost all of the women and children got to their feet, weeping with joy. They seemed lost and bewildered, but a feeble cheer rose up among them. Tears sprang into my eyes. The poor souls straggled towards the Prajekan road. By this time, more trucks had arrived and the marines on board handed out K rations. Lieutenant Havik pulled up in his jeep and ordered that the internees be sent to the rear of the column. We had to push on towards Prajekan, a short distance inland.

Prajekan was reached late in the afternoon and, after a brief but intense gun battle, we succeeded in capturing the sugar factory that was our objective. We had to halt and spend the night there.

In the fading light, I walked back to the truck for the rest of my things. Dog-tired and lumbered with the weight of my transport pack, I headed for the factory offices and joined the boys from the assault platoon poking around in the shadows for a place to bed down. One or two of the office cabinets were packed with mines and we felt uneasy enough to call in the Demolition Group. Disabling the mines turned out to be an impossible task. For want of a better idea, we carried them out as carefully as we could and laid them in the far corner of a large open-plan office. When that was done, we were finally able to make up our beds on the floor. Our only light came from tins of paraffin oil and small spirit lamps but the engineers kept working on the generators at the rear of the factory and within a few hours they managed to restore some power, which gave us electric light here and there. The mobile kitchens were working flat out, as all the men were in dire need of warm tea and coffee. For food we had to make do with more K rations.

Two .50 calibre machine guns were positioned at the door and guard posts were set up. I spread my poncho on the floor and laid a folded blanket on top. My knapsack, crammed with gun cartridges and hand grenades, served as my pillow. Still wearing my uniform and my boots, I pulled a second blanket over me.

At two in the morning I was woken by a dig in the ribs from one of my mates, whose watch I had to take over. I got up immediately, folded my blankets and poncho, and buckled everything, knapsack and all, to my transport pack. I grabbed my M1, strapped my fighting knife to my leg and headed for the machine-gun post to which I had been assigned. The gun had been set up to cover a wide stretch of the main road.

The sky was clear, moonless and full of stars. Beside me sat a seaman from E Company, whose watch ended at three. The boy seemed very edgy but when he saw I was an Indo, he relaxed a little and began asking question after question about life in the Indies and the customs and traditions of its peoples. We spoke in whispers.

When my watch was almost over, I went to dig another seaman in the ribs and tried to catch some more sleep, sitting because I could not face making up my bed again. Just as I was nodding off, the sound of both machine guns firing almost simultaneously jolted me awake. I grabbed my M1 and ran back to the guard post.

'I got them! Two of them!' my replacement shouted excitedly.

'Give me your flashlight. I'll go and take a look,' I shouted back.

More marines came running. With the flashlight in my left hand and my M1 in my right, I stepped out into the road. Instead of a couple of dead *pelopors*, I saw the body of a water buffalo.

'Hey, you just shot a water buffalo. Stone dead!' I yelled back. A few of the others came over to take a look and we creased up with laughter. The gunners looked more than a little sheepish.

'Oh well,' I chuckled, 'it's a better catch than that monkey I shot earlier.'

Before long, a couple of cooks appeared with their helpers. Armed with butcher's knives and dragging huge pots, they began carving the poor creature up. 'This will make fine soup. Enough for the whole column!' they shouted cheerfully. 'Fresh meat at last!'

Breakfast next morning was a piping hot mug of tasty soup, made from the meat and bones of our sad old water buffalo. It did me a power of good.

Breakfast over, we started preparing for the big push to Bondowoso and Jember, the region where my grandfather had brought vast tracts of land under cultivation a century earlier. I loaded my transport pack onto the truck along with a replenished supply of ammunition. There was a ditch across the road. The water was not clear, but good enough for me to wash my face and rinse my mouth.

Road blocks hampered our progress. Trees had been felled and landmines concealed under them. We finally made it to a strategic road bridge with a *kampong* on the other side. There, more hell broke loose. Every gun on our tanks and armoured vehicles spat murderous fire at the camouflaged enemy positions in the surrounding bushes and woodland.

When the resistance became overwhelming, we called for close air support. Before long, Fairey Fireflies came roaring over, unleashing rockets and machine-gun fire on the enemy's positions and bunkers. This wasn't much help and some marines wore orange patches on their backs so that our pilots would not shoot their own men from the air.

The full force of our infantry jumped off the trucks and advanced on the enemy. Fierce gun battles broke out. Our flamethrowers and bazookas went into action.

Along with a few marines from the assault platoon, I ducked into the bushes at the roadside and headed for the bridge to locate the source of the machine-gun rattle. We circled wide in an effort to outflank the enemy and attack from behind. Around fifty yards ahead, I saw a handful of extremists firing a double-barrelled machine gun on a double mount – as was standard on pre-war navy patrol boats. I crept up behind them and threw a hand grenade, then dived to the ground among the bushes. A violent blast followed and the machine-gun post was silenced for good, the bodies of five dead extremists lay scattered. More machine-gun posts were destroyed by other lads from the assault platoon.

The resistance was far from broken. We were still under constant fire from all directions. Now and then I saw our fighter-bombers strafing targets on the ground and soon after, our lads managed to take the bridge. The Demolition Group immediately moved in to disarm the mines planted under it. When their job was done, we surged across in the direction of the *kampong*.

I loaded my M1 with tracer bullets and fired at the *kampong* houses to set them alight. *Pelopors* came running out and were mowed down by waiting marines. The column ground to a halt not far from the bridge, the road blocked by felled trees and *chevaux de frise*. I could see booby traps among the spikes of the barricades. They had to be defused with great care. Some marines, equipped with light-weight jungle carbines, lost their patience and blew the booby traps apart. This made one hell of a racket and there was a danger of being hit by flying shrapnel.

Once the barricades were stripped of mines and booby traps, our tank-bulldozer came through to clear the debris and the column advanced once again. All the infantrymen continued on foot. We had to keep our eyes peeled, from the grass to the highest branches. Every now and then, a marine would shoot and a sniper would fall from a tree. A few of our men were wounded, but none seriously and we had suffered no fatalities.

Along the road, we had to look out for wires that might lead to more booby traps. Here and there I saw the bodies of women and children in the bushes. If we saw a woman's body on top of a man's, we shot them, knowing that *pelopors* often used women and children as shields.

I took a short detour and returned to the Bondowoso road to see a huddle of small boys and girls sitting on the ground, terrified. I asked them where I could expect further resistance from *pelopors* and, without hesitating, they told me the locations of enemy positions and an internment camp for women and children a mile or so up ahead. I passed this information on to the assault troops and asked Lieutenant Havik for back-up from BAR and tommy gunners. On the lieutenant's orders, a truck with a rifle squad of eight marines came to the fore. I jumped on, keeping low to use the sides of the loading platform as cover. One corporal stayed on his feet to man the .50 calibre machine gun. The truck was moving too fast for us to take aim, but he sprayed bullets left and right wherever we drew *pelopor* fire.

At last, I sighted a number of barracks on our right, fenced off with barbed wire. Our driver headed straight for them and pulled up outside. We scrambled down from the truck, guns at the ready, and walked up to the gate to find it secured with a heavy chain lock. Seeing faces at the window of the small gatehouse, I fired without hesitation. The others blew out the windows with their automatic weapons.

'*Keluar!*' I shouted. 'Come out and give yourselves up!' Moments later a group of men emerged with their hands above their heads. One was carrying a machete. I gunned him down and shouted at the others, '*Buka pintu lekas! Kalau tidak lekas, kamu saja bunuh!* Open the gate quick, or I will shoot you dead!'

In no time, the gate to the camp was open. We shot and killed the gatekeepers and kicked down all the doors. Crying women and children came out of the barracks. Some of the women fell to the ground and tried to kiss my feet. I was shocked by this and jumped back to stop them. The most wretched were seriously undernourished. We asked them to gather their humble belongings and walk to the main road. Any remaining guards who tried to escape were gunned down.

Two empty trucks arrived at the camp to collect the half-starved women and children. We used the *pelopors* we had arrested as pack mules. We put helmets on them, loaded them down with our heavy weapons and made them walk ahead as guides and decoys. When they began to slow us down, we killed them.

A mile down the road we arrived in Tengaran, the site of another sugar factory. More fierce resistance was waiting for us. Two armoured vehicles and a Sherman tank hit all the enemy's positions with artillery fire and .50 calibre machine-gun fire. As soon as the barrage was over, we attacked. The *pelopors* were well camouflaged among the bushes, some holed up in concrete pillboxes, built by the KNIL before the war and hard to spot. Flamethrowers and bazookas had to be deployed. The fighting was tough but we steadily wore down their resistance and ran to the sugar factory in formation to take the buildings while minimizing any damage. Between fifteen and twenty of us charged into the big factory hall, where *pelopors* were still planting explosives among the machinery. A brief exchange of gunfire was enough to wipe them out. In an adjacent hall, we came across two *pelopors* trying to set fire to piles of gunny sacks. I quickly shot them dead, found a fire extinguisher and put out the blaze. With a stick, I separated the smouldering sacks and doused them with the rest of the extinguisher's contents. Meanwhile I heard intense gunfire coming from the machine rooms. By the time I got there, six dead bodies lay on the floor, one of them a Jap.

The boys from the Demolition Group set about disarming the time bombs and booby traps among the machinery. We moved on, leaving behind a detachment of marines to guard the place until the main force arrived.

We continued our advance towards the strategic town of Bondowoso. Blue Column split up to attack in a pincer movement. I stuck with the assault troops. Our trucks drove straight through the residential areas. Whenever we drew fire, we stopped the trucks, leapt out and ran for the houses on either side of the street, giving as good as we got.

One by one, we searched homes and offices for military documents. I kicked down the door of a Chinese dentist's house to discover five blonde women, all of them Indos.

'What are you doing in this Chinaman's home?' I asked, seeing the fear in their eyes. 'Are you prisoners?'

They nodded. I turned to the dentist. 'Why are you holding these women against their will? What have they done wrong?'

He looked at me as if dazed, but said nothing. I hit him with the butt of my gun.

'I asked you a question!'

Groaning with pain he said, 'I kept these women here to protect them from the *pemudas*, to stop them being brutally raped. You know what I mean.'

'It's true,' one of the women whispered, 'but we have to pay him. We have no money left and he abuses us because we can no longer pay.'

The women burst into tears. Other marines entered the house and began a rapid search of the rooms. They returned with a Colt revolver and a Sten gun.

'Why do you have these weapons?' I asked the dentist.

'To protect my property,' he answered.

Suddenly one of those poor women shouted, 'No, sir! He is lying. He is an officer with the Indonesian National Army.'

One of the marines addressed me in Dutch. 'We'll take him outside and shoot him. Who knows what else he has been up to.'

'Be my guest,' I said.

As I was telling the women that they could pack their things and travel with our column, several shots sounded outside.

With the other marines, I carried out house-to-house searches for weapons and documents. Some were still occupied by armed *pemudas*, but we made short work of them. A handful of prisoners were taken and transported to the back of the column. The further we advanced, the more weapons we found. In the end we almost filled an empty truck with the revolvers, rifles, ammunition, grenades, portable cannon and mortar shells we seized. We left the explosives to the Demolition Group, who detonated them on the spot. All this meant it was late afternoon before we had control of Bondowoso.

Our next major objective was Jember, the city where my father was born. The column advanced through the villages of Grojogan, Tamanan and Sukowono and on to Kalisat, where there was a railway station. In no time, we had the whole complex under our control. And on we went.

Dead beat, we called a halt in the village of Arjasa. I asked a couple of farmhands to take me to the village head. The good man invited me onto his veranda and served me lemonade, biscuits and other treats. He was delighted to see Belandas again and told me how the entire population was suffering under all kinds of coercion imposed by the guerrilla units. The village head gave me a wealth of intelligence on troop movements in the area. Kalisat was not the only village being terrorized by the Indonesian Army. The commander of the column added this information to his map.

After an hour's rest, we were on our way again. The closer we came to Jember, the stiffer resistance became and the commander decided our best bet would be to cover the short stretch from Arjasa to Jember on foot. Minesweepers walked ahead and I followed with the infantrymen. We stuck to the verges, sometimes walking on grass or through dry gulleys, other times ploughing through the undergrowth. Snipers hidden among the dense foliage made life difficult for us. Some had even lashed themselves to the crowns of coconut trees. We also came under heavy fire from small *kampong* houses. We had to lie flat, then spring to our feet and run in a zigzag pattern. Bullets whistled unnervingly past my ears and left scratches where they glanced off the outer shell of my helmet. Even so, I managed to take out a few snipers. Their dead bodies hung in the trees above us.

A short distance from Jember, we were ordered to march to a small station, where a train was getting ready to depart. We reloaded our guns with armour-piercing rounds and soon eliminated the engine driver and the stoker. That train would be going nowhere.

I ran onto the platform and saw a *pemuda* take cover behind a woman with a child in her arms. He aimed his rifle at me and hooked his left arm around the woman's neck. The child let out a heartrending cry. I took a dive and fired at the innocent woman before I hit the ground. My bullets went straight through the child and the mother and the *pemuda*. I had no choice. It was kill or be killed. The sight of the three dead bodies turned my stomach. The mother and child had nothing to do with this war. I had taken a cruel decision, but there was no other way. That bloody moment will be with me for the rest of my life. Sometimes it jolts me from my sleep and I roll out of bed ~~and~~ primed to shoot, until the contours of the room become visible and I remember where I am.

A few miles from the centre of Jember, we drove through suburban streets lined with the grand homes of the wealthy. We jumped off the trucks to search the houses. I stopped at a house with a gilt-framed nameplate, home to some prominent Indonesian or other. As I opened the gate and walked up the path to the front door by the veranda, I caught sight of gun barrels sticking out of the windows. In a reflex, I opened fire and dropped to the ground. Spotting the danger, my mates did the same. From the ground, I blasted the front-door lock to pieces, then leapt to my feet and charged into the house. Three marines were right behind me. I entered the dining room in time to see a uniformed man clambering out of the window. Before he could jump, I fired two shots. He slumped forwards with a muffled cry and tumbled into the garden. I kicked in the doors of the adjacent rooms while my mates searched the back of the house. Shots rang out and I heard them swear loudly.

In one of the rooms, I found a beautiful Indonesian woman. She was sitting with tears in her eyes, shivering with fear. I prodded her chest with the barrel of my gun and snarled, 'Where are your husband's weapons? Hand over all the military and political documents in this house. Do not try to hide anything from me or I will blow your head off. Understood?'

Trembling, she went over to a wardrobe and took out a Parabellum semi-automatic pistol and cartridges, a samurai sword and a thick briefcase.

'Who were the men we shot?' I asked.

'The man you killed in the dining room was my husband,' she sobbed. 'He was an Indonesian Army captain. The four in the back of the house were his colleagues.'

There was no time for sentiment. I called to my mates and we left.

A little while later, we stumbled across an Indonesian Army barracks and were greeted by a volley of rifle and machine-gun fire.

We had to fight tooth and nail to gain control of the compound, one block at a time. I fixed my bayonet to my rifle, ready for man-to-man combat but the marines had no time to waste and wiped out the machine-gun posts with grenades and mortar shells so we could get on with sweeping the site. When it was all over, I trudged back to the truck, feeling suddenly exhausted and sickened by all the killing. At the outset I had carved a notch into the butt of my gun for every life I took, but by this time I had lost count. How many had I killed? A hundred? More? Yet I felt no remorse, except for the woman and her child. I was simply taking revenge for everything the Indonesians had done to me and those like me. I did not yet know how much killing I had left in me.

The main force of Blue Column advanced on the centre of Jember, and most of the Marine Brigade Security boys from SHQ-II went with them. I stayed with the assault platoon and E and F Companies. We stuck to the outskirts and at nightfall set up camp in a suburb, having cleared the area of extremists first.

We established a string of guard posts and tried to snatch some shut-eye in dry gulleys and by the sides of roads. My helmet was my pillow. But sleep was denied us. Shots rang out in the middle of the night, and we were fired on at close range and then from further off. Everyone was wide-awake and no one had even an hour's rest. When dawn broke, we were all miserable. There was no coffee. We had to make do with K rations and the filtered ditch water in our bottles. By way of breakfast, I cracked open a tin of chili con carne. It tasted fairly spicy and did me some good.

Back on the trucks, we headed for Mangli, where we stormed another factory complex, this time a large rice-husking plant. I ran into the machine rooms with two marines just as *pemudas* were about to detonate their mines. A very close call. Gunny sacks were ablaze in the storeroom. I ran in and spotted two *pelopors* making off across the steel roof beams. I waited until they were above the fire and shot them dead. Their bodies hung from the beams and as the flames grew higher there was the sickly smell of burning human flesh. I ran back to the machine rooms where the Demolition Group were busy defusing explosives, surrounded by *pemuda* corpses. Those boys risked their lives time and time again. We had the utmost respect for them.

We had gained control of the rice-husking plant. A small garrison of marines stayed behind to guard it.

On the road from Mangli to Rambipuji we encountered roadblocks and landmines, but little in the way of hostile fire. In Balung, six miles or so beyond Jember, we stopped for a while. A couple of our men had been wounded and one soldier was dead. We radioed for ambulances and reinforcements. Our intel indicated a strong enemy presence around Kencong and as we approached the village, our armoured vehicles moved ahead and began firing their on-board weapons. As the trucks drove parallel to the railway embankment, we began to draw heavy, long-range fire. We jumped off and lay along the embankment. Fanatical Hizbullah units came charging in from three sides and the order was passed from man to man: 'Go light on the ammo! One man, one bullet! Save the last bullet for yourself!'

I still had two hand grenades, three cartridge slings and a beltful of cartridge clips. I took the slings from around my neck and placed them on the slope in front of me. The Hizbullah fanatics came charging towards us screaming 'Merdeka' at the top of their lungs, most armed with only clubs and bladed weapons. We let them get within 150 yards or so, then opened fire. They dropped like flies. It was wholesale slaughter, so bad that we ran out of ammo. The bodies of countless fanatics were piled along the entire line and still they came. I had just fired my final cartridges when I heard the order: 'Prepare for bayonet charge!'

I fixed my bayonet to my rifle. Out of nowhere came the blast of heavier artillery. Our armoured vehicles had doubled back and were firing at the crazed Hizbullah charge. From the other side, F Company came to our aid. They finished off the last of the fanatics and we heaved a collective sigh of relief. It chilled our blood to see those Hizbullah fighters running straight into our line of fire. Not one escaped with his life, their bodies were stacked like sandbags. It was a horrific sight but there was no time to dwell. New supplies of ammunition and hand grenades were dished out. Here in Kencong too, a detachment of marines stayed behind. The plan to occupy all of Java's Eastern Salient rolled on.

From Kencong we advanced in the direction of Ambulu, another notorious stronghold of fanatical Hizbullah and Masyumi groups. They too were primitively equipped: only a small number had laid their hands on Japanese firearms. These fighters were led by bloodthirsty *kyai*, Islamic clerics whose only weapon was a sacred *kris*, its wavy blade smeared with a mixture of prussic acid and arsenic that turned the metal a dark reddish-brown. The slightest scratch would cause agonizing death within the hour, accompanied by raging fever and dreadful palpitations. The *kyai* were also festooned with amulets, signs of immortality and sanctity. To them, this was a holy war. They never took prisoners but carved their fallen enemies into pieces.

The area around the village was remarkably quiet, with only a few elderly villagers pottering about. Observing their looks and their movements closely, I realized that they were signalling to fighters concealed in the thick undergrowth around the many *kampong* houses. As a kind of pathfinder, I walked ahead and warned the marine closest to me, 'Signal to the men behind that we are completely surrounded by the enemy. Spread out and walk on. Do not stick too close together. Fix your bayonet to your gun. Save the last bullet for yourself!'

Then the fighting erupted. The bastards came at us from all sides, yelling 'Merdeka' in piercing howls that made the blood run cold. Before long, our attackers were dropping by the dozen in a hail of machine-gun bullets.

I found myself eye-to-eye with a fanatical *kyai*. He spat all kinds of curses and waved his sacred *kris* menacingly. Blind to everything around me, I slammed the muzzle of my gun into the sand and muttered a counterspell in High Javanese: 'Thou art made of dust and into dust thou shalt return!'

My gun was loaded with vicious phosphorus and tracer bullets. Still cursing the *kyai*, I walked towards him and fired twice in quick succession. The bullets hit him full in the chest and belly, and he fell backwards, groaning. 'So much for immortality,' I sneered in Javanese. I thrust my bayonet into the fanatic's belly and gave it a quarter turn, so when I pulled it out his guts came with it. The phosphorus wreaked burning havoc with the bloody mess at my feet. I looked up to see five enemy soldiers bearing down on me but the marines coming up behind made quick work of them.

I thanked my mates and fired a tracer bullet at a small boarding house. It caught fire. We sent everyone who came running out straight to hell. Again we found ourselves facing down charging hordes. The .50 calibre machine guns on every truck were blazing. Lying on my front, I looked up to see body parts flying in all directions. The sight made many a marine puke, but this was no time for compassion or self-pity. We fought on doggedly, our hearts full of hate. I felt nothing but exhaustion. Every muscle, every nerve in my body was straining. The threat of death came from all sides, hidden in the bushes and the trees, beneath roof tiles that could lift up at any moment.

Many marines took a bullet. A few were killed. The medics ran back and forth with stretchers. The warring sides were too close to allow air support, and we sent in the big guns. Our Sherman tanks let rip and eventually, even the most fanatical enemy fighters turned and ran.

We left a detachment of marines behind in Ambulu to keep control, while the main force headed inland to Bangsalsari, another hotbed of Hizbullah and Masyumi resistance. Night fell but there was no end to the fighting.

The marines had been trained for conventional warfare, but this was a guerrilla war and the advantage lay with the Indonesians. This land was theirs. They knew the terrain like the back of their hand.

I kept my bayonet fixed to my rifle, as did the infantrymen. We took it in turns to sleep, leaning against the wheels of the trucks, gun in hand and eyes half-open, plagued by armies of mosquitos. Man-to-man fighting broke out sporadically. I had cause to draw my fighting knife and my uniform was soon stained with blood. It was dawn before the fighting died down. We did not permit ourselves time for breakfast but prepared to move on again. To be sure, we left a larger detachment of marines behind this time and the company commander radioed for reinforcements from Jember and Bondowoso. Shortly afterwards, we received word that F Company was on its way. This left us free to push on towards Sumbersari and its many coffee, tea, rubber and tobacco plantations, some owned by Nolans, the legitimate heirs of my late father's family.

The road to Sumbersari led uphill. A thin mist lay over the land and the cool early-morning air was bliss. I was in the first truck with the assault troops from 2-INBAT. We tucked into our K rations and swigged cans of Pabst as we drove. For want of coffee we rinsed our mouths with beer. It left us feeling groggy.

A mile or so from the village of Sumbersari, our truck hit a landmine and lurched to one side. We were all thrown clear. The truck behind swerved to avoid us and ploughed straight into the *sawah*. We came under fire from a long way off. I recognized the sound of Japanese Nambu machine guns and the pre-war Brownings used by the KNIL. I scrambled to my feet and checked my rifle. It was clogged with mud and I cleaned it with water from the *sawah*. Other marines yelled at me to take cover. I yelled back that it was the enemy, not me, they should be worried about.

We took as much spare ammunition from the damaged truck as we could carry and continued on foot. My whole body was aching. I felt shattered and my head was pounding. We walked straight across the plantations towards Sumbersari and heard only a few distant gunshots on our way. We approached a huddle of plantation workers' houses. They stood deserted, damaged and looted. Fires were still smouldering here and there, and we saw the half-charred bodies of women and children.

Sumbersari behind us, we were finally allowed to stop and rest. I found a place to sit on the banks of a clear stream, where I rinsed and filled my water bottle, dropping in a couple of chlorine tablets. After a few minutes it was free of harmful bacteria and safe to drink. The tins of K rations were starting to taste better. I even ate the cabbage, though it left me feeling drowsy and constipated.

A dig in the ribs and it was time to move on. I have no idea how long I slept by that stream. The column travelled east towards Rogojampi, all the way to the Bali Strait. There we were to meet Orange Column, the marines who had landed at Banjuwangi and headed west. We hooked up at the agreed location late that afternoon, exactly as planned. We were allowed a long rest and treated to cans of Pabst beer. As if we weren't dazed enough already.

Away from the front

When we had purged those areas, scores of Dutch planters and industrialists were able to return and start rebuilding their enterprises. Even so, we had to keep up intensive patrols. The furthest reaches of East Java were rough, mountainous and densely wooded, and many plantations belonging to Europeans who had fled – the Nolan family among them – lay abandoned. Indonesian guerrilla tactics made occupying such a vast region a major problem, and we were fortunate to have the assistance of KNIL and Dutch Army units. We carried out sweeping operations and rounded up large numbers of prisoners. In Rogojampi near Banjuwangi, I submitted extremists guilty of slaughter to harsh interrogations before dispatching them to SHQ-II in Jember. I was ruthless in extracting all the military information we needed from the remaining prisoners, which enabled our commanders to pinpoint guerrilla activities on their maps. Prisoners of no real use to us were released immediately, while the genuine suspects accompanied us on patrol with orders to guide us to their comrades' positions. At the least sign they might be misleading us or manoeuvring us into an ambush, they were killed.

When a Marine Brigade Security Service detachment was established in Rogojampi, I was ordered to return to SHQ-II in Jember to recover from those tense weeks of battle. Lack of sleep had left me feeling wretched, a fate I shared with all of 2-INBAT's assault troops. It was the first week of August 1947. The First Police Action, code-named Operation Product, was at an end.

I took my leave of the lads from the assault platoon. Second Lieutenant Havik of the Marine Corps thanked me for the intelligence work I had carried out, though I had done more than interrogate people… I heaved myself onto one of five empty trucks led off by a jeep, a small column heading for Jember to pick up food and ammunition.

I arrived at SHQ-II late in the afternoon and was welcomed by Adjutant Mulder of the Marine Corps. 'So, Nolan, back at last,' Mulder said. 'We must seem like strangers after all this time. But I see you have brought us more than a few chests of documents and military items. Bravo! Oh, and Nolan, I have arranged a private room for you at the back of the building. A chance to unwind after weeks in the thick of it.'

Wearily, I shouldered my duffel bag and lugged all my gear to my room. Having put my things in order, I wandered through the building to check out the personnel and was amazed to see former prisoners doing housekeeping and admin for the Interrogation, Espionage and Documentation departments.

I found Bert Hermelijn and took him to one side. 'What on earth are those *pelopors* doing here, Hermelijn? Surely you are not letting those bastards in on our military secrets?'

'No, Nolan,' Hermelijn replied, 'I am not. "It takes a thief to catch a thief" is my motto. None of these chaps are guilty of murdering innocent civilians. The only one you need to watch out for is Wim Rompas. He was a member of the Kenpeitai under the Japs here in East Java.'

Hermelijn gave me the full tour. In the Interrogation department alone, I counted forty of those turncoats. There were also a few Indo girls hanging around, one of them Hermelijn's floozy. He told me I could bed her sister if I had a mind to, insisting that I was just her type. She had been cleaned up, he explained, so I was in no danger of catching some venereal disease. I declined politely.

Operation Harlot

Mulder came up to me one morning after breakfast. 'Nolan,' he said, 'I have a special assignment for you. Today you will be given a patrol of ten men and three empty trucks. Take a jeep, with Groeneboer as your driver. Your job is to arrest every whore in Jember and the surrounding area and load them onto your trucks. Bring them here for routine questioning and then to the city hospital for decontamination. I will have a word with the hospital governors beforehand. We need those whores to keep our boys happy. But don't be led astray and stay on the alert for gangs of guerrillas.'

I answered with a stiff salute and headed straight for my room. There I strapped on my truncheon, stuck my fighting knife in my right legging, grabbed my trusty M1 and slung a few belts of ammo around my neck. The three trucks were waiting outside, along with Groeneboer and his jeep.

I took Harry Tjong and a former Indonesian POW with me in the jeep. The rest of my patrol climbed aboard the trucks. Off we went. The POW knew the way and directed us to Jember's red-light districts. There we halted the column and conducted a thorough search of every house. The bounty was plentiful and our trucks were full within the hour. Those girls stank to high heaven! The fug of their perfume turned my stomach. We also searched their rooms for evidence of contact with guerrillas. When our little convoy was bursting at the seams, we drove our fragrant pickings back to SHQ. Other interpreters took over for questioning while we went back for another round-up.

When we returned with our second batch, the interrogation department was swarming and half the building reeked of whore. Questioning the women was a piece of cake, at least compared to interrogating guerrillas. They tried all kinds of seductive tricks on us, not least slipping out of their panties as provocatively as they could. The boys neatly typing up the interrogation reports looked more than a little hot and bothered. I took in the spectacle and laughed myself silly.

I signed off with Adjutant Mulder and went to my room. Throwing off my weapons, I lay down and fell into a deep sleep. By the time Jan Kraai came in to wake me for dinner, it was dark. The women with the worst infections had been carted off to hospital. The milder cases had been given injections and pills and sent home. One or two hung around and became lover girls for the Dutch marines.

Landmine No. 2

The following day I was dispatched with a pile of military maps and a new set of orders to the detachment in Bangsalsari. I hitched a ride with the food column. Other interpreters were sent on patrol to other towns, backed up by infantry.

A mile or so from Bangsalsari, our column had to cross a mountain pass and traverse a couple of heavily wooded slopes. Out of nowhere, a tree came crashing onto the road. The commander's jeep swerved to avoid it, hit a landmine and burst into flames. The blast catapulted lieutenant and driver from the jeep and left them badly wounded at the side of the road. The truck immediately behind the jeep hit a heavier mine and our truck was blown into the air along with it. Everyone was thrown clear. The other trucks managed to brake in time but we came under machine-gun fire from the hills on either side. Three lads from my truck died instantly. A couple of marines dived behind the .50 calibre machine guns and began spraying bullets in all directions. I lay dazed on the ground, feeling like someone had tried to pull my stomach out through my throat. My back was in agony. Bullets glanced off the road into the mud all around. I spotted my rifle and crawled a few yards to grab it, wiping mud and dirt from the barrel as bullets whistled past me. Directly ahead, in the tall grass on the hillside, a twin machine gun mounted on a gun carriage was spitting fire at the lads who lay scattered and groaning on the ground just a few yards away. I shot the gunner and his helper, killing them both.

'Don't just lie there whining for your mother!' I yelled. 'Shoot for fuck's sake! Blast them all to hell!'

Even though they were severely injured, they screwed up all their courage, got hold of their weapons and returned fire as best they could. Thankfully, the gun battle did not last long. The enemy fled, leaving their heavy artillery and dead comrades behind.

The danger gone, I almost collapsed from the pain. The marines who had escaped unscathed did their best to help their wounded mates. An injured truck driver had found the strength to radio for help, and an hour later around twenty marines arrived in a column of half-track ambulances and two trucks, into which the dead and badly wounded were loaded.

I scraped together everything intended for the detachment at Bangsalsari and we continued on our way. On arrival, I handed the commander the post and material he had requested and immediately slumped into a chair. He told me to report to the sick bay in Jember the next day.

A plan of action was quickly drawn up. The detachment was dissolved without delay and moved to Kencong to provide reinforcements for the Marine Brigade Security detachment stationed there. Meanwhile, reprisal expeditions were to be carried out around Bangsalsari the next day.

Before nightfall, I returned to Jember with the same column. My back and stomach were still raw with pain, and I turned in early without eating. The next morning I felt a little better and reported to Adjutant Mulder of the Marine Corps to request a place on one of the reprisal expeditions to Bangsalsari. My request was granted, not least because I would be able to point out where the ambush had occurred.

When we arrived at the scene, everyone except the drivers and the .50 calibre machine gunners leapt from the vehicles. The rest of us combed the area in rifle squads of ten, gunning down every armed man we came across.

With a rifle squad, I approached Bangsalsari *kampong*. A warm welcome awaited us: volleys from knee mortars and automatic weapons. We responded in kind. I started by scanning the trees and roof tiles for signs of movement. A *pelopor* opened fire from among the branches. I fired back. His sniper carbine with telescopic sight fell to the ground and he hung dead from the tree to which he had tied himself. Catching a flash of gunfire from the door of a *kampong* house, I circled round, lobbed in a hand grenade and dropped to the ground. One terrific blast and the firing stopped. I stormed the house with two marines and saw a bunch of wounded *pelopors* on the floor. My mates put them out of their misery, one bullet for each man. We piled their weapons at the door to be picked up by the marines behind us, and ran from one house to the next in quick succession.

I approached one of the larger buildings, where I thought Islamic clerics might be holed up. I kicked the door down and stood face to face with a *kyai*, brandishing a poisonous *kris*. I pumped two bullets into his chest and stuck my bayonet in his throat. Another *kyai* charged from the right. With no time to pull my bayonet from the dead man's body, I drew my fighting knife. The fanatical bastard ran straight at me, I kicked the *kris* from his hand and skewered his throat with my knife, withdrew the blade quickly and planted it in his chest. A faint crack of bone, a deep rattle and he sank slowly to the floor. Behind and to the left of me, my mates were fighting off fanatics who had leapt from the shadows. We could not fire for fear of hitting one another, but every last one of us escaped without a scratch from those poisonous blades.

By this time my back was giving me hell. I tried to block out the pain but to no avail. It was taking an age to clear Bangsalsari and the surrounding countryside. We were lucky that no marines lost their lives, though some of us were badly wounded. A number of prisoners were brought to me for interrogation and I did not spare them. They confessed that their group had rigged up 100-pound aircraft bombs as landmines. I flew into a rage and kicked their grinning heads in. Later my mates shot them dead.

Arriving back at SHQ-II in Jember, I went straight to my room and threw off my marching pack, before going to the commanders' office to report on our sweeping operation. The next morning after breakfast I went to the sick bay. I was examined by Dr Jacobus, medical officer second class, who diagnosed me with a form of sciatica. I thought this strange, as sciatica is almost unheard of in the tropics. The upshot was that I had to spend three weeks flat on my back in the sick bay.

I ended up on a large ward with seven men, all with relatively minor injuries. The eight men on the next ward had not been so lucky. We visited them on a daily basis to pump them full of hope and courage. Those Dutch lads did not have it easy. Some of them cried at night, calling out for their mothers and their loved ones in Holland.

Lying still for so long made me restless. Thoughts of my friends, my childhood and the violence I grew up with began nagging away at me. Dead and wounded marines were brought in almost daily, doctors and medics came and went, and the operating theatres were working round the clock. With a couple of mates, I sneaked into the mortuary rooms sometimes to see who had gone to meet their maker. I recognized drinking pals from my weekends on leave. It was horrible to see them lying there, half-mutilated or torn apart by machine-gun bullets. I swore revenge and asked to be discharged, but they told me I had not yet recovered.

A son returns from the grave

After a month confined to the Jember sick bay, I was discharged towards the end of August 1947 and given four days' leave to visit Surabaya. Since landing at Pasir Putih for the First Police Action, I had not had a single day to myself. I was in reasonable shape, though a little weak, and my back still hurt now and then.

I set off, unaware that my brother Karel had been to see Mama one evening after work. Ella and Poppy were there too. Karel summoned them to the dining room, along with Babu Tenie and Kokkie Tas and told them he had sad news.

Sitting at the table, Karel began, 'Ma, Ella and Poppy, *babus*, when Arto came to say goodbye to you all, he took me aside and said that if I did not hear from him in six weeks, I was to let you know that he is no longer with us. That time has come. I have had no word from him and must therefore assume that he is dead. I have asked the few marines I know for news of Arto, but no one could tell me anything. Many marines have lost their lives in East Java.'

Everyone, even Poppy, burst into tears. The *babus* were inconsolable.

Jan van der Burgt, a marine second class who worked at the Marine Corps bakery, paid occasional visits to Ella. During my absence, my sister had been liberated from the women's internment camp near Malang. Jan was having a fling with the woman next door, Mary Scheffer, whose husband was still a POW. When Jan stopped by a few evenings after Karel's announcement, Mama and Ella asked him to find out if I was really dead. The next day, he was taking the train to Bondowoso and Jember to deliver a consignment of bread and other supplies. The Marine Brigade Security Service detachment in Bondowoso referred him to SHQ-II in Jember but, instead of going there, he took the advice of a medic and went directly to the sick bay. That morning, the bodies of a number of marines killed in action were due to be transported to Surabaya for burial at Kembang Kuning military cemetery. Jan asked the staff about me. A sergeant consulted his paperwork and found my name, jotted down in error by another interpreter. Shocked, Jan slunk away and returned home, where the sad news plunged my family into grief.

Meanwhile, I was on the train to Surabaya. On arrival, I shouldered my transport pack and trudged out of Gubeng station. It was late afternoon but the heat was still stifling. I hailed a *becak* and slumped into the seat. The driver cycled slowly to Undaan Kulon, turned onto Heemskerkstraat and stopped outside No. 5. I paid the man, slung my trusty M1 over my right shoulder and dragged my gear onto the porch. I could already see Mama sitting there. She looked up and saw the ghost of her son. The poor woman had already rolled up my mattress and burned incense in my room. I had to shake her to convince her I was real. She began to cry.

I dumped my pack in my room, where the air was still thick with incense. In my confusion, I walked back into the dining room with my weapon still in my hand. The *babus* came to greet me with tears of joy. Then, through the window, I spied a child of around two years old playing in the back garden. A girl with slanted eyes.

'Who does that Japanese child belong to?' I shouted, and aimed my rifle at her. When the *babus* saw what I was doing, they flung themselves at me. My gun went off and the bullet missed the little Jap girl.

'*Jangan sinjo Arto! Jangan sinjo Arto! Minta ampun, itu anak tidak salah!*' they begged. 'No, Arto! Don't! Have mercy, Arto. The child is innocent!'

The two women clung to me so tightly that I could not raise my rifle. 'Enough, Arto!' Mama shouted reproachfully. 'That child has done nothing wrong! She was born to your sister Ella and Joshida, the Sakura Japanese she went out with after Kamei was killed. Arto, I order you, do not lay a finger on that child!'

'Where is Ella?' I shouted furiously.

'At the *pasar*!'

Mama told me how Dutch troops had liberated Ella and Ina during the Police Action, and that Ina had moved to Batavia with her husband and children.

'*Aduh*, you have grown even more heartless than you were as a policeman. I am shocked by your cruelty. How many people have you killed? Uncle Soen and Pah Tjillih are worried about you. Pah Tjillih has been asking after you. Go to see him! And leave poor little Josta in peace!'

It was gone six in the evening and already dark when Babu Tenie woke me. Feeling listless, I got up and took a refreshing bath, then put on my khaki dress uniform and headed for the Marines Club on Tunjungan. I went straight up to the bar and ordered ten shots of brandy. The Indo barmaid looked me up and down and said, 'I only serve blond, blue-eyed Dutch boys.'

Furious, I went in search of the manager and complained about the conduct of his personnel. He too was angry and took the girl to task. 'Hey, are you refusing to serve this marine because his hair is not blond and his eyes are not blue? What kind of nonsense is this? Serve him this minute, or take your things and leave. Understood?'

The Indo girl's cheeks turned red with shame. She poured my brandies, and I paid and took my full tray to a table by the loudspeaker at the corner of the dancefloor, where I settled down to enjoy my drinks to the music of Glenn Miller, Harry James, Artie Shaw, the Andrew Sisters, Bing Crosby, Judy Garland and, last but not least, Vera Lynn.

The incident with the barmaid heightened the feeling that I did not belong in this racist, colonial society. From an early age, I had seen all kinds of American movies and watched countless newsreels with glimpses of life in Holland. From my conversations with Dutch lads and letters from the Dutch girls who wrote to me, I had an idea of how people in Holland lived and what they thought of people whose skin was not white. That was where my future lay.

Buried alive

After a couple of pleasant days, it was time to return to the front. I signed off with the senior NCO at Firefly Barracks and was handed a bag of letters to take back to the lads at SHQ-II. A jeep took me to Gubeng station, where I caught the train to Jember.

On arrival, the first thing I did was read through the recent combat and counterintelligence reports. Gangs of Indonesian guerrillas had been on the rampage, all the more troubling since they were no longer sparing their own people. The local police had their hands full providing emergency assistance, while marines patrolled the region, day and night.

Late one afternoon, I was out on the front porch, smoking and shooting the breeze with a couple of the lads when a Chinaman came staggering into the compound, battered and bruised. A couple of chaps leapt up and went to his aid. They cleaned his wounds with boracic lotion, disinfected them with sulpha, and patched him up as best they could. As he was being tended to, he answered my questions.

He lived a mile or so from Mangli. That morning, nine guerrillas had appeared out of nowhere and proceeded to assault him. As he lay on the ground, groaning with pain, the attackers raped his wife and daughter and worked them over with knives and bayonets. His wife was killed, but his daughter, a girl of eighteen, survived. Those savages then decided to bury her alive before they moved on. The poor father staggered to the main road that runs from Mangli to Jember and was lucky enough to flag down a passing *dokar*. That was how he had managed to reach us.

Wasting no time, we formed an assault squad, eight-man strong. The Chinaman came with us. When we arrived at his house, I jumped out of the vehicle and helped him down, so that he could point out the spot where they had buried his daughter. Carefully, we began to dig. In the heat of the moment, no one had thought to bring a spade, so we had to scrape away the soil with our bayonets and helmets.

Sure enough, we unearthed the poor child… and she was still alive! A Japanese bayonet had been rammed through her pelvis. I was about to pull it out, taking the greatest of care, but one of the marines held me back. 'Leave be, Nolan. That's a job for a medic. We have already radioed for an ambulance.'

By the time the ambulance arrived, we had been hanging around for the best part of an hour. The lads had done their best to clean the girl up, rinsing off the mud and sand with water and tea from their flasks. Her mother's half-stripped body was lying in full view in the front garden. I cut some leaves from a plantain and laid them over her corpse. The poor Chinaman was inconsolable and sobbed the entire time. I searched for footprints and surmised that the culprits were probably Army guerrillas who had taken off in the direction of Rambipuji.

The Indonesian Army used intimidation of this kind to sap the morale of the locals. Fire-starting was also rife. The peasants were ordered to hand over at least eighty per cent of their harvest to the guerrillas, far more than they had ever surrendered to the Dutch. Anyone who failed to meet their demands was slaughtered.

The giant

A few days later, we received reports that a sizeable contingent of Indonesian guerrillas was terrorizing the local population near Genteng. Our commanding officers quickly drew up a plan of attack culminating in a night-time raid. We set out with twenty men. A mile or so from Genteng, we halted our attack vehicles and continued on foot, approaching the enemy with maximum stealth. With only yards to go, we spread out in a pincer movement and then swept through the village, kicking in doors. Every armed man or fleeing *pemuda* was gunned down. Women and children were spared.

Then I saw something I will never forget.

In the middle of the *kampong*, a giant of a man was standing motionless beside a *tong-tong*. He was shaking with fear, armed with nothing but a machete. I walked over to interrogate him but I had taken only a few steps when a sergeant charged past me and pumped a full magazine from his jungle carbine into the man's body. As if by a miracle, the giant remained standing.

In the moonlight, I counted fifteen holes in his bullet-riddled body. Burning with rage, I turned on the sergeant and yelled, 'What the fuck were you doing? The man was innocent! I was about to question him but you had to blast him to bits. And you didn't even finish him off.'

Over and over, the giant murmured, 'I'm innocent. I'm innocent.'

'Our orders are to shoot every armed man on sight,' the sergeant shouted. 'And from now on, stay out of my business!'

'Another screw-up like that and I'll have you reported!' I shouted back.

At that moment a corporal arrived to calm things down. I pleaded with him to draw his weapon, for God's sake, and show the poor man some mercy. The corporal aimed his tommy gun at the giant's forehead and fired a single, fatal shot. The man reeled back and hit the ground. Out of his misery.

Ill-fated prisoner transport

On 22 November 1947, Adjutant Mulder granted me a few days' leave in Surabaya, on condition that I take charge of a trainload of prisoners and hand them over to the Military Police at Wonokromo station. I gathered the interrogation files of the twenty-nine prisoners: mass murderers, rapists, saboteurs and arsonists. We knew from bitter experience that this class of criminal could expect to serve a maximum jail term of six months. We also knew that Judge De la Parra of the court in Surabaya had received death threats in the post: he, his wife, his children and his relatives throughout the Archipelago would be slaughtered unless he handed down lenient sentences to these hardened criminals. It was not uncommon for multiple murderers to be let off for lack of evidence. Verdicts like these did not go down well with the security services – with us, in other words.

I accepted this thankless task with great reluctance and Adjutant Mulder assigned three interpreters to assist me: Ong Thwan Hien, a former Chinese trader whose family had been massacred by *pemudas*, and Harry and Paul Madjoe. The Madjoe brothers were Manadonese and former members of the Indonesian Army. Though I took them on, I had my suspicions and made it clear I would gun them down at the least sign of sabotage. They were to shoot escapees on sight. A moment's hesitation and they could expect a bullet from me.

Groeneboer drove the four of us to Jember prison in his jeep. We reported to the guard with our packs and our weapons. In the office, I took the prisoners' files out of my knapsack and handed them over. The commander took note of the names, ordered a couple of soldiers to prepare those listed for transport and then checked the prisoners personally. Turning to me, he said, 'Marine, here you have the bastards, all twenty-nine of them. Stick them behind bars in Surabaya for a long, long time. And if you can't manage that, shoot them all to hell. I wish you and your helpers the very best of luck. Enjoy your leave.'

I thanked him and made the prisoners march to the station in rows of four. Rifles at the ready, we marched on either side of this criminal parade. At the station, I ordered my assistants to guard the prisoners while I arranged for the wagons we needed.

I approached the Van Gelder brothers, who I knew from our time together in the AMA Police Forces, and asked them for an open cattle truck. They relayed my request to Van Tilburg, their boss, but he refused and said I would have to take a covered goods wagon. I protested. Looking around the yard, there seemed to be enough cattle trucks available.

'Reserved for other purposes,' Van Tilburg explained.

I pointed out to him that I was transporting people, not meat, and that this would not be possible in a closed wagon with no ventilation.

'I am in charge around here, Nolan,' Van Tilburg bit back, 'and I will decide which wagons to allocate to prisoner transport. Right now, I have this one covered wagon and I will give immediate orders for it to be hitched to the Surabaya train.'

Left with no choice, I ordered my men to herd the prisoners into the wagon. Of course, I took care not to close the sliding door completely but left a gap of between 10 and 15 inches and secured the bolt with steel wire to allow enough air into the wagon once the train was moving. The four of us took up positions on either side of the small platform at the rear of the wagon, rifles poised.

November 22, 1947 was a scorching day and it was almost eleven in the morning when the train left the station. The next stop was Bondowoso, followed by Probolinggo. Even when the train was moving, the heat was stifling. In Probolinggo they had to stoke the locomotive and stopped for longer than normal. I jumped off the wagon and went over to some vendors to buy food and drink. As I was walking back, Ong Thwan Hien ran up to me looking rattled. 'Trouble, Nolan! Something's up in the wagon!'

I ran to the door, loosened the steel wire and slid it open. One of the prisoners sprang out and made a run for it. In a flash, I grabbed my M1 and shot him dead. My three helpers trained their rifles on the rest. Around five prisoners were lying unconscious on the wagon floor. I ran to the engine driver and asked him for a bucket of cold water. He gave me one and brought two more buckets himself. I threw the water over all of the prisoners and, to my relief, it seemed to do them good. I ordered my men to keep a close watch. By this time, the situation was attracting all kinds of attention. Gawping bystanders were crowding around the wagon and a few were bending over the dead fugitive. A Marine lieutenant from the tank division, also on leave, began to interfere. When my helpers were distracted for a moment, another prisoner made his escape. As I took aim, the lieutenant knocked my M1 upwards and I shot in the air.

'Why did you do that?' I snarled.

'Let the man run. He has already lost his mind. Just look at him!'

He had a point. I saw the prisoner scaling the barbed-wire fence around the railway yard. Just as he was about to jump, his strength failed him and he was stuck there. The more he struggled, the deeper the barbs dug into his skin. The officer stopped me shooting the unfortunate prisoner as a *coup de grâce* and he was left hanging from the barbed-wire to die in agony.

I called over a couple of street vendors and ordered them to give all their fruit, boiled rice dishes and biscuits to the prisoners. I paid them generously from my own wages and heard them say to each other that they had never got rid of their wares so quickly.

Checking the prisoners, I discovered that three were in a very bad way. It was another hour before we continued towards Pasuruan. As we crossed a bridge over a deep ravine, another prisoner jumped the train. Ong shot, but missed. I took aim and saw the fugitive plunge into the ravine.

In Pasuruan I looked in on the twenty-six remaining prisoners, only to find that three had succumbed to the heat. The sun was beating down mercilessly on our helmets. Again I called over a couple of vendors and ordered them to give all their wares to the prisoners. I compensated them generously.

At Bangil station, I took care of the prisoners in the same way. The heat was so intense that I left the sliding door half-open for the rest of the journey, though I knew it was an invitation to escape. Sure enough, between Bangil and Sidoarjo another two prisoners leapt from the wagon. They paid for their hopeless flight with their lives.

By the time we reached Sidoarjo, two more men had perished in the heat. This made a total of five. Yet another prisoner made a break for it. I fired a warning shot and, when that was ignored, I shot to kill: yet another casualty of the damned prison transport I had been forced to take charge of when all I wanted was to go home on leave.

Late in the afternoon, the train finally pulled into Wonokromo station in Surabaya, where the Military Police were waiting for us. I handed over the remaining eighteen prisoners and five dead bodies to them, along with the prisoners' files. Then I went to the stationmaster's office and called my senior commander, Captain Groeneveld of the Marine Corps. I gave him a brief account of the transport, the six fugitives and the five deaths. 'Nolan,' he replied, 'you have always shown initiative. Continue to do so now and act in good conscience. If you encounter any more difficulties, you can count on my support. Get the Marine Corps Military Police involved. Good luck, my boy!'

My next call was to the offices of the Red Cross in Surabaya, asking them to take care of the five bodies in the wagon. By this time, my helpers had begun to fret about the consequences of our ill-fated assignment. I did my best to reassure them and made another call, this time to the duty commander of the Marine Corps Military Police in Surabaya, and told him what had happened. By then it was dark and, not to complicate matters further, he suggested I should first take a day of leave before reporting to barracks to await further developments.

A couple of Military Police officers gave us a lift to the centre of Surabaya in their half-track. On the way we talked about what had happened. Those lads said it would have been better all round if every last prisoner had died. They dropped us off close to the Marines Club on Tunjungan and we thanked them for the lift.

I took my leave of the Madjoe brothers and Ong Thwan Hien, who went off to see their families. I scrabbled together my gear and my weapons and entered the Marines Club. First, I found myself a quiet spot close to the bar, put my kit down on a chair and my steel helmet on the table. Then I went up and ordered a dozen shots from the barmaid. She looked at me in surprise.

'Have you come straight from the front?' she said. 'What a sight! You look terrible!'

I gave her a dazed look and took the tray of shots back to my table. I swallowed down my order, taking a long time between drinks as my thoughts drifted back over the day's events.

Half-drunk, I left around ten. I waved down a *becak* and ordered the driver to take me home. I was in luck: Mama was already asleep. Babu Tenie was shocked to see the state I was in and prepared a bath for me. She washed my clothes and hung them out to dry.

I slept for much of the day and, even after waking, I stayed in bed staring into space. Kokkie Tas brought me food now and then. When Mama came to ask what was wrong with me, I told her I was tired. As evening approached, I ordered a *becak* to take me back to the Marines Club, where this time I got tanked up on whisky. Strangely, I saw no one I knew at the club that night. I left feeling uneasy and had a *becak* drop me at the barracks on Porongstraat. I staggered up to the barrier and reported to the duty officer.

'Hey Nolan, what's this I hear? Had a spot of bad luck with a prisoner transport? You're three sheets to the wind, man. Where's the good in that?'

'Bad luck? Yes, you might say that. Spoke to Captain Groeneveld on the phone yesterday,' I said. 'My entire leave is up the spout.'

'Well, if it's any consolation, you're in the same boat as a bunch of lads from another prisoner transport,' the officer continued.

'What?' I shouted, shaken from my stupor. 'There was another transport?'

The duty officer tried to reassure me, offered me a cigarette and a chair to sit down on. I badly needed that chair. A corporal came to sit with me and gave me a mug of strong coffee and a tin of K rations. As I wolfed down macaroni with ham and cheese, the officer told me that a second transport had left from Bondowoso after mine, with no fewer than one hundred prisoners on board. They had also been packed into covered goods wagons with no ventilation and half of them had suffocated.

After digesting that horror story, I wove my way down the corridor to the dorm. I dumped my kit next to my camp bed, hung my rifle in the belts and lay down, fully clothed, boots and all. I fell into a deep and immediate sleep.

The next morning I woke with a pounding headache. I stripped to my underpants and headed for the washrooms, where a long, cold shower washed away my hangover. In the mess, I met the lads from the second prisoner transport, including a lieutenant, a sergeant major and a marine first class. After breakfast we had a cheerless conversation about our situation.

At nine-thirty, we piled into a half-track which took us to Marine Military Police HQ, where they typed up a detailed report on each of us. We had no idea of the political shockwaves these events were about to cause or the international press coverage they would attract. Pending preliminary investigations, none of us were allowed to leave the city.

After questioning, I was assigned a defence counsel, Major Versteeg of the Marine Corps. The Military Police commander handed over my report and all other relevant documentation to him. I took comfort from the news that my commander-in-chief, Colonel Roelofs of the Marine Corps, was to attend the hearing of the court martial to defend his men.

It was getting on for December 1947. I was twenty-two years old. Major Versteeg of the Marine Corps had a reputation as a brilliant lawyer. Alongside my commander, Colonel Roelofs of the Marine Corps, I also had the backing of my battalion commander, Lieutenant Colonel Aberson of the Marine Corps. The involvement of these senior officers was reassuring, and the lads from the second prisoner transport were also able to count on their support. Everyone at the barracks was outraged by the big deal being made of the prisoner transports. Politicians and government officials were apparently less concerned about the countless Dutch women and children murdered by Indonesian freedom fighters. To us, it seemed perverse. Every man I met was griping, moaning and cursing about the situation.

Confined to the city pending investigation and trial, I kept myself occupied with intelligence work at GHQ. Adjutant Mulder came looking for me in the barracks dormitory one afternoon. 'Nolan, this evening you and the lads from the second transport will appear before the top brass at the Resident's Palace. Questions will be put to you. Dress in your best khaki uniform and wear a tie.'

I snapped to attention. 'Yes, sir!'

'Report to my room at approximately six-thirty this evening and I will take you there in the jeep. Let me tell you this in advance: Governor Van der Plas wishes to talk to you personally. He knows your family well. That is all, Nolan. See you later.'

I left barracks shortly after six, and made my way to the NCOs' quarters. On the way, I saw the lads from the second transport waiting for their truck to arrive. I knocked on Adjutant Mulder's door and asked him to help me knot my tie, as I had never worn one before. This made him chuckle, but he did as I asked. I looked up and was surprised to see Captain Groeneveld of the Marine Corps enter the room. I snapped to attention and saluted.

'Yes, Nolan, I have been summoned too,' Captain Groeneveld said. 'Rest assured that I have looked into this thoroughly. It will indeed be a case for the court martial, but given your actions on the front to date you have nothing to worry about. Everything you did was by the book. The Brigade Staff stands squarely behind you and the men from the second transport.'

Captain Groeneveld and Adjutant Mulder got into the jeep and I jumped in the back. In the foyer of the Resident's Palace, I saw many a staff officer from the various branches of the armed services. The mood was subdued. The truck carrying the lads from the second transport arrived soon after. They too were dressed in their finest. We exchanged uncomfortable glances. An army officer escorted us into a grand hall and gestured to us to sit down on a row of splendid chairs. From where we were sitting, we caught an occasional glimpse of the big conference room where the heads of staff were busy discussing our ill-fated transports. Among them I spotted General Spoor, Governor Van de Plas and Colonel Roelofs. None of us felt in the least at ease.

After a long wait, we were all admitted to the conference room and came face to face with the assembled top brass and political bigwigs. General Spoor and Colonel Roelofs spoke in our defence, as those responsible for both transports. They did so with conviction and with passion. The worst of it was not being able to say a single word on our own behalf.

When the spectacle was over, I was called into the library by Governor Van de Plas. I had a lengthy and gratifying conversation with that illustrious gentleman. Among the things he said to me was, 'I say, Nolan, I know your family well from my time in Jember. Before the war, I visited them on more than a few occasions. You are a son of which Nolan?'

'The lawyer Willem Nolan,' I answered. 'I am his youngest son. Did you know him? Many prominent men here in Surabaya knew my late father.'

'Indeed I did!' the governor answered. 'He was not one of the planters – I remember him now.'

He then asked me to give a full account of the events of my prisoner transport. I dredged up every last detail. A soldier serving as a waiter brought us cool drinks and cigarettes. When I was finished, the governor tried to impress upon me the nature of the current political situation. He advised me not to limit my view to a purely military perspective.

It slowly began to dawn on me that a soldier is nothing more than an instrument in the hands of politicians. At first, this made my blood boil. Then came bitterness and disillusion. I had hoped so fervently for a return to life before the war but this conversation robbed me of all hope, dashed every illusion. I had the feeling that we were losing the political game and could only win by military means. The conversation over, I snapped to attention and saluted. I thanked the governor and left the Resident's Palace feeling utterly despondent. I headed straight for Tunjungan and proceeded to drown my sorrows at the Marines Club.

'What on earth are we fighting for?' was the question that kept spinning around my head. There was little time to dwell upon these dismal events. I was given a post under the head of Department IV, Piet Dikotta. Although he was my direct superior, he treated me more like a younger brother. Whenever my mind was in knots or I was facing other problems, he was always there to lend a listening ear.

Court martial

The day of the hearing came for me and the lads from the second prisoner transport. We jumped on a waiting truck and set off for the naval court martial in Gubeng district, near the viaduct over the railway. A huge crowd had gathered. Journalists wielding cameras came and went, snapping photographs and scribbling notes. We were led inside and taken to a large waiting room. I was pleased and relieved to see not only our most senior commander, Colonel Roelofs of the Marine Corps – the tiger of the Gubeng Marine barracks – but also Lieutenant Colonel Aberson of the Marine Corps, commander of the second infantry battalion and Blue Column; Captain Groeneveld of the Marine Corps, my most senior commander within the Marine Brigade Security Service; his right-hand man, Lieutenant Brink of the Marine Corps; and of course Adjutant Mulder of the Marine Corps, commander of SHQ-II. Other staff officers of the Brigade were also in attendance. I even caught a glimpse of General Spoor, High Commander of the Land Forces in the Dutch East Indies.

My wait was mercifully short. Major Versteeg of the Marine Corps, counsel for the defence, entered the waiting room, singled me out and led me to the courtroom. There I caught sight of our very own Admiral Hellfrich. I halted before the dock, saluted and stood to attention until the judge gave me permission to sit. The prosecutor, himself a Marine officer, was clearly troubled by the notion of fellow marines being hung out to dry in the face of such intense political pressure. His indictment was brief and he made a procedural demand of ten years' imprisonment. Then it was the defence counsel's turn to speak. He presented as mitigating arguments the fact that I had given the prisoners food and drink during the transport, paid for out of my own pocket, that I had asked both Van Tilburg and the Van Gelders for an open cattle wagon and been refused, and that, having been assigned a covered goods wagon, I had protested at the lack of ventilation. I had improvised to the best of my ability but, during the long journey in excessive heat, I had been unable to prevent a number of prisoners from collapsing due to heat stress and lack of oxygen.

After the defence counsel, Colonel Roelofs and Lieutenant Colonel Aberson took the stand and spoke powerfully in my defence. The judge was convinced of my good intentions and acquitted me of the charges. I could have cried out with joy. The judge gave the command 'Dismissed!' and I was free to leave the courtroom.

Out of solidarity, I returned to my seat to await the verdict of the second prisoner transport. After their hearing, the lads told me that severe sentences had been handed down: eighteen months for the first lieutenant of the Marine Corps, one year for the lieutenant of the tank division, nine months for the sergeant major of the Marine Corps and six for a marine first class and another marine. We cursed among ourselves and had lengthy discussions with all the staff officers present, even the officers of the Big Shit.

When it was all over, the sentenced marines and I travelled in *becaks*, jeeps and *dokars* to the Marines Club. The place was packed. We drank heavily and the guilders flowed freely. The club resounded with our curses and calls for reprisals. Cries of 'Death to the Merdeka' rang out. To me it made little difference, I was already bent on revenge and even tougher action against the *pelopors*. I had read combat intelligence reports detailing our losses and how the bodies of marines killed in action had been defiled and hacked to pieces.

Bodyguard

I received orders to return to SHQ-II in Jember, where I was still head of Prisoner Interrogations Department III. I went to the quartermaster to replenish my kit and ammunition as usual, before going to Piet Dikotta's office for further counterintelligence instructions. I received a large sum of Indonesian currency for the espionage fund, then signed off with Sergeant Major Vestdijk of the Marine Corps. The dispatcher arranged for my transport and at the last minute I was handed a hefty sack of post for the men stationed in and around Jember.

Weighed down like a beast of burden, I heaved myself into the waiting M2 fighting vehicle, which joined a column at Wonokromo that was due to stop in Jember on its way to resupply frontline troops. It was early morning, not too warm. On long trips like this, I usually knotted a large handkerchief around my neck to protect my nose and mouth from the dust clouds, and wore sunglasses under my double-layer helmet.

By the time we reached Jember, late that afternoon, I was half-dead and caked in dust. Our vehicle first made a quick stop at the battalion staff's building to hand the postbags to the dispatcher, then headed for the SHQ-II building I knew so well. Harry Tjong, the Madjoe brothers and other interpreters helped me unload all the baggage, which included chests of ammunition and hand grenades.

I reported to Adjutant Mulder and was warmly welcomed by all and congratulated on my acquittal in the prisoner transport case. The *babus* and some of the boys' girlfriends prepared a hearty meal for me. At the dinner table, comrades crowded round to hear every last detail of the court martial.

Next morning, I heard from many of the boys that a bunch of Indonesian mass murderers transported to Surabaya to stand trial were already back on the streets after serving sentences of four to six weeks. This pissed us off no end. Some told me they had taken the law into their own hands. They had waited on a couple of those bastards at Jember station, accompanied them to their lodgings and executed them before they could kill anyone else.

*

A few days later, Colonel Roelofs of the Marine Corps and his staff paid SHQ-II a visit. He needed a bodyguard to accompany him on an inspection of all posts in the region held by the second battalion, including the Marine Brigade Security Service. Adjutant Mulder selected me for the job. Once I had prepared my marching pack, I reported to Colonel Roelofs. In accordance with protocol, I snapped to attention and saluted, but the Colonel could not have been friendlier.

'At ease, Nolan,' he said. 'It is good to see you here again. The news of your acquittal was most welcome. Let me be brief, the staff is implementing a reorganization and you are to help us as a bodyguard. I have every faith in you. Even Captain Groeneveld has a good word to say about you. Unfortunately he will soon be leaving. Were you aware?'

'No, Colonel,' I answered, 'and if that is the case I will miss him sorely, both as a commander and as a good man.'

'Come, Nolan.' In a fatherly gesture, Colonel Roelofs took me by the shoulders. 'Let us prepare to inspect the posts.'

Colonel Roelofs was a splendid chap: damn tough at times, but always fair. The crew stationed in Surabaya knew him as 'the tiger of Gubeng barracks' and he had certainly been ferocious in my defence at the court martial. I was proud to serve under such a man. As a high-ranking officer, he was accompanied by a rifle squad of eight infantrymen, mostly seamen with no combat experience, straight off the boat from their motherland. I felt sorry for those *barus*. During the First Police Action, many such lads had lost their lives. Some of the bodies we found had been mutilated beyond recognition or hacked to pieces.

The colonel inspected his retinue, told me to take a seat in the back of his jeep and gave the signal for us to depart.

From Jember, our route took in over twenty-five locations. The inspection as a whole lasted several days and, everywhere he went, the colonel held extensive discussions with the commanders of the detached units. The guerrilla activities of the Indonesian Army and other militant groups were gathering momentum and we came under fire as our column left Rambipuji for Bangsalsari, a notorious hotbed of resistance. Our colonel's jeep led the column, of course, his staff flag flying proudly in the wind.

In the middle of Bangsalsari, the colonel gave the sign to halt and got out of the jeep. The gunfire intensified. Down the length of the column, commands to return fire rang out. Accompanied by me and a few infantrymen, Colonel Roelofs walked straight through the *kampong* and had me lead him to where the shots were coming from. Cane in hand, he passed on his orders to his adjutant. The colonel trusted me blindly. Walking beside him, I saw a door ease open and the barrel of a rifle emerge. I ran towards the house, my M1 blazing, kicked in the door and fired in all directions. I quickly reloaded and fired shots into every room, then kicked the back door off its hinges in search of more guerrillas. I saw no one and retraced my steps to assess the damage. Three bodies lay on the ground, one still moving. I drew my fighting knife, stabbed the man in the throat and turned the blade forty-five degrees before pulling it out. I wiped my bloodied knife clean on his uniform, spat in his face, got to my feet and rejoined the colonel.

'Three fewer hostiles to worry about, Colonel,' I said. 'We can move on.'

'Well done, Nolan,' the colonel replied. 'I know who I can count on.'

Meanwhile, the other infantrymen had responded to the enemy fire and driven off our attackers. I gave the *barus* within earshot the usual warnings about snipers in the trees, landmines and booby traps. I saw them turn pale, but the sooner they learned, the better.

Near Umbulsari we once again came under fire, though less intense than in Bangsalsari. Both held painful memories for me as the places where my vehicle had hit a landmine, so I was more alert than ever. Searching houses as we went, I killed another few *pelopors*. In the direct vicinity of Kencong, our column was greeted by a salvo of whistling bullets, but as our vehicles approached their positions, the enemy fled.

At the next Security Service post, we stopped for lunch and the next meeting. As Colonel Roelofs' bodyguard, it was my job to stay close to him at all times. Many an intel officer shot me an envious look, but I shrugged them off. I was only doing my duty.

We set up camp for the night near Puger, on the south coast of East Java. After dinner, the colonel gave me permission to take a walk on the beach with a few of the marines.

The next morning we continued on our way to Balung, Wuluhan and Ambulu, where we came under attack once again. The M2 fighting vehicle bringing up the rear had to overtake us to mow down the *pelopors* as they ran.

Jenggawah and Mangli were next on our list. We were attacked near Mangli and again our combat unit responded with heavy fire. On we went, through South Jember to Wirolegi and then to Majan, where we stopped at another Security Service detachment for lunch and detailed discussions of the local situation with the commanders.

Some of my mates from that detachment were surprised to see me. 'Hey, Nolan, been brown-nosing your way into Colonel Roelofs' good books? You're fairly climbing the ladder.'

'I have never brown-nosed my way into any commander's good books,' I snapped back. 'The opposite if anything! I am the colonel's bodyguard and you know what that entails.'

Some low-ranking soldier piped up. 'I can see why they picked you for such a shitty job. You wouldn't catch me playing bodyguard to some big wig. I'd rather make it home with all my limbs attached. To hell with that crap.'

I held my tongue and found myself a quiet place to eat and drink. That afternoon, we began the return journey to Surabaya. Everyone was tired. Late in the evening the whole shebang ground to a halt at the gates of the Brigade Staff on Coen Boulevard. The colonel thanked me and I was free to return to the headquarters of the Marine Brigade Security Service.

There, the change of command had already taken place. Captain Groeneveld had been transferred to the Intelligence Section of A Division, to be replaced by Captain Galliër of the Marine Corps.

We were unhappy about this, as Captain Groeneveld was very highly respected, especially among the war volunteers. The air was blue with cursing and complaints. I will never forget the letter the Captain wrote to us, the men of Firefly Barracks.

Firefly, January 1948

FAREWELL AND REMEMBRANCE

To all those who regard the Firefly as their emblem.

Should you re-read this brief letter at some later date, may it give you cause to look back and reflect on all the comrades with whom you have shared the bitter and the sweet under the name Firefly. And as you look back, be sure to remember those who made the greatest sacrifice a man can make, and who did so for you and the cause for which we fought. Our thoughts turn to them, for they have borne the consequences of their ideals.

I reflect on the time we have shared in the deep conviction that we have worked in accordance with our beliefs and to the best of our knowledge. Duty, comradeship and honour: these three, in harmony with one another, have been our guides. Of course we have all made mistakes, most arising from the fact that error is inherent in the works of man and is therefore to be forgiven. Was it not our ideal to achieve perfection? Each of us knows for himself how close he came. The earliest memories of our small community lie in the United States, then in Malacca and then in our vision of the Indies. Those same Indies have brought us so many disappointments, yet have also made us men able and willing to bear responsibility under the most trying of circumstances, without the luxury of falling back on others.

In the States the Firefly was born, in Malacca it was baptized, and in the Indies it came to life and showed us the way from darkness into light.

Such are our memories, yet memories they would not be if old Firefly had not come to an end.

That time has come. And so we all go our separate ways, each man seeking out his own future, seeking to determine the path his life will take. We will be scattered across the world and dissolve into millions, yet all with a single memory. In these new circumstances, endeavour to show the spirit that made the Firefly bond so strong.

Wherever you may be, whatever trials you may face, try to hold on to your humanity.

To all those with whom these words resonate, I thank you for the comradeship I have found in you and from the bottom of my heart I wish you all the very best for the future.

GROENEVELD

Your dreams of the *babu*...

By mid-1948, many volunteer marines had reached the end of their tour of duty in the tropics. They were withdrawn from the front and stationed in Surabaya to await their homeward voyage. Their places were taken by marines fresh from Holland, young National Service conscripts who in no time had to be brought up to speed on the grim realities of guerrilla tactics and jungle warfare. I was still at SHQ-II in Jember when almost every Marine unit was recalled to Surabaya to be replaced by KNIL and Dutch Army units. This was to pave the way for the Second Police Action.

I was among those ordered back to GHQ in Surabaya. On arrival, I reported to my commanding officer, Piet Dikotta. It was all go at HQ. Spies and informers had already been dispatched to locations held by Indonesian Army units and other fanatical militant groups. Messages were coming back regular as clockwork and it was my job to assist in their evaluation. We made notes on our military maps.

Dikotta called me into his office one day. 'I say, Nolan,' he said, 'you will be leaving your position as head of interrogation and returning to the outposts for six months or so. You will start in SHQ-III in Lumajang under the command of First Lieutenant of the Marine Corps Flip Lichtenberg. He will send you out to Marine Brigade Security detachments in his area. Your role will be to keep a close eye on Indonesian troop movements. Send me your full counterintelligence reports on a regular basis. I have already informed Lieutenant Lichtenberg of your arrival. You know the drill.'

The next day I was on a truck to Lumajang with my full pack. Dusty and weary, I arrived at SHQ late in the afternoon to a hearty welcome from Lieutenant Lichtenberg. I stayed a day or two to go through the intelligence reports and receive instructions, before being temporarily relocated to Corporal Zijlstra's detachment in Tempeh.

The Tempeh detachment was a small-scale operation covering a limited area. Corporal Zijlstra was assisted by three interpreters and I became the fourth, but with a special assignment. The others were engaged in setting up native governance in the region and distributing textiles, food and medicine to the impoverished population.

I went out on patrol almost daily and covered the entire area. Here and there, I asked the villagers about movements by the Indonesian Army's guerrilla units and relayed counterintelligence reports to GHQ in Surabaya every other day. Our small detachment received frequent night-time visits from the *babus*. Those women had no use for undergarments, hence the song known to many a Dutch marine:

Your dreams of the babu *are made to last*
Just lift up her sarong and ogle her ass

Flash Gordon and the Jungle Princess

I was ordered to leave for Senduro, in the shadow of the great volcanoes Gunung Bromo and Gunung Semeru. At the Marine Brigade Security detachment there, I reported to Sergeant Gio Montagne of the Marine Corps, an Indo who was cocky beyond belief. He was a hard-core Sixteen Sixty-Fiver and was assisted by a Marine corporal and a private first class. I joined a team of interpreters that included Freddie Onsoe, my old buddy Ben de Lima and a lad called Jan Abas, who would later become my sworn enemy.

Unlike Tempeh, the situation around Senduro was tense. The countryside was swarming with guerrilla units. Our post was close to the base of W Company, which had recently undergone a reorganization. The company's first lieutenant was blond, six foot three and built like a truck. His favourite pastime was heading out on patrol at every opportunity, day or night. No wonder they nicknamed him 'Flash Gordon'.

The area around Senduro stretched all the way to the southern flank of Gunung Semeru, Java's highest peak. Deep valleys and ravines sliced through the rough terrain, home to mouse deer, venomous snakes, wild buffalo and black panthers. A paradise for hunters but given half a chance we steered well clear of the wildlife.

Flash Gordon turned up at our post one day to ask Sergeant Gio Montagne for at least two interpreters to assist him on a three-day patrol to Gunung Semeru. The objective was to find out more about Indonesian Army infiltrators and troop movements. Freddie Onsoe, Jan Abas and I were selected.

The next morning we were up at dawn, marching packs with double blanket roll, extra ammunition and hand grenades at the ready. With 75 pounds on our backs, we walked to the company post where Flash Gordon and his fifty infantrymen were waiting for us. We travelled on foot to the southern flank of Gunung Semeru with a ten-year-old Javanese boy as our guide. I walked at the front with Flash and the boy at my side.

The path grew steep and before long we were dripping with sweat. Then it petered out altogether. Only dense jungle lay ahead.

Three infantrymen wielding big machetes came to the fore and began hacking their way through the thick lianas. I pulled out my fighting knife, but those vines were too tough. Our young guide walked into a liana that turned out to be a twelve-foot python. The snake dropped and coiled around the poor boy's scrawny body with incredible speed. Three of us dived on that monster. A tough corporal with hands like coal shovels had the presence of mind to grab the snake by its head. Flash Gordon ordered us not to shoot, for fear of alerting the enemy, so we ripped into the snake with our bayonets and knives. I grabbed it by the tail and bent the end as far back as I could to relax the central nervous cord, but my own nerves were jangling so much that I ended up cutting the tail clean off.

Eventually the snake succumbed to the countless bayonet wounds and released its prey. Our young guide had lost consciousness. When he came to after a few minutes, I gave him a big gulp of coffee from my water bottle. Once he had recovered enough to get back on his feet, we continued our uphill journey.

The dazed boy looked up at me and said, '*Tuan*, the snake has crossed our path. Bad things will come our way. I am only the first to be touched by this ill fortune.' I looked him in the eye and nodded to let him know I understood. Thanks to Uncle Soen and Pah Tjillih, I was familiar with these superstitions.

After two hours of hacking away at lianas without a let-up, we had barely advanced a hundred yards. I asked the boy if he knew any secret trails that led to the southern ridge. He did know of one. We had to backtrack a few hundred yards and take a path slick from the water that flowed downhill. Slipping and sliding, we crept up the mountainside, cursing and complaining all the way. Late in the afternoon we finally arrived at a clearing and rested there briefly. A medic attended to our poor young guide, whose struggle with the python had left him with two broken ribs.

Having let the boy sleep for half an hour, we regrouped and continued to follow the slippery uphill path. We came to a flat section, which on further inspection turned out to be an abandoned road. But less than a hundred yards on, it dissolved into jungle foliage so thick that even our machetes were useless.

All our attempts to find other paths came to nothing. Dejected and disappointed, we gradually accepted that we had no choice but to turn around. By the time we made it back to our post, night had fallen.

From reports by his informers and spies, Sergeant Gio Montagne had learned that a guerrilla group was laying low in a *kampong* some three miles from our base. The group was terrorizing the entire village and was led by a *pemudi* – a female *pemuda* – who had climbed to the rank of lieutenant in the Indonesian Army. We dubbed her the 'Jungle Princess', as she was rumoured to be a beauty with hair that fell in waves to her waist. Behind this beautiful façade lurked a cold-blooded killer.

After a long morning meeting, Sergeant Gio Montagne went to the company post to obtain the assistance of a squad of marines. I made sure my phosphorus bullets were ready for use in the dark.

Our patrol set off late in the evening, as the sergeant wanted to catch the enemy as they slept. One of his informers came with us. We supplied him with an old Mannlicher rifle, some ammunition and a bayonet.

Conditions were against us: a full moon in a cloudless sky swarming with a million stars. We marched to the *kampong* in under an hour. Up front with Sergeant Gio Montagne, our informer pointed out a large wooden building with a thatched roof: a boarding house where around fifteen of the terrorists were billeted. At first, we saw no guards but we were mistaken. Our informer signalled that one guard was posted at the front and one at the rear. Quickly and silently, we took up our positions. I crept up on the guard at the rear and buried my fighting knife deep in his neck, turning the blade forty-five degrees and slicing through his jugular before pulling the knife out. He fell to the ground spluttering. Another marine similarly disposed of the guard at the front door.

The rest must have heard the dying men splutter, because muffled noises started coming from inside the building. I withdrew to my shooting position behind a couple of plantains. The others dived for cover among the thick bushes that surrounded the boarding house.

Sharp blasts from Sergeant Gio Montagne's jungle carbine signalled the start of the attack. My eyes were fixed on the back door. It swung open suddenly and two shadows came running out. Peering through my sight smeared with phosphor, I took aim and fired. One shadow hit the ground, then the other. More *pemudas* fled the building and were gunned down one by one by the other marines. Then I spotted the Jungle Princess emerging from the building, unmistakeable due to her long hair. She made a run for it. I aimed and fired. Two shots. Both missed. Five marines entered the boarding house, shooting anything that moved. When the battle was over, I stepped inside and counted six bodies.

'Damn it,' Sergeant Gio Montagne shouted, 'we let the Jungle Princess escape!'

'I had her in my sights but missed,' I admitted.

Disappointed, we tramped back to our post. On the way, Freddie Onsoe gave me a sly grin and asked if perhaps I hadn't missed on purpose…

'You know what, Nolan?' Sergeant Gio Montagne said the next day. 'It's time to live dangerously. I plan to dispatch five informers to track down what is left of that gang. One of them is the Jungle Princess's brother. However, it means arming them, and that's what's putting the wind up me. What's to stop those buggers walking out of here and turning our own weapons on us?'

I thought for a long time and finally said, 'It's a risk we have to take. But we need to know what route they are taking. If they break their word, they must be made to pay.'

The sergeant summoned the five informers, issued them with weapons and instructed them to locate the rest of the guerrillas.

Their assignment was to capture or kill them and return within forty-eight hours.

The informers left that same evening, well-armed and with a decent amount of ammunition for their Mannlicher rifles. Sergeant Gio Montagne handed the Jungle Princess's brother a Schmeisser submachine gun and two spare magazines. No sooner had they left than the sergeant ordered two more informers to shadow them.

A day and a half later, I gave the sergeant a worried look. 'Any sign of life from those five? I don't trust them one bit. Only twelve hours left.'

He nodded reassuringly.

In the meantime, my friendship with fellow interpreters Jan Abas and Freddie Onsoe began to sour. They were openly critical of the Dutch government and the military policy in the Indies, and I found myself doubting their loyalty to the Netherlands and the House of Orange.

The forty-eight hours ran out slowly with not a word or a sign from our five informers. Night had fallen: bright moon, clear sky. Feeling uneasy, I went to my room, fastened my belt, slid my fighting knife into my right legging, grabbed my M1 and went outside. In the distance, five shapes appeared carrying a stretcher between them. I approached the ungainly procession and saw they were carrying not one stretcher but two, cobbled together from branches and palm leaves. The five laid their stretchers on the ground in front of our post. Their leader pointed to the bodies and said, '*Tuan*, here lies my sister, the one you call the Jungle Princess. On the other stretcher lies the man who was her lover and second-in-command.'

I praised them and shook them by the hand. The other interpreters came and joined us. Sergeant Gio Montagne was visibly relieved as he took back the weapons he had lent the five informants. He went back inside, fetched a pile of banknotes bearing the head of Sukarno and paid them handsomely. They expressed their deep thanks and shook us all by the hand.

I took a furtive look at Freddie Onsoe and Jan Abas and saw pure contempt and hatred in their eyes as they observed us marines. Jan Abas in particular looked daggers at me…

The ravine

Unable to sleep one night, I went out onto the veranda to chat and drink coffee with a couple of men from the *kampong*. Ben de Lima joined us. I found myself thinking about one of the mysterious, almost incredible stories Pah Tjillih used to tell and I asked the villagers what night it was according to the Islamic calendar. This was in the early hours of Friday morning and they explained that it was *jumat legi* or 'sweet Friday'. I came up with the devilish plan of trying something Pah Tjillih had once told me. I went to the kitchen and found a lemon. Back on the veranda I said to Ben and the villagers, 'See those two dead bodies by the roadside, brought here on stretchers a few nights ago? Would you like to hear them groan in pain?'

The villagers knew instantly what I was talking about and nodded, but our lads looked sceptical.

There were still some patches of dried blood on the spot where the stretchers had first been laid. I cut the lemon into pieces and squeezed the juice onto the blood. Before long, agonized groans rose up from the ground. Even Ben and I were chilled to the bone, and the hairs on the back of our necks stood on end. I had never done such a thing before but I had always believed what Pah Tjillih had told me and it sent a shiver up my spine. The villagers heard the groans too and mumbled all manner of prayers for the salvation of the souls of the two terrorists who had been gunned down.

Whether it was due to the hatred shown by Jan Abas, my grisly prank on *jumat legi*, or the excessively gruelling patrols with Flash Gordon I do not know, but on one of those countless night patrols

I tumbled eighty yards into a deep ravine. I no longer remember how many infantrymen it took to rescue me from my plight and haul me back up again.

My landing had been so awkward that the pain in my injured back flared like never before. Sergeant Gio Montagne packed me off to Lumajang on the next mail and supplies truck, where I signed off with First Lieutenant Lichtenberg of the Marine Corps at SHQ-III. After the standard administrative rigmarole, a jeep was arranged to take me to the local sick bay. There I folded out my camp bed in a ward with five other marines with non-critical injuries. The medical officer in attendance, Dr Verbeek, was assisted by a senior nursing officer with the rank of sergeant.

One ward down from us were six Madurese soldiers from the KNIL's Tjakra Brigade. They had not been wounded in action but were being treated for venereal diseases contracted by messing around with loose women in and around Lumajang. Madurese soldiers had a fearsome reputation as fighters who were not to be trifled with, but before long I was on fairly good terms with them. We traded native goodies, with the Dutch boys treating the Madurese to cheese and other typically Dutch fare.

There was a lack of medical equipment at the sick bay. They had no X-ray machines or infra-red lamps. Every other day, Dr Verbeek gave me injections to combat my fever. It was a damnable treatment. I received a jab after breakfast and then lay on my bed shivering to the bone, despite the blankets piled on me by my fellow soldiers. After an hour or two the fever would subside, leaving me completely exhausted. My mouth was dry as sand and though I was dying with thirst, I had no appetite at all. By evening my body was burning up and I was so delirious it was as if a fever dream had taken hold of me. The medic appeared every now and then to give me two vitamin tablets. This went on all week and I was supposed to lie flat on my back as much as possible.

One feverish night, after hours spent tossing and turning, I went outside and lay on a low wall by the porch. Suddenly, all hell broke loose among the Madurese lads on the VD ward. Crazed with fever and pain, one of them had charged into our ward and started shooting up the place with his Lee Enfield rifle. Despite my wretched fever, I had the presence of mind to run back inside and jump that trigger-happy lunatic. I forced him to the ground and kicked his weapon out of reach. Grabbing my M1 from the rail on my bed, I pulled out my bayonet and rammed it onto the muzzle. I turned back to the incensed soldier, who by this time had recovered his Lee Enfield, and a life or death battle ensued. By this time, my roommates had tumbled out of bed. I saw them grab their weapons and run for the door, then my mind went blank.

I woke the next morning to a ward where the walls and mosquito nets had been ravaged by bullets. The medics and my roommates filled in the missing details.

'Don't you remember what you did to that Madurese fella last night?' one medic asked me.

'Well? What?'

'First thing we saw was that crazy Madurese charging into our ward, gun blazing,' said the medic. 'I was treating a fellow solider at the time. Jan, in the corner over there, couldn't get out of bed. The bullets ripped through his mosquito net and missed his belly by an inch. Poor lad was scared witless, couldn't move a muscle. Then you came storming in, jumped the Madurese from behind and wrestled him to the ground. You kicked his rifle away, grabbed your M1 and the two of you proceeded to knock lumps out of each other. Luckily you had the sense not to blow each other's brains out. Oh yes, and you jammed your bayonet on your rifle. It left an almighty gash in his belly and his guts came spewing out. Then another soldier whacked him with the butt of his rifle. You collapsed and your mates laid you on your bed, while the Madurese was carted off to the operating table. Dr Verbeek happened to be around that night and saved his life by operating straight away. His condition is stable. You can go next door and visit him if you like.'

I looked around in disbelief but the others all nodded in confirmation. That same morning I went to see my victim and was shocked to see his whole torso bandaged up. In halting Madurese I offered him my apologies. The poor bastard was unable to eat for days, that's how badly I had carved him up in my feverish delirium.

At last the day arrived when I was declared fit for discharge. Heaving a sigh of relief, I returned to the ward to pack my things while the nursing officer on duty called SHQ and asked them to send a jeep. After saying a heartfelt farewell to my fellow patients and the Madurese soldiers, I loaded my pack onto the jeep and was driven back to SHQ. From there I was given a lift on a supply truck back to the post in Senduro.

Following another few days with the detachment, Sergeant Gio Montagne called me in for a chat. 'Nolan,' he said 'the whole region is secure once again. People are returning to their normal lives and there is not a single *pelopor* for miles around. Tomorrow you will be transferred to GHQ in Surabaya. Piet Dikotta is in sore need of your assistance. There is more important work to be done. Preparations are under way for a second police action. Go to it, Nolan, and on behalf of us all, many thanks.'

A truck rolled up the next morning and gave me a lift to Surabaya. In my absence, the General Headquarters of the Marine Brigade Security Service had moved from Porongstraat to Karang Menjangan, a short distance from the navy hospital.

I arrived late in the afternoon and was greeted by Captain Galliër of the Marine Corps, the successor to Rob Groeneveld. I snapped to attention and saluted. Captain Galliër was a humourless man, small in stature. After informing the captain of the salient events in Lumajang, I saluted once more and headed for Piet Dikotta's office. He was pleased to see me again. 'So, Arto,' he said, 'you look peaky. How long were you banged up in that sick bay?'

'Over three and a half weeks, Piet,' I answered wearily.

Dikotta offered me a seat and poured me a whisky. 'As you may have heard from Sergeant Gio Montagne, I asked for your return and ordered him to pull you back from the front. Listen, Arto, you have seen enough combat. You are sorely needed here as head of Prisoner Interrogations, Department III. But I also want you taking care of counterintelligence for me, as head of Espionage and Documentation, Department IV. Your field of operations will be Surabaya and the surrounding area as far as Sidoarjo and Porong. I want you out there with the men on regular raid patrols. You know the score. Your office will be next door to mine and you can set up your camp bed there. When things are slack you can sleep at home, as long as you are ready to be dragged out of bed at a moment's notice. You can go through all the counterintelligence reports here in my office as usual: I need you to keep abreast of developments with a view to interrogating the various categories of prisoners.'

I eyed Dikotta suspiciously. 'There's more to this, Piet. Why did you recall me from the front? Come on, out with it!'

'Fair enough, Arto,' Piet sighed. 'Only don't fly off the handle, okay? While you were in the sick bay, Sergeant Gio Montagne reported you for using excessive force out there in Senduro and lodged a complaint with me. I took the decision to reel you back in. Meanwhile Sergeant Gio Montagne has been nominated for the Military Order of William, Knight 4th Class, primarily for ridding the Senduro area of extremist elements.'

'What a fucking nerve!' I shouted. 'I do all the dirty work and that bastard Gio walks off with the honours!

'Easy, Arto. Calm down,' Piet said in an attempt to placate me. 'Remember that courage and honour always win out in the end.'

'Say what you like, Piet,' I yelled. 'This kind of filthy trick makes me sick to my stomach!'

I leapt to my feet and stormed out.

Transport pack on my shoulder, I took possession of my new office. I unfolded my camp bed among the metal filing cabinets, set up the bamboo frame and camouflage mosquito net, then rearranged things so I had a place to sleep in one corner and a work space with interrogation room in the other.

Counterintelligence

Royal birthdays were usually cause for wild celebration in the Indies. Surabaya could be hell on those public holidays, so I tried to make sure I spent them out in the field. But on 31 August 1948, there was no escape.

Piet Dikotta had called me in to see him the previous evening. 'Arto, tomorrow is Queen Wilhelmina's birthday and there are festivities throughout the city. A military parade will roll down Palmenlaan and Simpang, cross Tunjungan to Pasar Besar and go on from there. I want you out on the streets tomorrow, unarmed and in your civvies. Mingle with the crowds, especially along the route, listen in on what people are saying. You know who is worth listening to and you have an eye for picking out infiltrators among the locals. Blend in and remember: no force of any kind! Resort to violence only if you are attacked or your life is threatened. And leave the ladies well alone! Report your findings to me tomorrow evening. Good luck, Arto.'

Why me? Most of the other interpreters were given leave on public holidays, especially those who were married. If something special needed doing, it was always down to this sucker. If the brigade commander needed a bodyguard on a tour of nearly every frontline post, yours truly was pick of the bunch. I could be off on some remote posting, and still they would find a way to rope me in. Who else would get landed with a counterintelligence assignment on a public holiday? The job was not without its dangers and my only weapon would be my trusty fighting knife.

I set off straight after breakfast dressed in my civvies, a brightly coloured shirt hanging loose over white trousers to conceal the knife on my belt. Hiring a *becak*, I took in all the *pasars* and mixed with the crowd, spotting countless spies and infiltrators among the local Indonesians. I strolled among them as nonchalantly as I could, and eavesdropped on their chatter. If I suspected someone of being an Indonesian spy, I struck up a conversation and soon came to the unsurprising conclusion that most had a deep hatred of the Dutch. They wanted Merdeka at any cost. These encounters left me feeling uneasy. One or two let details of sabotage plans slip and, when I felt I had enough information, I went in search of a radio car belonging to our Military Police. If I was unable to find one, I walked into a shop or a pharmacy and asked to use the phone. I called GHQ and spoke to Piet Dikotta, who would arrange for one or two senior officers to meet me at a rendezvous point within forty minutes so that I could pass on my findings. On and on it went, and the Queen's birthday dragged deep into the night.

As the Second Police Action approached, every department at GHQ went into overdrive. Long lists of names appeared on the bulletin board, complete with unit and mission, so that everyone knew what part they were going to play. I searched eagerly for my name on the lists of men assigned to the landing at Glondong but found it nowhere. Deeply disappointed, I strode into Piet Dikotta's office. 'Hey, Piet, why isn't my name on that list?' I asked. 'I want to be part of the landing at Glondong. Can't you review your decision?'

'No, Arto,' he said resolutely. 'Like I said before: I need you here. Aren't you tired of fighting yet, man? You've seen enough action and your back is already halfway to hell. Do you want to end up an invalid? Now come on, help me sort out the admin and let's make sure the lads who are being deployed receive their instructions. A number of interpreters will be placed under your command. They will interrogate all prisoners and send them to Werfstraat Prison. It will be your job to instruct them and supervise their counterintelligence work. Before long I want you all to form raid patrols in the city. It's no mean feat keeping Surabaya free of subversive elements, Arto. There is danger enough right here. Now get to work.'

The mood at HQ wiped the smile off everyone's face. Even my best friends among the interpreters looked troubled. Weaponry had become a major focus of attention. Between the First and the Second Police Actions, many battle-hardened volunteer marines had returned home to be replaced by conscripts with no experience at all. You could recognize them by their uniforms. The word *Nederland* was sewn into their badges, while ours said *Netherlands*. Our dress uniforms looked American, while the rookies wore British-style suits.

The ranks of the Marine Brigade Security Service were also home to plenty of *barus*. As Indos with experience of jungle operations, it was up to us to teach them the combat tactics they were going to need and familiarize them with native customs and traditions. The transition to local food always gave the Dutch a bad case of the trots but the skin diseases were even more of an ordeal. Those new boys were used to the strictest hygiene back in Holland but, unfortunately for them, the Indies was a different matter. Typhus and malaria were also rife. Even I fell prey to the curse of malaria from time to time, despite taking plenty of Atabrine tablets.

I got to know a marine from Limburg, who was on guard duty at the Brigade Staff. Piet was his name, and he was all skin and bones. The doctors at the naval hospital had all but given up on him due to his recurring problems with malaria tropica, the most dangerous strain of the disease. He had been given permission to sail for home but, having developed a fondness for the country and the people, he refused.

'Hey, Intel Marine,' he addressed me, 'you're a native of this country, aren't you? I've been suffering from malaria tropica for a while, or so the docs at the naval hospital tell me. They've been shoving Atabrine tablets down my throat and alternating them with quinine, but it hasn't helped. They've even put me on light duties, which is why I'm here standing guard and bored out of my skull. You wouldn't know some medicine man or hocus-pocus guy who might be able to cure me, would you?'

'I think I can help you,' I said, 'but you mustn't get ahead of yourself. Let's ask permission from your doctor first or you could end up slapped with a court martial.'

'I don't give a toss about that bastard,' was his frank reply.

'When do you get off duty?'

'This afternoon, at four.'

'Right then, Piet. I will meet you at four and take you to see my mother. She has cured me of that damned malaria often enough, so she should be able to do the same for you.'

I met Limburg Piet by the Big Shit at four and we took a *becak* to my house. Mama looked surprised to see me in the company of a blond Dutchman. I introduced Piet and explained the problem, mixing Dutch with her potpourri of Malay, Javanese and Chinese. Wasting no time, she sent Babu Tenie to cut some leaves from the papaya tree and pound them to a paste in a cast steel bowl. The *babu* then pressed the moisture from the crushed leaves into a glass and added salt. She stirred the dark-green liquid and handed the glass to Mama, who passed it to Piet and told him to drink. With all the bravura he could muster, Piet took the glass from Mama and swallowed down the contents. He pulled one of the ugliest faces I ever saw.

'Fuck's sake, Nolan,' he said. 'That mother of yours is out to poison me.'

I burst out laughing. 'You have to repeat this treatment two or three times a day here at my house,' I explained. 'In a matter of days, I swear you will be completely cured of malaria. It's filthy stuff, I know – I have trouble choking it down myself sometimes – but it's better than all those bloody tablets put together.'

Piet did as he was told. He visited Mama two or three times a day and drank the dark-green juice. By the fourth day, he was already feeling better. To be sure, he had his blood checked at the sick bay and they found that the malaria parasites in his blood had decreased considerably. He began to get his appetite back. Feeling like a new man, he went back to see Mama and thanked her profusely. The colour had returned to his pale cheeks.

'Fuck me, Nolan! Your mother's only gone and cured me of fucking malaria! I'm fit as a fucking fiddle and back on regular duties. The doctor couldn't believe his eyes, just mumbled some crap about native herbs sometimes being better than all our chemicals put together. Fucking hell, Nolan, I'm happy as fuck and so fucking grateful to you and your mother. Come on, let's fuck off down the fucking Marines Club and get drunk as a fucking skunk.'

'No,' I replied. 'I am going to take you to the best Chinese restaurant in the city.'

On 18 December 1948, I waved off Piet and the others at the forecourt of Marine Brigade Security Service headquarters. They climbed aboard the trucks with their transport packs and left me behind feeling rotten. I hated each and every one of those commanding officers for not letting me be part of the operation.

I felt a hand on my left shoulder and turned to look Piet Dikotta straight in the eye.

'Come on, Arto,' he said. 'Back to work.'

That same evening I had to go into the city on raid patrol. We made dozens of arrests and worked deep into the night. I hardly got a wink of sleep before it was time for the team to interrogate our suspects. Some I released under the motto 'it takes a thief to catch a thief'. The days that followed were exhausting; my body was crying out for sleep. We were on duty all day, every day, and every last one of us was complaining. Going through the daily combat intelligence reports, I saw that we were suffering heavy losses on all fronts. Far too much time had elapsed between the First and Second Police Actions, of course, and the Indonesian forces had used this lull to their advantage. First, they had built up their arsenal with smuggled weapons. Second, they had watched and learned from our combat techniques. Third, it had given other Indonesian units ample opportunity to plant mines and block access roads to their strongholds. Fourth, the enemy were able to spring ambushes wherever they wanted. And to cap it all, we were going into battle with far too many inexperienced boys from Holland in our ranks.

One-man war

Meanwhile, I was engaged in one dangerous counterintelligence assignment after another. At the barracks, I could come and go as I pleased and even spend the odd night at home with Mama. Whether I was out in combat uniform or civvies, I was always well-armed. At this time there was a rise in the number of infiltrators, as more members of the Indonesian Army were tasked with guerrilla activities aimed at disrupting life in Surabaya. Sabotage was among their objectives. My main job was to identify and shadow these infiltrators, then alert our standby raid teams and direct them towards the enemy with a view to capturing or eliminating them. This struck me as a roundabout way of doing things, but those were my orders.

One evening, I was patrolling the market in the notorious Pacar Keling neighbourhood. I was in my civvies and armed with only a small, flat FN pistol, no great shakes as a weapon. I was sitting at a stall eating *soto Madura* when three Indonesian soldiers sat down at my table. We greeted one another and they ordered *soto* too. I recognized one of them instantly from a composite photo: Lieutenant Colonel Djarot Soebiantoro, commander of the Indonesian Army's notorious 113 Battalion. As a marine, I knew all too well that his soldiers were a tough nut to crack. We slurped our *soto* and struck up a conversation. My trigger finger was itching to blow the three of them away but, under orders to avoid bloodshed unless absolutely necessary, I sat there powerless in the face of adversaries who had the lives of so many marines on their consciences. Seething with rage and hatred, I resigned myself to being an effective spy and gleaning as much information as I could from those three, which to some extent I managed.

I reported back to Piet Dikotta that same night; he was still hard at work in the staff office. The raid team was alerted immediately and set off for Pacar Keling, with me as their guide. One of the three men had been foolish enough to visit a local prostitute and it was not difficult for me to trace him and have him arrested.

Under interrogation, we discovered that the Indonesian Army was planning sabotage and guerrilla attacks on military and police barracks.

The next evening I ran into my brother Karel. I was on patrol in Kapasan district, wearing my utility uniform and armed with a Colt .45 pistol. My knife was tucked into my right legging. At this time, Karel was a senior police officer in charge of maintaining law and order in Kapasan. We went to a Chinese stall for something to eat. 'Look over there, Bro,' he said out of nowhere. 'Those Javanese beauties in the corner have been giving us the eye.'

'Let them,' I replied. 'If they want anything from me they can come and get it. I have other things on my mind, military secrets I cannot share with you.'

No sooner had I spoken than, to my surprise, one of Karel's beauties got up and made her way over to our table. With the sweetest of smiles, she very politely invited us to come and join them. Feeling apprehensive, I tried to catch Karel's eye, but his brain was already addled by the womanly charms on display and, before I knew it, he was trotting along behind her, meek as a lamb. I followed him to their table. Karel did not waste a second and was soon flirting like mad with two of those Javanese beauties. Even as a boy, my brother had been girl crazy and fancied himself as a regular Don Juan.

The third beauty lured me over to her place, an impressive house not far from the Kapasan *pasar*. There she plied me with refreshing palm wine and all kinds of Javanese treats. We flirted briefly and she led me to her bedroom, where the oil lamps were burning low. She blew out the lamp at the window and as we lay down naked on her bed, a voice inside warned me to keep my pistol within arm's reach. As we were making love, I caught sight of two hooded figures passing her open window, followed seconds later by fumbling at her front door. My lover wrapped herself tightly around me and stirred the flames of passion, yet still I felt uneasy. Suddenly the bedroom door swung open and a man carrying a Sten gun peered in. In a flash, I grabbed my Colt and fired. He doubled over and fell down dead. I pressed the pistol to my lover's throat.

'You filthy bitch!' I hissed.

'No, don't shoot,' she cried out in fear. 'I do not know this man!'

'Then why did you blow out the lamp at the window?' I snarled.

I leapt from the bed and pulled on my underpants, just in time to see another man enter the house. Before he could aim his tommy gun at me, I shot him dead. Then I turned my pistol on the woman and put a bullet between her eyes. She was thrown back onto the bed and, with a rattle in her throat, she died. I quickly pulled on the rest of my clothes and – pistol in my left hand, knife in my right – I ventured outside. I scanned the street for *pemudas*, but saw only a few curious bystanders. I went back inside and retrieved the Sten gun and the tommy gun from their dead owners. With both weapons slung over my shoulder, I made for the main road and took a *becak* back to barracks.

The guard at the gate looked at me in surprise. Then the duty commander appeared and asked suspiciously, 'Hey, Intel, are you out there fighting a one-man war?'

Hadji

One morning they brought in an important political prisoner for me to interrogate. Like Sukarno, he was a qualified engineer and they had been exiled together under Dutch colonial rule. Piet Dikotta ordered me to treat this prisoner with all due respect. On no account was I to rough him up. To interrogate such a man effectively took thorough preparation and I had a stack of books brought to my room: works on politics in Indonesian, High Javanese, Malay, English and Dutch. My office-cum-sleeping quarters became a library, complete with musty odour. It took me a month to skim through all those pages. This friend of Sukarno's was a Muslim who had made the pilgrimage to Mecca, so I called him Hadji. He was given his own room at the rear of our headquarters but was warned in no uncertain terms that he would be shot dead if he tried to escape. I gave him ten notebooks and a fountain pen and told him to write a full account of the political situation of the period. Every so often I would read what he had written and, if I thought he was lying, I would punish him by denying him meals for a couple of days. Then I would send one of my informers to bring me the tastiest Chinese dishes from local restaurants so that I could torment Hadji by eating them right in front of him. Eventually, he could stand it no longer and begged me to give him some food.

'Hadji, I will bring you the finest meals imaginable, but only after you write down what you know about the political objectives and military targets of Masyumi, the Communists and the Nationalists. I will go through everything with a fine-tooth comb and if I discover a single lie, you will not be given so much as a grain of rice. Is that clear?'

I even forced the man to write through the night until he fell asleep with the pen in his hand. Eventually, I was able to extract the truth from him about every political matter of relevance to us. Piet Dikotta passed on these comprehensive and complex reports to the highest naval authorities.

Crocodile fodder

The reports arriving daily at headquarters were none too encouraging. A column of marines had been mowed down by Indonesian Army units. A squad of nine marines on sweeping operations had been ambushed by a company commanded by the notorious Major Djarot Soebiantoro. Their limbs had been severed, their genitals cut off and stuffed in their mouths. They were then tied to plantain trunks and thrown into the infested waters of Kali Solo as fodder for the crocodiles and iguanas. Another reconnaissance patrol found itself outnumbered and was all but wiped out. A single marine, an Indo by the name of Kling

Logeman, lived to tell the tale and ran to seek help, hand pressed to his bayonet wound to stop his guts spilling out. He passed a couple of *kampongs* on his way, but the villagers pelted him with stones. In desperation, he staggered on, found his way back to the main force and was able to report what had happened before collapsing. A mobile sick bay saved his life.

Meanwhile, I was conducting raids in the most notorious *kampongs* around Surabaya. Our team arrested and jailed entire gangs of infiltrators and double agents. Interrogating them was tough going. Flushed with victory, our captives knew that the world was turning against the Netherlands and that decolonization could no longer be stopped. We were sore losers and subjected those extremists to ever more punishing treatment. Christmas came and went in a cycle of raids, arrests, interrogations and incarcerations.

The first day of 1949 was fast approaching and with it came a lull in our activities. Good news from the front was scarce. Indonesian forces had stepped up their guerrilla operations and the Big Shit was casting around for fresh tactics. I was given New Year's Eve off to go home and celebrate with Mama, Ella and the rest of the family. I turned up in combat uniform, armed with rifle, bayonet and fighting knife. Mama saw the glazed look in my eyes. 'What's wrong, Arto?' she asked. 'Your thoughts are far, far away and not with us.'

'I don't know any more, Mama. All this hunting, killing and fighting… when will it end? I have many friends among the marines. They have told me about life in Holland, how people there are not put down for being brown-skinned or born out of wedlock. Life there is so very different, Mama, and I am starting to feel like I don't fit in here. I no longer feel *senang*. This country, this people, all these wars. Every minute of every hour of every day, I have to fight to stay alive. My enemies are everywhere. But come, Mama. It's New Year's Eve. For what it's worth, let's celebrate together.'

Mama said nothing. Tears welled up in her eyes. That dear woman could sense that we were drifting apart.

In those days, fireworks were strictly forbidden. The only loud blasts to be heard came from a rifle or machine gun, wielded by friend or foe. The mood was grim and, though people celebrated across the city, there was little in the way of elation or spontaneity. I didn't even wait for the clock to strike midnight, but took my leave of Mama and the rest shortly after eleven and flagged down a *becak* to take me on a long detour to headquarters on Karang Menjangan. Traffic was light and most of the traders had shut up shop. Only restaurants, bars and other places to eat and drink were still open. Here and there, I saw drunken marines and KNIL soldiers staggering across the street. The police were out in force and could occasionally be seen chasing down suspects, guns blazing.

I asked the *becak* driver to stop outside the Marines Club, gave him a hefty tip and told him to wait for me. With my M1 at the ready, I crossed the street and tracked a group of shooting policemen. A marine came up to me and shouted, 'Look out! *Pelopors*! I heard shots from the dark alley by the Aurora store!'

We ran into the alley together and I asked one of the policemen ducking for cover where the enemy was located. He pointed in the direction of Pasar Blauran. I told my fellow marine that we had better return to Tunjungan, since hunting down infiltrators among crowds of shoppers would be a hopeless task for the pair of us. I wandered back to the Marines Club only to find driver and *becak* gone.

For want of something better to do, I walked into the club and got tanked up on booze. Though everyone was wishing each other Happy New Year, the atmosphere was muted. I felt miserable, like a ship cut adrift, and my mood was no better by the time I arrived back at headquarters in the wee small hours. Clearly no one there had felt the need to sleep a wink. Wide awake, they all wished each other a prosperous 1949 and every strength for the battles ahead. Many a marine remembered his fallen and wounded comrades.

I had little chance to mull things over. The call for 'standby' went up again and in no time we were back in our fighting vehicles on the way to carry out raids in some godforsaken neighbourhoods of the city. Tips from informers, double agents and assorted scum led to several arrests. All interpreters present had orders to interrogate suspects on the spot. None of us held back.

A hole in the ground

On the first of January yet more prisoners were transferred from the front to headquarters. My department was tasked with interrogating a Jap by the name of Toshiba. In his glory days, he had belonged to the Sakura organization and after the capitulation he became a foreman, constructing bunkers and other fortifications for the Indonesian Army. He also trained their Demolition Group. I was ordered to attend to him personally.

Toshiba had an arrogant, cynical air about him. He blanked my every question with an emphatic silence. After a while I lost my patience, pulled him from his chair and screamed at him to stand to attention. This he did. I struck him repeatedly in the face until he fell over backwards. As he fell I kicked him in the chest. He croaked and spluttered in pain, and the sight of his bloodied face gave me satisfaction. All the while, I saw myself hanging on the scaffold while a merciless Kenpeitai thug pounded my back with a baseball bat. I could not banish his savage grin from my memory.

The next morning Toshiba became more obliging. Useful intel began to escape his lips in fits and starts. After questioning him a while, I took him into the back garden, where I had noticed a spade propped against one of the outbuildings. I handed it to Toshiba and motioned to him to follow me over to a spot by the tennis court. I pulled out my fighting knife, outlined a rectangle roughly six feet by three, and ordered Toshiba to dig a hole three feet deep. I left him in no doubt that he was digging his own grave. I registered shock in his eyes, but he said nothing and began to dig. When the hole was deep enough, I ordered Toshiba to lie down in it to make sure he would fit. Trembling from head to toe, he obeyed. I nodded my approval and let him clamber back out.

I felt a hand on my shoulder and turned to see Captain Galliër standing behind me.

'I say, Nolan,' he said calmly, 'do you want to serve twenty years for murder?'

'Murder?' I asked indignantly. 'This slant-eyed piece of shit is a war criminal. He has trained *pemudas* to systematically massacre marines. Some of our lads have been fed to the crocodiles. Give me the pleasure of slitting this fellow's throat and booting his damn body into that hole.'

'No, Nolan, I won't have it,' Captain Galliër insisted. 'A ceasefire has been announced. This bastard is to be taken to Batavia and put on a transport back to Japan, where he will face trial. An Allied tribunal has been installed there.'

I obeyed orders reluctantly and barked at Toshiba to return to his cell.

On patrol with brother Karel

One evening I told Piet Dikotta I was going to the Chinese district downtown on a counterintelligence patrol. I put on my utility uniform, borrowed a Colt .45 pistol from the quartermaster and strapped on my fighting knife, tucking the sheath in my legging. I signed out with the duty officer and walked from Karang Menjangan towards Gubeng Viaduct. On the way I hailed a *becak* to take me to Kapasan, one of the city's more notorious neighbourhoods. At the 5th precinct police station, I got off and strolled in to see my brother Karel, who was on duty till early morning. In his office, we chatted over a few cups of strong coffee and the sweet taste of *perut ayam* and *kue lapis*. He suggested going on patrol together in and around Kapasan Pasar. The market was always teeming with hardened criminals, opium smugglers and whores, not to mention spies and Indonesian Army infiltrators.

Once Karel had finished his paperwork, he buckled on the holster that held his Colt service revolver and rounded up three

Javanese policemen armed with old-fashioned Mannlicher rifles to join him on patrol. Shooting the breeze, we walked in the direction of the *pasar*, still buzzing with life late in the evening. We feasted our eyes on the stalls as we ambled past. I was able to pick out the infiltrators even in their civvies. They did their best to blend in but when I looked at them long and steady, their nerves gave them away. They were all too familiar with a Marine uniform.

'Damn it, Arto,' Karel blurted out, 'it was so busy at the station, I forgot to ask why you only have your fighting knife strapped to your right leg. Why aren't you carrying a firearm?'

'The quartermaster issued me with a Colt .45 and four spare magazines. It's in my right trouser pocket. Only officers are permitted to wear a gun belt.'

Our conversation ended abruptly as Karel's men alerted us to a vicious fight a few stalls along. Karel and I rushed over to where a man lay squirming on the ground. His eyes had been gouged out, but I recognized him as one of my best informers, Achmat. The culprit, a Chinaman, stood only a few paces away. His right hand was sticky with blood.

In a mixture of Chinese and Malay, Karel asked him what had happened. Still seething with anger, he replied that Achmat had slept with his prostitute without his knowledge and a fight had broken out. As a precaution, I drew my pistol and released the safety catch, ready to fire. Karel turned pale. 'Careful, Arto!' he called to me in Dutch. 'This man is a notorious *kuntao* fighter.'

Sure enough, the Chinaman was readying himself to attack, cursing the Marines in his native tongue. He ran towards me at speed, the fingers of his right hand poised to stab me in the eyes. Even before Karel – a first-class *pencak* fighter – could intervene, I put a bullet straight between the man's eyes. He fell back with a short cry, all set to join Achmat on the road to Valhalla. In a blind rage, I pumped all eight rounds from my magazine into his quivering body, then pulled out a fresh magazine and reloaded my pistol. At the sight of this bloodbath, Karel turned white as a sheet and threw up. His constables, who had witnessed the whole thing, stood there speechless, knees knocking. 'You surprise me, brother,' I sneered. 'This much blood never used to turn your stomach You beat me till the blood poured from my nose and mouth. I don't remember you throwing up then.'

'Shut your mouth, idiot!' Karel snapped at me.

I grabbed him by the shoulders. 'Come on, Karel. Now you've finished vomiting, what do you say we head down the road for a beer? You look like you could use one.'

Non-active duty

In January 1949 a truce was agreed and the Second Police Action was coming to an end. Conferences were being held to settle political differences and every serviceman was beginning to feel that he had fought on for nothing. Commands, routine orders and marching orders were relaxed. The intelligence units of the Marine Brigade Security Service and the KNIL switched their focus to gathering political intelligence instead of military intelligence, though the enemy were constantly breaching the truce and continued to wage their guerrilla war. More than ever, Surabaya found itself confronted with an influx of Indonesian Army infiltrators and other militants. Interpreters and marines continued to lose their lives, and we laid them to rest in the Marine cemetery. A sense of defeat began to weigh on us.

My father was buried not far from the military cemetery. I paid regular visits to tend his grave, pray and put fresh flowers in the marble vases by his headstone.

At this time my duties mainly consisted of office work: interrogating prisoners and translating political pamphlets and documents. In the evening, I engaged in counter-espionage and went on the occasional raid patrol.

Six months later, all interpreters and marines were pulled back from frontline positions to GHQ. Everyone had to hand in their weapons, combat gear and transport gear. Interpreters and informers alike were put on non-active duty from July 1949. As interpreters, we were given references and three months' additional pay. Informers received a bonus of sorts, paid in rupiah banknotes that bore the face of Sukarno, and were granted permission to return to their *kampongs* in the city or the *desas* beyond. Those chaps were at risk of being liquidated and some of them, with permission of course, chose to stay on at the barracks and do household chores.

At a short ceremony, Captain Galliër gave me my references and thanked me for services rendered. Many of us struggled to hold ourselves together and, as I handed in my weapons to the quartermaster, tears were rolling down my cheeks too. This was not lost on the corporal in question. 'Ah yes, Nolan, I can well imagine how you must feel,' he said sympathetically. 'Through the years you and your weapon have become one. You used it often and maintained it well. Without your M1, you would have rotted away beneath the sods long ago. Saying goodbye to your weapon is tough, but it will come to us all before long. Those *pelopors* will soon have their Merdeka and there's bugger all we can do about it. Damn it, man, it's a lousy state of affairs. Soon I'll be on the boat home and then what?'

'At least you Dutch lads can look forward to a safe passage home. What about all the Indos who have fought so hard for Queen and Country? Where do we go? I have been fighting ever since the Japanese occupation, and what thanks do I get? The chance to hang around here and be gunned down with not a single marine for back-up? Politics is a filthy game. All through the ages us soldiers have been left to do the dirty work for our lords and masters, men who have never heard a bullet whistle past their ears.'

Bitter and in the lowest of spirits, I headed for Piet Dikotta's office. He saw me coming through the open door and came to meet me like a true brother in times of need.

'Arto, come and sit down,' he said. 'Wait, let me pour you a stiff drink first.'

It was the last thing I wanted, but I accepted out of courtesy. 'I say, Arto,' Dikotta went on, 'I am being transferred to the Intelligence section. Captain Groeneveld has asked me to work under his command. I need a man out in the field, an informer I can trust. You are the first man I thought of. It's a dangerous assignment: you will be shadowing some sinister characters and you will not be armed. At most you will carry a fighting knife. Assistance from KNIL patrols will only be available when you report back and you will be paid according to the value of your intelligence. What do you say, Arto? I'm telling you straight, not everyone is cut out for this kind of work.'

I thought about it for a while and accepted the job of informer, having first complained bitterly about going into the field unarmed. Dikotta was right, this kind of work wasn't for everyone. Only for a man as tired of life as I was.

A long-held wish was finally fulfilled. The war had put the process on hold, but at last I was able to change my name. At the offices of the town clerk, a note was made in the margin of my birth certificate. From that moment on, I would go through life as Noland, and not 'Nolan' in quotation marks. That one letter changed me from within, set me apart from the colonialist taint of the Eurasians and the fair-skinned Dutch Indo elite. It made a new man of me, you might say. I relished the chance to go through life as a Dutchman born of the Indies, loyal to the House of Orange. To me, 'Noland' simply had a nice ring to it. I was oblivious to the fact that my new surname suggested I was stateless.

At GHQ, I asked Captain Galliër if I could pay for my own passage and sail for the Netherlands on one of the Marine transport ships. The captain passed on my request to the staff, but it was refused. My hopes crushed, I returned home. To my amazement, I discovered that there were Dutchmen in the ranks of the Marine Brigade Security Service who were very reluctant to sail home. A few went looking for good civilian posts while others were offered jobs in the enterprises of East Java. I continued to operate as an informer for the intelligence service of A Division under Piet Dikotta and Captain Groeneveld. It called for steady, slow-paced detective work.

My first big fish was First Lieutenant Hoenholtz of the Marine Corps. Although officially out of service, I was allowed to frequent the Marines Club and the staff there still treated me as a marine – a boost to my flagging morale. I got talking to Hoenholtz at the bar one evening. He was an Indo, every bit as brown as I was, much darker in fact, and he spoke Dutch with a marked Indies accent. After a few drinks, he began to sound off about the Royal Navy, cursing the discrimination against coloureds that was apparent throughout the ranks. Unfortunately, I could only concur with his hatred of this injustice, but as the conversation went on, I began to draw him out. He started cursing the Royal Family, the Dutch government and the Dutch people as a whole. I held my tongue and let him blow off steam, filing his comments away at the back of my mind as a good story for my counterintelligence report. I ordered more booze and let Hoenholtz do the drinking. The floodgates opened and he began listing a whole catalogue of names, marines who had defected to the Indonesian Navy. Among them was a name I knew well: Freddie Onsoe. His defection did not surprise me in the least. When Hoenholtz was well and truly plastered, I made my excuses and left. He saluted with a cry of '*Tetep*!'

That was a term used only by members of APRA units, a militia group for which I had a certain sympathy. They were pro-independence but also federalists, fiercely opposed to President Sukarno's dictatorial regime.

I drew up a substantial report and submitted it to Piet Dikotta. He was not surprised by Hoenholtz's shifting allegiance and ordered me to continue shadowing him.

One evening, standing at the corner of Simpang and looking towards Ketabang, I saw a military column approaching on Palmenlaan. Six motorcyclists from the Indonesian Military Police led the way on their Harley Davidsons, followed by two magnificent American convertibles. In the front car, who should I see but

Hoenholtz, sporting an Indonesian Navy uniform. From the badge on his immaculate khaki jacket, I could see that he had the rank of commodore. Running at full speed, I followed the autocade and saw it halt in the grand garden of the former residence of Rear Admiral Koenraad. The front steps were bustling with officers from the Indonesian armed forces, all of them quartermasters. As the Dutch forces were gradually withdrawing and preparing to leave this beautiful country, every gap they left behind was being filled by the Indonesian military.

My old school pals

31 August 1949: a date I will never forget. Even with the Dutch on their way out, Queen Wilhelmina's birthday was cause for celebration. On Simpang, the governor and assorted dignitaries lined up to take the salute at a military parade. In addition to the Dutch armed forces, a number of Indonesian units joined in as a show of reconciliation between the two sides. This robbed me of any desire to celebrate. It was almost noon by the time the troops marched past the seats of honour. First came the Marines, immediately followed by the Navy and a whole series of Army units. Then came the various branches of the KNIL, followed by units from the Indonesian Army and Navy. As the enemy forces went by, I stared in amazement at the modern firearms on show, the spoils of smuggling. The sight of those *pelopors* on parade left a bitter taste and my blood began to boil. It was ludicrous: many of the Indonesian soldiers marching past had no shoes, yet they were armed with better bazookas and mortars than the Dutch Marines. I cursed the lot of them.

Once the parade was over, I took a *becak* through some of the city's shadiest downtown neighbourhoods. There I met some of my old Indonesian pals from Queen Emma School – Soekaton,

Soedjono, Soetjipto and Soemarsono – every one of them dressed in Indonesian Army or Navy uniforms. They embraced me and we went to a Javanese cafeteria to sit, eat and talk.

Radèn Soekaton said to me, 'Arto, we are now free to wear our uniforms and carry weapons. Soon we will have our Merdeka and colonial rule will be gone for good. We could not be happier, yet we see great sorrow in your eyes. Why, Arto? You too are a child of this country. We have been comrades ever since our schooldays. Remember all the mischief we got up to? How we resisted the Japs? Yet when our revolution came, you fought on the side of the Dutch. We believe you were wrong, but you are still one of us. To us, you will always be a friend, a brother even. Arto, now that you are no longer in service, what's to stop you from joining our side?'

I gave him a pitying look and sighed. 'Sorry Soekaton, but I hate your armed forces. I despise their cruel and inhumane attacks on innocent civilians. The way they carved up the bodies of soldiers. You should not forget the horrific massacres committed by countless freedom fighters when President Sukarno proclaimed your Merdeka. I saw them with my own eyes.'

My words left everyone silent. I could see that my Indonesian friends were struggling to reconcile themselves to these facts.

'But Nolan, Arto,' Soetjipto tried to excuse himself, 'in every revolution, in every war, innocent lives are lost. Those sacrifices have been made throughout human history. You know that.'

'I agree. But the way our innocent civilians met their fate can only be condemned. Standing someone against a wall and shooting them, I can understand. But to rape them first, to kill them slowly, then hack them to pieces and feed them to the crocodiles – what kind of barbarism is that? To bury someone alive? These things are beyond me. Surely you understand that?'

'Come on boys, my brothers,' Soemarsono intervened, 'let us talk of brighter things. The war is over now. We should do our best to forget this cruelty.'

I had no desire to dwell on those atrocities either. Once again, the company of my old pals left me torn inside.

Blacklisted

Government talks in both the Indies and the Netherlands were not going smoothly, but all the signs suggested that the Netherlands would soon be forced to capitulate, not least due to pressure from the United States. Before long, the Dutch East Indies would cease to exist and the Republic of Indonesia would be born. Our armed forces would be compelled to relinquish all the territory they had captured and hand it over to the Indonesian Army, withdraw to the major ports in the Archipelago and sail for home.

I was at home with Mama one afternoon when a telegram arrived from Piet Dikotta:

Drinks this evening at my home.
Old friend wants to see you.

I knew what such a telegram meant. At least, I thought I did. That evening, I rang Piet Dikotta's doorbell. His wife welcomed me in and escorted me to her husband's private study. Who should be sitting there but Captain Veenhuizen of the Marine Corps.

Captain Veenhuizen stood up and greeted me. 'Good to see you, Nolan. You are one tough soldier. How the devil are you?'

I shook his hand. 'I am reasonably well, only I miss my time in service. I long to be a marine again and to continue the fight.'

'Well, Nolan,' Captain Veenhuizen answered, 'you will soon be a marine again. But not with the aim of fighting on…'

'All in due course,' Piet Dikotta interrupted. 'First, let's enjoy a drink together. Whisky for you, Arto?'

His wife filled our glasses.

'And so to business,' Captain Veenhuizen said.

Piet Dikotta got to his feet, opened his safe and removed a document. 'Here, Arto,' he said. 'Read this carefully.'

It was a routine order with a list of names attached. It bore the stamp of the Indonesian Army's notorious high command and was signed by President Sukarno himself. Among other things, the document stated that everyone on the list was a wanted man and was to be killed. The first name listed was Piet Dikotta's. The second was mine.

'Let the *Staf Satoe* send their death squads,' I said. 'Give me weapons and I will shoot them down. It is high time I became a marine again, Captain Veenhuizen.' I turned to Piet Dikotta. 'How did you come by this blacklist?'

'It was given to me by a reliable Indonesian informer with a grave warning that everyone on it should fear for their lives. Arto, I should also warn you that your Timorese friend Jan Abas has defected to the Indonesian Army. Watch out for that traitor – I have a nasty feeling that he is gunning for you.'

'That comes as no surprise.'

'Listen here, Nolan,' Captain Veenhuizen continued, 'you have an outstanding service record with the Marine Brigade Security Service. You have given your all for Queen and Country, and have done so of your own free will. The Dutch Royal Navy is duty-bound to ensure your safety. I am giving you forty-eight hours to talk things over with your mother and the rest of your family, and then to decide where you want to make a life for yourself. You have no choice but to leave this country along with the rest of the Dutch armed forces. We can give you passage to the Netherlands or to New Guinea. I have the authority to place you under military discipline. From this moment on, you are once again a marine. It is late now, but you can report to the quartermaster at Willemsoord Barracks in the morning and pick up your full kit. In the meantime I will arrange a decent, quiet place for you at barracks. Send me word of your decision, tomorrow if possible. Agreed?'

'Captain Veenhuizen, along with my sister Ella and half-sister Poppy, it is my duty to look after my old mother. It will be very hard for me to abandon her. But I have taken your warning and Piet's words very much to heart. I will give you my decision tomorrow.'

Unarmed, I had an uneasy *becak* ride home. As soon as I arrived, I discussed the situation with Mama, Ella and Poppy. All of the women in the house burst into tears, including the *babus*. It was only then that I felt their love for me, but it was too late. Mama regained her composure and said, 'Go to Holland. In that distant land you can study and build a decent future for yourself. What is there for you to learn in the jungles of New Guinea?'

'But Mama,' I protested, 'I can stay here and join the APRA militia. I can carry on the fight against the Indonesian Army. I have many friends willing to join me in the struggle against Sukarno and his savages. The main thing is to be close to you, to help you out with food and money.'

'Arto,' Mama said, 'I do not doubt how much you love me and the others. I will miss you, of course I will, but it is better for you to live in safety far away than to be near me and at risk of being killed at any moment. I know that a number of your friends have betrayed you and want you dead. Listen to you mother, Arto. Pack your things tonight and take a *dokar* to your barracks early in the morning. God will bless you and protect you.'

That night I packed my things. Of the few books I owned, I took only my school textbooks. My spoils of war, consisting of two samurai swords, a *kris* and a .38 calibre Smith & Wesson revolver, I tucked away carefully in my trunk. Worry kept me from sleep and, knowing I might never see my mother again, my heart bled for her and tears welled up in my eyes. I prayed to God but no answer came. All my childhood memories ran through my mind like a film. My harsh but beautiful life under the tropical sun was over.

The next morning, Babu Tenie hailed a *dokar* for me. With a heavy heart, I loaded my meagre possessions. I kissed my mother's cheeks and told her to be brave. Then I climbed aboard and headed for Willemsoord Barracks.

The barracks was in fact an extended complex of houses that had once been commandeered by the Dutch. Arriving at the barrier, I unloaded my things and paid the *dokar* driver. A couple of willing marines helped me carry my baggage to the third house in the complex.

My abode was an empty kitchen with a metal-framed bunk bed and a couple of chairs. The kitchen counter served as a writing table. This would be home until I could board a ship to the Netherlands.

Having settled in, I reported to the office of Captain Veenhuizen of the Marine Corps. 'Captain, I have discussed this matter at length with my mother, my sister and other family members without compromising any military secrets. My mother has urged me to go to the Netherlands because there I will have the opportunity to study and build a prosperous future.'

'Very well, Nolan,' Captain Veenhuizen answered, 'I will have the necessary papers and documentation drawn up. You are once again a marine, under military discipline. We have need of your counterintelligence reports and you will resume your close collaboration with Piet Dikotta. Go to the quartermaster and collect your full kit. Aside from that, you will be expected to perform your regular duties in the mess. After work you are to remain here on standby, awaiting orders. Dismissed!'

When I was not hard at work in my office, I found myself battling conflicting emotions. My sorrow at the prospect of being forever separated from my loved ones ran deep, yet now I could live in hope of a new life in the peaceful country for which I had sacrificed so much. Exhausted by the bloodshed, pain and misery I had endured – the torture, the betrayal, the landmines, my fall into the ravine, the whole sorry tale – all I wanted now was rest.

I had bought myself a rudimentary bicycle on the black market – no headlight or taillight – and regularly cycled down to the docks to see the men embarking on the voyage home. As I stood on the quayside, watching the Dutch soldiers waving to the crowds as they filed aboard to the accompaniment of a military band, I felt angry and sad by turns. And then there were the pregnant Indo girls, crying and waving, calling out to the soldiers: 'When will you come back? When will we be married?'

After a few days at Willemsoord Barracks, I cycled back to my mother's house one evening. Mama was standing on the porch, waiting for me. There were tears in her eyes. Her whole body trembled as she told me, 'Jan Abas and four of his cronies came calling a few days ago, waving their guns around. They are looking for you. They want to kill you! I told Jan Abas that you had left for Holland weeks ago and called him a coward for pointing the barrel of his gun at an old woman. I ordered him to shoot me on the spot, but he was ashamed and he and his henchmen left. What do you plan to do, now you know this about Jan Abas?'

'That's simple, Mama,' I answered. 'I am going to hunt him down, him and his friends.'

'Arto, Arto,' Mama sighed, 'when will your killing end? I have come to fear you.'

Evacuation

A few days later I received another call from Piet Dikotta. I went to see him that same evening and he sent me directly to the home of First Lieutenant Knegtmans of the Marine Corps, a few streets away from Willemsoord Barracks. I reported there and was given a sensitive and highly dangerous mission.

'Nolan, I have summoned you here because you are Surabayan born and bred and know this city like the back of your hand. Your job will be to save as many former interpreters as possible and bring them and their families to Willemsoord Barracks. I will supply you with a full list of those who live in and around Surabaya. Their lives are in danger and they must be brought in as soon as possible for their own safety. This rescue operation cannot be done on a large scale or it will lead to unrest. But it needs to happen fast. I will give you money for transport and other expenses. Use your initiative.'

'I will, Lieutenant,' I answered, 'but I must have an M1 with sufficient ammunition and a number of hand grenades.'

'First thing tomorrow, I will contact the quartermaster with orders to supply you with whatever you think you might need,' Lieutenant Knegtmans concluded.

In every corner of Surabaya's bustling city centre, the mood had turned violently anti-Belanda. Inside the barracks complex, every possible provision was being made to accommodate those in danger. Large army tents were even being set up here and there, a number already occupied by former interpreters who had managed to flee with their families. No sooner had they fled than their homes were ransacked. There was a power vacuum in the city. Law and order had completely broken down. Police officers were still on the streets but, other than directing traffic, they barely lifted a finger. Some flirted openly with loose women. The conduct of these native officers made me sick to my stomach.

It was October. I spent most of my time at the barracks and ate in the mess. Late one afternoon, I signed out with the duty officer and, fully armed and dressed in my utility uniform, I set off on my bike for the city centre. All the lads on duty and in internal services knew of my mission. 'If you need back-up, just give us a sign,' they assured me. 'We're spoiling for a fight.'

The home of my mate Jan Kraai was my first port of call. He and his family lived on the edge of town near Ujung district, where all kinds of secret routes used by Indonesian infiltrators converged. As the crow flies, it was a distance of round five miles. I took my time to make sure that I arrived after dark. Even so, I was sweating profusely and stopped along the way for a few refreshing glasses of ice with grated coconut.

I arrived at Jan's door around six-thirty in the evening, puffing and panting in the heat. Night had fallen but he saw me arrive and came out to meet me. I dismounted and got straight to the point. 'Jan, I have terrible news. You and your family have to leave immediately. I have orders to help you evacuate. Here is a copy of a death list given to me by Lieutenant Knegtmans. Read for yourself, your name is on it.'

Jan's eyes scanned the list and he turned pale.

'But Arto,' he cried in despair, 'how can I? I live here with my mother and my wife's aunt. They're too old for all this, man. You can't just drag them along. And even if we make it to safety, what then?'

'Come on, Jan, there is no time to waste. Let's go inside and I will discuss things with your family.'

Jan gathered everyone in the dining room and left the talking to me.

'Ladies, children, as I told Jan here, I have come to help you all evacuate. We must leave now. Begin packing immediately. You will travel with me to Willemsoord Barracks in Darmo, where you will be housed in a large army tent. Take only the pots and pans you need. Furniture and bulky possessions must be left behind. If you stay here, your lives will be in danger. A number of former interpreters and their families have been found murdered, their possessions looted or destroyed by fire. So hurry up and pack. Jan and I will go out to hire a bunch of *dokars*.'

The women and children were unable to hold back their tears but they did as they were told. I turned to Jan. 'Did you know that Jan Abas and Freddie Onsoe have defected? Abas has betrayed the entire Marine Brigade intel system to the Indonesian top brass and now he is leading a death squad. They have already come looking for me at my mother's house. I plan to give those bastards hell when I get the chance, because I know they will be back. I have friends in the APRA militia.'

Jan looked horrified. 'Bloody hell, I would never have expected that of Jan and Freddie. Can I join you?'

'No, Jan,' I answered resolutely. 'You have your wife and children to think of. The night before last, Ong Thwan Hien and his whole family were massacred and their house was razed to the ground. Wim Rompas and his family have been killed too, though I have no pity for Rompas. He was a Kenpeitai informer under the Japs.'

Jan and I were only able to hire six *dokars*. We packed them full of people and possessions. I got on my bike and led the caravan through the quiet, dimly lit streets to Willemsoord Barracks. At the barrier I said a hasty goodbye and cycled to Dinoyo *kampong*, where Wim Soemajow lived. It was almost eleven by the time I arrived and the whole house was in darkness. I knocked on the front door. Wim's face was puffy with sleep when he finally answered.

'Jesus, Nolan!'

'Wim,' I said resolutely, 'I have come to fetch you and your family. Now, this minute! Your lives are in danger! Former interpreters and their families have been murdered. Their homes have been looted and torched. I have orders to evacuate you and take you to Willemsoord Barracks.'

Suddenly Wim Soemajow was wide awake.

'My God, Arto!' he cried. 'I live here alone with my wife. She is asleep. We have no children.'

'In that case, wake her. Tell her to pack your bags while we arrange transport.'

While his wife gathered the bare essentials, Wim and I went in search of *dokars*. We found three. Just as we were loading the baggage, revolver shots rang out at close range. I grabbed my M1, ordered Wim and his wife to run inside, and crept round to the back of his house. I saw three shadows prowling, aimed my gun and fired. Two of them fell and I heard a loud groan coming from the third. Then came the sound of more voices and at least ten hooded figures appeared.

Seeing in a flash that they were Indonesian soldiers, I reached for a hand grenade, bit on the detonator ring and pulled out the pin. I lobbed the grenade among the pointed black hoods. An almighty blast was followed by screams and groans. Down the road, I saw a *kampong* house go up in flames and took cover in Wim Soemajow's house.

'Do you know whose house is burning?' I asked.

'It belonged to an informer for the Netherlands Forces Intelligence Service. But he's long gone, as far as I know.'

'Jesus, Wim!' I burst out. 'This place is crawling with infiltrators. You and your wife have to hurry. Where do the Madjoe brothers and the Bolang brothers live?'

'Keputran *kampong*, near Dinoyo. Why? Do you have to pick them up too?'

'Of course I do, man! Tell you what, Wim. I'll see you safely to Darmo Boulevard first. From there you can find your own way to the barracks. Then I'll hurry over to Keputran *kampong* and collect the brothers and their families.'

We had barely left Wim's house when more shots rang out. Minutes later, fire began licking the walls. Wim and his wife had tears in their eyes as they watched their home go up in flames. While their *dokars* rode on, I leaned my bike against a lamppost, took my rifle from my shoulder and grabbed another hand grenade. A mob of *pelopors* had formed in front of the burning house, egging each other on. I tossed the grenade among the rabble, aimed my M1 at anyone running towards me and shot to kill. Then I turned and ran, grabbed my bike, slung my rifle over my shoulder and cycled at full speed to catch up with Wim and his small column of *dokars*.

At the crossroads of Darmo Boulevard and Coen Boulevard, I called to Wim and his wife to ride on to the barracks. I turned off towards Keputran and went in search of the houses where the Madjoe and Bolang brothers lived. There too, I had to bang on doors to wake them, order them to pack, hire *dokars* and lead them back to Willemsoord Barracks. It was three in the morning by the time I arrived at the barrier with this third column. The marines on duty escorted the brothers and their families to one of the army tents.

Night after night I set off, fetching more former interpreters and their families from their homes and escorting them to the barracks. I eventually succeeded in tracking down most of the Marine Brigade's interpreters and bringing them to safety.

One evening, however, I decided to seek out the traitor Jan Abas and his cronies. I asked the quartermaster to issue me with a Colt .45. That impressive pistol soon lay heavy in my hand, along with four cartridge clips; eight bullets per clip, forty shots in total. This time I left my bike and took a *becak* to the city centre. The driver dropped me amid the bustle of Tunjungan. Mingling with the crowds of shoppers, I saw drunken Dutch servicemen staggering across the street, blaring that all was lost now they had to sail for home. I spotted Indonesian soldiers too. Thankfully, they were unarmed.

I walked the full length of Tunjungan, heading south towards Simpang. I peered into almost every shop, café and restaurant, but there was no sign of the traitor Jan Abas.

But I did meet a member of his death squad. I asked him if he knew Abas. His face lit up and, beaming with pride, he told me how he had executed marine informers on Abas's orders. I smiled and told him how right he was. Then I invited him to take a walk with me, as I was keen to know more about the reprisals he had carried out.

We were not far from the Marines Club. Across the street, an alley called Gang Butteweg ran down the side of the Aurora department store to Blauran, another shopping street. We entered the dark alley and I let the young man walk ahead, bragging all the while about how he planned to murder pro-Belanda elements. I drew my Colt pistol. He glanced back and I registered the surprise on his face as I shot him between the eyes. He fell backwards like a dead weight. I looked at my watch. It was almost midnight.

I walked back to Tunjungan, hailed a *becak* and returned to barracks, cursing my luck at not having found Abas himself. The next evening, I cycled all the way to Sawahan, the district where I had lived as a child. By chance I saw the Lodz brothers walking down the street. Bert and André Lodz turned out to have contacts with APRA, an underground guerrilla group which often operated under the guise of Darul Islam and fought against both Dutch and Indonesian forces. I gave the Lodz brothers the details and antecedents of Jan Abas and his death squad, and asked them to kill those bastards on sight.

Bert Lodz told me at length how APRA groups had carried out armed assaults on Indonesian Army supply transports and ammunition depots. He asked me if I was interested in joining these raids from time to time. It would mean putting on a Darul Islam uniform over my Marine uniform and donning a pointed black hood. It sounded to me like the raids had been inspired by the ruthless hardline tactics employed by the Special Forces Corps headed by Captain Westerling of the KNIL. Without committing myself, I kept the option open. I first had to give it some serious thought, not least because I was back under military discipline. It was quite a dilemma. I relished the chance to fight on against the Indonesian Army, but I was for Queen and Country while APRA backed a federalist Republic of Indonesia and opposed the Indonesian Army as the military apparatus of Sukarno's dictatorship.

It was mid-December and the Dutch government in The Hague was immersed in talks on the final transfer of sovereignty to Indonesia and the consequences this would bring. Former interpreters and informers of the Marine Brigade continued to arrive at the tent camp at Willemsoord Barracks with their families in tow, but we also received reports of former intelligence contacts who had been murdered. Our senior officers continued to come up with new rescue operations, in which I was deployed along with others. Often we arrived to find houses burned to the ground and charred bodies among the ruins. The death squads sent out by the Indonesian top brass were thorough in their reprisals. They spared nothing and no one, not even pets or caged birds. Everything was hacked to pieces and set alight.

Farewell to my brothers

Cor Matagora, a friend who served with the KNIL, had once introduced me to his mother, brother and sisters. They lived at No. 96 Simpang Dukuh. To reach their home, you had to take a narrow path that led off Simpang, around the back of the main thoroughfare. This made it a good place to lay low and Mother Matagora had offered me her help. She understood why I hid so many things from my own mother and occasionally she would let me spend the night after my perilous wanderings in the city, tracking down defectors and spies working for the Indonesian top brass.

Mrs Matagora helped me arrange a meeting with my brothers at her home. Her daughter Marie brought Jacob and Karel to the house, and Mrs Matagora joined us at the bare dining table. I looked my brothers in the eye and began to speak. 'Jacob and Karel, I have asked you here because it is the last time I will be able to see you. As you know, I will soon be leaving. I am going to Holland, where an uncertain future awaits me. But more importantly, you know that I have always supported Mama financially, as is the custom in the Indies. When I am gone, I will no longer be able to fulfil this role. Mama is as much your mother as she is mine, so show your love and give her what you can!'

My brothers' eyes were wet with tears. After a moment's hesitation, Jacob spoke first. 'Arto, it is a great pity that you will soon have to leave us for good. But I promise you that I will help Mama. I mistreated you as a boy, but it has made you the brave man you are today. God bless you, Arto.'

Then Karel said, 'Arto, I will miss you terribly. I too mistreated you in the past. But at least now you have become a strapping lad. You are a brave marine, something of which I can be very proud. I too will try to help Mama now and then.'

After coffee and biscuits, I said farewell to my brothers. We embraced. There was not much to be said by way of goodbye. But at least there was no more hatred and resentment between us. They left the house and I walked with them as far as Simpang, where I bade them farewell once more. Everything inside me hurt. It was all I could do to maintain my composure. Hanging my head, I returned to the Matagora family home and fell sobbing into Mother Matagora's arms.

Choices

Christmas was fast approaching. I continued to head out from Willemsoord Barracks every evening, often in the company of Ben de Lima. One evening, I set off with an interpreter by the name of Preyers. He wanted to introduce me to his sisters, who lived next door to the southern district telephone exchange on Kaliasin. His elder sister was courting an army man and was expecting his child. With his younger sister Evelyn, it was love at first sight. She was single, a pretty girl with a sweet face and a gentle nature. She took the initiative almost every step of the way. I was consumed by doubt, constantly weighing my options. Pending repatriation to Holland, I was roaming the city like a hunted animal, still hoping to settle scores with defectors and traitors, and I worried that my love for Evelyn might leave me soft-hearted and weak. Yet being with her was bliss, so much so that I had to tear myself from her arms.

Ben de Lima also started courting. A friend of Evelyn's, by the name of Jo Petten, won him over with her charms. These amorous escapades caused me to lose touch with reality. From a double agent, I received word that a Marine corporal had defected to the Indonesian Navy. I went to report this fact to Piet Dikotta the next morning at barracks, but he was nowhere to be found. His rooms were empty.

I bumped into Major Veenhuizen, who had since been promoted from captain, and inquired after Piet. The major looked at me in surprise. 'But Nolan,' he answered, 'I thought you knew. Piet Dikotta and his family have already left. They boarded an American transport ship yesterday, bound for the Netherlands. He went looking for you before they embarked. Nolan, it has not escaped my notice that you go into the city night after night. Be careful.'

'Thank you for your concern, Major Veenhuizen,' I replied, and felt a surge of relief now that no ill could befall Piet Dikotta in Surabaya.

*

The exodus of most of the former Marine Brigade Security Service personnel bound for New Guinea began on Christmas Eve 1949. The transition camp for former intel personnel and their families was a hive of activity. Everyone was busy packing and preparing for the voyage. They were due to leave Willemsoord Barracks that evening, under cover of darkness. A great many trucks, including the Marine Brigade's Tapeworm Express, had been commissioned. Everyone said their goodbyes with the hope of meeting again in a dim and distant future. It felt unreal to be taking leave of so many of my intel comrades.

Escorted by countless Military Police in jeeps and on motorbikes, the column wound its way to the naval docks at Ujung. There a couple of ships lay at anchor, ready to take the evacuees to New Guinea where, after arriving in Hollandia, they would be dispersed across the island. My heart went out to those boys and their families as they set sail for a destination unknown to them.

Four members of the Marine Brigade Security Service stayed behind: Ben de Lima, Harry Rijckaerdt, Jonker Laperia and me. None of us knew which transport ship would give us passage to the Netherlands.

New Year's Day 1950 had only just come and gone when I was summoned to the office of Major Veenhuizen of the Marine Corps. I sprang to attention, saluted stiffly and reported for duty. The major offered me a seat.

'I say, Nolan,' he began, 'I have here a summons of sorts for you to appear in court regarding the possibility of Indonesian citizenship. I suspect that it has come from our government in The Hague, but I can't say I understand it exactly. You are serving in the Dutch Royal Navy, after all, and that makes you a Dutch citizen. Why you should have to opt for Indonesian nationality under these circumstances is beyond me. All these years you have fought against all things

Indonesian. Anyway, here is your summons. Go there, in uniform of course, and fight your case. I wish you every success, Nolan, and if you should find yourself in a bind, legally speaking, ask for a postponement and return here so that I can arrange for a Navy lawyer to accompany you to the next hearing. There's something fishy about all this.'

*

On the appointed day, 20 January 1950, I appeared before a judge by the name of Hampel. He was a mild-mannered, friendly man, with the air of a contented Indo about him.

'Mr Nolan,' he began, 'I have before me a document sent by the Dutch government in The Hague asking you whether or not you wish to accept Indonesian nationality. You have, after all, been born and raised in this country by parents who have their roots here. You have received a good education, not to mention military training. In the newly founded Republic of Indonesia, we will have need of men like you, from both a social and a political perspective. You can count on every possible support from our political leaders. What is your answer?'

'Your honour, I have fought against your people. I have been tortured, starved, humiliated and trampled underfoot. I cannot and do not wish to accept Indonesian citizenship. My answer must therefore be no, Your Honour. I do not wish to become an Indonesian. I am a marine, as you can see, not a traitor. Since boyhood I have pledged allegiance to the Royal House of the Netherlands. I am loyal to the House of Orange and will remain so. I have fought for Queen and Country and will soon set sail for my fatherland, and that is the Netherlands. While I have been born and raised in this land, I do not feel at home here, however strange that may sound. Whenever the Netherlands calls on me to take up arms, I will do so.'

'Your statement is clear. The clerk of the court has taken note of everything you have said. I will pass judgement accordingly. You are free to go, Mr Nolan.'

Much relieved, I left the court building, hailed a *becak* and rode back to Willemsoord Barracks in Darmo district.

It later transpired that legal procedures of this kind had to be initiated for almost all Indo-Dutch, on the orders of the government in The Hague, with the aim of ensuring that as many Indos as possible would assimilate into the Indonesian population. For me, this would have been an act of high treason.

In cahoots with the enemy

January 1950 was nearly at an end. Almost all of my comrades had been shipped off to New Guinea and I wondered how they were getting on there. When not on duty, Ben de Lima and I could be found in the city. Our first stop was the southern district telephone exchange, more specifically the adjacent pavilion where Evelyn Preyers lived, with her sister and her sister's fiancé. Evelyn and I were very much in love but I could not ask her to marry me. She already knew that I would soon have to leave this beautiful country. Ben de Lima had told her too much for my liking about the role I had played in the Marine Brigade Security Service, even that my name was on Sukarno's blacklist. Often with tears in her eyes, Evelyn begged me to stay and make a new life with her. Her tears were hard to resist, and I held her close and promised her the moon. But I knew that ultimately I would have to leave her. My mother's words of warning about falling for an Indo girl were also playing on my mind.

Above all, my heart was still full of hatred and the desire to take revenge on the *pelopors* of the Indonesian Army. I was determined to fight on, if need be with one of the splinter groups that were rife in Surabaya. Of course, these were things I did not share with Ben de Lima, Harry Tjong or Jonker Laperia. I often thought back on my last conversation with Soedjono and my other old pals in that Javanese café. At the very least, I wanted to know what they were up to.

*

One afternoon I let Ben de Lima know that I would not be going into town with him that evening and asked him to give my regards to Evelyn. Good-hearted Ben did as I asked. Evelyn made no attempt to disguise her disappointment. She shot Ben a piercing look and asked, 'Why isn't Arto coming? I am worried about him. He is restless – he is hiding things from me. Is he cheating on me or is he out there courting danger again?'

'I honestly don't know, Evelyn. It's true, he has been very evasive of late. As far as I know, there is no one else. Arto loves you deeply, but I think something is troubling him. I have often tried to get him to open up, but he avoids my questions.'

That afternoon, unarmed and dressed in my khakis, I had a *becak* take me to the Javanese café where my friends Soedjono, Soekaton, Soemarsono and Soetjipto met at set times. There Soedjono introduced me to a Javanese man in a black uniform and pointed hood, who went by the name of Djojo. I eyed him suspiciously but Soedjono told me I had no cause to worry.

'He is a member of Darul Islam,' Soedjono said, 'and he has invited us to take part in ambush raids on Indonesian Army supply columns. We need their weapons, ammunition and food supplies for our battle groups. Darul Islam and the APRA militia are one.'

'How does that work?' I asked Soedjono. 'I don't understand you. Ever since the Japanese occupation you have all been crying out for Merdeka. So why support APRA units bent on undermining your own Indonesian Army?'

'Arto, deep in my heart I am against the policies of President Sukarno,' Soedjono declared. 'My sympathies lie with Muhammad Hatta. Political revenge is behind these ambush raids with Darul Islam. Soekaton, Soetjipto, Soemarsono and Soekaton are with me on this. We all come from Queen Emma School, after all. If you wish to join us, I will give you a black uniform that is easy to pull on over your Marine uniform. You will be armed with a tommy gun and a Colt pistol. What do you say?'

After eating and drinking together, I accompanied them deeper into the unsavoury neighbourhood where two dark-blue American limos were waiting for us. Soedjono introduced me to two Javanese sitting in one of the cars. They wore the emblem of Darul Islam, the head of a bison in a red circle.

We drove at high speed through the city centre towards Dapuan and stopped outside a hovel where a number of Chinese and Indonesians were snorting opium. There we put on black uniforms. Djojo lifted a few planks from the wooden floor and handed round weapons and ammunition. The plan was to take out all of the men on the supply column and seize control of the vehicles and their cargo. I was introduced to yet more Indonesians. Together we formed a group around fifteen strong.

After dark, we set off in three big American cars, first towards Grissee and then on to Lamongan. Between these two towns, the Indonesian Army ran supply columns at set times. The aim was to spring an ambush between Lamongan and Deket, an ideal stretch of road lined with trees and dense undergrowth.

At a suitable spot, we steered our cars onto the verge, camouflaged them with leaves and branches and took cover in the bushes, waiting until we heard the low hum of engines in the distance. One of the Darul Islam fighters quickly smeared his face and forearms with chicken blood that he had wrapped in greaseproof paper and folded in a banana leaf, so it looked like he had been seriously injured in a gun battle. More blood was spattered on the asphalt and he lay down in the middle of the road.

The column consisted of a jeep occupied by four Indonesian soldiers, followed by four Chevrolet trucks, each with two men in the cabin and three or four armed men riding in the back. The beams of the jeep's headlights hit our decoy and he groaned for help. The column stopped and all the men got out or jumped from the back of their trucks to take a look. That was our cue to open fire. Within seconds not a man was left standing. Every last one lay dead on or at the side of the road. Our group wasted no time manning the vehicles. Then we split up. Djojo travelled back to Surabaya with me, Soedjono and his driver in one of the big American cars.

A few days later, we met again at a contact address somewhere in Dapuan district. I was surprised to see defectors from the KNIL among the group. The weapons handed out to us had been obtained in raids on Indonesian Army depots. That night we employed the same simple tactics on the road between Jombang and Ngimbang, seizing a column of three Dodge trucks and a Master jeep. All of the occupants were killed. Days later we carried out an identical ambush on a column between Mojokerto and Krian.

And so it was that I found myself fighting alongside mutinous officers of the Indonesian Army I hated so deeply, officers who sympathized with the APRA militia and Darul Islam. Oddly, it felt good to be reunited with my old school friends, as if we were back fighting the Japs. But when they asked me to take part in operations near Westerbuitenweg and Ujung, I refused. Knowing our navy was still based there, I asked my newfound brothers-in-arms not to go ahead with their plans.

One evening I joined a twelve-man ambush of an Indonesian Army munitions depot in Grissee. The raid was child's play. We piled onto two large trucks, drove up to the entrance and opened fire with our automatic weapons. Within minutes, every last guard had been riddled with bullets. I was back in my element and dearly hoped to find that bastard Jan Abas among the dead. I was still determined to finish him off. We managed to load almost all the weapons, ammunition and grenades from the depot onto our trucks, except for the rapid-fire guns, which were too heavy. Tired and fulfilled, we returned to Dapuan. At the contact address, I shed my black Darul Islam uniform and went to a local restaurant with Soekaton and Soedjono. I returned to Willemsoord Barracks around midnight, sanctimoniously sporting my khaki dress uniform.

The following day I left the barracks early, without a word to Ben de Lima or my other mates. At the end of Jambistraat, I took a *becak* to Dapuan, where Soekaton lived. To my surprise, I was met by his little sister Kartini. Soekaton had just left. Kartini was roughly two years younger than I was. She looked absolutely beautiful. Before I knew what was happening, she had pulled me over to a quiet corner of the porch and kissed me full on the lips.

'Hey, what's all this about?' I asked her softly. 'Where are your parents? What if they see us?'

'I love you, Nolan,' Kartini murmured solemnly and continued to hold me close. Then she bundled me over to a rattan bench and just about welded her body to mine. Once again, my feelings got the better of me, and I had no idea what to do with myself. That Indonesian girl's loving ways were like nothing I had ever experienced. For a while she even drove all thoughts of Evelyn from my mind. Soekaton returned before long, and grinned from ear to ear when he saw his little sister Kartini so close to me and so clearly in love.

'Hello, Nolan, Arto!' Soekaton called out. 'It does me a power of good to see how much Kartini loves you. For years I have told her and my parents all about you. You are so very different to most Indos. They are arrogant and lord it over us Indonesians but you, Arto, have always treated us as equals. You are more like a brother to me, and not only to me but to Soedjono, Soetjipto and the others. We all love you. Behind your hard exterior as a fighter, you conceal a kind nature. Many people do not see you for who you are, but my little sister succeeds where they have failed. She has laid her soul bare and I ask you not to disappoint her.'

His words struck me as too much of a good thing. As if that wasn't enough, Soekaton continued to lavish praise on me. With a mixture of pride and awe, he told his sister how I had gone into battle the previous night at the munitions depot in Grissee. While everyone had ducked for cover as they shot at the guards, I had charged forwards with my tommy gun blazing. None of the others had shown such contempt for death.

Soekaton tried to convince me to accept Indonesian nationality and marry his sister. I did not want to offend him, so I kept him guessing. As long as I was with him or his family, my feelings for his sister ran deep. But as soon as I left, I did my best to forget Kartini. Not only did I still have Evelyn, but I also had to keep fighting and remain loyal to the House of Orange at all costs, even if it meant my downfall. Once a marine, always a marine.

I stayed in touch with my Indonesian friends. We had fought side by side under the Japanese occupation, and that meant something. We knew where we stood with one another. Day after day, I wrestled with my conflicting emotions. I had sent countless Indonesian freedom fighters to Valhalla, yet I still had many friends among those same freedom fighters. It was nothing short of inner turmoil. To defect to the Indonesian Army would be to commit high treason towards the Netherlands. That was something I could not countenance. If my number was up, I would die as a marine, not as a traitor. My participation in the Darul Islam attacks had been fuelled by the hope of gunning down the traitors and defectors among former members of the Marine Brigade Security Service.

My mother's parting shot

One afternoon as I was signing out with the duty officer to head into the city, I was accosted by two military policemen, who ordered me to accompany them. I had no idea what it could be about. They took me to their commanding officer, who in turn referred me to Major Veenhuizen. 'So, Nolan,' he said after a cordial greeting, 'I have some damnable news. You are to come with me for an audience with the Commander of Naval Forces. Apparently the admiral has a bone to pick with you.'

Completely at a loss, I accompanied the major to the office of the Commander of Naval Forces. We entered the room and the blood drained from my face… Opposite the admiral sat my own mother, her gaze more forbidding than I had ever seen it.

I sprang to attention. The admiral turned to me. 'Nolan,' he said, adopting the severest of tones, 'as you can see, your mother has paid me a visit. She has lodged a personal complaint about you and testifies that you have taken part in raids on Indonesian Army transports and depots, carried out by APRA and Darul Islam. Is this true? You are addressing your most senior commander, so lie at your peril!'

Mama spoke. 'One of your Ambonese friends came to see me. He told me you have been taking part in ambushes and gun battles with the Indonesian Army, even though a peace agreement has been signed. Arto, you know I cannot stand for this. You have to listen to me! I want you to leave and find yourself a good future in Holland as soon as possible. I have always opposed your overwhelming urge to fight. And now it must end, once and for all.'

'Right then, Nolan,' the admiral resumed, 'what's it going to be: twenty years behind bars or a bullet for desertion? The choice is yours. Speak up, man!'

'Admiral,' I answered, 'it is true that I took part in raids on Indonesian Army transports at Mojokerto, Jombang and Ngimbang and attacks on depots in Grissee and Lamongan. I acted out of frustration. We have had to stand down on all fronts. It feels like cowardice. I cannot bear the thought that we have lost so many of our fellow soldiers for nothing, while many former members of the Marine Brigade Security Service have defected to the enemy. They have betrayed us, sold us down the river. Surely that is unconscionable?'

'I cannot argue with your conclusion,' the admiral replied, 'but you are still a marine under military discipline. When you are ordered to lower the flag, you are expected to follow that order. I understand you, Nolan. You darkies are damned good fighters, but orders are there to be followed. On this occasion, I will let you off with a warning. But from now on you will only leave the barracks in the company of two or three of your fellow marines, and you will refrain from every unnecessary show of force, unless compelled to defend yourself. As for you, Veenhuizen, keep a close watch on our man Nolan here. And pass on this order to every commander who has anything to do with him. I will now continue my conversation with his mother. Nolan, dismissed!'

A Dutch subject

Not long after my refusal to adopt Indonesian nationality, I went to the government building on Pasar Besar to apply for a passport. A charming Indo girl at the counter was there to help me.

'You require a passport for the Netherlands, Mr Nolan?' she asked sweetly.

'I do indeed, Miss. Here is the court's statement regarding the matter of my nationality.'

'Oh, but Mr Nolan,' the girl replied, 'I see here that you have refused Indonesian nationality. Why, Sir? I have chosen to accept *warga negara*. A bright future awaits me here, as an Indonesian citizen. My father is an Indo and a member of the Indo-European Alliance. He has told me all kinds of terrible things about the Dutch government and the colonial administration in the Indies.'

I had no desire to discuss my future with the daughter of a defector and asked the girl to help me obtain a passport for the Netherlands as quickly as possible. A few days later I received word that my passport was ready for collection. At the same time, Ben de Lima, Harry Rijckaerdt, Jonker Laperia and I were asked to report to the Red Cross on Tunjungan to pick up winter clothing ahead of our voyage.

Our first stop was the government building. I went up to one of the desks and a female civil servant handed me my passport. The cover was green, not blue, and inside it gave my status as 'Dutch subject'. In other words, I was still not officially a Dutch national. All I could do was shrug indifferently.

The three of us then headed to the Red Cross for our winter clothes. The whole building was buzzing. A few helpful ladies took our measurements from head to toe, and once they had our sizes we were all issued with two long-sleeved undershirts, two sets of long johns, three shirts and a thick pair of black woollen trousers. We took one look at the underwear and burst out laughing. Other Indos began laughing too. 'Ghost suits' we called them, those comical long-sleeved undershirts and underpants that reached all the way to our ankles. Suits and overcoats were not in stock, so we had to do without. Lastly, we were all handed two scarves. We left the building in high spirits and went over to the Marines Club for a drink.

Back at barracks, I ran into the senior NCO and showed him my passport. He almost choked on his anger. 'Fucking hell,' he burst out, 'how can those swines not give you Dutch nationality? You are in the service of the Royal Navy, you are under military discipline. You are a Dutchman, damn it! In the eyes of the entire navy you are a Dutchman. Are those fucking idiots fucking— How the fuck— Oh, fuck the fucking lot of them!'

Springtime in Holland

The year was 1950. The date was 21 March. Someone told me it was the first day of spring in Holland. I had no idea what spring was. Early in the morning, I went to the mess with Ben de Lima, where we spotted Harry Rijckaerdt and Jonker Laperia. There we sat, the last human remains of the Marine Brigade Security Service, awaiting repatriation to the Netherlands. We exchanged sympathetic looks and said little more than 'good morning', each of us lost in his own thoughts. We had been granted permission to leave the compound and say our last goodbyes. Our final departure from the homeland had been set for the following day. Our trunks had already been carted off to Tanjung Perak and lay in the hold of a troop ship called the *Great Bear*.

After breakfast, Ben de Lima and I left for our final round of farewells. We signed out, walked down Jambistraat and hailed ourselves a *becak*. Our first stop was a house on Darmo Boulevard, home to Ben de Lima's sisters. Brotherly and sisterly advice was exchanged, messages were relayed. When it came time to part, many a tear was shed. It made me miserable. I embraced Ben's sisters and walked teary-eyed back to the street in search of a *becak*.

By this time it was late morning and the hot sun felt good on the crown of my head.

Ben de Lima and I then paid one last visit to the cemetery at Kembang Kuning. Barely able to contain our emotions, we walked past the graves of the fallen, many of them our mates. We paused at each headstone and prayed for a moment. I left Ben waiting at the gates to the military section, hurried over to my father's grave a short distance away and took my leave of him with a murmured prayer.

In silence, Ben de Lima and I walked down the driveway to the cemetery entrance and back to Darmo Boulevard. We got into a *becak* and continued our farewell tour, heading for Heemskerkstraat in Undaan Kulon district. Unfortunately Ella and Poppy were at work, but Mama was home.

'Arto, my dearest son,' Mama sobbed, 'we both had to make this momentous decision but it was my will that sealed our choice. It is better for you to live far from me than here where death might come at any moment. You have sacrificed yourself for the Netherlands, a country entirely unknown to you, and now the Netherlands will receive you into its fold. Arto, once you are there, work hard to build a future for yourself. You have spent many years at war and have fallen far behind with your studies. Show the Nolan family that their illegitimate son is now the rightful bearer of another name and that you can succeed in Dutch society. In my prayers and in my soul, I will be with you.'

With tears in my eyes I took Mama in my arms. All I could say was, 'Oh Mama, I will not be gone forever. I will return. I want to be with you, Mama, to go on taking care of you. That is all that matters to me.'

I knew it was a promise I could not keep.

'Keep your heart strong, Mama. Pass on my goodbyes and best wishes to Ella and Poppy,' I cried out at last.

Babu Tenie and Kokkie Tas came to me in tears and I embraced them both. These servants were far better people than all those folk who bragged about their European blood.

Once Ben de Lima had said his own fond farewell to my family, we took leave of our city with a quick walk through the streets of Undaan Kulon. Then we took a *becak* back to Tunjungan.

It was already late afternoon. We had the driver stop outside the Marines Club and went inside to drink our fill of whisky and brandy. Ben and I were half-drunk when six marines from other units came in and got tanked up on beer and hard liquor. We had a fine old time with those Dutchmen, bursting into song after song, each man more tuneless than his mate. Then all eight of us staggered out into the street. Luckily we were not the only drunken marines around, though there were less and less of us in the city and passers-by stared in our direction.

Night had fallen, and Ben and I went looking for a Chinese restaurant. Following Ben's directions we found a small place off Embong Malang, which he swore served the best pork in town. The first thing we did was order a large glass of strong coffee and wait until we felt a little less drunk before ordering our final meal: an elaborate selection of Chinese dishes, including a special pork dish I had never eaten before.

After dinner, Ben suggested we go to Evelyn's house to say goodbye. We left the Chinese restaurant and wandered listlessly down Embong Malang to the southern district telephone exchange near Hotel Sarkies. Jo Petten was there too and she ran into Ben's arms and smothered him with kisses. I received the same treatment from Evelyn. It felt fine, even if she did begin with a playful slap in the face because I reeked of booze. Amid these caresses on the porch, Evelyn begged me to stay with her forever. No matter what, she wanted to bear my child so that I would always be bound to her. I almost cringed in fear when Evelyn said these things, choking on her tears, but I swallowed hard and regained my self-control. 'I'm sorry, Evy,' I said softly, 'but I can't. I love you very much but I am still under military discipline. If I stay with you, they will shoot me as a deserter. Later, if you have the chance to sail for the Netherlands, write to me and I will wait for you there.'

It was close to midnight when Ben and I finally found the courage to tear ourselves away from the girls we loved. We kissed our sweethearts one last time, then ran all the way to Simpang. We were in luck: the good old Tapeworm Express was easing round the bend to Kaliasin. We raised our hands and the driver slowed her down enough for us to take a running jump. The linked trucks snaked their way past Willemsoord Barracks where we hopped off and strolled up to the guard at the barrier.

We were wakened at six the next morning. After a long bath, we dressed and immediately started packing. Each of us had a duffel bag and a suitcase. Breakfast over, we returned to our sleeping quarters in our khaki dress uniforms with cap, checked our baggage and humped everything to the parade ground, where some two hundred marines had gathered, ready for the overseas voyage. At the parade ground, Major Veenhuizen introduced me to Major of the Marine Corps Van Tielrooy, who was to sail with us as transport commander.

Late in the morning, fall-in was sounded. All two hundred marines lined up, raring to go. The barracks commander gave a short farewell speech on behalf of the Commander of Naval Forces. We were then issued with every possible instruction and at last were able to march out onto Jambistraat, waved off by the few who remained behind.

Two four-truck Tapeworm Expresses stood ready to take us to the docks at Tanjung Perak. Our route led through the centre of Surabaya and I feasted my eyes on the city one last time, absorbing every detail. A deep sorrow came over me but I did not let on to my fellow passengers. In every neighbourhood, people waved as we passed. It was left to us to wonder why.

After an hour or so, our column arrived at the docks and approached the quay where the *Great Bear* was moored. In no time, a bunch of us had christened her *The Grizzly*. She was a liberty ship, bought from the US by the Dutch government, and had seen her fair share of wartime action. We gathered our baggage and walked slowly in the direction of the ship. A military band had appeared and began playing a series of marches and patriotic songs. Many of the servicemen were over the moon to be sailing home at last, but many were not. I trudged sadly up the gangway to the ship. A crew member pointed the way to my bunk. I threw down my bags, returned to the deck and leaned over the railing, looking down at the quay.

Among the crowd I spotted Evelyn in her lacy white summer dress, standing with her sister and brother-in-law. I was overcome with emotion and waved to her. I called out that I would wait for her in Holland, if ever she were able to make the passage. She stood there and did not move a muscle.

I heard the ship's horn blast once, then twice. Crewmen walked over to the hawsers and cast off. By the time the horn sounded a third time, their job was done. The *Great Bear* left the quayside and slowly sailed away. I went to the bow of the ship and took in the panoramic view of the city where I was born. Off in the distance I could still see the tower of the government building and far behind it the district of Undaan Kulon, where Mama lived.

Suddenly I felt a hand on my left shoulder. I turned to see the sympathetic eyes of Major Van Tielrooy.

'Let your tears flow, Nolan,' he said, full of feeling. 'I know what it means to say goodbye in such wretched circumstances. My men have informed me well. I know about your family. You have given your all for Queen and Country, and from this moment on the Royal Navy has a duty to take you under its wing. You are no longer safe on your native soil, as well you know, not only because of your allegiance to the House of Orange, but because you have given more than the Netherlands had a right to expect.'

I nodded my thanks and kept staring at the spot on the quayside where Evelyn Preyers stood. I felt the urge to jump overboard and swim back to shore, but instead I continued to stare until I lost sight of her.

The *Great Bear* sailed north, full steam ahead through the narrow strait between Java and Madura. She then bore west, setting a course for Semarang. Early in the morning of 23 March 1950, we cast anchor in Semarang harbour. Navy motor launches ferried a few hundred KNIL soldiers, many with their families, from the quay to the ship. From Semarang our voyage continued westwards to Tanjung Priok, where the *Great Bear* was able to dock. Ben de Lima and I ambled across the deck and could just make out the distant city skyline of Batavia. I thought of my sister Ina, living her life somewhere beneath those roofs. The *Great Bear* lay at anchor for a full day and night to give more KNIL soldiers and their families the opportunity to board. It was almost evening when the old tub left Tanjung Priok, heading west past the island of Sumatra. She moored one last time at Sabang, off the coast of Aceh, where we took on drinking water and supplies. Lost in thought, Ben de Lima, Harry Rijckaerdt, Jonker Laperia and I gazed out across the city.

V

CODA

Paper in a munitions chest

Someone had tracked me down, sent me a letter enclosing photographs of a mysterious chest. I contacted the sender and travelled to a provincial town, where I was met by old acquaintances of my father's from the Indies. They fed me *nasi rames*. The man was an Indo and told me my father was all swagger and bluff back in his Java days. This he knew from tales told by people from Surabaya, where my father had apparently enjoyed a degree of notoriety. Unfortunately, the man could name no one who featured in my father's anecdotes or memoirs. His wife was a Dutchwoman who only cooked Indies-style, recipes handed down by her mother-in-law. I was taken aback to see a white woman taking care of her Indo husband in this way. Later, it was my own perception that struck me as strange.

Once we had eaten, they fetched the battered chest from the attic. It was a faded navy blue, rather heavy and, not counting the two reinforcement strips on the lid, measured roughly eighteen inches by fourteen by twelve.

On the lid and the back, bold white capitals, emphatically punctuated, read:

TO CTD. DPT
MARNS. ROTTERDAM.
A. NOLAN

Printed diagonally on the sides in the same colour and font and were the words:

HOLD LUGGAGE.

On the front was my father's destination, an address in The Hague:

A. NOLAN
PARALLELWEG. 169.
DEN HAAG.

NOLAN, not NOLAND. Which means he didn't go by the name of Noland back then, at least not in the eyes of the Marine Brigade. The chest couldn't have travelled with my father on his voyage from Indonesia to the Netherlands, as he had docked in Amsterdam with a cabin trunk from which he claimed two samurai swords had been stolen in transit. This smaller chest must have been shipped to the Netherlands separately, through the port of Rotterdam.

My hostess told me the chest had been left with her late mother-in-law, a woman from the Indies whom my father often visited. I had no idea who she meant and I can't say it interested me much. The chest had never featured in my childhood. The bottom was lined with a musty, yellowed Dutch-language newspaper from 1950, the year my father arrived in the Netherlands. But what about its contents? Had the Marine Brigade simply sent it on as a memento?

I wrote to my father asking him if I could keep the chest as a souvenir. I never received an answer. Strange, as he was usually quick to reply to letters.

It was my brother Phil who identified it as an old-fashioned munitions chest, carried on the patrols the Eagle went on with the Dutch marines. He was in no doubt that it had once contained hand grenades, cartridges and the like. The Eagle had probably lugged that heavy chest, slung around his shoulders on two loops of rope. These days it holds the many letters my father left me before he departed for Spain – letters he once sent to the authorities with complaints about Child Services, about the governors of the children's home in Voorschoten, about Ma, Frau Eva, Renate and the Spanish bride who did a runner two weeks into their marriage. I also keep old photos in the chest, the handful that escaped Frau Eva's vengeance. And of course the manuscript I once deposited in his letterbox, yellowed and dusty now. He later rewrote the whole thing, a more concise account, which I keep in the munitions chest too. It was completed in 1985, the year the Eagle turned sixty. By coincidence a war monument was unveiled in Bondowoso, East Java that same year: Monumen Gerbong Maut A memorial to the prisoners who perished on a train from Bondowoso to Surabaya in 1947. In 1985 I was about to make the crossing to Indonesia myself, to stay with my Aunty Ella for a while. Not a single publisher, not even one of the six hundred Indies associations in the Netherlands, had shown the least interest in the manuscript my father never tired of sending out. These days I often feel like its custodian, especially when I plonk myself down on the old chest to strum my guitar.

The manuscript is at Phil's now. Typical twins we are: the younger primed to have a go at the elder, always on the offensive unless he happens to be in a good mood. My relationship with Phil is not unlike my relationship with Ma. Normal conversation barely gets a look in. It's all friction, sarcasm and sometimes downright hostility, echoes of the old family home where the first-born son had to make sure his siblings were home on time and all the rest of it. I was little more than the reluctant extension of my father's will. That makes me the Smart Arse in Phil's eyes, the brother who always thinks he knows best. And I see Phil as the Inquisitor, forever poised to take up his hammer and chisel to chip my wavering character into a sculpture of steadfastness. We share a city, live less than half a mile apart, yet we seldom see each other in the flesh. Email and webcam are our channels of choice.

Our mother too, after a vagabond existence that took her to Helmond and Zoetermeer is – to use the Eagle's words – back in the 'city of the damned'. When Uncle Willem passed away, she chose to spend her final years in Dudok's housing estate of all places. Whenever I cycle through Zuider Park and see those streets looming up ahead, I feel a tremendous urge to turn around and pedal for my life. How I hate that place.

Phil and I see Ma once a year at most, unlike Arti, Mil and Nana. Those three live up in Amsterdam, but still visit her more than we do. As for Ma, she visits no one. She sits there glued to the TV and couldn't even tell you where we live. Pa refuses to return to the Netherlands to see his grandchildren. What a family! Mil is the only one who visits Pa down in Malaga. Our sibling relations are dominated by feuds: sister snubs brother who shuns brother who offends sister and on it goes. Being the eldest, I sidestep much of the animosity that divides the other four but, even so, it's beyond my power to bring the five of us together. Looking back, Pa didn't do too badly on that score. He never managed to unite the entire clan for Christmas or his birthday, but there was the odd occasion when he succeeded in gathering four of us around him in that grim little Haarlem flat of his.

I can't help wondering how that old *katjong* keeps it up, knocking around his no-man's land of a life, stranded between the past imperfect and a dead-end future. First thing tomorrow, in the concrete tourist trap he retreated to however long ago, will he toddle down to the kiosk on that unsightly Spanish boulevard for the thousandth time to buy the latest edition of that rag of a Dutch newspaper? And after downing a *kopi tubruk* at his regular haunt – some dodgy Chinese café – will he toddle back to his flat, put a magnifying glass to his worn-out eyes and while away the hours cutting out articles that expose racism in the Netherlands? How many of those have I received in the post? Photocopied snippets accompanied by his standard handwritten message:

Leave that hateful country full of racists!
Come and live here, in southern Spain!

Boy, wouldn't that be fun? A front-row seat for his tales of woe about the Queen, Child Services and Ma all over again. Granted, I moan about the Dutch often enough myself, but then I was never about to fight to the death for them, the House of Orange least of all. The Dutch understood that the day I failed to make it to the end of my National Service medical: that's how quick they were to declare me 'permanently unfit for service'. Sister Mil told me Pa now has scrapbooks full of clippings on racism in the Netherlands, the country where he never found his feet. I could tell him I have never found my feet here either but that would be no comfort to him, only his cue to trot out the same 'at least you were born here' bullshit I've heard more times than I care to remember. He and all the Indos shipped over from the colonies never tire of telling me and my generation we don't belong among them because we were not born *over there*. So where exactly *do* we belong? As I write, thousands are flocking to The Hague to attend a festival called *Summer of the Indies*. Don't ask me who it's for. The organizers' neocolonial mindset even stretches to dishing up the world's biggest *rijsttafel* on the main square. When every last vestige of cultural sensitivity is gone, there's always the *Guinness Book of Records* to shoot for. Do they even know the *rijsttafel* is the culinary symbol of colonialism at its most opulent? Beats me. My father never had much time for the upper classes in the Indies. And here in Holland he much preferred Chinese cafés to Indo cafés – precious few of them left in The Hague these days. Most are being taken over by Indonesians; I wonder what Pa would make of that. For the average Dutchman there's no difference between Indo and Indonesian food. And these days even us post-war children pass for Indos, genuine Indos – once an insult, now an identity – but of course we will always be fakers to my father's generation with their *tempo doeloe* schtick. A while back, I read a book by one Wim Walraven Jr, a young man with an irascible scribe of a father by the name of Willem Walraven. Walraven Senior was a Belanda journalist who married a Javanese woman and lived in a house in the tropics, waited on by Indos galore. And in the stack of letters he wrote to a friend, 'those Indos' come in for torrents of abuse. Unfortunately the man could write. His own little Indo pride and joy, Walraven Jr, went on to scale the dizzy heights of professional lunacy. Wound up in America, a little house in the middle of nowhere. And when the memories of his father got too much for him he would head out into the desert and have himself a right old scream. I'm a screamer too. I scream when I practise a deadly technique at the *dojo* where I train. A scream the Japanese call *kiai*. At an age when tai chi would make more sense, here I am devoting myself to the martial art of jujitsu: a shrimp propelling myself backwards through life or so it sometimes seems. I put it down to a need to confront my fear of violence. At any rate I do not fear the Eagle any more. Luckily for him, I came to jujitsu thirty years too late to bounce him off every wall in that flat of his, with his shitty war books that stank of mothballs, his filthy *obats* on sticky little tables and his ridiculous Indo textiles on the walls. I appear to be a decent enough guy, even a high-minded human being in the eyes of a new-ager or two, nobly imbibing the principles of the *I Ching*. That'll be what's stopping me from boarding a plane even now and sending the Eagle to the eternal hunting grounds once and for all. He could be there already, for all I know. In which case he can give my best to that family of his and tell them what an almighty bastard he has been to his children, though if they've been paying any attention up there they'll have worked that one out for themselves by now. Then he can brace himself for a flogging with his mother's whip and her brother Soen can rub vinegar into the welts on his back, assuming acid has a place in the sweet hereafter. And they can all praise the Lord that they've been spared this miserable *Autumn of the Indies* in The Hague, for you can bet your bottom dollar that the world's biggest *rijsttafel* will be washed away by a Dutch monsoon. No one wants that to happen, of course. No one but me. Tragic how the depleted, rollator-bound platoon from the Indies totter into the spotlight time after time and let the Belandas make a spectacle of them. In that sense they really are the immortal film stars the folks back in Indonesia take them for: kow-towing to the director and saving their complaints for when they wipe off their make-up behind the scenes. Indos never form a front. Rival splinter groups are all they have ever amounted to, incapable of agreeing on anything. The Eagle knew that all along. But that hard-wired inferiority complex of theirs means they will always listen to a Belanda, even a Belanda who knows bugger all about the history of the Indies. Attention at last! Understood by the Belanda, the *tuan besar*. Those losers and their *tempo doeloe*. That said, most of my best friends are Indos. 'Birds of a feather…' as The Eagle used to say. It's one thing Pa and I agree on: he always despised that *tempo doeloe* nonsense too. Not that his own taste was so refined. The daily dose of American drivel he consumed on his black-and-white TV was a legacy of the starry-eyed obsession he contracted in the damned Dutch East Indies. In that sense, the Eagle was a Belanda himself. The Australian radio stations in the pre-war Indies drooled over everything their American big brothers did and copied them by broadcasting Hawaiian music. It caught on and the Indos adopted the Hawaiians as their musical brethren. Uncle Karel played a damn good steel guitar and once came second in the Surabayan championships, if I remember rightly from the tales the Eagle told us back in the day. Then again, it might not have been a guitar at all but the *sia*, the three-pronged weapon he wielded with such skill as a *pukulan* fighter. Or maybe he was second best at both… could be. Karel made his little brother sweat on the high bar in the garden, taught him how to kick and punch, but I don't think Arto was ever really one for hand-to-hand combat. A true fighter turns up his nose at pistols, rifles and cannon. Not the Eagle. He had no qualms about pulling out his stupid pistol and gunning down a Chinese martial arts fighter at a street market. An act that even made his brother Karel sick. Martial arts versus weaponry that has been refined over generations. The lone wolf versus the military industrial complex. No contest. But I will always take the side of the lone wolf who hones his martial arts skills year in, year out. Can I help it if my chosen tradition is Japanese? Am I honour-bound to make the Eagle's old enemies my own? Of course he damned them all to hell, the bombers that reduced his family home to rubble, but his main objection seems to have been that they were Japanese. Never did I hear him say he was happy that his mother, brothers and sisters had survived the bombing. All he could whine about for years on end were the twelve man-sized Chinese vases that had been blown to bits. True, they were worth money, but his sisters' beautiful bodies brought in the readies too, didn't they? What a disgrace in his eyes, Ella and Ina serving in a restaurant where Japanese officers got smashed on sake every night, his own sisters letting themselves be used as hostesses. Oh, the shame! 'Comfort women' is the term they use today, at least when a woman was coerced by the occupier. A term off limits to a woman who needed to earn a crust by trading love for money, lest she incur the wrath of the society for the protection of comfort women. There are comfort women who have formed groups to demand an apology from the current Japanese government – an apology and a hefty payout. Who wants payment in arrears from their abuser? Keep your money and stick it where the sun don't shine! I would not take the Eagle's money. Not a penny. My sister Mil would be happy to, but then he only hit her once in her life. Pa's sister Ella told me, as an old woman bowed with sorrow, that she had truly loved the Japanese officer who frequented their family home. She told me this on the porch of her home in Surabaya, where I stayed for a month in the hope of hearing something about my father's war. What I heard was precious little, nothing at all in fact. 'My little brother was always home with me,' she said without blinking. As if she had never endured two years in a women's internment camp. In the end, love pays no heed to war – just look at those films about the Nazi who loved a Jewish girl or the unrequited longing between a German officer and a French piano teacher. The Eagle's romance was with Holland. He was crazy enough to hang a portrait of Queen Wilhelmina on his bedroom wall in defiance of the Japs. His whole family berated him and waited wisely for better times to come; he was the only one to side with the Dutch. The fact that his mother was nothing but his father's concubine turned out to be a blessing in disguise, allowing him to walk the streets with his Chinese ID and a Chinese badge on his lapel. Chilling when you think about it, the double role he played, like his Uncle Soen come to that, who went about his day-to-day business with Indonesians while helping his nephew fight them. It's hard to grasp. Pa and his schoolmates signing up for the Demolition Corps, I get that. Unfortunately, he was captured by the Japanese and tortured. Yes, I know what they did to him, he showed me the scars on his back often enough. Was it just a cowardly case of siding with the big boys? Once the Americans had dropped their atom bombs on Hiroshima and Nagasaki and long-faced Japanese soldiers were roaming the streets of Surabaya, he skewered them with his *takeyari* under cover of darkness. The city had been in chaos ever since Sukarno had declared the Republic of Indonesia: the Javanese were crying out for their Merdeka, their freedom, and anti-Belanda and anti-Indo slogans were daubed on the walls. But what was going on inside the Eagle? His Javanese friends never tired of reminding him that the Indos – or at least his late father's highbrow coterie – had always looked on him with contempt. Amid the throes of revolution, surely his choice should have been clear? But off in the distance, the cannon of the British Royal Navy could be heard. With a red-and-white emblem on his shirt, he misled the Indonesians and offered his services to the British. He went out on patrol as a truncheon-wielding constable first class. And then the Dutch came blundering back onto the scene in the naive conviction that Indonesia was still theirs. To the Eagle's regret, the revived Municipal Police offered him little chance to kick up a rumpus, but then came the Allied marines, trained in Carolina. The next best thing to American cowboys, the real deal. As a young *katjong*, he fell in love with their uniforms and their high-tech weapons. There were more boys like him, interpreters all. They too spoke Chinese, Japanese, Javanese, Malay, Dutch, English and goodness knows what else. Many were childhood friends of his: Indos,

Chinese, Ambonese, Manadonese and even Javanese with personal motives for fighting against the Indonesian freedom fighters. Indonesian captives were interrogated by the Eagle and his mates, beaten and tortured. Nice work if you can get it. The Dutch delegated the torture to the interpreters. Interpreters? Talk about misrepresenting the job! The Eagle even climbed the ladder, became head of Prisoner Interrogation, which means he must either have been exceptionally cruel, or smarter than his fellow interpreters. In the meantime it became clear that the world was turning against the Netherlands, with the Americans leading the way: after all, a return to the Dutch colonial monopoly could only be bad for business. While the Eagle and his mates were playing the thug, beating one prisoner after another till they could barely walk, the top brass were sitting around a conference table with their filthy hands sheathed in immaculate gloves. Arto was but a common soldier and it began to dawn on him that he had backed the wrong horse. And still he didn't want to know. With the hatchet buried and decolonization looming, even his Dutch mates told him he'd be better off staying put. There, on Java! He never committed it to paper, but he did let it slip to me once. But what are you supposed to do when you're second on a blacklist signed by Sukarno? The Indonesians were always going to hound him, and hound him they did, all the way to his bedroom in Holland. I hope he packed up those phantoms and took them with him when he left for his Spanish costa, though sometimes I wonder. Especially when they visit me in my dreams. I am in my element alone with a guitar in my hands or with a pupil sitting opposite me. My father thrives alone with a typewriter on his lap and a framed portrait on the wall opposite. I am the captive guitarist who turned the tables and interrogated him endlessly on my visits to his flat in Haarlem, almost as persistently as he interrogated his prisoners, minus the physical abuse of course. His response was to hand me his memoirs, the rewritten version no less. For years I pushed them aside, simply could not bring myself to read them. And now the time has come. He always thought it was Arti who shoved those three parcels through his letterbox that night. I never told him the truth, that I was the one who had returned his original manuscript to him. Because I wanted to find out how often he got things wrong. Completely and utterly wrong.

What about that manuscript of his? Is it a black book? A blue book? A black-and-blue book? A feeble joke, but then he was the one who told me the Indonesians tore the blue stripe from the Dutch tricolour and gave it to the Indos for their repatriation to Holland. Which is why we were dubbed 'blues' in the fifties and sixties. Relatively mild as racial slurs go, though less flattering accounts exist. Are his memoirs nothing more than a written defence of all the misery he inflicted in his homeland, an apologia that got out of hand? One long plea for more military honours than the single medal he ended up with? As I recall, the Eagle stopped carving notches on the butt of his rifle when his personal death toll reached a hundred. If even ten per cent of what he lists is true, it makes him a mass murderer and all his Dutch mates along with him.

I let a couple of friends read the manuscript and asked them to gauge its truthfulness. Now it's with Phil, who has yet to respond. I value his judgement more than anyone's, more than the opinion of a couple of pals who reckon it's half truth, half embellishment. If that's the case, we might as well call it fiction. A novel based on real-life events. Something like that. Faction as a counterpoint to fiction. Of course, the Eagle would be mortally offended by such a label. For him it's all about the truth, the whole truth and nothing but the truth, a condition from which many of his generation suffer. Which brings us back to that old cliché: their story was never heard. No one bothered to listen. I hate to say it, but my father's generation have a point, from the upper echelons to the lowest of the low. Holland loves the cliché of the 'silent father from the Indies'.

I once saw a TV documentary about a remorseful Dutch veteran of the war of independence. He visited some Indonesian village or other and assembled all the villagers. They stood around a podium while he blubbered his heart out, apologizing for what he had done.

The Indonesian villagers listened in silence, asked him no questions. But if you looked closely, you could read the words in their eyes: *What is this Belanda whining about? Didn't* we *win the war? This man must be confused. He thinks he's still the boss around here, that colonialism never went away. Kasihan, how sad for this man, yes indeed.*

I am so sorry I lost the war to you. I'm so very sorry, my esteemed victors!

What an embarrassing spectacle. Even now, I can't bring myself to laugh at it. In spite of it all, there's one thing I have to give my father and his generation credit for: they never – and I mean *never* – apologized for fighting for the House of Orange. No Dutchman can fully understand what a motto like 'In the name of Orange' meant to people from the Dutch East Indies and Indonesia, with their sovereigns, sultans, princesses and goodness knows what else.

Webcam chat

AL: 'Hey, have you dived into Pa's past yet or are you still too busy messing about with that computer and synthesizer of yours?'

PHIL: 'I got the PDF of Pa's manuscript you sent me and I'll get stuck in one of these days. I never really read his memoirs properly…'

AL: 'Has a nice ring to it, Bro… get stuck in…'

PHIL: 'I scanned the odd page at random on the computer. Haven't been able to find the original since I dumped all my paperwork in the skip outside the flat.'

AL: 'But you must have read how he bumped off one guy after another… Or didn't you?'

PHIL: 'Yeah. But is that news? He told us that when we were kids.'

AL: 'And you believe that shit?'

PHIL: 'Why wouldn't I?'

AL: 'Why would you?'

PHIL: 'Look, if you don't like my answers, don't go twisting them into questions and firing them back at me. You know I hate that. Let me put it another way, Mr Smart Arse: to me his memoirs feel genuine.'

AL: 'Genuine! Ha! Since when did you let your feelings do the talking, Mr Inquisitor? Ain't you supposed to be the man of reason, a disciple of logic? And still you believe that shit?'

PHIL: 'Like I said, I haven't given it a thorough read yet, but Pa's descriptions strike me as honest, candid and authentic. Spiced up a little here and there maybe. No law against that, is there?'

AL: 'But where does fact end and fiction begin?'

PHIL: 'Does it matter? If anyone's life should read like a novel, it's his. Am I wrong? What gets me most is that he only ever showed us one side of himself: the tyrant. But in the memoirs there's a romantic side to him.'

AL: 'Yeah, a romantic brandishing an M1 rifle.'

PHIL: 'Are you trying to tell me romantics are all about love? I thought you were our resident man of letters? Why don't you go and pluck at your guitar or something? In fact, that's exactly what you should be doing! I'll give Pa's document another read, a proper read this time. As you can see and hear, I'm loaded with the cold right now.'

AL: 'You're just like Pa, with those colds of yours. Remember when we stayed in that filthy Indo boarding house and Pa bombarded us with letters asking us – no, telling us – no, commanding us – to come and look after him? The man came down with a new ailment every other day. And off we'd trot, back to dreary old Voorschoten to do his shopping for him. In winter, his place always reeked of cajuput oil, ginger, lemon, peppermint, liquorice and noodle soup. Do you remember how he used to make noodle soup? He'd fill a big pot with water, chuck in a frozen chicken and a whole pack of margarine, a stock cube, a few big onions quartered, chili paste, soy sauce, MSG and a pack of chopped mixed veg from the supermarket. Bring it to the boil, then turn down the heat and have himself a nice long shower. After an hour he added the noodles, dropped three raw eggs into the murk and a pack of beansprouts for good measure. And… God it tasted good! Delicious! Unbelievable how you can make such good noodle soup without so much as giving a toss.'

PHIL: 'I'd forgotten all about that! He always had the flu, didn't he? Never missed a winter. Okay, have it your way, I'm Pa for a week. But before I collapse on the couch again, I'd like to say something about Ma, our wannabe sitcom star from Helmond who would have liked nothing better than to order us a UFO and send us back to whatever planet she thought we came from. When we were kids, Ma always told us Pa was schizophrenic. Split personality, she said, though she was never very clear which personalities she was talking about. I reckon I can shed some light on that. Basically, Pa was a man of feeling. But in the outside world he had to operate as a man of reason. Of course, that threw up all kinds of problems – he was going against his own nature. I'm not saying Ma was right. She was too stupid to be right, always has been, always will be. She didn't understand Pa at all. Every night he sat there typing away at his Remington, but I don't remember her ever being curious enough to sit down beside him. What can you do with a wife who never takes the slightest interest in what you have to say? Right then, I'm off for another lie down.'

AL: 'Get well soon, Bro. By the way, Ma and the rest of us always thought Pa was studying. She knew nothing about his memoirs. Anyway, let me know when you've finally read through that shit of Pa's.'

PHIL: 'Shit? Smart Arse here continues to call Pa's memoirs shit? Prose is what they are, brother.'

AL: 'Off you go and hang that head of yours over a steaming bucket of Vicks. You'll see Pa's phantoms rising up before your teary eyes soon enough.'

PHIL: 'Hey, there's a thing: Vicks! Wasn't that the stuff Pa used to chuck boiling water over? Then he'd hold your head above the bucket, throw a wet towel over you and clamp one hand around your neck, camp commandant style. It worked though, didn't it? You'd be back at school the next day.'

AL: 'Hey, Bro, one more thing. Do you know what a *buaya* is?'

PHIL: 'Animal, vegetable or mineral?'

AL: 'Animal. Pa ate turtle meat during the war, so why not crocodile?'

PHIL: 'Is that what *buaya* means? Crocodile? Hmm, I think he told us once that he ate crocodile.'

AL: 'He ate everything, even rancid pork. To toughen himself up for World War Three.'

PHIL: 'Was that why he did it? I thought he was just too tight to buy it fresh.'

AL: 'Could be. Or a bit of both. He would buy butcher meat for next to nothing when it was past its sell-by date. And he had this strange preoccupation with what he called the smell of corpses. Couldn't eat a piece of meat without reminding us it came from a dead body. He got a weird kick out of eating that rancid pork. Anyway, the Indies had a few names for crocodile. There's *baya* and there's *buaya*. In the old Dutch colonial classics and Malay pantuns, verses which have made their way into *kroncong* music, *buaya* stands for womanizer. Suits him down to the ground, don't you think?'

PHIL: 'Christ, that man's been through a ton of women.'

AL: 'The second time I stayed with Pa in Voorschoten, when things were okay between us for a while – it was summer, he was always easier to take in the summer – a new woman from some personal ad or other would show up on the doorstep every weekend. Pa subscribed to a magazine published by a German dating agency and he always managed to learn the language of whatever woman he was writing to within six weeks: Polish, Portuguese, Spanish, Swedish – the man was a regular polyglot! He must speak around twenty languages by now. Once an interpreter, always an interpreter.'

PHIL: 'One time when you weren't there, Pa double-booked. The bell rang and I opened the door. It was a Dutch woman, not much of a looker, though that never seemed to bother Pa. I'm still amazed at how quickly he managed to manoeuvre those women into his bedroom. Probably told them it was easier to talk in there, so his sons couldn't hear. We were part of his gambit, I'm sure of that. Anyway, no sooner had he locked his bedroom door, than the bell rang again. His next victim was so beautiful even I wouldn't have minded. I didn't know what to do and eventually sat her down in the room we used to stay in. I kept her talking for ages in the hope Pa would soon be done with that desperate damsel from Den Helder or wherever she came from. I made Number Two a cup of tea, apologized till I was blue in the face and put on some lute music to spare her any grunts and squeals from the other room. We sat there for an hour. I spent an hour gazing at the most beautiful woman Pa had ever blown it with because of his own stupid fault. I finally saved his honour by escorting her back to the bus stop. Her honour too, of course. Pa could have kicked himself when he found out later.'

AL: 'And laughed that stupid laugh of his, I bet?'

PHIL: 'Yes, people were little more than objects in his universe. Even if he had made a go of it with that blonde stunner, he would have wound up knocking her about too. That's what happened with his third wife, that German bird.'

AL: 'Renate.'

PHIL: 'Yeah, she left after an incident like that. Warned him from the start, one slap and I'm gone. But then she came back and he never hit her again.'

AL: 'She stuck with him for a while, even moved to Haarlem with him. There she spent a lot of time in bed, maybe life with him was starting to get her down. She called me once from Germany, after she had finally left. She wanted to say goodbye to me, but she sounded tired – tired of life and, above all, disappointed in love. I was fond of her. She knew all about flamenco music, and a fair bit about literature and world history.'

PHIL: 'When was that?'

AL: 'I can't remember. I do remember being there when they

got married in Voorschoten, I was the only family member in attendance. What a poor excuse for a wedding that was! When it was all over, we had a meal at that Chinese restaurant across from the children's home. And later, after you had moved to Geneva, he married that Spanish woman. She had her old man with her, one of those proud, old-school Spaniards, and her young son from a previous marriage. Pa used to play weird games with that little boy. He would hold him by the ankles and dangle him with his head just inches from the floor, that kind of thing. It was only then it hit me how strangely he behaved with little kids. There was always a dangerous edge to his games. Didn't Ma always say he was a sadist? Swinging a child out over the edge of a ravine in Indonesia, or dangling them over a balcony railing in the Netherlands. Pa kept dangling that son of hers upside down and just before the kid's head went smack on the floor, he would stop and give this strange little laugh. That old Spaniard's face was rigid with suppressed rage and eventually he took his grandson on his lap. Man, was I ashamed! His Spanish bride was on cloud nine and danced flamenco to gramophone records she had brought with her from Spain. Within seconds the downstairs neighbours came charging up to complain about the racket her high heels were making. Pa just about beat the complainers from his front door. Christ, that was some wedding day.'

PHIL: 'How long did that one last?'

AL: 'A few weeks, if that. It was easy to see that coming. Hey, do you remember that beefy Portuguese woman he had, the one who used to be an opera singer? She would do her vocal exercises all day, ha ha. Her voice echoed through the flat. He sent her back to Portugal but he couldn't get rid of her and eventually Pa got you to write and tell her he'd been committed to an asylum, ha ha ha!'

PHIL: 'Ha ha, yes! It's all coming back to me! Must have been quite a letter. We never heard another word from Portugal.'

AL: 'What language did you write it in anyway?'

PHIL: 'Pa dictated something in Portuguese and I made up all kinds of other shit, in French, ha ha! About him being locked away in some loony bin, under investigation for trafficking in women. That we, his children, had had him committed – that was his idea.'

AL: 'Oh, hang on, and a week later I went to visit him in Haarlem and this really sweet Swedish woman had moved in. She literally used to tiptoe around so as not to disturb Pa. She wanted to do everything for him, but he was always taking over her chores and doing them himself. Odd, that. Man, she was sweet. Such a sweet lady.'

PHIL: 'And?'

AL: 'Never saw her again.'

PHIL: 'Do you remember how Pa always used to blame everything on his sign of the zodiac? Like he was proud of it?'

AL: 'Yeah, he infected us with that too, with his books on astrology. Claimed that as a Libra his reason and his emotions were always in balance. Not a word of truth in that. Then again, he never could make up his mind: should I hang this up here or over there? And eventually he'd hang one of those *batiks* of his on this wall, only to take it down ten minutes later and hang it on that wall after all, ha ha.'

PHIL: 'Astrology was just a plaything to him. He used it to juice up his letters to all those women, but he didn't know the first thing about it. Did you know that the ancient astrologers only worked with nine or ten signs of the Zodiac? With the rise of the natural sciences, a line was drawn between astrology as an occult science and astronomy as a modern science. The astrologers were stuck with a gap between Virgo and Scorpio, and for want of a smooth transition they came up with Libra. The scales. A strange symbol when you think about it. Libra, along with Aquarius and Gemini, is an air sign. As humans, the water-carrier and the twins still have a place in the Zodiac menagerie, but there's nothing human, never mind animal, about Libra. A set of scales is an instrument, a machine, an inanimate object! A perfect instrument that merely responds to commands.'

AL: 'Look, you really need to read that shit… sorry, that prose of his. Put a weight on the scales and the balance tips: could a government ask for a better soldier? That's your style, to explain away Pa's actions in terms of astrology. But however much you explain, it's what you can't explain that really counts.'

PHIL: 'Well then, stick to your guitar. Music needs no explanation. You chose the right gig.'

Esteemed Smart Arse (1)

Yesterday evening, I skimmed and scanned my way through Pa's memoirs from start to finish. Then I spent the whole night dreaming about them. Jesus, I thought it would never end, one dream after another. It was only this morning, after I got up and took a shower that I finally had a proper kip on the couch. Hats off to you for digging around in Pa's past the way you have. I would rather have spent a year in the isolation cell at our old children's home in Voorschoten.

Philip Noland

No virus found in this message

My Dear Inquisitor

In that case, how about a little food for thought so we can put our heads together and work out how realistic Pa's version of events is? Three weeks after what Pa called the second prisoner transport, the head of the Navy's top brass sent a letter to the Minister of Defence. In it, he referred to that transport as – wait for it – *the Corpse Train*… A Dutch TV journalist thought this was in such bad taste that, fifty years on, he decided to make it the title of his book on the subject. He tracked me down – you were still living in Geneva at the time – and came round to poke his nose into Pa's manuscript while I was in the room next door giving a guitar lesson. He skimmed and scanned too, and only extracted the pages about that miserable prisoner transport of Pa's. With my permission, he photocopied them and set to work, collecting the declarations and eyewitness accounts of former marines from Brabant and Limburg. And, so he claimed, secret documents and recordings stored in a safe at the Ministry of Defence. He said there was a typed transcript from Surabaya of Pa being questioned at the time. Did they even use tape recorders in those days? Pa never mentioned them.

To save you reading the book, here's a brief summary of what the journalist wrote about the Corpse Train. Pa's prisoners were on a separate transport, remember – let's call that one 'the Ghost Train'. As you will see, the journalist's version differs substantially from Pa's account. Pa doesn't sketch the political background, to which he was oblivious. Let's face it, what man on the ground knew the score back then? Allow the universal soldier to eavesdrop on his puppet masters and he'll run a mile before you know where you are.

It all begins in London 1943, where a bunch of commanding officers acting as advisors to the cowardly Dutch government-in-exile hatch a plan to win the Dutch East Indies back from the Japanese. In Camp Lejeune in the US state of North Carolina, the first four hundred Dutch marines, drummed up from all over the world, are given special training. After the liberation of the southern Netherlands, a major recruitment campaign persuades a bunch of volunteers to join the force. By May 1945, there are already a few thousand American-trained Dutch marines. Atom bombs are dropped and Japan capitulates. Oh well, time to dissolve the Marine Brigade before it has even gone into action. But then the goalposts are shifted: with the Indies stampeding towards independence, this brand-new Brigade can help bring the wayward colony back under Dutch control.

When at the end of 1945, thousands of marines armed with heavy, modern American weapons set sail for the Dutch East Indies, they are not allowed into the country. The British, who have been given temporary charge of the Indies, believe the situation is fine as it is and have no desire to see tensions rise. How right they were. After a few weeks spent sulking and cooling their heels on an old plantation in Malacca, the marines are granted permission to land in the Indies after all. An instant recipe for trouble, as the Marine Brigade is attached to the army's A Division. This strips the naval commanders of all direct authority and the Brigade is assigned East Java as its field of combat, the very region where the relatives of Pa's father Willem Nolan own vast plantations.

The army's primary focus was strategic, whereas the Marine Brigade saw themselves as a bunch of action heroes. In no time, Pa and his comrades have a whole swathe of East Java under their control but as Pa writes in his memoirs, they are reined back in for the sake of detente, though no agreement between the Dutch government and the newly declared Republic of Indonesia actually materializes. Meanwhile, the financial burden of maintaining a 100,000-strong Dutch army overseas begins to weigh heavily on the government in The Hague. A decision is taken to acquire significant assets by capturing as many stretches of fertile land as possible by force. This is done in the hope that capital will once again start to flow. All with the aim of steering the former colony to independence on terms set by the Dutch, rather than simply entrusting the process to the Indonesians.

A code name is dreamt up for the battle plan: Operation Product. A military offensive sold back in Holland as the First Police Action – a deceptive term that will stand the test of time. This job is given to the Marine Brigade in East Java, and they get it done in a matter of days. But their success is largely down to the Indonesians pulling out of many areas in preparation for a guerrilla war. Even as a lad of 22, Pa more or less sussed that out. He and his comrades also took over police operations in the city and this generated a lot of ill will among the Indonesian police, many of whom joined the guerrillas out of sheer frustration.

Pa was with the Security Service of the Marine Brigade and they were tasked with intelligence work. Little wonder that the army quickly lost sight of what he and his cronies were up to. With their typical Marine zeal, they made far too many arrests, and the prisons were soon full to overflowing.

The Marine Brigade Security Service began to get a bad name. In East Java they became synonymous with torture and cruelty. 'Everything's under control' was the official line sent back to The Hague, but those on the ground knew damn well that things had turned very messy since the First Police Action. As Pa discovered in his prisoner interrogations, the dyke had burst and there was no plugging the leaks. Around this time, the Marine Brigade asked to have its remit extended, most notably to include summary executions. Thankfully, the Commander of A Division failed to issue a response, otherwise the havoc wreaked by Pa and his comrades in East Java would have known no bounds. The army and the marines had never hit it off and there was even talk of disbanding the Marine Brigade altogether. It's clear that they were a bunch of maniacs in any case.

The plan to disband the Brigade was shelved, but its numbers were reduced to three battalions of 1,300 men each. That left around 3,900 men in total. Let's round it up to four thousand: who knows whether Pa and his 'native' comrades were even included in the official figures.

The journalist who wrote about the Corpse Train zoomed in on the prisoner transport which left after Pa's train. Of the hundred prisoners on board, forty-six were dead on arrival in Surabaya. Pa's transport was an earlier train, a Ghost Train that never made the news.

The prisoner transports were needed to ease the pressure in the overcrowded prisons. In Bondowoso there were almost three hundred people in custody, one hundred over the limit. It was therefore essential that one hundred prisoners be transported to Surabaya. The wagons for the Corpse Train were ordered the previous day, while Pa had to make arrangements for his Ghost Train on the day itself. The lieutenant in charge of the Corpse Train clearly had a remarkably low IQ and did something Pa would never have done: he shut all the doors tight and secured them with steel wire.

Into one of the wagons of the Corpse Train, a prisoner has smuggled a couple of bananas and a fork, which he uses to prick a hole in the floor. A banana leaf is rolled up to serve as a straw through which the prisoners take turns to suck a little oxygen into their lungs on what meteorological records later reveal to be the hottest day of 1947. When the train arrives at Wonokromo station in the south of Surabaya after a journey of nearly 140 miles – eleven hours without water, without food, with no ventilation and a debilitating lack of oxygen – the Military Police are unable to open the third and last wagon. Railway personnel have to be called in to lend a hand. The door opens at last, and the hush inside is immediately apparent. Initially, the military policemen think it's a silent protest, though the surviving prisoners from the first two wagons are already beginning to stagger onto the platform. When the second sergeant major realizes that the third wagon contains nothing but dead bodies, he collapses – a luxury not afforded to the survivors from the other wagons, who are given the absurd order to drag the corpses of their fellow prisoners from the train and lay them out on the platform. The Military Police count forty-six dead prisoners and fifty-four survivors. The bodies are loaded onto trucks. The living have to sit among the dead and carry the corpses into the hospital on arrival. Then they are thrown into Werfstraat prison, except for the eleven who are in such a bad way that they are admitted to hospital for treatment.

Have you read the *Memorandum on Excesses*, Phil? The Dutch government's investigation into war crimes committed by its forces during Indonesia's war of independence. Perhaps you've never even heard of it. Demands have often been made for a new version, a new farce if you like, since the so-called excesses it details were standard practice. That piece of shit document was published the year I stood at Pa's front door and he asked:

'Why did you forsake me?'

I assume Pa has never read it and neither have you. In pursuit of his Corpse Train, the journalist took an investigative trip to Java and writes that the *Memorandum on Excesses* devotes only a few paragraphs to what it calls the 'Bondowoso Affair'.

When the press finally got wind of the Corpse Train, the Marine Brigade issued a communiqué stating that over fifty previous transports had taken place and that over 2,800 prisoners had been relocated without a hitch. The focus therefore came to rest firmly on the Corpse Train, though Pa's Ghost Train travelled almost exactly the same route and certainly encountered a hitch or two.

According to the journalist, who wastes relatively few words on Pa, four Indonesians died on his Ghost Train, in a covered goods wagon that was sealed tight. He makes no mention of the first prisoner who made a run for it when Pa opened the door in Probolinggo, the man Pa says he shot dead on the spot (death number one). No mention of the second prisoner who tried to escape and wound up hanging from a barbed-wire fence (death number two). No mention of the third prisoner who tried to jump from the train as it crossed a bridge.

Ong shot, but missed. Then I took aim and the fugitive plunged into the ravine. (Death number three.)

No mention of the two prisoners who tried to jump from the train between Bangil and Sidoarjo and who were shot dead by Pa and his helpers (deaths four and five). And no mention of the prisoner who tried to flee in Sidoarjo and was gunned down by Pa (death number six).

Pa reports that three prisoners had succumbed to the stifling conditions by the time the train reached Pasuruan and two more come Sidoarjo. Of the twenty-nine prisoners, Pa delivered eighteen alive and five dead to the Military Police.

Eighteen plus five makes twenty-three. That leaves six missing prisoners: five shot while escaping and one caught in a barbed-wire fence and left for dead. The numbers in Pa's version add up. Which makes me wonder whether the Military Police checked that tally properly against the paperwork Pa was supposed to hand over.

The total of five suffocated prisoners who Pa says were dead on arrival at the final destination is one more than mentioned by the journalist. And what did the Military Police make of the six who never arrived at all?

The journalist states that the facts surrounding the four deaths on Pa's Ghost Train were known to the head of the Marine Brigade, the Commander of Naval Forces, the Public Prosecutor and the Minister for the Overseas Territories. Yet at the time, the minister claimed he knew nothing about the incident until he received a telegram from Governor Van Mook two weeks later, which suggests that the minister deliberately omitted these facts when informing parliament. The *Memorandum on Excesses*, published around twenty years later, makes do with a vague statement that on the day before the Bondowoso Affair another prisoner transport had run into problems but that no further attention was paid to the incident.

In short, the journalist's reconstruction of Pa's Ghost Train is as follows:

Adjutant Mulder had decided that the prisoners should be transported by train and put Nolan (without a *d*), a 'young man of twenty-two from the region', in charge of the transport. Was this a job for an interpreter? That question doesn't seem to occur to the journalist. Did he even know that Pa was an interpreter? The journalist names the three guards allocated to Pa as stated in the memoirs. He also describes how Pa's request for an open cattle truck was denied by the stationmaster. In addition, Pa reportedly asked for permission to smash two barred windows in the side of the wagon to give the prisoners some air. Why doesn't he mention that in his own account?

At half past ten in the morning, the prisoners were herded onto the train in the blistering heat at Jember station. The wagon stood for forty minutes in the burning sun before the train departed. A survivor of the Ghost Train recalled that, even at the station, conditions in the wagon were unbearable and a few of the prisoners quickly lost consciousness. According to the journalist, Pa first assessed the situation at Klakah station, had the guards throw water over the prisoners, purchased rice and fruit with his own money and sent one of the guards to buy drinks. And not, as Pa says, only 19 miles further on in Probolinggo. The journalist says all of the prisoners were revived in Klakah, but one man suffered a nervous attack and Pa decided to hand him over to the Military Police to be admitted to hospital – a damn sight more humane than shooting him in cold blood. But in his memoirs, Pa doesn't even mention Klakah as a stop on the journey, let alone handing a prisoner over to the Military Police. According to the journalist, a prisoner asked for more room in Probolinggo and Pa agreed, allowing seven sick men to lie down while he ordered twenty-one men to climb aboard another wagon. None of this is described in Pa's memoirs either. From Probolinggo on, the wagons were left open, while the guards kept their weapons trained on the doors. In Pa's version, one of the prisoners made a run for it and died hanging from a barbed-wire fence.

As Pa tells it, when his Ghost Train arrived in Wonokromo – around seven-thirty in the evening after a nine-hour journey – he immediately made a phone call to report the incident. He was then questioned by two corporals from the Military Police, who drew up their own report. According to the journalist, he was then taken to barracks and ordered to make himself available for further questioning. In Pa's version, he first went to see his mother and slept well into the next day. Then he headed for the Marines Club and downed a dozen stiff drinks. You know our father has never been able to hold his drink. One glass of fruit wine and his head was spinning. Maybe the Dutch climate sapped his tolerance for alcohol, who knows? From the Marines Club he returned to Firefly Barracks. Of course, the journalist might have dispensed with these details as irrelevant to the case.

The wagon of Pa's Ghost Train was some twenty-three feet long and made of wood. But a layer of asphalt on the roof caused the temperature to rise dramatically, especially at the smaller stations with insufficient cover. Pa was indeed heard by the same panel that handled the case of the Corpse Train. According to the journalist, he was not given a ten-year suspended sentence, as Pa writes, but was unconditionally acquitted with immediate effect, having taken every measure within his power. Contrary to his own account, Pa did not have to appear before the court martial. The journalist writes that only the suspects from the Corpse Train were summoned to appear, the aim being to hush up what had happened to the Ghost Train Pa cursed so bitterly.

The journalist argues that this is why neither the general public, parliament, nor the international press ever found out what had occurred the day before the Corpse Train drama. Even the Republic of Indonesia was never told about Pa's Ghost Train. And if no one knows, then it never happened. At best, his story would always be dismissed as fiction. I should add that the journalist only managed to interview one Ghost Train survivor.

Alan Noland

No virus found in this message

Esteemed Smart Arse (2)

I received your email – epistle, should I say. I even read it. Counting corpses now are we? What's got into you, man? You'll be digging them up and dissecting them next. Don't be taken in by some sanctimonious TV journalist who spreads lies for a living. Screaming bloody murder at the government by day, only to meet up with ministers by night to chow down on lobster at some swish brasserie. It's a report churned out by an ageing hack who booked himself a tax-deductible trip to East Java fifty years after the fact, where he managed to interview all of one survivor and poke around in a bunch of so-called secret archives, which he labels reliable or unreliable according to whether or not they suit his story. Pa's memory might not be all that clear, but at least he was *there*. So who has more right to the truth? You'd pick the journalist because, as he tells it, Pa didn't shoot a single prisoner. But Pa was the man on the train. The man charged with transporting those prisoners. It could well be that they doctored the documents Pa submitted, altered the number of prisoners on the Ghost Train without his knowledge. And who says Pa had any paperwork to hand in? This was war: corners were cut all the time. Oh, and learn to read while you're at it… Pa's account mentions a procedural demand of ten years' imprisonment. That was a sentence in name only and didn't amount to anything. Why don't you stick to music? Play guitar instead of lugging Pa's past around with you. You'll collapse under the weight of it if you don't watch out. Be Zen… Zen, I tell you! But I know what you're like, so let me dig around and see if I can't find us some official documents. There's something fishy about those job titles: guide, interpreter, marine, member of the Marine Brigade Security Service, informer, spy and what have you. None of it adds up. Watch this space. Amen.

Philip Noland

No virus found in this message

Waiting

As the missives from the Costa del Sol gradually peter out, I wonder if the Eagle is sitting there waiting for death. Literally sitting and waiting. Apparently there are people who consciously wait for their own death, and who wake up every morning deeply disappointed. Meanwhile others are locked in a constant battle to beat the shadow of death from their door. Take Ma, for example. She would wring death's neck with her own bare hands given half a chance. It has never occurred to her what a hell eternal life must be. Not that I'm waiting for the Eagle to die; I would like to talk to him again. Not about the things we have never been able to talk about. Just about his life there, the little things that make up his everyday existence. How long has it been since we saw each other? Fifteen years? What kind of father and son are we anyway? I remember the last time I dropped by to see him unannounced in that desperate hole of his in Haarlem – he was happy as a kid to clap eyes on me again. That surprised me. Really surprised me. I had stayed away a long time, ever since that Christmas when he and Arti spread the festive cheer by threatening each other across the dinner table with a knife and a pair of scissors. As the eldest son, I stood up, walked out, drove off in my car and left them to stab each other to death. Phil was living in Switzerland by that time and wanted nothing more to do with any of us. I had no idea what was wrong with him, knew only that he lived on the 27th floor with a view of Lake Geneva. When you're up that high, you've clearly had enough of other people's crap. We called each other once a year, if that. The day after their festive face-off, the Eagle and Arti called me up. I was sleeping when the phone rang, lifted the receiver and my Boxing Day began to the sound of their voices on speakerphone. I listened and said nothing, left those two hardmen to wonder out loud if there was something wrong with the line. I felt relief that thank God their macho bullshit had not resulted in an actual stabbing, then crawled back into bed without a word, leaving the line open. I did not say goodbye to Pa when he was all set to trade one country for another for the second time in his life. I don't remember why. Perhaps I didn't want to say goodbye. Perhaps I didn't want to believe he was actually leaving for Spain. Perhaps I'm incapable of goodbyes. They say it's something you should learn at an early age. It's not something you learn when you've been dumped in a children's home from one moment to the next.

With the passing of time, a kind of indifference has come over me, one the Eagle must feel too. Neither of us sent a card when the year 2000 arrived. Does that consign our story to last century? I'm happy to say I haven't feared him for a long time. He's too old for that now. I practise the martial arts; he wouldn't stand a chance. I am not the coward he was, the kind who hits women and children.

Nor do I hit old people. Hitting back is something I should have done at twenty-one. I carried a pocket knife back then, tucked in my boot, ready to cut his throat. A deed I had already done in my darkest thoughts. I would catch the bus to Voorschoten, where he lived at the time and, standing at the entrance to his flat, I would take the knife from my boot and clasp it tight in my right coat pocket. Up the stairs I go, ring the bell, he opens the door… What kind of person are you, if you knife your father in cold blood?

At times I wonder what it will be like when he is dead. Will my hatred die with him? Will I become as witless as every other mortal, for whom nothing is simpler than honouring the dead? So cheap, so easy… It never meant much to him when someone he knew was buried six feet under and left to rot. Sarcasm was his standard response to another man's death. In that sense too, he was more colourful than your average guy. Imagine everyone being as neurotic, troubled and traumatized as him and me – it doesn't bear thinking about. Ha! 'Him and me.' The two of us in one sentence! I'll need a moment to process that, Mr Ex-Marine! 'Him and me' but not quite 'us'.

The dead live on in us, or so they say. But do we live on for the dead? If so, would he still want to hear me? See me? Read over my shoulder? Does it honestly make a difference to me if he is alive or dead? For us, I mean, for him and for me. He has still not replied to my letter about that munitions chest of his. He has stopped sending his racist newspaper clippings. His incessant urging to come and live in Spain has ceased.

At a Spanish hotel they once ushered him to the front of a queue of around thirty white Dutch people. That was before he moved there. A spot of preferential treatment he cherished almost as if it was a military honour. Do they still treat him that way, those Spaniards? His birthday cards have stopped arriving too. Not that I'm one of those loyal sons who sends his dad a card every year. Cards lie. They're small change compared to genuine attention. What's the big deal about sending a card once a year, prompted by the birthday calendar that hangs in your toilet? Nowadays it's a digital calendar that does the prompting and, if Phil is to be believed, the whole process will be automated before long. Does Pa even have an email address? I doubt it. I will go and see him. It's about time, even though I reckon a visit from him is long overdue. He has a couple of grandchildren he has never even seen, yet still he refuses to come. A worthless grandfather. Just like his own father, a drunk who lived out his last, miserable days holed up in a room at a colonial clubhouse. Even so, it's time I went. Little Sister wants to come with me, but Big Sister is having none of it: Mil and her mysterious bond with Pa, based on nothing more than the fact that he named her after an old flame of his, a name I cannot find in any of his manuscripts. She kicks up a stink anytime she gets wind that we are planning to go and see him. If we can take her word for it, she and her two woefully neglected kids are down there all the time, at Pa's side whenever we discuss our travel plans. After his worthless inheritance, no doubt. The family vulture circling above the battered figure of the Eagle as he drags himself across his lonely desert. Oh well, good luck to her.

Little Sister, our Nana, *is* still afraid of him. Terrified that once he's dead he will appear at the foot of her bed night after night and blame her for all kinds of things. Things that war-crazed mind of his has no right to blame on anyone. Strange, that fear of Nana's. She was much too young to fall into his clutches, only six when we were deported to the children's home, to use the Eagle's words. Yet still she has that fear. He's done a good job of stirring up anxiety in his children, or driving a wedge between them and the world. For Brother Phil everything – absolutely everything – is part of some conspiracy. He hates all things American and takes great pleasure in hacking into US websites. Pa must know what a website is by now, surely, or does he still wallow in front of the TV all day, like some washed-up sea lion? Mil says that telly of his is blaring away from six in the morning, which means he's still living on Java time. Meanwhile Brother Arti is celebrating his third decade as a heroin addict, an achievement of sorts. Thanks to the scores of minor offences that come with a life of addiction, that boy has seen the inside of every jail in Holland. He keeps trying to kick the habit but abstinence almost instantly brings out the tormented adolescent in him. A life story made for the small screen! As we all know, the life story of the Eagle himself is beyond compare, even when rendered in the second-rate Orange-tinted Indo prose of a conflicted soldier. Perhaps that's why he began to hate the Belandas: because they had no desire to read it. He used to look up to those loutish Belanda soldiers back on Java. For all their shortcomings, they came from the land of his late father, though the man was born in Jember and only went to Holland to attend high school and study law. Even so, the Eagle felt abandoned when his father died. But what's all that about? What did he want to find in Holland? Footprints in the clay? Yes, he was forced to flee, we know that. But what drove him to the point where fleeing was his only option? That's the real question. Try as I might, I cannot distil the essence from those writings of his. Was it being forced to be a baldy bastard up to the age of twelve? Whenever he's at a loss to explain his actions, he resorts to the notorious 'native' state referred to in dusty old colonial literature as *mata gelap*. The dark mist of rage. Yeah, sorry, I went a bit *mata gelap* there for a minute, can't be helped. What's going on there? Try trotting that out at the war tribunal here in The Hague and see where it gets you! If his memoirs had been shot through with the motif of the son's admiration for his father's Eurasian origins and status, I might have understood it, to some extent at least. But raging like a madman simply because you've sided with the House of Orange? No, I just can't buy it. What did his father really mean to him? *That's* what he needed to write about! He was probably unaware that his father refused to speak Dutch when he conversed with plantation owners. I heard that from Daatje, with whom I share a grandmother. She is a granddaughter of Sie Swan Nio's first marriage, while I am a grandson of Sie Swan Nio's non-marriage to that father of Pa's. When I visited Yogyakarta during my stay with Aunty Ella, Daatje told me that my grandfather preferred to speak English in the colonial Indies, and imported his own whisky. Our esteemed legal practitioner saw himself as a Scot first and foremost. And he despised the Dutch. But why? The Eagle spoke Dutch because he felt himself to be a Dutchman born of the Indies and now hates the Dutch as much as his father did. And yet he fought for them... Let's just say he wound up hating them and leave it at that. And truth be told, the Hollanders didn't exactly shower him with gratitude. They wouldn't even salute him in the street! If only he had been allowed to strut around the streets of Holland in uniform. Not far from where I live, there's a first-generation Indo who does exactly that. He walks the streets in jungle camouflage gear with a red beret on his head. Paratrooper. Steeped himself in war for an additional half a century. The man is lean, with the hunted eyes of a predator, and he constantly mumbles to himself as he walks. Listen closely as he passes and you'll catch him bad-mouthing both the Belandas and the Indonesians in Malay. Now and again he calls out to me, forgetting for a moment that I am second generation and worthy only of his contempt because we barely speak a word of the old tongue. I happen to know where he lives. His house, like Aunty Lique's back in the day, has a window display. It hangs full of newspaper clippings about the conflict in Indonesia and his own face features in one or two, from the time when local newspapers still used to cover the colonial war.

Forty years as an Indo, trudging through the muck and mire of the Netherlands, must have been a heavy price to pay for Pa, tantamount to torture. One by one his old friends vanished in the mist and no new ones presented themselves. Yes, there were women. They came and went. Until he grew dog-tired of this country, tired of all those women, and reached sixty-five and retirement at last. And when night after night his three sons stood as apparitions at the foot of his bed, it was time to flee again, this time to Spain. Dear God! Apparently he slept with an axe under his bed in that Haarlem flat with the two spare bedrooms in which none of us ever slept. One thing sent shivers up his spine more than any other: the delusion that Arti would creep into his flat one night and slit his throat. Why Arti? That boy missed Pa just as much as Pa missed his own father. Suppose our Arti had turned up one night, simply to tell his father how much he missed him, would Pa have buried that axe in his skull and sent his youngest son to an early grave? I thought we Indos were supposed to fight unarmed? At most clutching a girlfriend's lipstick holder or a bunch of keys in one fist. Axes are for Russians. A man filled with hate should never betray his roots. The Eagle was a coward. He ran away from us, his own sons, his own flesh and blood. And from the wind and rain and chill of cosy old Holland… that too.

The night

Meanwhile there's a question that will not leave me be. Do the nightmares of the father infect the son? Do I share them without him even knowing? When I go to sleep, it's never with my back to the door… still frightened as a child in the dark. It has made me a night owl. I play and teach guitar in the afternoon and evening. At night I write these words. Or read a novel. Or – a real talent this – I stare into space and talk to myself. Dialogues not monologues, because a voice inside me answers. Not a ghost or a stranger. The voice is my own.

The night is my enemy, my father's paladin, and so I stay awake. A vigil that lets me keep a close watch on the night. Heir to the Eagle, who slept with his eyes half-open. Days bore me, if I'm honest. They are not my friends. Tolerable at best, when summer brings sun enough for the beach and the slosh of the sea. Otherwise the days here in Holland are hellish grey. Yet as soon as I cross the border, I live by day, rejoin the rest of humanity: Indonesia, Greece,

America, France… Even the likes of Germany, Austria or Scotland, where the cold can be just as cruel. Another indication that something's up. Then again, perhaps it makes perfect sense… My father's war raged overseas, but for me it is set in Holland. And so it's only in Holland that the night is a threat that keeps me watchful and wary. One strange noise is enough to send me creeping up or downstairs in search of an intruder. Sometimes I grab the *sai,* the three-pronged Japanese weapon Uncle Karel handled so well, or the *bō*, the Japanese staff I wield for my kata moves at the *dojo*. There I stand, primed to beat any trespasser to a pulp. All out of fear – fear of whom? The Eagle, my father, is thousands of miles away. Yet he is the only one who comes to mind.

Given the crimes he committed, the Eagle's fear that some *kris*-wielding Javanese might burst into the bedroom and slit his throat is understandable – for an adult, not for a child. But the fear that seizes me is too complex, I cannot explain it to anyone. Like my old man, I have been through dozens of girlfriends. Sadly, I have turned out to be an impossible creature, barely capable of cohabitation. Each and every girlfriend got to hear my list of bedtime instructions: dos and don'ts in case she woke to see a maniac dive out of bed in the middle of the night and cower in a corner, trembling. Do not run to me. Keep your distance. Do not touch me, or my fear will turn to violence. Call me by my name. Then I will hear that you are a sweet woman with whom I have shared a loving embrace. And not the ghost of my childhood, the Eagle who stalked me when I sleepwalked and pelted me in the face with cold wet flannels.

Whacking your sleepwalking son in the face with a wet flannel, is that an act of paranoia? A paranoid man has no time for games, seems to me – what, with the government, neighbours, friends and family breathing down his neck. Or in this case your son, an eight-year-old boy whose bed was never his friend, only a place from which to run. At the children's home, surrounded by the other boys in the dormitory, I did sleep through the night. And never once walked in my sleep.

How the Eagle used to hate my sleepwalking. One night I walked clean out of the house and rang the neighbours' doorbell. A kind couple, they opened the door and even let me in. Their home was nice and warm, a peaceful house where no war was raging. My freedom was short-lived. Ma fetched me back and, with a dazed look in her eyes, handed me over to the former prisoner interrogator: *'What were you up to, over there with the neighbours?'*

Was I too pro-Indonesian for him even then? He must remember the critical questions I asked as a kid, unable to grasp why he had fought for the Dutch against his own people. A beating was the only answer he gave me.

But the very last time I asked him whether he might have fought on the wrong side after all, he hesitated and then replied 'Yes... Perhaps I did, yes...'

It was shortly after he had handed me his memoirs, typed again from scratch. Believe me when I say I hope he didn't mean it. I could never wish that on him: the horror of realizing that everything he did was wrong.

Little Sister told me he wants his coffin to be draped in the red, white and blue of the Netherlands. As arranged in his last will and testament, with Big Sister as his sole beneficiary because his other four kids are clearly good for nothing. Even as a dead expat in Spain he wants to show that he fought for this cold, damp country. Funny, I always thought he wanted to be buried here in Holland. I still have a letter from him, with a copy of his funeral insurance policy. I have no idea whether it's still valid or whether he has since made other arrangements. It wouldn't surprise me. Six feet under, Dutch mud is sure to be so much colder than the soil of Spain.

The Dutch flag... Does he really think those Spaniards give a toss about a war between the Netherlands and Indonesia? They probably don't even know what the Dutch flag looks like; the red-white-and-blue comes a very distant second to the orange shirts of the Dutch football team. It's not like any of the Dutchmen and women he fought for will be standing at his graveside. The vast majority have no idea what really happened over there on the other side of the world, and those that do deny it. I know, there I go again, riding my hobby-horse into the ground. The family killjoy.

Does he refuse to come to Holland because he hates this country? Or is it just that he can't be arsed? He is one of a rare breed of grandfathers, one who has never seen his grandson, let alone heard him play guitar. He has never asked after him in any of his letters. My son is curious about his unknown granddad, asks about him now and then. The answers I give are circumspect. I am not about to follow in my crazy father's footsteps and burden him with all the shit that's going on in my head.

Hack

Here you are, Mr Smart Arse. I have purloined a secret document or two from the confidential archives, the sewers of the colonial war. 'Hacking' to us geeks. I have read Pa's memoirs, three times no less, from A to Z. And unlike your good self, I am completely on Pa's side. To you, dear brother, I say grab another torch and let your little light shine on other people's bullshit for once. Take a look through Pa's eyes and leave the Dutch and the Indonesians to swap their fairy tales. The official history is a lie in any case. In those interminable emails of yours, you ask me who to believe: Pa or a journalist who flies all the way to Java for one sweaty interview with a little man from a *kampong* and then tries to flog it as the scoop of the century. You don't want to see Pa as a murderer. That's your problem, and not your only one. Unlike me, you have never been in military service. You didn't even make it to the end of the medical! They took one look and knew you weren't fit for the army. You'd have been out there in your foxhole strumming your guitar and serenading the enemy. Riddle me this, Smart Arse: can anyone in military service, who has been given a licence to bump people off, honestly be called a murderer? Was our very own Soldier of

Orange, immortalized on stage and screen, a murderer? No? Then what was he… a hero? Oh, so what does that make Pa? Read the confidential documents attached. Wait and watch this space for an email about something Pa kept to himself. And wait means wait! Don't bug me in the meantime. I'm working on a synth track in 11/8 time.

Philip Noland

No virus found in this message

Secret

THE ROYAL NAVY OF THE NETHERLANDS
Marine Corps

Surabaya, 12 March 1947.

No. 220/3/47/509
From: Commander of the Marine Brigade
To: Commander of Naval Forces in the Dutch East Indies
Subject: Payment of civilian interpreters
Ref.: Your letter No. A2 3a/1/3 dated November 1946

I have the honour of informing Your Excellency as follows.

1. At the time of your above-mentioned correspondence, the following salary scale applied to Civilian Interpreters in the service of the Marine Brigade.

1st class:	65 guilders per month
2nd class:	95 guilders per month
3rd class:	155 guilders per month
4th class:	200 guilders per month

2. It transpires that the designation of 'interpreter' is an inaccurate representation of the military nature of the work carried out by said personnel. Allow me to draw your attention to the fact that the majority of them engage in the same work as military servicemen

on the front line. They are both uniformed and armed, and given the particular nature of their work, are often exposed to even greater risks than the men of the infantry patrols.

Such circumstances had not been envisaged at the outset.

In other respects too, most notably the interrogation of prisoners of war and the drawing up of reports and/or recommendations, their work goes far beyond the duties that the service originally had in mind for them.

3. It therefore appears to me to be not only desirable but also essential that the personnel in question be paid to a level that reflects their present role.

As regards distribution across the four classes, I would like to maintain the current distinctions but bring them in line with the levels of pay given to Marine First Class, Corporal, Sergeant and Sgt Major or Adjutant, i.e. approx. 100, 155, 225 and 300 Dutch guilders per month respectively. Such an arrangement would, in my opinion, result in a fair pay structure.

4. This arrangement is solely intended to apply to the uniformed and armed section of these employees.

For those to whom this does not apply, the existing payment structure should be maintained.

I would like to request that you look kindly upon this proposal and notify me of your decision as swiftly as possible by telegram.

Commander of the Marine Brigade, Colonel of the Marine Corps,

[signature]

Reply

2 June 47

R.168/4/17

CIVILIAN INTERPRETERS.

----

1. In response to your correspondence of 12 March 1947 No. 220/3/47/509, I have the honour of informing you, my distinguished colleague, that I was struck by the fact that a number of the civilian interpreters are uniformed and armed.
2. While such a situation is understandable, I am compelled to point out that it runs counter to their position as civilian public servants and may place both the service and the individuals concerned in considerable difficulties.
3. Having accepted the proposal that the interpreters in question should be given the status of military personnel, I request that you provide a list of the surnames and given names of the individuals concerned, accompanied by date and place of birth, nationality and the military rank that, in your opinion, they should be given within the Marine Brigade. In the event that they already have military status, please state their current position and/or rank and the relevant section of the armed forces.

I would also appreciate a copy of the security screening report for each individual.
4. My aim is to incorporate the civilian interpreters into the naval forces, in accordance with Art. 99 of the military service regulations for the Dutch East Indies (I I.V. XIV) and in a rank befitting the authority they are to exercise, or compatible with the services required of them.
5. In the event that one or more of these men are currently in military service with a branch of the armed forces other than the Royal Navy, the necessary measures will be taken at this end to bring about their transfer to the naval forces.
6. Another possibility for calling up these individuals for military service is contained in Military Regulation No. 157, a copy of which is attached for your cognizance.
7. If you would prefer these men to be drafted and brought into

service by the Marine Brigade in accordance with the above regulation, might I request that you inform me accordingly.

The Vice-Admiral,
Commander of Naval Forces in the Dutch East Indies,
signing on his behalf:
The Head of Department I,
Naval Captain,
Commander of the Marine Brigade
S u r a b a y a.

[signature]

Special Service Employees

Dear Mr Smart Arse,

At *kenpō* school, I recently trained with three generations of the same family: son, father and grandfather, an old man from the former Dutch East Indies. That old man, the school's founder, was the embodiment of *zanchin*. He sat there on the couch surfing the net on his laptop, but nothing escaped his notice. The second his son or grandson missed a beat in the demonstration, he was up on his feet correcting them. I got talking to the old man and he asked about my name, like they always used to with Pa: if it was Nolan without a *d*, you know the story. He was Ambonese and knew Pa from back in the day, though the difference in their ages meant they never fought alongside one another. Under colonial rule he was registered as a 'native', which gave him no incentive whatsoever to side with the Dutch. Pa with his semi-European status was at least one rung up the social ladder, at school if nowhere else. Our native boy from Ambon could just as easily have fought for the Indonesians, if they had been the ones to shove a rifle in his hands. His only thought when revolution broke out was that he needed a weapon and fast. It barely mattered to him which side he fought on, as long as he was able to defend himself. It was sheer coincidence that he ended up with the Marines, where he and Pa crossed paths once in a while.

Here's where it gets interesting... Do you know what they called him and Pa and all those other 'native chaps'? Special Service Employees. That was the official name for the interpreters. It's a title Pa never uses. Understandably, because for him it was all about being a marine. Being a marine meant he was somebody. As a Special Service Employee, he was nobody.

When soldiers arrive in a strange land and can't speak the lingo, they need to enlist local interpreters and guides. This was also true of the Dutch Marine Brigade, dispatched to Indonesia when the Netherlands refused to relinquish sovereignty.

Pa and the *kenpō* teacher were boys from East Java, cut adrift in the aftermath of the Japanese occupation. They spoke several languages, knew the local customs, were able to distinguish between the various sections of the population and were ready recruits for those macho Dutch marines. Those secret documents prove that their role went way beyond that of guide or interpreter. For the British they were guides, for the Dutch they were interpreters with an extremely broad remit. Reason enough to keep them out of the history books, quite apart from the fatherland's general reluctance to bring up the matter of colonial violence. As Special Service Employees, they did not qualify as members of the military, but they *were* armed. A crafty job title, Special Service Employee: it covers a multitude of sins, as those boys found out to their cost.

In the grand scheme of things, you would expect the marines to go in and attack a village, round up any suspects and haul them back to base for interrogation, where the interpreters would be waiting. But an army is little more than a hastily assembled bunch of lads who given half a chance would rather be splashing about in the *kali* with the local babes. So they send the Special Services Employees on ahead as cannon fodder and follow along behind providing cover. According to the *kenpō* teacher, the SSE boys were more heavily armed than the average marine. That explains those photos where you see them wielding daggers, cutlasses and sometimes even samurai swords, alongside their modern firearms and hand grenades. For years you thought the Dutch asked the questions and all Pa did was interpret and type it all up. And yes, that's how it was supposed to be. Poor Pa, sitting at his typewriter, looks on as Indonesian rebels are horribly tortured and it drives him mad. That's what you want to believe. Only that means pushing Pa's memoirs aside, dismissing them as fiction. But, by definition, war is not the way things are supposed to be. War is anarchy dressed up, a masquerade of uniforms, ranks and chains of command.

The *kenpō* teacher reckons there were 130 Special Service Employees like Pa, most of them assigned to the Marine Brigade Security Service, which was involved in the Police Actions. But before, between and after those campaigns a host of covert operations took place, such as Pa's hunt for the Jungle Princess. Even after a ceasefire was agreed with the Indonesians and an official demarcation line was drawn, Special Service Employees were sent across it to seize enemy fighters. An ugly business, because officially those SSE boys were not military servicemen, nor would they ever be. Some were decorated, some were not, but in the end those trappings count for nothing.

There was no military pension for Pa in recognition of what he did for his so-called fatherland. There was no psychological support in the fifties. Special Service Employees were kept under wraps. Pa could well be the only one who committed his memories to paper, to show that he and his comrades existed. What son wants to read that his father set fire to villagers' houses with rounds of phosphorus bullets and shot down anyone who fled, in the very region where he had been nursed back to health as a baby by his aunts and uncles? You don't want to know. I do. War is war, and it's as old as the human race. War is part of life. You shrink from life, and that's why you only come out at night.

*

At the end of the war, a number of Special Service Employees defected to the other side, and the Indonesians cobbled together a blacklist from the names in the defectors' notebooks. Pa's name was on there. So was the name of the *kenpō* teacher. When the first Special Service Employees were murdered, an unwritten law kicked in: 'once a marine, always a marine'. They may not have been marines, but the SSE boys were colleagues, comrades. And so the marines took them under their wing, without government permission needless to say. It was left up to Pa to fetch them from their homes, risking his life in the process, but at least the Navy commanders decided to get the SSE boys out of East Java, knowing it couldn't be left to some Queen's envoy or other. It was the Marine Corps who made sure Pa was decorated, a tribute from his comrades.

Several dozen Special Service Employees came to the Netherlands. Others went to New Guinea and wound up God knows where. In any case they were scattered to the four winds and their history was never told. The rest were dead.

Read the history books and you'd swear the war in Indonesia was all about the Royal Netherlands East Indies Army: the KNIL, the whole KNIL and nothing but the KNIL. Who in the Netherlands has ever heard of the interpreters who worked with the Marines? Pa tried to shine a light on them. So from now on you can shut up about it. Case closed.

Philip Noland

No virus found in this message

Arto, come unto us

Arto, my *anak mas*, this is your mother. Prepare yourself, my son. The time has come for us to release you from your hell on earth. Things will be better for you here than in Malaga, where you have retreated into solitude, as so many old soldiers have done in the world I left some fifty years ago. The heat in Malaga appears to be as fierce as it was back home in Surabaya. Here we reside in the cool of the mountains, the same mountains your first-born son can see in the motif on the Chinese vases I sent you care of a naval officer, a farewell gift when you had to flee Indonesia. Your first-born is burdened by your memories of the war; he bears part of your cross. Not long ago he had another nightmare about you. It was full moon, rabbits were asleep on the beach and your son saw one of those long-eared creatures wake up. Then you were in the jungle and he had to find you. Your son felt no fear – this was a game, nothing more. He wandered, searched and found you in an open meadow. But then the game was over. You wanted to fight and his fear of you returned. You laughed at his lack of practice, you jeered at him because you were young and nimble once again, dark eyes shining above your sneering mouth. Your son fell on the warm earth and his scream echoed through his bedroom. There was no one to calm him. He hurried downstairs in his dressing gown and drank a glass of water. Beside him on the couch lay a gramophone record with an army of rabbits on the cover. *Multiplication*. Your son placed the record on the turntable to listen to the guitarist. But your spirit continued to fill the living room while your son murmured to himself:

'When will you die and be damned, man? You have tormented me long enough, just as your victims have always tormented you from beyond the grave. One day they will rise up before your dying eyes, led by the first dead man on your conscience. Who was he? An old schoolfriend perhaps who sided with the enemy, who did not want to fight for the Hollanders you saw as the brothers of a neglectful father who had refused to recognize you. Perhaps your sleepless nights are filled with endless repeats of the moment when you felt your blade slide into your old friend's body as you lay retching on top of him because he had grabbed you in the panic of his death throes and would not let you go. You tore yourself away, looked around and ran from him as fast as you could. And no one except your mother saw that the innocence had gone from your eyes. One year later, at that same dark hour, your old schoolfriend appeared at the foot of your bed, elusive as a cockroach and about to multiply. The next year, he returned as two apparitions who divided into four. And the year after that, the four divided into eight. And so, after years of unfettered multiplication, a whole army inhabits the kingdom of the dead that is about to receive you and they sing in chorus: *Welcome home, Surabaya hardman, welcome into our midst!* We are many now, and still we fear you. Tell us what we did wrong, other than fight each other in a colonial war. When our war was over, we continued to pray for you as you hacked a hopeless path through the brick-and-mortar jungle of distant Holland, where closed doors can never be kicked down because a baffling power is in place to prevent such things, a power infinitely stronger than the magic of the smartest man from our youth in the Indies, the *dukun* who only welcomed death when he knew the Belandas had finally gone for good…'

Arto, I, your mother, can no longer bear to look on as my grandson is visited by visions of your old enemies feeding you to the crocodiles. The crocodile no longer swims in the *kali* of the city where you were born. Now it is only found with the shark in the Golden River on Surabaya's coat of arms. Your son has been to the river on a pilgrimage, and perhaps he will return to scatter your ashes on the water. Your friends are among us too, those who sided with the Dutch but saw the error of their ways and later fought for Indonesia. Like all of us here, they know no rancour or hatred. There is no more reason to ward off death as it rattles around your house in the hot nights of Malaga. When you are here, your son's nightmares will cease and he will forgive you for everything your war-crazed mind, your belt and your bloodied fists inflicted on your wife and children. In time he will understand that your romantic soul wanted only to fight for a white queen who, in your imagination, sat on a throne all day while her subjects bowed around her, as it was in the olden days. He will come to see that how we are born and the paths our lives take are not within our mortal grasp. Fight no longer in your dreams, Arto, but come unto us, and together we will watch over the path your son has yet to walk.

An announcement in HTML

His death was not printed in the paper. Or on a mourning card trimmed in black. It was announced on a web page designed by Phil. Mil wanted an old-school obituary, but given that his old acquaintances, distant relatives and comrades from the Marines are scattered across the globe, Phil posted the news of his passing online, and promptly got the date wrong. Pa's death was mired in confusion, in miscommunication and rows sparked by delayed messages from Mil, who had shot off to Spain as soon as she heard the news. The patriarch falls away and the family descends into anarchy. Only Nana managed to hop on a plane in time to attend the funeral with Mil. Phil couldn't have selected a better photo, a snapshot taken by Nana when the Eagle was sixty-five or thereabouts, shortly before he emigrated to Spain. Veiled in cigar smoke, the very picture of *senang*. He wasn't much of a smoker – one cigar a day perhaps. An old Nolan tradition? The family plantations in Jember had mainly grown tobacco. Nana and I always thought Phil hated Pa. It turns out we were wrong. We were right once though. When did Phil stop hating his father? After reading his memoirs? Of course, Phil's hatred has now been deflected towards our mother, who in his eyes has come to symbolize everything the Dutch don't want to know. My twin has done the old man proud. The web page is a thing of beauty, a labour of love even. The text is concise but it sings. And the dates give food for thought.

*****

Arend Noland

Surabaya, Indonesia 28 September 1925

Málaga, España 28 September 2005

Have a good

journey through space
and
time for another life

Your children and grandchildren…

[etc.]

*****

Phil has turned that contented portrait into a planet trailing cigar smoke. In the background, the Earth is suspended in an indigo sky. Distant planets twinkle and circle beyond. Pa has entered a celestial pantheon, or so it would appear. I think Phil believes in something akin to a life beyond this mortal coil. Gazing at his digital artwork, I'm almost inclined to agree.

The doctors and the authorities in Spain say there is nothing to indicate suicide. Let's face it, that's the first thought that comes to mind when a worn-out old soldier dies alone on his birthday in an anonymous Spanish apartment and is found one morning by the lady who cleans the place and fetches his groceries. Phil and I attribute the timing to the air of mystery that has always surrounded his life. My son is sad that he will never have a chance to meet his grandfather. My hilarious accounts of grandad's slap-dash, soldierly approach to cooking with frozen chicken, margarine, noodles, stock cubes and a shitload of MSG send him into fits of laughter.

Sura & Baya

The Spaniards gave Pa a stylish and efficient burial, Nana says. As far as I'm concerned, they could have thrown him to the crocodiles and sharks of Surabaya, where he came into this world. Not out of revenge for whatever he inflicted on whoever, but as the ultimate journey home. Perfect recycling. All the rage now, apparently, in his beloved America: an environmentally friendly death. The terminally ill wander off into deserts or swamps to be devoured by vultures or alligators. Not really an option in Surabaya now that such carnivores have vanished from its waterways.

Surabaya was founded in 1293 by one Radèn Wijaya, or so the story goes. The city owes its name to the shark *sura* and the crocodile *baya*, the two creatures locked in an eternal battle on Surabaya's coat of arms, against the blue background of Kali Mas, the Golden River. On my one visit to Indonesia, I went there to see for myself. The Golden River looked more like a murky Amsterdam canal heated to 32 degrees Celsius. I had no trouble imagining crocodiles swimming in the water, but that shark must have taken one hell of a wrong turn.

Still, it's not impossible. Kali Mas flows to the sea, so shark and croc might have met one day in the brackish water. Here in Holland they once found a whale in the Rhine and guided it safely out to sea. Very humane when it comes to animals, the Dutch. As was my father, judging by his memoirs.

Now that the Eagle is dead, there's not much left to hate. There are even moments when I think back on him with something that resembles love. I appear to be one of the great unwashed after all, a mere mortal who never speaks ill of the dead. I missed his funeral and the chance to lay my warm hand on his cold forehead. Strange, but since he died my nightmares have left me. And I have started to join the rest of humanity and live by day again.

Pa's grave is insured for five years and Little Sister and I have hatched a plan. When the five years are up, we will have our father cremated, coffin, flag and all. I will fly to Java with an urnful of his ashes, and place them in his mother's grave. But perhaps it would be more fitting to go to the Red Bridge over Kali Mas and scatter him on the water.

*

I recently came across a blurred photo of me taken on the Red Bridge in Surabaya. My little cousin, the grandson of that murdered Japanese pilot, accidentally moved the camera when he clicked. It's as if a ghost is leaning over the railing, looking deep into the water. Without intending to, I had followed in my father's footsteps. I was a stranger, I felt like a stranger there. My father had travelled a long, long way, an eternal stranger who rose like a monster from a cold, grey sea he thought could wash away his past. Many were those he left behind: beaten, raped, murdered, floating in the *kali* that reeked of death and guided him to the harbour from which he set sail, at the mouth of a river on the northeast tip of Java. Night after night he told me his war stories, the way another father might tell his children fairy tales. He told me how he and his soldier buddies unleashed death and destruction on the villages of his boyhood. Was he out to obliterate that boyhood with flamethrowers and grenades, to wipe out the traces of shame and disgrace that clung to the bastard son? He was never recognized by his father, but his mother did not give him life so that he could destroy the lives of others. Deep inside, was he always that little boy who was happiest shooting bats and rats and mice, only to be handed better weapons and told to hunt bigger prey? The tables turned and the friends of the men he had hunted came looking for him once hostilities between the Netherlands and Indonesia had officially ceased. Dutch marines gave him safe passage. For six weeks he sailed across the sea, and the sight of Holland made him so desperate that he had to fight the urge to jump overboard and swim straight back to Java. Did war make him crazy or was he born crazy? The madness must have been in him. All it took was a set of circumstances that gave him free rein. Karma. Ill fortune. A curse. Whatever. Does it matter in the end? Us humans have no say in how we are born, in how we carve a path through life. My father sailed to his fatherland, I took a plane to his motherland. Without having read his manuscript, I crossed from one end of Surabaya to the other, not knowing the names of all the streets, lanes, squares and *kampongs* he mentions. On Jembatan Merah, the Red Bridge over Kali Mas, my guide told me about the mythical struggle between shark and crocodile that once coloured the water red. I looked down at the stinking, shit-brown river. At the poor Javanese grubbing around on its banks. That water has a long history. If I scatter my father's ashes there, I will be as old as he was when he completed his memoirs. For a long time, I fought his madness like a madman. Today I am a weary bridge, hunched over the past, blind to my own reflection in the water. I will stop now. This fight is at an end.

GLOSSARY

#

'606'
another name for a Salvarsan injection to combat venereal diseases

A

aduh
an exclamation of pain or surprise

Allied Military Administration, AMA
a semi-military organization tasked with the restoration of civil administration and law under Dutch colonial rule after the capitulation of Japan's occupying forces in the Dutch East Indies at the end of World War Two; formerly known as the Netherlands Indies Civil Administration (see also NICA money)

amtrac
short for 'amphibious tractor'; an assault/landing vehicle capable of moving on land and water

anak mas
favourite child; the apple of mother's eye

APRA
Angkatan Perang Ratu Adil
the Legion of Ratu Adil or the Prince Justice Legion, a militia opposed to the Republican government of President Sukarno and encompassing many factions

attap
dried palm fronds used in thatching

B

babu
nanny or female domestic servant in colonial times

BAR
abbreviation of Browning Automatic Rifle, a US-made machine gun

baru
a greenhorn, a newcomer; nickname for a marine fresh off the boat from Holland

Batavia
the capital of the Dutch East Indies, now Indonesia's capital Jakarta

batik
a Javanese method of creating patterned textiles by covering parts of the material with wax and dyeing the parts left exposed in various colours; also a fabric dyed in this way and a pattern produced by this method

becak
a cycle rickshaw, mainly used as a form of taxi

Belanda
Dutchman or woman

Berlage, Hendrik
(1856–1934)
a prominent Dutch architect perhaps best known for his stock-exchange building in the heart of Amsterdam, but also for a cubist-expressionist kiosk in The Hague which now has listed status

Bersiap
the name for the period of chaos and violence that erupted in the power vacuum in the Dutch East Indies following Japan's capitulation at the end of World War Two; literally 'to get ready'

Big Shit
nickname for the staff of the Marine Brigade

BKR
Badan Keamanan Rakyat
People's Security Body, a government-run force made up of fighters previously trained by the Dutch and the Japanese; a forerunner to Indonesia's armed forces

Brabant
a province in the south of the Netherlands; much of Brabant was liberated by Allied forces in September 1944 as part of Operation Market Garden, while other parts of the country had to endure a bitterly cold winter with severe food shortages under German occupation before liberation came in May 1945

Bung Tomo
another name for Sutomo

bushidō
the code of conduct of the Samurai or warrior class in feudal Japan

C

Celebes
the former name of the Indonesian island of Sulawesi

cheval de frise
a portable frame covered with many long spikes or spears, used in warfare to block an enemy advance

Croc City
Krokodillenstad
a nickname for Surabaya

D

Darul Islam
an Indonesian resistance army founded on strict Islamic principles, which fought against both Dutch colonial rule and the Republican forces of the Indonesian Army; literally 'House of Islam'

desa
village

Destruction Corps
Vernielingskorps
an organization in the Dutch East Indies set up to sabotage industry and equipment to prevent them being of use to the invading Japanese

dojo
a building for the practice of Japanese arts of self-defence

dokar
a two-wheeled horse-drawn carriage

Dudok, Willem (1884–1974)
a Dutch modernist architect put in charge of the urban redevelopment of The Hague after World War Two

dukun
medicine man, traditional healer

Dutch East India Company
Verenigde Oost-Indische Compagnie, VOC
a Dutch trading company founded with government backing in the Netherlands' Golden Age with a monopoly on trade to and from the Dutch East Indies; still used as nationalist shorthand for Dutch maritime and mercantile power and the enterprising attitude that went with it

E

Eurasian
in the Dutch colonial context, a person of mixed blood in the Dutch East Indies who was recognized by their Dutch father and who held a Dutch passport; paternal recognition gave children of mixed blood access to privileged European status in some aspects of their lives

F

First Police Action
Eerste Politionele Actie
a Dutch military operation (codenamed Product) launched in July 1947 with the main aim of regaining control of commercial plantations and other assets on Java and Sumatra
(See also Police Action)

G

GHQ
abbreviation for General Headquarters

guna-guna
black magic

gunung
mount

H

Hatta, Muhammad (1902–1980)
a close ally of President Sukarno and vice-president under his rule, though tensions between the two eventually resulted in a rift

Heemskerk, Jacob van (1567–1607)
a Dutch admiral and explorer who commanded voyages to the East Indies and established trading posts there

Hein, Piet (1577–1629)
a Dutch admiral and privateer whose most daring deed was capturing the Spanish silver fleet in 1628

Hizbullah
a militia recruited from various Muslim groups and ready to give their lives for God in the fight against Westerners

Hollandia
a settlement in Western New Guinea when it was part of the Dutch East Indies; now the city of Jayapura in the Indonesian province of Papua

I

INBAT
abbreviation for infantry battalion

Indo (adjective)
word to describe a person of mixed European and Indonesian blood without European status in the Dutch East Indies; also a cultural description for both whites and Eurasians steeped in the characteristics and customs of the colony

Indo (noun)
someone born of a European, in most cases Dutch, father and a 'native' (i.e. Indonesian) mother in the Dutch East Indies; once a racial slur, it was later adopted with pride by the post-war generation in the Netherlands, an act of rebellion against the first-generation immigrants from the Indies who referred to themselves as 'Indo-Dutch'

Indo-Dutch
the designation given to (and readily accepted by) first-generation immigrants from the Indies to the Netherlands

Indo-European Alliance
Indo Europeesch Verbond, IEV
a social movement and political organization founded in 1919 by the Eurasian community of the Dutch East Indies to campaign for race equality and a political say in how the colony was run

Indonesian Army
Tentara Nasional Indonesia, TNI;
previously known as *Tentara Republik Indonesia, TRI*

Indonesian Communist Party
Partai Komunis Indonesia, PKI

Indonesian National Party
Partai Nasional Indonesia, PNI

Indonesian Navy
Angkatan Laut Republik Indonesia, ALRI

Indonesian People's Revolutionary Front
Barisan Pemberontakan Rakyat Indonesia, BPRI
a militia formed to fight for Indonesian independence

Indonesian police
Polisi Negara

Indo-Peranakan
a child born of an Indo father and a peranakan mother
(See also peranakan)

K

kampong
also spelled kampung
a village or poor, semi-rural quarter of a city

kacang ijo
mung beans

kali
river

kamar kecil
toilet

kasihan
also spelled kasian
an expression of pity, compassion; poor thing!

kata
basic exercises or formal practice used to teach and improve the execution of martial arts techniques

katjong
a street urchin, little rascal; a teasing term for an Indo boy who acted like a 'native' (Indonesian) boy

kebaya
a light loose tunic commonly worn in the East, often with a sarong; Chinese women always wore a white kebaya

kecap
Indonesian soy sauce

Kenpeitai
the secret police of the Japanese Imperial Army

klewang
also spelled kleywang or kelewang
a single-edged sword that gets wider and heavier towards the point

knee mortar
a light and easily portable discharger used by Japanese forces to launch grenades in short-range combat

KNIL
Koninklijk Nederlands-Indisch Leger
See Royal Netherlands East Indies Army

KNIL air force
Militaire Luchtvaart Dienst, MLD
the Royal Netherlands East Indies Army Air Force; the KNIL operated independently of the rest of the Dutch armed forces and therefore had its own fleet of aircraft

kokkie
a kitchen maid, sometimes also referred to as *babu*

kopi tubruk
unfiltered ground coffee with sugar and hot water added

K rations
small packages of emergency rations

kretek
a cigarette made with clove-flavoured tobacco, widely smoked in the Indies and Indonesia

kris
a dagger with a wavy blade, strongly associated with Indonesian culture

kroncong
Indo style of pop music with old Portuguese influences, reminiscent of Hawaiian music

kue lapis
a traditional Indonesian cake, colourful, layered and steamed

kukri
a curved knife, broader at the point than at the handle, used by the Gurkhas of India

kuntao
a term for the martial arts practised by the Chinese across Southeast Asia, particularly the Malay Archipelago

kyai
also spelled kiai
an Islamic cleric and scholar respected in Javanese communities, some of whom took on the mantle of sacred warrior and spiritual leader during Indonesia's struggle for independence

L

Limburg
a province in the south of the Netherlands, partly liberated in September 1944 while the major cities such as The Hague, Amsterdam and Rotterdam in the west of the country remained occupied until May 1945

LST Landing Ship, Tank
a vessel designed to carry tanks, vehicles, cargo and troops and land them directly on shore at locations where ships are unable to dock

M

mandor
a foreman or overseer

Marine Brigade
Mariniersbrigade
a US-trained Dutch fighting force founded in 1943 and disbanded in 1949; often operated independently from the rest of the Netherlands armed forces in the Indies in a special forces capacity

Marine Brigade Security Service
Veiligheidsdienst Mariniersbrigade, VDMB
the intelligence branch of the Marine Brigade, which employed large numbers of the local population in their efforts to gather useful military and political information

Masyumi
a militarized Muslim political party with its origins in a council of Indonesian Muslim associations set up by the Japanese during their occupation of the Dutch East Indies

mata gelap
blinded by rage; literally means 'the dark eye'

Merdeka
the battle cry for revolutionaries demanding Indonesian independence, also used to refer to the revolution itself; literally means 'free'

N

nasi goreng
fried rice

nasi rames
white rice accompanied by a range of side dishes, including meats, vegetables, peanuts, eggs and fried-shrimp crackers

Netherlands Forces Intelligence Service, NEFIS
a Dutch military intelligence and special operations unit that was mainly active during Japan's World War Two occupation of the Dutch East Indies

New Guinea
a former territory of the Dutch East Indies, now the Indonesian

province of Papua; it remained under Dutch control for some time after Indonesia gained independence, which is why Dutch sympathizers wishing to remain in the region were shipped there when the Dutch pulled out of Indonesia

NICA money
currency issued by the Netherlands Indies Civil Administration, a semi-military organization, established in April 1944 to restore civil administration and law under Dutch colonial rule after the capitulation of the Japanese

nona
a young Indo or Indonesian girl

nyai
a 'native' housekeeper, companion or concubine in the Dutch East Indies

O

obat
an Indo or Indonesian herbal medicine or ointment

P

parang
a Balinese machete, over half a metre in length and broader at the end than at the base

pasar
market

pelopor
an anti-colonial fighter; from the Dutch *voorloper* meaning pioneer or scout; the 'e' is silent (See also plopper)

pemuda
a young fighter for Indonesian nationalism; literally 'youth', a term that took on added significance as part of the indigenous population's new outlook on the road to independence for Indonesia

pencak silat
a fast-moving, elegant form of martial arts that originated in Madura

pendek
underpants

pendekar
a master of the martial arts, especially *pencak silat*

peranakan
anyone born of Chinese parents in the Dutch East Indies, including people of mixed Chinese/Malay descent; under Dutch rule the Chinese occupied an intermediate position between the indigenous population and the Europeans

perut ayam
traditional Javanese cake made from a length of fried dough curled into a circle; takes its name from its shape, which resembles the entrails of a chicken

pikolan
yoke of wood or bamboo, placed across the shoulders to carry a pair of pails, baskets etc.

plopper
a corruption of *pelopor*, used by soldiers to refer to Indonesian freedom fighters and later by uninformed Dutch people to refer to Indos in the Netherlands (even in literary texts) (See also pelopor)

Police Action
Politionele Actie
a term coined by the Dutch authorities to refer to the military campaigns launched against Indonesian nationalists in their struggle for independence; though still widely used, it is a euphemism designed to suggest the restoration of peace and order rather than the reassertion of colonial rule by military force

Political Intelligence Service
Politieke inlichtingendienst, PID
an organization set up by the Dutch authorities in the Indies which recruited members of the indigenous population to provide intelligence on possible subversive elements

pukulan
a style of martial arts that mixes *pencak silat* and jujitsu, attributed to pre-war Indos in West Java

R

Resident
the governor of a residency, an administrative division in the Dutch East Indies

rijsttafel
a lavish meal consisting of a wide selection of Indonesian dishes served with rice

Robinson, Tjalie
(1911–1974)
an alias adopted by Indo intellectual and writer Jan Boon, a post-war Indo activist, writer and champion of Indo culture

rōmusha
a forced labourer during the Japanese occupation of Indonesia

Royal Dutch Indies Airways
Koninklijk Nederlands-Indische Luchtvaart Maatschappij, KNILM
the commercial airline of the Dutch East Indies; all of its aircraft fit to make the trip were evacuated to Australia when the Japanese invaded

Royal Netherlands East Indies Army
Koninklijk Nederlands-Indisch Leger, KNIL
the Netherlands' main military force in the Dutch East Indies, defeated by the invading Japanese in World War Two; the KNIL was not part of the regular Dutch army but a separate force founded specifically to establish and then defend Dutch colonial interests in the region

S

sakura
cherry blossom, the national symbol of Japan and the emblem used on the badge of the Kenpeitai, the Japanese Army's secret police; also vernacular for Japanese soldiers

sarong
a garment consisting of a length of cloth usually wrapped around the waist

sawah
an irrigated rice field

Scheveningen
a former fishing village near The Hague, later a popular seaside resort

Second Police Action
Tweede Politionele Actie

a Dutch military operation (codenamed Crow) launched in December 1948 with a view to retaining as much influence as possible in the face of impending Indonesian independence (See also Police Action)

Senjata makan tuan
A set phrase meaning to backfire: the weapons turn on their user

sembah
a greeting in which the palms are placed flat against one another as if in prayer and then brought to the forehead

senang
comfortable; at peace, at ease

SHQ
abbreviation for Surabaya Headquarters

sia
a three-pronged martial arts weapon mostly used in pairs

Sixteen Sixty-Fivers
Tweede Politionele Actie, 1665'ers
a small section of the Dutch Marine Corps made up of professional marines, most of whom had joined up before World War Two and were highly experienced combat soldiers; named after the year in which the Dutch Marine Corps was founded

Soldier of Orange
Erik Hazelhoff Roelfzema (1917–2007), a Dutch war hero whose autobiographical account of his wartime exploits entitled *Soldaat van Oranje* (Soldier of Orange) was later turned into a film and a musical of the same name

soto Madura
Madurese beef soup, eaten with rice

Staf Satoe
the senior staff of the TNI (Indonesian National Army)

Sutomo (1920–1981)
a military leader in Indonesia's war of independence against the Netherlands, who played a leading role when Surabaya came under attack from Allied Forces in 1945

T

takeyari
a bamboo spear used by the Japanese

Tapeworm Express
nickname for a truck with covered, half-open trailers attached; operated by the Marine Brigade as a shuttle service for its personnel in Surabaya and fitted with running boards so that marines could jump aboard while it was moving

tempo doeloe
a period of history in the Dutch East Indies covering the late 19th and early 20th centuries and viewed with nostalgia; used figuratively to mean 'the good old days'

Tennō Heika
His Imperial Majesty the Emperor of Japan

Tjakra Brigade
Korps Barisan Tjakra Madoera
auxiliary forces of the Royal Netherlands East Indies Army (KNIL)

tonarigumi
a neighbourhood association during the Japanese occupation

tong-tong
a wooden block that could be used to send signals when struck with a wooden hammer

trassi
also spelled trasi, terasi
fermented shrimp paste, dark in colour and with a strong flavour and smell

Tromp, Maarten
(1598–1653)
an admiral and naval hero of the Dutch Golden Age, celebrated for his victories over the Spanish and the English

tuan
a form of address used as a mark of respect

tuan besar
a colonial boss, a gentleman of means, a big shot

U

UN Committee of Good Offices
a United Nations peacekeeping initiative involving military observers from Australia, Belgium and the United States with the aim of monitoring and reporting on the conflict between Indonesia and the Netherlands in the time leading up to independence

W

warga negara
Indonesian citizenship

war volunteer
oorlogsvrijwilliger, ovw'er
Dutchmen who volunteered to go and fight in the Dutch East Indies with the aim of bringing the colony back under Dutch rule

Z

zanchin

sharp as a tack; watchful, alert

A note on spelling

In his novel *De tolk van Java*, Alfred Birney spells Indonesian words using the colonial-era spelling system based on Dutch. For the sake of simplicity, this translation only uses the Dutch-based system for the names of characters. Place names, street names, the names of prominent historical figures, and general words and phrases have been rendered in modern Indonesian spelling wherever possible.

ABOUT THE AUTHOR

Alfred Birney was born in 1951. For *The Interpreter from Java*, he was awarded the Libris Literature Prize, the Netherlands' premier literary award, and the Henriëtte Roland Holst Prize. He lives in the Netherlands.

CENTRAL 17-11-2020